BY THE ORDER OF THE KING

Shelby Ann Harms

Author Note

Welcome to the world of Adamas! The four kingdoms of Orellia, Norfell, Evenend, and Mistivas make up this dark, fantasy continent, and I'm excited for you to explore the lands. I really do hope you enjoy this book and the story it contains.

The reason for this note is that, while this story is purely fictional, it contains content some readers may find harsh or disturbing. Please check the following page for a list of content warnings, and read this book with care.

And now, let us proceed into the world of Adamas, where mysterious secrets and powerful abilities beyond compare await!

Content Warnings

This book contains content that some readers may find triggering such
as:

Kidnapping
Violence
Homophobia
Alcoholism
Abuse
Interrogation
Torture
Familial death
Fatphobia
Sexism

Please read with care

By the Order of the King
Playlist

Prologue- Runaway by AURORA
Chapter 1- Amas Veritas by Alan Silvestri
Chapter 2- Barracuda by Heart
Chapter 3- Game of Survival by Ruelle
Chapter 4- Numb by LINKIN PARK
Chapter 5- The View Between Villages by Noah Kahan
Chapter 6- Little Girl Gone by CHINCHILLA
Chapter 7- I'm Not Okay (I Promise) by My Chemical Romance
Chapter 8- Another World by Ruelle & UNSECRET
Chapter 9- Nightmare by Halsey
Chapter 10- Just A Girl (From The Original Series "Yellowjackets") by Florence + the Machine
Chapter 11- Smells Like Teen Spirit by Nirvana
Chapter 12- Nobody's Soldier by Hozier
Chapter 13- Will I Make It Out Alive (feat. Jessie Early) by Tommee Profitt
Chapter 14- Who We Are by Hozier
Chapter 15- Gives You Hell by The All-American Rejects
Chapter 16- Teeth by 5 Seconds of Summer
Chapter 17- Supermassive Black Hole by Muse
Chapter 18- BIRDS OF A FEATHER by Billie Eilish
Chapter 19- Famous Last Words by My Chemical Romance
Chapter 20- Shake It Out by Florence + the Machine
Chapter 21- Another One Bites the Dust by Queen
Chapter 22- Brain Stew by Green Day
Chapter 23- Eat Your Young by Hozier
Chapter 24- Versions of Violence by Alanis Morissette
Chapter 25- Madness by Ruelle
Chapter 26- Welcome Home, Son by Radical Face
Chapter 27- ...Ready For It? by Taylor Swift
Chapter 28- Fighter by Christina Aguilera
Chapter 29- Emergence by Sleep Token
Chapter 30- Until We Go Down by Ruelle
Chapter 31- Know Your Enemy by Green Day
Chapter 32- Iron by Woodkid
Chapter 33- Headstrong by Trapt
Chapter 34- Dangerous by Sleep Token
Chapter 35- invisible string by Taylor Swift

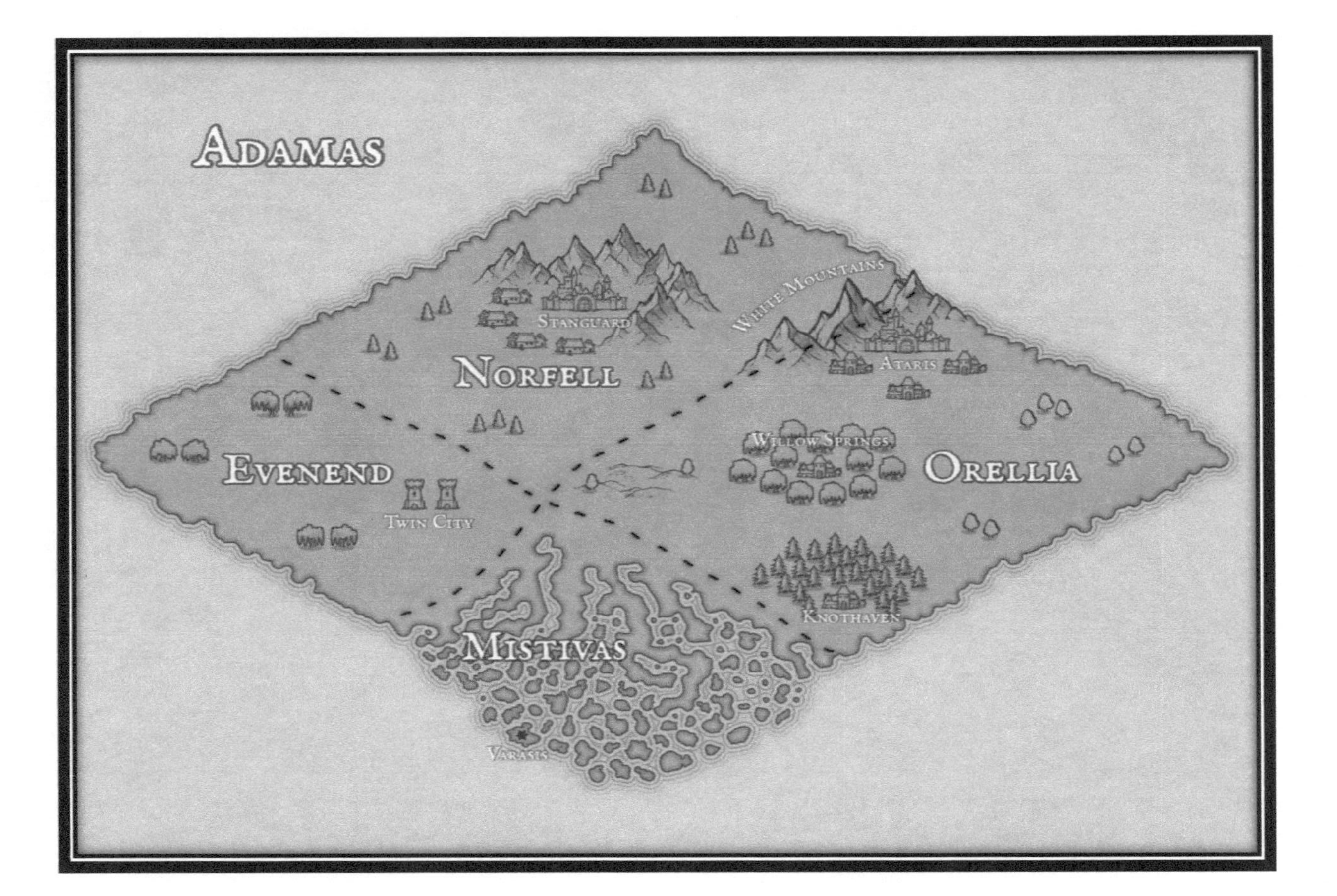

ADAMAS
WHITE MOUNTAINS
STANGUARD
NORFELL
ATARIS
WILLOW SPRINGS
ORELLIA
EVENEND
TWIN CITY
KNOTHAVEN
MISTIVAS
VARASIS

To those who also crave escapism.
I see you.

Prologue

They're dead. I know it. I don't have to look back to know it. Even though I'm far past the point of looking behind me and still being able to view my home.

My heart beats so hard in my chest, it's on the verge of exploding.

I run as fast as my feet will take me in my pale slippers. Although I doubt they are still the light, ombre colors after my trek through this forest.

Voices sound behind me, far enough away to where I can barely make out what they're saying.

I try to pick up speed but it's difficult as a fresh wave of tears start flowing down my face.

I let the salty liquid run down my cheeks, and I bob around a tree. I know this forest well enough but at night, and with my vision blurring from the wetness, it's hard to tell exactly where I'm going.

Something lies on the ground a few paces away from me, a fallen tree I assume, and I jump, sailing over the obstacle.

The brush surrounding me closes in tighter, the forest thickening. The spaces between the tall trees narrow. The bushes clump together. Maneuvering around them has sticks and thorns pricking my bare legs.

They won't be able to stay on their horses much longer. They'll have to begin chasing me on foot. Although, their armor will give them an advantage I don't have in my thin nightclothes.

I weave around two more trees, veering ever so slightly right.

I hope the forest is on my side, and the maze of nature confuses them, forcing their search to end.

My feet keep moving, and I pump my arms, pushing myself harder than ever before.

I'm not ready to face death today. Not before I've been able to live a full year as a teenager.

I blink my eyes repeatedly, trying to force away more oncoming tears. It doesn't work. My sight is fuzzy again when I squeeze in between two trees, the rough bark snagging on my nightclothes.

I pause, bending over to catch my breath behind the massive trunks. Then, I finally peer back.

No one's there, and there's no sign of lights in the distance. Everything is entirely pitch black. I shut my eyes, listening closely for any sign of movement. A branch snapping, leaves rustling, anything. But no noise comes.

My throat tightens and I let out a strangled breath, sliding down the coarse bark of the trunk.

I bring my knees up to my chest, hugging them as more sobs break free. I try to keep them contained, muffling any noises into the fabric of my robe and nightgown.

I hope if they are still, somehow, following me, they don't hear my crying. But I can't make it stop. It hits me again, like a boulder to the chest.

They are truly dead. Both of them.

The King's Guards have killed my parents.

Chapter 1

...11 years later

As I hear a breeze rattling the old window pane above my desk, I look up to see fire wielders feverishly lighting the posts along the gravel-covered street in order to beat the setting sun. I shake my head and giggle to myself; they do this every year in the fall when the sun begins setting earlier. It's as if they forget the seasons change.

I close my journal and stand up, stretching. I flick my hand, disposing of the light ball I had placed in its lantern in the corner of my desk.

Walking out of my bedroom, I shut my door behind me and head into our small yet functional kitchen. With my aunt busy running the apothecary downstairs, I decide to make us a quick pot of stew.

After rustling around, I retrieve vegetables picked from our extensive garden out back, chopping up a russet potato, two carrots, and a small yellow onion.

I turn on the stove and stick a flaming match into the gas underneath a pot, cursing my abilities, wishing I was able to wield fire at a time like this.

A selection of herbs, which are always plentiful in our kitchen, is added with the vegetables and broth I plop into a pot. My palm hovers over the mixture and I close my eyes, focusing on the liquid molecules of the broth, stirring the contents with a wave of my hand.

After letting the stew simmer and giving it a taste test some time later, I descend the stairs on my left, carrying two steaming bowls into the store.

Aunt Rowena has various candles lit all around in order to keep the store from drowning in darkness now that the sun has officially set.

Setting the bowls on the counter, I smile at the customer on the opposite side. The man my aunt has a "thing" for, although it took weeks for me to get her to admit it.

"I really can't thank you enough for this," he says, holding up a clear jar filled to the brim with a variation of herbs.

"It's no problem. After all, you are one of my best customers," my aunt replies, shyly smiling at him. She is never this coy. Only he brings it out in her.

He turns to me then. "Hello Aurora, I hope you've been well."

"I have, thank you. How about yourself, Lee?"

"Well, this damn leg is giving me the same old problems. So you know, the usual." He chuckles lightly as he taps the wooden peg leg I know is beneath his pants.

I've seen it on many occasions when my aunt has experimented with new creams and elixirs she made specifically for his poorly amputated leg. The scarred, maimed flesh of what was his left leg causes him tremendous pain. He once said the injury was from a skirmish in the White Mountains, at our shared border with Norfell, eight years ago.

Lee was a high-ranking general in the King's Guard, but after his injury, he was thrown out with no regard for his time spent loyal to the crown. He battled infection after infection before it finally healed.

Over the years, he's told us how he spent his entire adulthood working his way up the chain of command, serving first under King Amos and becoming one of his best generals, then under his son, King Kairos, after his death.

Then to be discharged from the guard after a lifetime of service with an unhealed amputation? What *else* would be expected of King Kairos?

I snap out of my thoughts of the King.

The tyrant doesn't deserve to take up any further space in my mind.

"I'll let you ladies get to your dinner now. Thank you again for your help, Rowena."

"Any time, Lee. You know you're always welcome here."

Lee turns and slowly limps to the front door of the store, my aunt close behind. She shuts and locks the door before flipping over the sign to state we're closed.

"'You know you're always welcome here.'" I repeat my aunt in a sing-songy voice while batting my eyelashes.

"You shut your mouth over there! I was just being polite!" She turns, wagging her finger in my direction. A deep belly laugh takes me over.

"You've had a crush on him for forever! Why don't you just ask him out already?"

"I have *not* had a crush on him 'for forever'!"

A blush creeps up, turning her cheeks a rosy pink.

I know her as well as I know myself, if not better. My usually sassy, confident, spirited aunt turns into a puddle of mush around Lee. No matter how much she wishes to deny it.

"Oh, whatever. Now, what did you make us?"

Of course she's avoiding the topic.

I sigh, giving up on the subject. "I threw together a stew."

"Why thank you, love."

We sit down on our respective stools behind the wooden workbench that stretches across the back of the store and dig into our meal.

"By the way, I'm going out tomorrow night so you don't have to wait up for me," I tell her after slurping up the last of my stew.

She raises an eyebrow at me. "You know I'm going to anyways."

"I just don't want you worrying about me. I can handle myself."

"I know you can. I taught you everything you know," she says with a wink. "However, it's my job to worry about you. You may be an adult now but I will forever be responsible for you. I owe your parents that much."

I roll my eyes, even as a smile blooms on my face. I don't know how I'd live without her.

"Why don't you head upstairs. I have a few things to clean up here," she continues, shooing me away, then gathering her brown curls at the back of her head, tying the strands off her neck.

Bowls in hand, I ascend the stairs, shouting down a good night. I hear her echo the same when I form an orb of brightness in my palm to light the way through the evening darkness.

I place the illuminated ball into a lantern beside the kitchen sink when I enter our apartment.

Dishes cleaned and dried some time later, I gather the light and head to my bedroom, changing into pajamas.

I move the glowing orb into the lantern next to my bed, and grabbing the book from my nightstand, I open it to where I left off. All I remember is reading a handful of chapters before I eventually drift off to sleep.

When I wake in the morning, I hear the mourning doves cooing as the sun peeks through the redwoods outside my window.

As I sit up to stretch, I hear flushing coming from the bathroom down the hall. I move to peek out my bedroom door, asking my aunt why she's up so early when it's my day to open the store.

"Oh you know me, I don't sleep well, so I'm up with the birds," she says, hands on her hips. "You know, I will forever be grateful for indoor plumbing. I'm glad it became standard before I started my cycle when I was a girl."

She gestures to the bathroom she stands in the doorway of, then moves to tie her light brown hair atop her head.

"When I was really little we had to use chamber pots. It was a disgusting mess. You better be grateful you've never had to use one," she pauses to wag a finger at me. "If you ask me, it's the greatest invention of my lifetime."

I stare at her, bewildered. I rub the sleep out of my eyes. It's too early in the morning for this conversation.

"Anywho, I'll make us breakfast then tend to the garden. So don't you worry, you'll still be running the shop today." She winks at me. I roll my eyes.

"Are you sure you don't need any help in the garden? I don't want you spraining your wrist again." I point to her left wrist which she's injured not only once, but twice from pulling carrots out of the ground.

"Oh you hush, don't make me seem older than I am! I am fully capable of handling those damn carrots!"

I shake my head at her and sigh. "Fine, if you say so."

She humphs at me and stalks into the kitchen.

I back into my room and shut the door. The ball of light in my bedside lantern went out when I fell asleep last night, but plenty of sun peeks through my windows to see.

I step over to my dresser, pulling on a pair of dark pants, jumping into them as they hug my curves. I tug on a light, long sleeved tunic then lace up a black bodice over top, tying off the ribbon at the top of my breasts.

After brushing and plaiting my caramel waves, I finally slip on socks and boots before heading out to the kitchen.

Aunt Rowena slides a plate of jam covered toast and fruit across the counter to me as I walk up to a barstool.

As I eat, she rambles on about how the carrots in the garden will "not get the best of her this time around" while taking bites of her own breakfast. I quietly nod my head along, listening to her carrot monologue.

She snatches up my plate the moment I finish, her vegetable rant uninterrupted.

"I'm going to go open up shop now," I slide in when she pauses for the briefest of seconds. "Thank you for breakfast. You can definitely beat those carrots this time around!"

I scurry out of the kitchen after kissing her suntanned cheek, before she can continue on about those damn vegetables again.

I flip over the welcome sign when I enter the shop under our apartment.

Before pulling out a stool from under the main workbench, I grab two small pots of nearly ready to harvest lavender. I place them down and get to work growing the plants the rest of the way.

I place my hands on either side of a single pot, wiggling my fingers, adjusting, feeling for the earth, the roots of the sweet smelling plant. The plant begins to grow under my touch, the vibrant purple springing to life.

The bright flowers blooming from the tips always make me smile.

Removing my hands and retrieving a pair of sheers, I snip the stems.

Deciding to use the buds from the second plant for tea, I set my palms on the next pot. I grow this one slower than the first, ensuring to stop before the buds open to reveal the colorful flowers.

My fingers tingle with the use of my favorite power.

We have a plethora of glass containers in the storage closet, so I move to find a small one for the buds and a tall one to fit the stems.

I look up when the door bell jingles after placing the pieces of lavender into their respective jars. Our first customer of the day.

Mrs. Cromwell, a loyal customer who has about a decade on my aunt, smiles brightly at me.

How do these women always manage to be cheerful so early in the morning? I'm tired, regardless of the amount of sleep I get.

"Good morning Aurora! How have you been, dear?"

"I've been well, thank you. How are you? Here for your usual?"

Every Friday for nearly three years, she's visited our shop for the same order: a small jar of pain relieving salve and a large pouch of dried chamomile for her daily tea.

When she was a young woman her then boyfriend, a fire wielder, purposely burned her hands and feet so horribly she could no longer wield her ability. She told me she had once wielded air, and how she believed it to be the most freeing of the seven abilities—air, earth, fire, water, light, shadow, and the mind.

The loss of her power placed her with the non-wielders, who only made up a fifth, perhaps even a sixth, of the population. A part of the population who were treated as less than in some areas of the world.

It's unimaginable, being able to use powers one day then be stripped of them the next. I can't fathom what I would do if I lost even one of my abilities. I wouldn't be able to pick one I would be fine living without.

All Mrs. Cromwell knows is that I wield earth, like my aunt. It's all anyone knows, aside from my Aunt Rowena. And while her earth skills didn't always translate to wielding light, water, or the mind, she did her best to have me practice, in secret of course, all of my abilities once I came to live with her.

I had discovered all of my powers before my parents passed when I was thirteen.

Triggered by anything throughout puberty, frustration, nerves, anger, shock, or even trauma can bring about one's abilities. One day a child will have no abilities at all, then the next they're blasting fireballs, tendrils of shadows, gusts of wind, or even trying to see into your mind, and succeeding.

And although genetics decide what ability, or abilities, one wields, many people's personalities are seemingly reflected in their powers.

I always had my money on my aunt being a fire wielder, had she been born with anything more than earth.

"Yes please, my dear."

Her words pull me from my thoughts and I grab her order from under the counter, where we keep items for our most loyal of customers.

Handing the items over, she places them in her bag and reaches out a scarred, deep crimson hand, coins loose in her palm. I take the money, placing it in our collection box.

"Unfortunately, I can't chit-chat today. Even though you know I enjoy our conversations," she explains, throwing me a wink. "I have to pick up a special package for Mr. Cromwell this morning. Thank you, as always, dear."

Relief had washed over me when Mrs. Cromwell told me the story of how she met Mr. Cromwell, only a year after losing her abilities.

She said from the moment he locked eyes with her across the dance floor at a Yuletide celebration, she knew he would be the one. And in her words: the rest was history.

I can only hope to find a love like theirs one day.

"Of course, Mrs. Cromwell. Any time," I tell her with a wave as she exits the store.

Aunt Rowena joins me in the afternoon several hours, and dozens of customers, later, triumphantly holding up a bundle of carrots by the stems as she walks in.

"I told you those carrots wouldn't get the best of me this time!"

"I suppose you were right. I'm glad I didn't make a bet against you," I laugh out.

She snorts. "Damn, I wish *I* had placed a bet with you!"

After giggling about her root vegetable debacle, I return to the tending of the shop.

A few hours later, the sun had moved beyond the redwoods in the distance, illuminating the sky with barely a drop of pink before fading into shades of violet and sapphire.

With the shop empty, I move to flip over the open sign, accidentally breaking the thin chain holding it aloft.

Jumping back to spare my toes any damage, the sign crashes to the ground.

I grunt, retrieving and inspecting the metal plate. Out of instinct, a ball of light forms in my hand as I inspect it more closely.

A shriek from behind me has the sign dropping to the ground again and the brightness fading from my palm. I spin to find my aunt, mouth agape.

"Aurora! What in the world are you doing?" she whisper-yells.

"What? It was dark."

"You could have been caught light wielding! You're right by the front windows!"

"Relax, no one saw me. There's no one even out on the street right now." I glance out the window to ensure what I was saying was, in fact, correct.

"See?" Gesturing with my hand, I wave towards the street, empty for as far as the eye could see.

"It doesn't matter! It's one thing to use your other abilities upstairs but don't do it in the shop where you could be seen," she scolds, fingers pressed to her forehead in exasperation.

"Ok, ok, I'm sorry. I won't do it again," I give up, hands raised in defense.

She strikes a match, lighting a lantern.

I collect the sign and move to sift through the tools beneath our long tabletop for pliers. After finding a pair, I connect the chain together again and walk to the door, placing the sign back in its proper spot.

"I'm grabbing my bag then heading out to meet Alessandra, Jonas, and Zavier," I tell my aunt, walking upstairs. I hear her sigh and I pause on the third step.

"I just want you to be more cautious, please," she calls out.

"I know, I know," I say, waving her off and continuing up the stairs.

I stop in our bathroom to brush the work day out of my hair, tying my caramel waves half up.

Then snatching my waist bag from off of my dresser, I head right back downstairs.

"We're having dinner and drinks at Greystone's so I'll be back late," I explain, looping the belt around the curve of my hips, resting the pouch at my side.

"You guys and that damn tavern. Why don't you go to any of the other places in town? That place doesn't always have the best sort of people hanging around."

"My friends and I like it there. It's fun." I shrug. She rolls her eyes at my response.

I continue before she can add in anything else. "Well, I love you and I'll see you later, because no matter how many times I tell you, you're still going to wait up for me, even if I have my keys. Aren't you?" I tilt my head, giving her a look.

She beams back at me, a few wrinkles crinkling around her light brown eyes.

"Of course I will be. Have fun, but not too much fun, please."

"Yeah, yeah, will do."

I turn around and wave her off.

Shutting the shop door behind me, I hold up my keys through the window for my aunt to see.

I jingle them lightly as she shakes her head before locking the door.

The loose gravel of the street crunches beneath my boots as I place my keys in my bag while laughing.

That woman, I can't live with her but what would I do without her?

Chapter 2

"That pot roast was the shit!" I slump in my creaky, wooden chair, close my eyes, and rest my hand on my stomach.

Zavier and Jonas laugh from either side of me. Alessandra giggles into her drink as she brings it to her lips.

"What? It was!" I declare, sitting up straighter.

"Excuse me?" Zavier asks, flagging down a nearby waitress. "Can we get another round of drinks?"

We've already had two rounds thus far. Seems like I might be getting a bit tipsy tonight.

Too many rounds of various liquors later, Alessandra and I are leaning against one another in a corner booth, cackling, the sound reverberating in my ears.

I don't remember what prompted our chuckling, but it feels too good to stop. My belly hurts in the best way. Tears build in my eyes as I clutch her arm, and she tightens her hold on mine.

"Oooooh, he's cute!" Alessandra drawls, pointing to a tall, dark-haired man.

He leans against a wall, waiting his turn as he plays darts with another man. Zavier and Jonas stand beside them at the next dartboard over.

The man's head turns towards us and I feel my eyes go wide.

We are *definitely* being too loud.

But my head is floating and my body feels light. I throw my head back and start laughing anyway.

"Crap! I th- think he saw me point at him," she slurs.

I throw my hand over my mouth in an attempt to quiet my chuckling, although I'm not sure if it's not entirely helpful.

The dark-haired man looks Alessandra up and down, then winks at her before facing his dartboard. She leans into my shoulder, trying to hide her blushing cheeks.

"You *have* to go talk to him now! He winked at you! He's obviously interested," I encourage her, nudging her with my elbow. She lifts her gaze to mine.

Looking her in the eye, I use my whole arm to point in his direction and say, "Go."

"Nooo I don't have the balls! I'm nothing special anyways," she pouts.

It may be more common than not to have an ability, and while she may be a part of those who don't, discrimination towards non-wielders is rare in these parts.

She is also beautiful. Striking features, blonde curls, thin, delicate, and petite. Nearly my opposite, particularly in size. The curve of my hips are wide, my stomach is soft, my chest is much larger than hers, and I stand notably taller than the average woman.

She perks up, grinning. "I have an idea! *You* go talk to him for me."

"You're ridiculous," I sigh, but swiftly give in, the liquor swimming through my veins making me all too agreeable. "I *suppose* I could go for a game of darts."

Sliding out from the booth and striding up to Zavier, I congratulate him on his win as his arms raise above his head in victory, then ask if I can play him next.

A scoff sounds behind me.

"Yeah, let the loud, drunk bitch play with weapons."

I whip around.

The friend of the flirty guy.

He looks at me up and down, disgust in his dark eyes.

"I wouldn't go there if I were you," Zavier butts in. Jonas, being the more level-headed one, carefully watches the interaction through narrow eyes.

"I find it funny *you* didn't have the balls to say something to me. *Drunk bitch,*" the man says to me, a slight slur to his own words.

I step closer to him, looking up, directly into his eyes, daring him. He steps in, closing the distance, leaving less than a foot between us. In my peripheral, I see Zavier step closer too.

Then, I pry my way into his mind. Not a shield in sight.

Stupid, drunk *man.*

Once inside his head, I claw my fingers down the side, pushing in flashes of those darts, *weapons* he called them, flying into his carotid before he collapses to his knees as blood drips down his chest.

I smile wickedly when his eyes widen and Adam's apple bobs, gulping at the images.

He shakes his head when I release my grip on his mind. Then, all hell breaks loose.

He snarls, forming a flame in his palm, attempting to blast me with it.

I dodge to the right, sliding around him.

I splay my fingers out, feeling for the earth below, and pull vines up through the wooden floorboards of the tavern.

Throwing my hands forward, I command the crawling plants. The greenery wraps around his wrists, pulling them behind his back, restraining him.

It doesn't last but a few seconds as he lights the entirety of his balled fists on fire, turning the vines to ash.

"Hey! No wielding in here!"

I hear the bartender's yelled command but I ignore him, sending another wave of vines at this asshole.

Zavier then ignites a flame in his own hand, throwing it.

Flirty boy steps up, wielding shadows and dousing Zavier's fire with a sphere of darkness.

I guess he's not so cute anymore, Alessandra.

Grunting, Zavier turns to flirty boy and launches a fireball in his direction.

In the same moment, I bend to the ground, place my hands on the floorboards, and shake the land beneath.

As the ground rapidly shakes and my attacker tries to gain his footing, I force it down, cracking and sinking a few floorboards. One of his feet catches between two boards. I smile to myself.

"Enough! Get *out* of my tavern!"

The huge, burly owner of Greystone's steps through the kitchen doors.

His massive frame towers over me. I lift my hands off the floor, more than intimidated, stopping the shaking ground. Rising from my crouched position, I peer down at the man whose foot I trapped in the earth between floorboards.

Level-headed as usual, Jonas corrals Zavier and me towards the tavern's door while Alessandra gathers our belongings at the table.

"I'm sorry, we'll be leaving now," Jonas apologizes, a hand on either of our shoulders. Zavier and I spy one another, passing a look of frustration back and forth.

Alessandra catches up to us, carrying Zavier's cloak and my discarded waist bag I don't remember taking off.

I briefly twist, seeing what must be another one of my attackers friends using earth wielding to remove his foot from the boards. A giggle bubbles up my throat at his predicament.

"Dammit, you guys! It's time for you to go home and sleep. You've had *far* too eventful of an evening. And *far* too much to drink," Jonas scolds Zavier and me while we walk down the street.

"Well, he shouldn't have called me a bitch. *He's* a bitch." I cross my arms over my chest.

"His friend was a little bitch too," Zavier chimes in, nodding at me. I chuckle.

"I suppose he wasn't very cute after all." I peek at Alessandra over my shoulder to see her rolling her eyes.

The crisp midnight air cools the rage of the fight. My head feels light once more, fuzzy even, and I beam ear to ear as we continue walking down the gravel pathway until we reach the shop.

"Thank you for a fun night!" I gather the three of them together into a giant group hug.

"Alright, alright. You go get some much needed sleep," Jonas says into the huddle. We pull apart and Alessandra hands me my bag. I didn't realize she was still holding it. Mentally, I thank her.

I dig through it and grab my keys when the three of them take off.

Inside, I notice light coming down from the stairs at the back of the store and shake my head. I knew she'd wait up for me.

Locking the door, I head over to the dim light at the bottom of the staircase.

I step onto the first stair and my vision swims, sending me stumbling to the side.

Perhaps I *did* have a little too much to drink.

Slowly making my way up, I lean against the wall for support. Reaching the top, I see my aunt sitting in one of the barstools, facing me.

"Seems like you had a good night." She brings a cup of tea to her lips, eyeing me over the edge.

I fight to hold back a giggle. Be *nonchalant.* "Yeah, it was fine."

"Fine? That's all?" A questioning look covers her aging face, slightly tan from her time in the garden.

I repeat myself, covering my blooming smirk as I start walking past her, into the hallway leading to our bedrooms. I can practically hear her rolling her eyes in response.

"Good night, hun," she calls after me.

"Good night, love you," I respond, and enter my room.

Blindly wandering around my dark space, I strip off my clothes and change into the first pair of pajamas I find in my drawers. And when my head hits the pillow, I'm out.

"What in the *world* is the matter with you!"

My eyes snap open, nearly bulging out of my skull at the sound of my aunt's screaming.

I fly up, which was not a good choice. Now the room is spinning.

"What are you talking about? And why are you yelling so early in the morning?"

And now my head is pounding.

"Do you want to know what I've just been told by a customer? About your 'night out' last night? You got into it with a group of men at the tavern!"

Oh yeah, that.

"What? It was just some assholes doing asshole things. Well, mainly one asshole. But it wasn't a big deal."

"It *absolutely* is a big deal when the whole damn town is talking about how you started destroying the tavern with your powers!"

Ok, I'm sure it's not the *whole* town.

"That sounds a little dramatic." My palm presses between my brows, where it's now throbbing.

"You were *kicked out* of Greystone's! It is not dramatic!"

"Ok, ok. I got it, it won't happen again."

Now I feel like vomiting.

"I cannot believe you! Get up and get dressed! It's nearly noon and I need you to watch the shop while I go to the next town over for some ingredients." She spins, stomping out of my room and slamming the door shut behind her.

The sound echoes, bouncing around in my skull. Everything is *so* loud.

"About damn time," she huffs at me when I arrive downstairs some time later.

The shower I took before coming down here has yet to help with my nausea and throbbing head.

She unties the apron she dons while making the various elixirs, creams, and tonics we sell, telling me of her plans. "I realized we're out of a few key ingredients and no one in Knothaven sells them. Give me a few hours and I'll be back."

"No problem. I've got the shop handled."

"Like you had things last night handled?" She eyes me suspiciously.

I sigh. "I'm sorry, okay? I promise it won't happen again."

"Do you understand now why I worry about you? All I want is for you to be careful."

She walks over to me, placing a hand on my shoulder. I look down at her, thinking about how I definitely didn't get my height from my mother's side of the family and giggle to myself.

As if she read my mind, she questions me aloud.

"Are you giggling at my height again? You know, I may only be five-foot-two but I assure you, I can pack a punch." She removes her hand from me and throws a punch into the air in front of her, laughing.

A chuckle escapes me and I shake my head. Cloak and satchel in hand, she turns, pointing at me from the doorway.

"Now, don't you go burning the shop down while I'm gone, alright?"

"Yeah, yeah. I promise," I say, folding my arms over my chest.

The hours pass by in a blur. Dozens of customers pass through the apothecary's doors. The afternoon bleeds into evening with orange and scarlet hues seeping through the shop windows.

I look up from my work when the door's bell chimes, signaling someone has entered.

"That took way longer than I expected," my aunt sighs out, carrying a large sack.

"I thought you were only getting 'a few key ingredients' not buying a whole second store."

She chuckles, placing down the bag on the counter in front of me.

"They were having a sale. I couldn't resist! And now, I won't have to go back for a while," she explains, promptly turning back around to flip over our open sign and lock the door.

I shake my head. She is something else.

"Tonight's going to be a long one. Refreshing stock," she trails off, opening and pulling products from the sack. "Oh! I also have a few new experiments I want to test out."

The rest of the night consists of doing exactly that.

Raw ingredients are organized away in the storage closet and in drawers behind our workbench, new herbs hang upside down to dry, and experiment after experiment are tested until she settles on a few new ones to keep in stock.

By the time I flick away the ball of light in my palm, which I'm sure to use solely upstairs, I haphazardly crawl into bed, my head muddled with thoughts of elixirs and tonics.

"Aurora! Wake up!" My aunt whisper-yelling my name has me stirring awake. I swear I only *just* fell asleep.

"What's going on?" I sit up in bed, abruptly, confusion rising in me when I look out my window to find it still dark out. Why is she waking me up *again*?

Then I hear it.

Glass shattering and shards crunching beneath a shoe as someone walks over it.

I scramble out of bed at the sounds.

My aunt's eyes widen in the near total darkness. I instinctively create a light ball to see her fully.

"Put that out," she hisses.

Dammit, she's right. If there's someone breaking in and they see me, they'll learn about my other abilities.

I snuff out the illumination with the formation of a fist.

My aunt runs to her room, and returns holding a small, lit lantern as I slip on my socks and boots.

"I am *not* about to let some low-life thieves steal everything we've worked so hard for. Let's go," she spits angrily.

We slowly tiptoe to the stairs and start down them. As we reach the bottom we turn, and come face to face with four large men standing in the middle of our shop.

My eyes go wide when I realize…

I recognize three of them.

My attacker from Greystone's and his flirty friend, as well as the one I briefly saw using earth wielding to unstick my attacker's leg from the floor. All of them are in different clothes, their ones from the tavern nowhere to be seen.

My attacker takes a few, slow steps towards us, grinning widely. He ignores my aunt, looking me dead in the eye before stopping only a pace in front of me.

"Well, hello there, *multiwielder.*"

Shit.

Chapter 3

"Who the hell are you calling a *multiwielder?*"

I whip my head to my aunt, surprised she's giving these intruders sass. Gulping, I wait for their reply.

Raising his hand, he lights it on fire. The flames lick up his wrist, his forearm. Slowly turning his head towards her, he smirks.

"Does it look like I'm talking to *you*, old hag?"

Disrespectful ass. I've had enough.

Light beam forming, I spear it at his face.

He stumbles back. His palm covered in fire goes out in an instant as my brightness temporarily blinds him.

His earth wielding friend throws out his hands, the window behind me shattering. Vines spring past the broken glass, wrapping around my wrists and ankles, yanking me backwards.

A gust of wind slams into me, throwing me flush against the wall with the shattered window. My head hits the window sill as I'm dragged to the floor by the deep green plants.

A daze stirs through me, sending my head pounding.

Vines sprout up from between the floorboards at the hands of my aunt. The crawling plant flies at flirty guy.

He whips out tendrils of shadows, twisting them around the strings of green earth. The vines slice in half, dropping to the floor, useless.

The man controlling the vines spiraling around my limbs and the fourth man I hadn't recognized brood their way towards me, the latter holding two sets of metal cuffs and a thick, metal collar.

Fuck.

With as much force as I can muster, hot, white brightness shoots from my palms.

Both men come to a screeching halt to shield their eyes.

The vines wrapped around me fall lifelessly to the ground.

Springing to my feet, I release an assault of light balls, one after the other.

Heat begins slithering up my legs not even a moment later. I peek down to find a ring of fire encircling me, the flames already reaching my thighs.

Stretching my fingers out, I take ahold of the vines hanging limply from the broken window. Aiming them at my attacker from Greystone's, who smirks as the flames he controls climb even higher, I send the plants flying.

My vines successfully wrap around his wrists, yanking him to the ground before he has the chance to burn them.

As he's pulled to his knees, the fire keeping me captive goes out.

I throw more vines his way, twisting them around his chest and upper arms.

But before I can complete his entrapment, another blast of wind hits me, sending me flying.

Crouching down, I dig my heels in to avoid slamming into the wall again. I skid to a stop just before reaching the wood paneling.

A fireball hurls my way the moment my body halts.

I drop to the floor completely and roll to the side, feeling the heat of the flame brush past my face as it narrowly misses me.

On my stomach, I peer up to see the three men making their way towards me.

I yelp when a strong stream of wind from above pushes me into the floor, forcing the breath from my lungs.

My head slams into the ground with the impact, my cheek scraping against the floorboards. I try to scream but all I can do is gasp for air.

The feeling of slithering tickles along my left wrist and I spot vines twisting around me, further securing me to the ground. The pieces of earth slither up my arm, around my back, and down my other arm, trapping my entire upper body.

I try to focus on my breathing, try to get air into my lungs. Everything begins to numb from the lack of oxygen.

Panic surges through me.

My chest aches and my head pounds.

A tear slips out of my eye against my will, its saltiness landing on my top lip.

Then, the air assault stops.

My entire body buzzes. My head throbs.

One of the men steps over my arm, squatting over my back. My hands are swiftly forced together behind me, secured in metal cuffs.

The vines around my upper body go limp, no longer holding me in place, and I take in a full breath for the first time in what feels like hours.

A second pair of cuffs snap around my ankles then, and my head is yanked up, his fist full of my caramel hair, craning my head back so I'm forced to look him in the eyes.

It's the earth wielder, and he's smirking down at me.

"You didn't *actually* think you'd get away from us, did you?"

I don't give him the pleasure of a response. He laughs at my silence to his question.

He drops my head and I hear the clanking of more metal behind me. He lifts my head again, as if I'm a doll he can yank around.

Shoving my messy, braided hair to the side, he clicks the two sides of the collar together at the back of my neck.

Then, he stands up over me, grabs my bound wrists, and jerks me to my feet.

As I shake my head to shift loose strands of hair out of my eyes, my gaze lands on my aunt.

My eyes widen as fright courses through my veins.

The flirty, shadow guy stands behind her, her light brown hair bunched up in his grasp and neck exposed. Covered in ribbons of shadows, her arms are pressed to her sides, her legs tightly held together.

And my fire wielding attacker stands in front of her, a dagger to her throat.

"Please, don't," I croak out, attempting to breathe normally.

He pricks her neck with the tip of the weapon, letting a bead of blood out, and watches it drip slowly down.

"No!" I screech at him and move to lunge forward, only to be held back by the earth wielder.

"I don't want any resistance from you on our way to the capital. Or else I'll come back here and finish this cut," the man says, slowly dragging the tip of his blade across her throat.

I glare into his eyes and try to push into his mind. Nothing happens.

Why can't I enter his mind?

The heaviness of the collar swiftly becomes apparent and I try to glance down at it. It's about two inches from touching my neck, but it feels as if it's choking me.

"What's this collar for?" I have my suspicions, but I want them to confirm it.

Devilish grins cover their faces.

"It's so those of you who can use *any* abilities with your mind, can't," the fire wielding man says with a smirk.

The man whose shadows twist around my aunt chuckles maniacally at his friend's explanation.

I've heard about the metal cuffs stopping people from using their abilities, but never collars. These must be a newer invention.

"Do we have an understanding? You will cause us no trouble on the way to the capital, or else," the fire wielding man questions as he taps my aunt's throat with his dagger.

I grunt when my restraints are yanked. "Yes, I understand."

A tear rolls down my aunt's cheek and I force myself to look down.

I can't watch her cry.

The fire wielder paces to the front door, which lies hanging off one of its hinges, commanding the rest to follow.

I'm shoved forward, the earth wielder holding the back of the collar and my bound wrists.

"How did you know?" I grunt out the question before I can think better of it. The men stop and spin to face me.

"I've had my fair share of experiences with mind wielders before you, sweetheart. I knew you had been in my head before you even left that tavern. Then when you used earth abilities, and I knew you were *exactly* what we were looking for," my fire wielding attacker answers.

He twists back around and struts out the front door, the air wielder following him like a puppy dog.

I view my aunt as the shoving begins again.

She's bawling now. She shouts at the men through her cries, incoherent to me aside from the curses she throws in.

The ribbons of shadows remain strapped over her body and flirty boy starts pushing her along behind the rest of us.

Outside, an enclosed metal wagon pulled by two white horses resembling a dungeon on wheels more than anything, awaits. Beyond the carriage, I spy the shocked faces of dozens of onlookers.

It hadn't dawned on me earlier. The fighting was loud enough to draw people out of their homes in the middle of the night.

These weren't just any people. These were our neighbors, many of which we called friends. These were the people I've been around for nearly half of my life. They watched me grow up.

Scanning the people's faces, I find Alessandra with her hands covering her mouth and tears running down her cheeks.

I hold my head high, even as I hold back tears of my own.

I'm led to the back of the wagon where a door is held ajar by the fire wielder, who wears a wide grin on his lips.

Another push hits my back between my shoulder blades. As I place a foot onto the single step leading inside, I turn to survey the audience one last time.

My Aunt Rowena, still bound by shadows, is crying quietly now. Alessandra, who's moved to the front of the crowd and sits on her knees, sobs into her hands. The rest of the faces I've known for so long, including Lee and Mrs. Cromwell, are covered in looks of shock and disbelief.

"Let it be known: multiwielders belong to the King. They rightfully belong in his army, as stated by law. If you are hiding, we *will* find you," the fire wielder proclaims to the crowd, his voice booming, bouncing across the redwood landscape and our town's buildings.

I finally notice then, the crest, on a patch at each of the four men's jacket shoulders. A golden crown, sitting atop a white shield with the emblem of an oak tree inside of it. All lying within a large, maroon shield.

The symbol of the King's Guards.

The King's Guards, otherwise known as those who wish *they* were multiwielders. Loyal, single wielders, the majority of whom desire to be a soldier in the King's special multiwielding forces: the King's Army. Only for their lacking number of abilities to stop them from such a dream.

Landing hard on my stomach, the wind is knocked out of me as I'm thrown into the dungeon-on-wheels, the door slamming shut behind me.

In the darkness, I wiggle my way up to lean against a solid, cold bench running the length of the wagon, then push my way to my feet. I peek out the small, barred window inlaid on the door.

Zavier and Jonas sprint down the street towards the crowd. They push their way to the front and the surprise on their faces as we make eye contact through the window makes my chest ache.

Zavier's face slips into vexation. Not at me, but at the men surrounding my new, gilded cage. Jonas's face morphs into sadness, his eyes becoming glossy. They spot Alessandra sobbing on the ground and race over to comfort her.

My aunt is thrown to the gravel-covered road as the shadows unwrap from her body. The shadow wielder stalks away, leaving her there as if she was a piece of trash he's discarding. Rage stirs in my gut at the man Alessandra once thought was attractive.

Lee moves to her as she kneels on the ground, softly crying. She leans into him. His arms wrap around her instantaneously.

I can no longer see any of the King's Guards. Rustling and horses neighing sound from the opposite side of my wheeled cage. They must have gone around to the front.

From the sound of it, there must be more horses than the ones pulling the wagon. Reins snap and the death carriage jerks forward.

Taking one last look at the people I love, I inhale a deep breath before shutting my eyes and turning away.

What have I gotten myself into?

Chapter 4

A fresh wave of tears start rolling down my cheeks when I plop onto the metal bench built into the side of this dungeon-on-wheels. The tears swiftly descend into choking sobs. I double over, trying to catch my breath.

My stomach churns, nausea rising within. Chest aching, my heart feels like it's being torn in two.

I don't know how long I sit this way, folded in half, trying to breathe through the sobs and the pain. It could be a handful of minutes or several hours, time is lost on me.

I only sit back up when I'm able to inhale without the air immediately expelling from my lungs and no more tears are able to squeeze out my eyes.

I attempt to put my bound feet up onto the bench on the other side, a few feet away. Even with my longer than average legs, it's a hair too far away. Groaning, I slam my boots back on the floor, frustrated.

Memories of my aunt flood my mind. How she often called after me when I would accidentally walk several paces in front of her. "Hey, legs! Slow it down!" she would holler.

I would tear up at the memory, but I don't have any left in me.

Instead, I investigate the bench under my butt.

Icy, hard, but overall wide and long enough for me to probably lay down on. Deciding to test it out, I lay down on my left side, stretching my feet towards the door. Still having enough wiggle room above my head and behind my back, I turn to lay flat on my stomach, since my back isn't an option with my wrists restrained behind me.

Mentally, I thank whoever designed this dungeon-on-wheels. They made these benches *almost* wide enough for my fuller hips and thighs, even if the metal edge slightly digs into my flesh.

Maybe I deserve the dull pain after all I've put my aunt through.

I lay my head on its side, facing the opposite bench.

The light rocking and shaking caused by the gravel roads we're taking doesn't make for the best of sleeps but I eventually drift off, exhausted from the night's events.

Some time later, light shining in through the barred window of the door blinds me awake.

I struggle to rise. After lying on my stomach, I hadn't thought about how I'd sit back up with my hands being of no use.

Deciding that rolling onto the floor is going to be my best option, I land on the floor with a thud. The groan accompanied is reminiscent of two stones grinding against one another.

The sunlight hits my eyes and I squint, grabbling my way, albeit slowly, back onto the bench I rolled off of. I scoot my way to the end closest to the door and crane my neck up in an attempt to peek out the barred window.

The sun is high in the sky, and bright; more white than yellow. We're still amongst redwoods, which isn't saying much as they are rather expansive in this area of Orellia.

I've always loved the strength of the reddish brown trees; tall and mighty. So massive it's impossible to wrap your arms around one of them, let alone several people doing so. The rich, cinnamon-like color bark of the trunk is one of my favorites, second only to the stunning deep green of the leaves flaying outward from the branches in a bristly fashion.

Inhaling, I take in the earthy, slightly spiced, fresh smell of the trees, realizing I will soon no longer be able to.

Resting my head against the side wall, my eyes automatically close.

And of course, now I need to pee.

It's going to be fun trying to convince these King's Guards to let me out of here.

I holler for the closest guard on his horse, whose tail tip I saw flicking around when looking out the window.

"Hey! I need to use the bathroom!"

A scoff is my only response.

"Please? I won't take that long but, I've been in here for a long time now! Nature calls!" I force a laugh, hoping to be persuasive.

The horse comes to a stop as the wagon continues on. A second later, I meet the eyes of the earth wielder, whose face is dark with annoyance.

"Please?" I ask again in my sweetest voice.

He follows behind my death carriage, holding eye contact with me. I scrounge up the largest, pleading gaze possible.

He finally sighs but calls ahead, "Hey, Griffin, can we stop for a minute?"

Grumbles sound up ahead before we slowly roll to a stop.

A horse knickers and the clomping of its hooves comes closer. Around the side rides the fire wielder, Griffin, I assume, atop his steed. Glaring at me through the window with a grumpy expression, he questions me.

"What's your problem?"

"I need to pee. I've been in here a long time," I repeat what I told his friend.

"No, I don't think you do," he scoffs.

"Yes I do. I'm serious. I have to pee. Come on, be human. Have some empathy."

He rolls his eyes before turning back to the earth wielder, pointing at him as if he's scolding a child. "Fine, let her go but *you're* dealing with her, Reid. And make it quick."

Griffin then pulls the reins on his horse and trots back to the front of the wagon.

The earth wielder, Reid, climbs off his steed. He shuffles around with what sounds like a bunch of keys and clicks the lock on my door open.

I squint as it swings open, revealing bright light beams streaming through the redwood branches.

"Come on," he grumbles, grabbing my bicep and pulling.

I stumble out, nearly falling on my ass but held up by his grip on my arm. I'm surprised to hear him mumble a "sorry" as I right myself from my near flop on the ground.

My eyes roam over him but he avoids them, focusing on starting us towards the nearest tree instead.

We reach the giant redwood and he motions to the trunk. "Go ahead."

I stare at him, confused.

"For starters, my hands are behind my back. Also, I can't just 'whip it out' like you guys can, even if I did have access to my limbs. I'll need to go *behind* the tree."

His face reddens at the realization and he freezes, scanning our surroundings and the other guards.

"I'm not going anywhere. I don't even know where we are," I try convincing him, taking a step closer. He looks around again, unsure of himself, before deciding.

"Well, I can't take your cuffs off."

"You can at least switch them to where my hands are in front of me. I do have pants I need to remove after all," I push, taking another step towards him, lightly brushing my breasts against his chest.

This better work, my arms are aching being stretched behind my back.

He audibly gulps as he briefly looks down at my chest, eyes wide, then peers off to the side. "Fine, just… make it quick."

I smile up at him, fluttering my lashes, as he clanks the key ring around, finding the correct one. I turn and he uncuffs my left wrist, takes hold of my forearm, and brings my hands together in front of me as I twist back to face him.

He doesn't meet my gaze when snaps the cuff back on.

"Thank you," I say, my voice sugary sweet as I scurry behind the massive tree.

A few minutes later, after struggling to pull my pajama pants down with my hands bound, then back up again when finished relieving myself, I reluctantly make my way back. "All finished!"

Reid grips my arm once more. Pushed towards my cage again, I notice the air wielder slumped over on the seat at the front of the wagon, reins loose in one hand with his head resting atop the fist of his other. He points me a brief, dirty look.

Griffin and the flirty shadow wielder stand a few paces away, speaking in hushed voices, their horses beside them.

While behind the huge redwood, I considered the possibility of escape, but the image of a knife against my aunt's throat replayed in my head. I swiftly pushed the thought away. I didn't want to find out if they would hold true to their threat and go after her if I did something stupid.

Reaching my cage's door, I pause to eye Reid. "How much longer until we reach the capital?"

He glances at the guards still in conversation and yells, "About how much longer 'til Ataris, Mathias?"

The shadow wielder lifts his head to respond. "About three more days. Depending on how many stops we make."

He looks pointedly at me with the second half of his response.

I roll my eyes and step up into the wagon, Reid slamming the door shut behind me.

Knothaven is nearly on the other side of the kingdom from Ataris, but I haven't done much traveling so the distance has no meaning to me.

These guards have traveled so far, solely with the hope of capturing a multiwielder for Orellia's bastard King. What do they see in him? Why do they continue to do his bidding?

These are questions I realize will probably never be answered. Even if they were, my ears wouldn't be sympathetic to the answers.

"Thank you," I tell Reid through the bars, truly genuine in my tone this time, even if it's only an ounce.

He peers at me with a small, closed lip smile. "Sure thing."

Then, his eyes move down, locking the door, officially securing me back into my dungeon-on-wheels.

Chapter 5

Several hours later, the sun has set, and a deep, navy darkness has set in.

The redwoods are considerably more spooky at night. I may love admiring their beauty during the day time, but they become an impossible labyrinth to navigate once the light fades.

I only ever dared entering the forest after dark when I was with my aunt, foraging for specific supplies for the store; her exquisite navigation skills are something I *definitely* did not inherit.

The wagon eventually slows down and veers to the right before coming to a complete stop.

Out the window, I spy Griffin with a ball of fire in one hand and the reins of his horse in another. He and Mathias lead their steeds to a redwood in the small clearing we've stopped in, securing the animal's reins to the tree. Reid immediately does the same with his own horse.

On the edge of the clearing, a creek weaves through the giant trees.

My stomach growls at the possibility of fish swimming among the current.

Lost in thought, I hadn't noticed Reid approaching the wagon, keys in hand. He reaches the door and gives me a smile.

"I spoke with Griffin, you can come out for the night."

My eyes widen as surprise surges through me. Apparently, batting my lashes at Reid earlier worked to my advantage.

Stretching my arms and legs as best as I can with cuffs restraining movement to both, I step out.

I stare at the clanking between my ankles. While I know some people can, I have never personally been able to wield my abilities with my feet, so this seems excessive. Although, I suppose it does help stop people from running. Walking in these is manageable but running is definitely not a possibility.

To my left, in the middle of the clearing, I see the air wielder and Griffin building a fire.

"What's his name?" I ask Reid, gesturing to the man with air abilities.

"Oh, that's Aiden," he explains before gripping my bicep and leading me over to the fire burning brightly, thanks to Griffin's powers.

I plop down, pulling my knees in so my legs cross in front of me.

"Grab the sleeping bags," Griffin orders without even looking up at Reid. The man glowers but does as he's told.

The shadow wielder, Mathias, heads our way, arms full of supplies. He drops various bags and canisters into a pile between Griffin and Aiden.

The three of them dig through the bags, hauling out bread, dried meat, apples, and oranges. Griffin snatches up one of the canisters, taking a swig from it before pulling away with a sour look on his face.

"Damn. That's some strong shit, Mathias."

I roll my eyes at him.

He must take notice because a glare points my way, then a hunk of bread is chucked at me. I barely catch it before it hits the ground.

The jerk couldn't even hand me my own food?

"The King sure is going to be happy with us, now that we have you to turn over to him. He's always elated each time I bring him back a new soldier," Griffins says, smirking.

I bite down on the inside of my cheek to stop myself from spewing a snarky retort. Staring off into the distance, I ignore him to the best of my ability.

"No witty comeback? I'm surprised," he drawls.

I bite harder into my cheek, and taste the metallic tinge of blood.

I need to find an excuse to walk away. Glancing at the creek, I devise an excuse.

"I need to relieve myself, if you don't mind," I snarl as I stand up, cuffs clanking.

"I'm sure you do," Griffin scoffs.

At the creek, I bend down, peering into the clear water and smooth stones lining the bottom. Pushing my palms into the icy cold, I bring up a handful to splash my face clean.

Feeling the water makes me long to wield it. It's such a strange feeling to be able to submerge my hands in it, but I can't feel its energy or harness its strength.

The coolness drips down my neck from my face. I lean back and tip my face towards the sky, closing my eyes.

"Let's not go too far from camp, okay?"

I spin to find the owner of the question and see Reid, his fire-colored hair dim in the night.

"You don't need to follow me around. Cuffs, remember?" I hold up my bound wrists, jiggling the metal so it clacks together. He frowns.

"I'm just trying to protect you from anything that could be out here in the woods."

A scoff scrapes from my throat before I can think better of it.

"Protect me? You're one of the people who captured me from my own home! If I should be worried about anything in these woods, it should be you lot!"

I snap around, moving to continue down the length of the creek and away from him.

Before I can take my first step, he tightly grips my shoulder, spinning me to face him. He looks down his nose at me and snarls.

"How dare you? I've been nothing but nice to you all day!"

"This is what you call 'nice'? Showing me the slightest bit of human decency? How low is the bar? Is it underground?" Sarcasm dripping from my tone, I investigate the ground, trying to find said bar. "Do you see it? I can't seem to find it."

He flares his nostrils and the sting of a sharp slap runs across my cheek, flinging my head to the side.

My head hangs to the right, caramel hair covering my brow. I take a moment to compose myself. Then, I shove him.

A splash rings out, echoing off the forest. Reid sits, waist deep in the creek, soaking wet, and glaring up at me with furious, wide eyes.

"Maybe you'll find the bar in there," I say, and turn back to the clearing before he has a chance to respond.

I stomp away, clanking the metal cuffs loudly.

Upon reaching camp, I fling out the nearest sleeping roll from its tight form. Crawling inside, cuffs and all, I notice Griffin, Mathias, and Aiden eyeing me strangely. I turn over, giving them my back.

Sloshing stalks up behind me, followed by a cacophony of belly laughter.

"Take a nice dip, Reid?" I hear Griffin slur out. Hollers follow his sarcasm.

"I'm *not* talking about it," Reid responds, frustration filling his tone.

Refusing to flip over and confront any one of them, I lie still, hoping sleep will take me soon, but alas, my mind races with the events of the last twenty-four hours.

I've been attempting to count the number of trees we've passed over the last few hours, solely to try keeping my brain occupied. But I stopped once I reached a thousand.

Bored out of my mind, with only the thoughts of my fate once I'm presented at the castle running through my head, I start to investigate the cuffs binding my limbs.

The late morning sun hits the metal through the barred window of my wagon.

A gleaming, gray metal, they slightly scratch around my wrists and ankles. A few inches of chain made of the same light gray material hold the two cuffs on my arms together. At my feet, the linked chain between my ankles is slightly longer than the width of my hips.

While the view of the collar around my neck is extremely limited, it seems to be of the same metal. And to my knowledge, they are a rather new idea. I wonder when the King decided that these were necessary.

And collars? Of all things? *Kinky*, King Kairos.

The cuffs are infamous; known for stopping the wearer from using their abilities. But I've never seen a pair up close before. Whether or not the exact science of the mineral is known has never been revealed to the public.

I doubt it ever will be.

I know the metal they're made of is mined exclusively in the White Mountains, near the capital. And only in Orellia is such a substance found.

Non-wielders or single wielders who committed nearly any crime were shipped to the mines when they were found guilty, giving the King a consistent source of free labor. Any multiwielders found guilty of committing a crime are taken to join the King's Army instead.

I can only wonder of the fate of those who end up in the mines.

Kairos' father, the ruler before him, King Amos, discovered the mineral in the mountains. King Amos assured the kingdom it would only be used on prisoners who possessed abilities, and he kept to that promise.

Obviously, his son, who was crowned after his passing, did not share those same ideals.

In a show of force and control, as soon as he was named King, Kairos assigned his predecessor's guards to capture those found with multiwielding abilities. As the years went on, most people in Orellia learned to hide the fact they were multiwielders.

Myself included.

Although I wouldn't have even been given the chance to do so if it weren't for their sacrifice.

My mind races back to that night eleven years ago.

And how the shouts of the King's Guards combined with the screaming of my parents. Then, the adrenaline rush I felt as my mother swiftly ushered me out the back door of our cottage. Even the sound of horse's neighs that echoed through the woods still rings clear in my memories.

A beam of sun shines into my eyes from the window above and I look up from examining my shackles, pushing the thoughts away.

The redwoods outside are sparse as we approach the edge of the massive forest. The ground around the remaining trees starts to fill in with a thick, lush, green grass, foreign to the majority of the typically dirt-covered forest floor.

The last few dozen redwood trees pass by in a blur and I'm met with sprawling fields. The blades of grass grow fuller and taller than I've ever seen before. The sunlight reflects off the vibrant green, making the whole field shine.

This place is so different from the forest I have come to love. It's so much brighter, warmer.

Breathtaking grassy fields stretch as far as the eye can see, pale flowers sit in small bunches ready to pick, graceful willow trees scatter the space, waiting for people to take cover under after a long day in the beaming sun. Their long wispy branches nearly touch the ground and swish side to side, as if they're waving hello to me. It's truly the epitome of spring.

I stare at the rolling green for a long while, taking it in. Some time later, the sound of the guard's voices pick up on the wind, floating their way to me, only partially coherent.

"…village for more supplies."

"I agree but we…"

"…be fine."

"Before meeting the King…"

"…days away."

Their voices drift away but their plan is clear. We will be stopping at a village before reaching the King's castle.

What a joy. A pit stop to put off my inevitable doom.

Chapter 6

When the carriage jostles and the clomping of horse's hooves loudens, I peer out my barred window at the town we've entered.

All of the buildings are made of a reddish-brown brick and light cream stucco, giving a rough texture to the walls. Deep chocolate wooden beams run vertically and diagonally across the pale stucco. People line the streets, some standing in front of the warm brown doors of their homes and shops, the roofs of the buildings matching in color. The path below consists of pale white, light gray, and soft peach inlaid cobblestones.

Dozens of men and women walk in either direction, some in pairs or groups, many of them carrying some kind of supplies or food. Baskets full of fruits and vegetables are placed upon women's heads and hips. The fresh scents of apples, pears, pumpkins, and squash combine, wafting into my carriage and filling my nostrils.

We pass multiple men hunched over, rolling dark wooden barrels on their side down the street.

Carts selling various foods and goods are spread out on either side of the path, mostly occupied by older men and women who sit behind them in order to face customers. A few of them begin to close down for the night as the sun heads west.

I hear the laughter of children before they race past. Four of them, by my count, chasing a scrappy dog who looks like he's having the time of his life playing with the children.

Down a side street, an open top wagon pulled by a horse and full of hay comes our way. We travel past several more, piled high with various items, pulled by both horses and donkeys.

We reach what seems to be the town's center: a large, square area opening at least four or five times the width of the cobblestone paths. More carts line the square's edges, and more people travel in every direction.

In the middle of it all stands a huge, white limestone fountain, three tiers high. My jaw drops open at the sheer sight of it.

The wagon slows to a stop near a cluster of bustling shops. A mother and her young son make eye contact with me, and her eyes go wide as she forcibly turns his head away and pulls him along, away from me.

I gulp, ashamed.

A jolt of the carriage rumbles my seat before the dismounting of horses sounds.

I notice more people beginning to stare at me, the wagon, and I would assume, the four King's Guards accompanying me.

Griffin approaches my window with a smirk. "We're just stopping for supplies. Don't get yourself into any trouble now, okay?"

Rolling my eyes, I stare anywhere but at him.

A while later, after the sun has begun its descent behind the tops of the village's buildings, I hear a commotion.

Rising to my feet, I peek through the bars to see a scramble of people coming down the path we took to reach the town's center, right towards me. As they approach, the scene becomes more clear.

A young woman around my age with deep brown skin and dozens of long, dark braids is thrashing around as she's being dragged this way by two men. The ends of her braids swish back and forth a hair below her elbows as she fights against them.

One of the men is tall, bulky, and middle aged, with dark skin much like the woman's. The other man is similar in age to me, with pale skin, shaggy blonde hair, and lanky limbs.

She writhes around, pulling and yanking against their hold on her. She yells incoherently, doing everything she can in an attempt to get out of their grasp.

My mouth hangs ajar as they close in. Her yelling is no longer incoherent.

She's cursing at them, one expletive after the next, as she slams against the two men.

Then, after a particularly long string of profanity, she takes in a deep breath, cranes her head back, and blasts a breath of fire out of her mouth, into the sky.

I feel my eyes go wide at the sight. I've heard of powerful wielders possessing the skill of fire breathing, but I've never seen it with my own eyes.

She's remarkable.

The lanky, blonde man jumps back, loosening his grip on her arm. He spins slightly and I notice the crest on his shoulder. He's a part of the King's Guard.

My mouth gapes wider at the sight unfolding before me.

I bet she's a multiwielder.

The restraints she has around her wrists and ankles match my own, but she's missing a collar. That's why she can still breathe fire.

Breathe fire.

Astonishment courses through me at the pure strength of her ability.

The young guard tightens his hold again once the girl ceases shooting heat into the sky. The older man seems unfazed by her actions, and continues dragging her closer.

She kicks, aiming to knock both of the men's legs out from underneath them. She slams her toned shoulders into them, left, right, and back again. Her restrained wrists in front of her stomach pull tightly in either direction, as if she can rip the cuffs in half.

Griffin, Mathias, Reid, and Aiden run into view only a split second later, Griffin with a collar in hand. As soon as he reaches her, he snaps it around her neck. She thrashes against his touch, but it's too late.

The two men with ahold of her arms throw her to the ground, huffing and puffing as they stare down at her.

She falls to her knees, then onto her stomach. She swiftly flips around, onto her back, staring up at the now six men surrounding her.

The town's center has gone eerily quiet, everyone frozen in place, watching the scene.

"You disgusting little bitch! I'm so glad to be rid of you! Let the King's Army deal with your ass!" the older man yells as she snarls at him from her place on the cobblestones.

I *am* right, she is a multiwielder, but a cold chill runs down my spine at his words.

"Fuck you!" she spits back at him.

"You are *filthy*, and you don't deserve to live in my house any longer," he drags out, his words slightly slurred.

The realization hits me then, slamming into me like a brick wall.

He's her *father*.

And he's *turning her in* for being a multiwielder.

"Good luck surviving without me! You can't do anything on your own!" she rips into him.

He moves to kick her, but Aiden holds him back with a shove to the chest.

"You're a disgrace!" he screams.

"Okay. We got it from here," Griffin steps in, voice booming. He stands in front of her father, forcing him back.

Her father digs his feet into the ground and sways to the side a bit, trying to stare Griffin down.

"I'm tired of your theatrics. Leave us," Griffin orders him, crossing his arms over his chest in a powerful stance.

The man huffs, looks back and forth between the young woman and Griffin, and spins around, heading back in the direction they came from.

A breath releases from deep in my chest as the man finally stalks off into the distance.

Griffin pulls the young, blonde guard aside as Aiden holds out a hand to the fire breathing woman. She reluctantly grabs his open palm after staring at it for several long seconds. His grip moves to her bicep once she stands.

She starts to writhe against his grip but Mathias appears, grabbing her other arm. She slows the stirring as they approach my door, her eyes widening when they connect with me through the window.

I move to the bench I was on before this whole commotion started as Aiden and Mathias give her a small shove inside. She stumbles in, attempting to catch herself on the opposite bench before falling completely.

Her gaze locks with mine as she pushes herself upright and flops down across from me.

"I- I saw what happened. Are you okay?" I ask tentatively. I realize it's a stupid question, but my brain hasn't formed a better one yet.

"Yeah, I'll be fine," she says, wiping blood off her lip.

She has a split lower lip freely bleeding. She stares at the red, now on her hand, and wipes it across her fitted black jeans.

A bruise is forming above her right eye—her rather stunning eyes, now that I notice them. They're a deep honey brown, with bright golden rings encircling both of her pupils, unlike anything I've ever seen. They're not only bright, but fiery too.

Like her, I suppose.

She is quite beautiful, with a slightly oval face and full, pouty lips. She's tall, around my height if I had to guess, and an athletic build from what I can tell with her snug, black pants and cream, sleeveless tunic. Her black hair is split into dozens of small braids. She moves a few to the side and I whip my gaze away, realizing I've been staring.

"I'm so sorry about what happened to you," I tell her, facing her once more. I may not know the whole story but I saw enough to know, whatever it is, it's horrible.

She laughs. "It's not your fault. You don't need to apologize."

"I guess you're right, it's not...," I trail off but begin again. "Anyways, I'm Aurora."

"Rowan," she smiles, the blood finally starting to clot on her lip.

"Nice to meet you. Although, I suppose I do wish it was under better circumstances," I laugh out on a huff, eyeing the dark, metal wagon.

"I can't disagree with you there," she chuckles to herself. "Are you from around here?"

I shake my head. "No, not really. They took me from my home a little over a day and a half ago. I live in Knothaven, deep in the redwoods."

She nods her head. "I'm sorry."

"It's not your fault," I repeat back to her, a genuine chuckle bubbling up.

"I've never seen a redwood tree, but I hear they're beautiful."

"They are. I miss them already," I say, memories of home springing into my mind.

I shake the images of Knothaven away as swiftly as they arrived and gesture around.

"Anyways, welcome to my humble abode. I even decided to include extra seating for any potential visitors," I say, eyeing the metal bench she sits on with a giggle.

"Ah, yes. Thank you for thinking of guests such as myself." She laughs, matching my sarcasm.

"Please, make yourself at home."

I chuckle, and her own laughter builds.

We inspect the inside of this dungeon-on-wheels and fall into simultaneous fits of laughter before we know it. Laughing about our meeting, the misery of our circumstances. A fit of laughter because what else are we supposed to do? Cry? I've already done my fair share. Wallow? I've done some of that too, and it's not going to help where I'm at right now.

Maybe laughing is the only thing I can do in this moment to cope with everything that's happened.

After some time, we catch our breaths and wipe away spilled tears from both of our eyes. Composure regained, I tilt my head back, leaning it against the cold, metal wall.

We sit in silence before I begin to think more about Rowan and her circumstance.

Why would her father turn her over as a multiwielder? That information about me couldn't be tortured out of my aunt. She would have done anything to protect my secret. Why wasn't Rowan's father the same? I always assumed people would protect their multiwielding loved ones as fiercely as my aunt had protected me.

I suppose that was extremely naive of me.

My chest aches for her, and my stomach flips as the questions spin around in my mind. Removing my head from the wall, I look at her incredulously.

"I-," I start but stop myself. I shouldn't.

She narrows her dark brows at me. "What is it?"

"Um, nothing. I don't want to pry," I say, turning away.

"Well, since we're roommates now, I suppose we ought to get to know each other better. So, spill it."

My gaze roams over to see her sitting smugly, hands folded in her lap, as if she's waiting. I warily answer her demand.

"I was going to ask you why he would turn you in for being a multiwielder. That was your father, right? And you are a multiwielder?"

"Yes, that was him. And yes, I am."

So I *did* guess those two things correctly.

She sighs, continuing. "And he turned me in because he caught me kissing another woman."

My eyes widen, nearly bulging out of my head. "Seriously? That's the most ridiculous thing I've ever heard. I'm so sorry."

My mind goes to my aunt, who was always supportive of me. I've dated men and women, some of whom she ended up meeting, and she had loved me all the same.

I couldn't fathom not having that kind of support, especially from a parent or loved one. I know not all people receive the same as I did, but to use hatred as a reason to turn them over for the King's Army?

The ache in my chest expands at the thought.

Rowan takes in a deep breath and lets it out before continuing. "Yeah, I had a feeling he wouldn't like it so I never brought any of the women I've dated around him, which isn't exactly hard to do since he's gone half the time."

I sit quietly as she tells me her story.

"He's a drunk. A useless, idiotic drunk. He'll go out for a drink at one of the pubs or taverns in town and won't come back for the next several days."

She stops briefly before continuing.

"I used to worry about him. In the beginning, I would search all over town for him. It was embarrassing, having to ask around if anyone had seen him. I would visit each of his regular spots in between my shifts at The Wild Willow, the *one* tavern he would never visit, of course." Rowan shakes her head at this, rolling her eyes.

"He didn't like it when I got a job there when I turned eighteen. But I needed work, and he was fired from his own job a few months prior, not long after my mother died."

She pauses after this reveal, sighing before going on.

"We needed a way to pay the bills and he was of no help. He hasn't bothered doing anything, besides getting wasted of course, since she passed a little over four years ago. And these benders, they started off being one or two days but lately they've been getting longer. Up to a week now. I don't know or care what he does during them at this point. Today was day four."

She shakes her head again, leaning it back to rest against the wall.

"Of course he had to come home when I had Myla over. He slammed the door open, nearly taking it off the damn hinges before going on his tirade. Screaming at us, cursing at us."

Rowan's hands in her lap curl into fists as she speaks.

"I led her out the back door. Then, after she left, things got physical and he eventually dragged me out of the house. I had no idea what he was thinking when he took the argument outside. Not until we got further down the street and rounded a corner, when he spotted a guard. That's when he started yelling he had 'found a multiwielder for the King' hoping the guard would look over at us. And of course he did. And, well… you know the rest."

She brings her head off the wall, her eyes landing on mine, and shrugs.

I don't even know where to begin. My mouth is wide open, and I have no clue what to say next.

"I- it's insane… that you went through that," I tell her. It's all I can come up with, even though it's a completely useless thing to say.

"Yeah, tell me about it," she laughs out before resting her elbows on her knees, clasping her palms together.

I look at her, narrowing my brows as I try to figure out more to say. After a minute, I continue.

"I'm so sorry, again. I know I've already said it, but I am. Truly. I know how hard it can be to accept yourself, let alone tell others about that part of you," I pause, swallowing a gulp. "What he did was terrible. It may not mean much but know you'll always have me and my support. We're in this together now, stuck in this dungeon-on-wheels."

I reach my restrained hands across the space between us, setting them gently on her folded ones. Gazing at her, I give her what I hope comes across as a hopeful smile.

Her lips tilt upward. "Thank you. I appreciate it."

The wagon dips then, a sign I've come to know as Aiden climbing onto his seat. Neighs ring out a split second later.

"Off we go," I joke to Rowan.

"Oh, *goodie*," she responds with a chuckle dripping in sarcasm.

Scanning the outside before we pull away, I spy the sun officially setting beyond the village, sending flame-like streaks of gold and pink across the sky.

Chapter 7

There's not much to see in the darkness. The sliver of a moon is high in the sky, a stretch of shining stars scatter on either side, illuminating the fields of green outside. I slump back from peering out between the bars and sigh.

"I'm hungry," I tell Rowan, exasperated.

"Me too."

"And I need to pee, so I could definitely use a stop right about now!" I shout loud enough for the guards to hear.

Rowan snickers at my comment.

Griffin slows his horse and starts trailing behind us. He narrows his eyes at me. I give him a proud, toothy grin in response.

"We will stop soon. And not because of you two, so don't flatter yourselves. The horses are starting to tire."

"Yes, I'm sure they're *also* tired of your shit," I say, holding my wide smile. Rowan covers her mouth with a fist to hide her chuckle.

Griffin doesn't bother with a response before rounding the side of the wagon, disappearing from sight.

Rowan and I hold on to our respective benches to stop from falling onto the ground when our death carriage screeches to a harsh halt.

Griffin eventually arrives, a small ball of fire lit in one hand and with his other, he unlocks our door, swinging it open.

"You're welcome," he snarks at us as we pass him with no comment, stepping out of our wheeled cage.

After Rowan and I relieve ourselves a safe distance away behind some willow trees, I take in our surroundings.

The grassy clearing is significantly smaller than last night. On the left, a dozen or so willow trees sit in the shape of a crescent. A small stream, only as wide as the wagon, crosses through the clearing on the right, going so far off into the distance I can't tell where it ends.

The two of us walk upstream and begin to rinse what we can with our restraints.

"Have you tried to escape yet?" Rowan whispers.

I stare over at her hunched figure beside me in disbelief.

"I'm flattered you think I'd be able to take on all four of them without my abilities, and with my wrists and ankles restrained." I hold up the cuffs at my wrists in show.

"They also threatened to go back and harm my aunt if I gave them any problems. So, while I have thought about it, it's just not realistic. I don't want her harmed and I wouldn't know where to go anyways. These guards have spent years traveling all over the kingdom, have you noticed they don't even use maps?"

"Damn, I understand. And you're right, they must know the kingdom quite well by now," she says with a sigh. She splashes water on her face, scrubbing at the dirt and blood from the day.

"We don't have our powers, there's four of them and only two of us, and I truly have no idea where we are or how to get back," I tell her, realizing my hopelessness as I say it aloud.

She nods. "We're powerless with these cuffs on. And they keep switching around that key ring, so I have no idea who has it at any time."

"I've thought about trying to steal the keys at night, but one of them stays up to keep watch. I overheard them discussing it as I fell asleep last night."

"Damn," she grumbles.

"I know, we're fucked."

We fall into a bout of silence, washing in the cool water. Eventually, with a wordless look, we head over to where the four guards sit in a half circle around a fire and. I survey the food they pull out of pouches.

"What's for dinner?"

"For you? Bread. Maybe more if I'm feeling generous," Mathias answers me snarkily.

"Here," Aiden follows, holding up two hunks of sourdough and two red apples. I snatch them up, handing half to Rowan and giving him a nod. Rowan and I flop onto the ground, eating quietly after the long day.

The King's Guards proceed to consume their dinners, along with whatever alcohol is in the two canteens they pass around. Their talking swiftly turns into hollering, led by Griffin, the drink taking effect.

Eyeing Rowan, I lean over to whisper as close to her ear as possible.

"I slept outside last night, but they weren't nearly this rowdy."

Her gaze bounces to them, then back to me. "Maybe sleeping in the dungeon-on-wheels tonight is a better idea?" She quirks an eyebrow.

I dip my chin in agreement.

Some clanking around and two sleeping rolls later, we're each lying on our rock-hard metal benches, attempting to get comfortable.

Rowan speaks up after our flipping and flopping stops.

"Can I ask you something?"

"Of course."

"Does it make me a bad person if I no longer care about my father's fate?" She turns her head to me, pondering.

"That's… not what I expected you to say," I tell her honestly, flipping onto my side to face her.

She releases a small laugh at my candor.

"No. No, I don't. Especially after what he did to you today," I say simply.

She's a good one, I know it.

Her lips turn into a solemn smile before looking up at the ceiling.

"Thanks," she says after a minute.

"Of course, Rowan. Good night."

"Good night."

The next full day and night pass in a blur. Rowan and I only leave our dungeon-on-wheels a few times to relieve ourselves or stretch our legs before climbing back inside.

We woke this morning with stiff backs for the second day in a row after sleeping on our metal benches, but it is decidedly better than spending another second with the drunken King's Guards.

It's hard to believe only three nights have passed since we've left my village, and my aunt.

It feels like a lifetime.

And it feels as if Rowan and I have known one another all our lives.

Rowan shares she not only worked at a tavern in the evening, but as a seamstress's assistant during the day in order to get by. I inform her of my aunt's shop, and the concoctions we created then sold to help with various ailments.

She tells me of her mother, who passed four years ago after being sick for a number of years. I describe the first time the King's Guards tried to kidnap me, when I was a child, and how it resulted in my parents' deaths.

Needless to say, there were more than a few tears shed as we traded stories.

Last night we stopped on the outskirts of the capital, barely able to make out the outline of the city in the distance.

Those outlines are now full-fledged buildings.

I let out an audible gasp as I take in the sight of it all through our little window.

Variations of plain beige, muddy brown, and drab charcoal gray buildings line either side of the narrow street. Old, deteriorating brick makes up the foundation of several of them. Some buildings tower to what looks to be three, or perhaps even four, stories.

I've never seen any *that* tall.

As I investigate closer, I notice the buildings are a mixture of shops and houses. Some even have a store on the first floor and an apartment above them, similar to how my aunt and I lived.

I smile as the memory floods my mind.

Like Rowan's village, the homes and shops are stacked right on top of each other. Roofs connect in some areas, made of either shingles or tiles in the same bland tones.

Below, the wagon's wheels bump along uneven, dark gray bricks.

The city seems to stretch forever. The only backdrop being the King's castle, so far off in the distance I can barely make out its shape, with the staggering, foggy white mountain range beyond it.

"The capital is huge," I say in awe to Rowan, who remains sitting across from me.

"I remember it being massive. I'm sure being six or seven years old made everything look bigger than it is, but the city still stretched on forever."

Rowan mentioned earlier today she visited Ataris once before with her mother and father. She said she doesn't remember much about the trip, aside from tasting the best chocolate cake she had ever eaten.

The carriage jerks, and I plop into my seat, gripping it, waiting.

As we travel further into the city, the louder it gets.

Rowan and I stand, squished together in front of our barred window to investigate the noises.

The streets are busy, vendors shouting at passersby to buy their items for sale. Stands of fruits, vegetables, baked goods, ceramics, and fabrics are packed densely along the walkways, directly in front of other businesses.

While these stands are similar to that of Rowan's village, the quality is poor. Flies buzz around the food. The wear and tear of the items is apparent, even from here.

The sellers are also harsh, yelling at people, talking over neighboring stands. The energy is high. People rush through the streets, briskly walking past the stands as if they're on a mission. Most people hustling and bustling up and down the street ignore the hollering. They must be used to it.

Our wagon isn't drawing nearly as much attention as it did in Rowan's village either; most don't give us a second glance.

People dart back and forth across the packed street. Other wagons narrowly pass by, heading in either direction.

I spot another dungeon-on-wheels, a twin to our own, and my stomach jumps into my throat.

I wonder… are there more multiwielders in there? Or others? They carry criminals, too. Or in the King's eyes, are we one in the same? If we've been hiding our abilities in order to escape the King's Army, are we considered criminals, too?

There are people who follow his absurd law, turning themselves in to him at eighteen. Loyalists, they're called. Believing it's their rightful duty as citizens of Orellia to serve the King in his *special* multiwielder army.

I couldn't agree less.

The King's a *bastard*. A hateful, power hungry man, believing we're his rightful property.

He's the reason my parents are dead.

A spark of rage flames within me at the thought of him. My hands ball into fists before I can stop myself. Squeezing my eyes shut, I rest back onto my cold, metal bench.

"I can't stop thinking about what might happen when we get there," I say, my breath shaky as I try to stomp out my rising temper.

Rowan sits, then leans across the distance between us, putting her hands on mine just as I did when we first met.

"Everything will be okay," she says through a tentative smile.

I give her a look, raising my brows. "Don't lie."

"Well, if you think about it, it doesn't seem like he'll kill us, right? He wants us for his army, which means he needs us alive."

"What a *comforting* thought Rowan. Thank you," I answer, sarcasm heavy in my voice.

She grins brightly at me before saying, "I'm glad I could be of some assistance."

I roll my eyes, smirking, and she removes her hands.

We surge forward a moment later, coming to a rough stop, nearly tumbling off our benches.

Shouting echoes, above what we've come to know as the normal level of volume here in the capital.

"What now?" Rowan asks, standing and moving to the window.

I stand, following her lead.

A scuffle between three men rounds the side of the carriage. Two of them wear the guard's crest in the shape of a shield on their shoulder, a crown sitting atop a smaller shield, the emblem of a tree in it. The third man is hidden beneath a long, black, hooded cloak. Only wisps of warm, brown skin, and dark curls under the hood are visible amongst the wrestling.

One of the guards unleashes a bolt of fire at the cloaked man.

He narrowly avoids the blast and whips pitch black shadows back at the guard.

The second guard shoots out a gust of wind, attempting to block the darkness from reaching his partner.

Too late, the shadows twine around the guard's body, like a vine crawling up a tree, forcing his arms to his sides.

Griffin, Mathias, Reid, and Aiden run past our wagon then, straight into the fight.

Griffin immediately sends a fireball for the cloaked man's head, with Mathias right behind, fighting his own shadows with the ones wrapped around the guard.

Aiden fires off a blast of wind as Reid bends to the ground, placing his hands on the bricks, and sends a ripple coursing through the ground. Shaking then cracking, the man is pulled down as if he's in quicksand.

The shadows around the restrained guard evaporate.

And the cloaked man sends a flurry of wind to his slowly sinking feet.

He lifts his boots out in a flash, jumping out of the hole.

He pushes the air harder into the ground, flying backwards several paces, and lands steadily on the ground.

"He's a *multiwielder*." My jaw drops when I state it aloud.

"And a ballsy one at that, attempting to take on *six* guards," Rowan mumbles, eyeing the scene.

The man's hood falls off. His face is young, around my age, perhaps a bit younger. He sends out gusts of wind with one hand and shadows with the other.

I guess he isn't afraid of them finding out now.

Griffin throws flame after flame at the man, uncontrolled and sloppy.

Mathias and Aiden fight with their matching abilities, but come up short, their shadows and air proving useless against the man's same powers. Blending together, they create swirling cones of darkness and wind.

Reid, palms still flush against the cobblestones, rips the ground apart further.

But the cloaked man has catlike reflexes. Dodging and weaving, he blocks every blast coming from all directions with his own shadows and wind.

He's brilliant. *And powerful.*

Attack after attack, he doesn't look to be slowing down.

Smoke fills the air from the burning flames. Tendrils of black whip in waves. Walls of wind send debris flying.

Then, the ground rumbles once more.

Reid crumbles the stone beneath the young man's heels.

The back of his feet sink down, throwing him off balance and onto his back.

From their back pockets, the guards pull out cuffs, snapping them onto his wrists and ankles in a flash. Griffin appears with a collar in hand

and after yanking him by the cloak, the metal shines, connected around the man's neck.

Mathias and Reid haul him up, starting towards us. The young man kicks and elbows as they drag him.

Griffin shouts at them to halt, and they pause. He frisks the man, pushing his hands into the depths of his cloak.

When Griffin's palms leave the man's body, they each hold a thick stack of star-shaped daggers, five sharp metal points on them all.

Damn.

With a jerk of his head, Griffin urges them onward once more.

Despite the mess they made while attempting to capture the man, the guards don't seem to notice—or care.

The people on the street have scattered, hiding in buildings or behind stands. As they slowly peek out to survey the damage, their eyes go wide, and mouths gape.

The ground is in ruins, thanks to Reid. The bricks have cracked and crumbled into rubble. Vendors' stands are singed from the fire, and black burn marks scatter the ground. Blasts sent items flying. The once neatly stacked fruits, vegetables, and baked goods now lay smashed among the cracked bricks.

"Get back," Griffin yells, reaching for the carriage.

Rowan and I back away, and onto our benches.

Keys jingle and the door swings open, letting in a wave of bright, warm sun. Mathias and Reid throw the man in, shoving his shoulders.

He lands at our feet with a bone crunching thud.

I cringe at the sound. I'm positive it hurt.

One of the guards slams the door shut before locking and stomping away, leaving us with our new, powerful, multiwielding friend.

Chapter 8

"That was one hell of a fight out there. You okay?" I glance at Rowan as she questions the young man.

He responds only with a grumble as he rolls and shifts around until he's sitting up, struggling with his hands restrained behind him.

He scoots to the far wall of the wagon, opposite of the door. Curling up, he rests the side of his head against the metal, staring down at his boots.

"You're welcome to come up here, if you'd like," I suggest, motioning to the empty space next to me on the bench.

He forcefully shakes his head, folding himself in smaller.

I lean down, a bit closer to him, trying to feel out his temperament. He only huffs out a sigh.

"Ok then..."

I raise a brow at Rowan. She shrugs her shoulders at me.

A loud bang sounds against the metal of the wagon, as if someone is slamming their hand against the door, sending a vibration running through my entire body.

Griffin peers through our barred window, not at us, but at the curled up figure sitting on the floor. "So, you're not just a multiwielder, but a thief too? That kind of crap won't be tolerated in the King's Army, you got it?"

Rowan and I exchange confused glances.

I peek at the young man out of the corner of my eye. He sits, unmoving, an emotionless look plastered on his face, ignoring Griffin's remarks.

Griffin's eyes narrow, staring him down, then lets out a frustrated huff.

"This is what you get for stealing, little guy," he says snarkily before stalking off.

The young man's eyes briefly flash over, noting Griffin had left, before returning his gaze downward.

"That was Griffin. He's always rude. Don't mind him," I say to make conversation.

I give him a smile, hoping for a response.

He lifts his dark eyes to mine, and just as I think he may say something, he glances back down.

I try one more time. "What's your name?"

"You could at least tell us that much," Rowan chimes in, hopeful.

That gets his attention. He turns his head to Rowan and gives her a mysterious look. His eyes roam over to me before grunting his answer to my question.

"Sebastian."

"Nice to meet you, Sebastian. I'm Aurora, and this is Rowan," I tell him, motioning with my head to Rowan.

She gives him a small smile, slumping back in her seat. I give him a matching one, hoping it looks encouraging.

He nods his head in acknowledgement before staring at his boots again.

I finally give up on trying to get him to talk when our dungeon-on-wheels lurches forward.

The three of us sit in silence for a long while. During that time, I listen to the sounds of the capital.

Other wagons squeak past us, pulled by nickering horses and snorting donkeys. Children's squeals echo off the buildings around us. Some people who pass tread lightly, casually, while others are fast and heavy on their feet as they sprint past.

The smells also hit me. The scents of freshly baked bread and sweet citrus fruit, occasionally mixed with horse or donkey dung, at which I bring my hand up to cover my nose and mouth.

Smells of warm soup and smoked meat fill my nose when we pass by restaurants. As does the pungent reek of spilled beer.

The wagon sways to the side as we turn left, right, and left again.

I adjust on my hard bench, wiggling and crossing then uncrossing my ankles multiple times. My unrest only gets worse as time goes on, knowing we're only getting closer to the King's castle. Anxiety rises in my stomach, sending my insides tumbling.

To force myself out of my head, I stretch up, looking out at my surroundings.

The further we stray from the city's edges, the fewer people crowd the streets. The number of stalls selling goods drops by half, and the people working them aren't yelling. It's more peaceful.

While there's still hustle and bustle, it's smoother. People aren't as frantic. They walk with purpose but don't rush. The children passing by have their hands held by parents. Tailored pants and shirts cling to men's bodies while unique dresses cover women's.

As I study the pathways, I notice they look cleaner too. They're less trafficked than the outskirts. No horse or donkey dung is swept to the sides, either. The wagons we pass are only drawn by horses anyways—not a donkey in sight.

Groups of King's Guards walk up and down the streets, patrolling the area with a watchful eye.

The shops and homes are spaced out, and appear to be of higher quality too. Hand painted tiles surround doorways. Once drab, dull gray buildings are replaced with crisp white ones. Colorful shutters line the sides of windows in shades of green, blue, and red. No cracked bricks or deterioration of any kind is to be found.

The stark differences of the capital become clear as we draw closer to the castle; the city is well taken care of *only* where the King can see it.

It's where he puts more money and builds a better economy. Of course he wouldn't care about the sight of his capital if it's too far away from him to see.

What a bastard.

I turn to Rowan, telling her my thoughts on the observations.

"It's probably areas like this where most of the loyalists come from too," she says when I finish my rant on the King and his capital.

I swear I hear Sebastian scoff at the end of my tirade too. I investigate him but he doesn't move or make a sound when I do.

Between the bars, the sun begins to lower itself behind the White Mountains that split our kingdom and Norfell.

"The view is, admittingly, very beautiful," I say to Rowan, motioning her over. She slides across her bench and peeks up to look out with me.

"You got that right."

Tears begin building in my eyes as I face her.

At the thought of what's to come. The unknown, the things they may put us through in order to become a part of the King's Army.

Trying to shove the thoughts and the tears down, I take a deep breath in to calm myself.

"We're gonna be okay. Everything will turn out okay," she whispers to me. A single tear escapes as she reassures me. I nod, forcing myself to think positively.

"I've cried too much in the past few days. It's all been out of my control. No more," I laugh out, wiping the stray tear away.

"We'll get through this together. And we'll see what we can do about getting you some control back once we get there and see what they want with us," she declares with a grin.

I dip my chin to her. "You're right."

"Ah yes, some of my favorite words."

I roll my eyes at her cockiness. However, my lips can't help but rise into a smile.

I feel another pair of eyes on me and I twist to find Sebastian staring at us. As soon as I catch him, his eyes go wide and he looks back down.

The wagon then takes a hard turn, forcing us all to hold on to anything within reach.

Once we're steady again, I peek back out to see castle gates being closed behind us by two guards. Iron, castle gates that are no longer off in the distance, but right in front of me.

My mouth goes dry and my heart plummets into my stomach as I realize: We're finally here.

Chapter 9

Griffin's grasp tightens around my arm and I'm yanked from our dungeon-on-wheels; Rowan and Sebastian are hauled along after me.

Tilting my head up, I inspect the monstrosity before me.

A chill runs down my spine, but I'm unsure if it's from a breeze passing through or if it's accompanying the knot forming in my stomach. As much as I'd like to say it's the former, I don't find it likely.

The White Mountains tower above either side of the castle; the distant mountains splitting Orellia from Norfell being the only thing the palace backs up to.

Sunshine bounces off the granite walls of the castle, forcing me to squint my eyes. Sharp lines of gunmetal gray roofing tiles stretch up and back down at varying heights, splitting the estate into sections.

High above, several specks of deep red sway with the wind—the King's banners at the top of each tower's peak.

To my left and right, the building stretches far beyond what I can see. It's never ending, eventually seeming to run into the surrounding mountains.

A wide set of stone stairs leading up to a pair of double doors begins a few paces ahead.

As I examine the castle, the tall, wooden doors leading inside creak open outward at the hands of more King's Guards.

Gulping, I peek over at my death-carriage companions, who are also taking in the massive, looming palace. Before I can process anything further, Griffin smirks viciously and tugs me forward, escorting me to the steps.

The escort is more of a show of force, with Griffin practically dragging me to the doors. Stumbling, I do my best to keep my feet under my body.

The guards holding the doors open give those of us in chains seething looks, but I don't have time to return the glare as I'm dragged through the entrance and down a lengthy corridor.

Dark, slate gray walls extend over us as we make our way towards a second set of doors at the far end of the hall. Sconces filled with floating balls of light line either side of the long hall, but are unsuccessful in truly brightening the dark, foreboding corridor.

"You know, we do have our own feet to walk on," Rowan barks at Mathias, who's firm hold is around her elbow.

She stumbles as she sasses him. A scoff and rolled eyes is his only response.

Sebastian is positioned between us, with Aiden and Reid gripping each of his restrained arms tightly.

The two of them have a grand time pushing him forward in an effort to make him move faster. He shoves and jerks against them each time, staying silent as he does so.

As we approach the ominous set of massive doors, Griffin speaks up.

"You are not to speak once we're in there. You will only speak *if* you are spoken to and *if* a response is required. Got it?"

I glance over at Rowan, and our eyes meet before I turn to Griffin and smirk.

"Sure thing," she mocks sweetly.

She *definitely* won't be listening to those orders.

And I'm on the exact same page.

Sebastian doesn't reply, no surprise there.

"The King will see you now," a guard announces as he swings the ornately engraved wooden doors open.

The fear and uncertainty once held within me dissipates, and is replaced with a burst of rage. My stomach warms, my chest tightens, and my teeth clench together as a grand throne room is revealed.

At the opposite end, atop his sleek, black throne sits none other than the bastard himself—*King Kairos Amos Aragon.*

My eyes narrow in on him, taking in his features.

His dark, black hair is neatly slicked back beneath his golden crown. His face is all hard lines and angular; it's not necessarily ugly, but aged, and full of distaste. And his eyes are a deep, unforgiving brown.

Though his face may not be entirely unbecoming, hatred radiates off him in waves, seeping from the deepest parts of his soul.

His posture is rigid; his spine a metal rod. He wears a deep red, velvet garb, draped over his body like a cloak, flowing down his arms. Black, flowy material makes up the pants covering his lower half. Shining, black dress shoes follow, fitting his feet as if they were custom made. Stacked golden rings cover all of his tan fingers sitting on either arm rest of his throne.

My vexation intensifies the closer we get, and it almost makes me miss the men standing on either side of the King.

To his right is an older man with long, gray hair and a matching beard, with a face aged much older than the King's, with wrinkles weighing heavily around his light colored eyes. His cream, shapeless, floor-length linen robe swishes as he taps his foot against the floor impatiently.

My eyes then swing to the other side of the throne, where they land upon a devilishly handsome man radiating regality.

Emitting a dark, dangerous aura, he stands with his spine as straight as the King's, hands behind his back and feet spread slightly apart; the stance of a well-trained soldier.

His black long sleeves and pants hug his muscled form tightly. Shining dark boots complete his look.

His deep chocolate, wavy hair cascades onto the top of his shoulders. His eyes, a beautiful mixture of bright blues and tinges of silver, survey us harshly. The lips below sit in a perfect bow shape. And his tan face is stone cold; emotionless.

I look him up and down, and back again, only for his eyes to meet mine as I investigate him a third time.

We hold eye contact before his gaze trails down, observing me closely, the way I did him.

I blink away, fixating on the King once more.

"Welcome, multiwielders," he starts with a villainous, toothy grin.

My insides twist at the sound of his gravelly voice. My hands ball into fists and shake, rattling my restraints. My throat tightens and bobs, begging to formulate a response.

"*Fuck you*," I roar before I can process what's coming out of my mouth.

Griffin shoves me down as soon as the words leave my lips.

On my knees, I glimpse up to see the King smirking down at me.

"You should be grateful to serve your King and your kingdom," he sneers.

The infuriatingly handsome man on his left squints at me, tilting his head in speculation. I meet his gaze for a split second before I hear Rowan shout, and whip my head to view her on my right.

"Fuck you *and* your bullshit army!"

Mathias swiftly pushes her to the ground.

My eyes float to Sebastian on my other side, where I swear the slightest hint of a grin grows on his lips, but he remains quiet.

"You're a bastard! And I am *not* grateful to serve you," I bite out before spitting towards the base of his throne.

Out of the corner of my eye, another ball of spit flies at the King's boots and I smile, knowing without having to look over that it's from Rowan.

The King's face reddens and his eyes bulge. He springs to his feet in a second, stretching his hands out towards us.

As he does, against my will, my body leans forward, bowing to him. My face hovers barely an inch from the sleek, white marble tiles. Black veining runs through the shining white stone, reminding me of spiderwebs caught between a pair of trees.

My head then twists, forced to the side, and my cheek presses down into the icy cold flooring.

Damn him.

He's slipped into my mind with ease, able to control my movements.

I attempt to fight against his hold, but the shield I try to keep around my mind at all times is gone; the collar's blocking out my abilities, causing it to disappear altogether.

"Now, that's more like it," he hisses.

I slump to the floor, catching myself with my forearms when he releases his hold on my mind.

Satisfied, he smiles smugly, perching on his throne once more.

"Don't get used to seeing me on my knees. For you, it will *never* happen willingly," I snap.

Rowan chuckles, and a rough cough follows, seemingly from Sebastian, who tries not to join her.

"Make them shut up," King Kairos orders with a flick of his hand.

The handsome, young man on his left dips his chin to the King, stepping over to us, before shadows pour out from behind him, spiraling in our direction as he maintains his soldier-like stance.

Strips of pitch black darkness fly at Rowan, and in an instant they've ensnared her, forcing her arms to her sides. They slither up her neck and wrap over her mouth, silencing her. She struggles against the bonds.

Something brushes against my leg and I glance down.

Onyx ribbons rapidly bind my legs together. They climb up my torso, restraining my arms, before reaching my throat, twisting over my mouth and head.

A scream crawls up my throat, but nothing comes out.

The man inspects his handiwork on Rowan then moves his eyes to mine, investigating me, his face flat.

His gaze then floats to the King, now bored with his given order.

King Kairos narrows his eyes. "I do hope this attitude will be worn off in training. Or else we will have a *serious* problem."

His hand lifts, waving again.

At the silent command, the shadows unravel from our bodies, flowing back to their source before vanishing completely.

In awe, I stare at the alluring, shadow wielding man whose hands remained behind his back.

Did he wield those with his mind?

But he doesn't have a moment to move to his original place beside the King before I let another piece of spit go flying.

It lands in the dead center of his dark tunic.

His eyes flood with silver, bursting wide as his body tenses.

That's the only show of emotion from him, with the King raising his voice once more. "Guards, take them away. I'm tired of dealing with them and their attitudes."

Griffin grabs under my arm, yanking me up, and shoves me toward a door to the far left of the throne room I hadn't noticed earlier.

Manhandled by Mathias, Aiden, and Reid, my carriage buddies are pushed in the same direction.

Behind it lies a hallway. Then another. And another. We're guided, or rather, forced, down a series of corridors taking lefts and rights, followed by sets of stairs, then even more hallways.

I'm positive we are lost but the guards obviously know their way.

We descend lower and lower until I have no choice but to believe we're underneath the primary estate of the castle.

This place is a labyrinth.

After what feels like hours, we turn right down one more corridor, occupied by three guards at the end, who stand post at a large set of metal doors.

"We brought in more multiwielders to be trained," Griffin boasts.

My eyes roll at him and his ever apparent ego.

The three of us are led inside, arriving in an expansive room filled with dozens of thick, square mats spread out on the floor.

Off to the right is a wide open doorway, leading to a dining hall full of metal tables and chairs.

A handful of shut doors line the distant wall at the back along with the one on my left.

Several sets of people are crouched on the mats before us and even more stand beside them, chatting, but they all come to a deafening halt to watch us enter.

A tall man with near-white blonde hair faces us, arms crossed over a broad chest. Sides of his head shaved, the snowy hair solely down the middle is braided back, the end resting on the top of his back.

His light green eyes narrow in examination, and one of his pale fingers taps against his bare bicep.

He wears a black sleeveless shirt tucked into matching, form fitting pants and dark boots, of which the right one is tapping too.

"Luca, I have some new meat for you," Griffin states.

Rowan speaks up first. "It's so *not* nice to meet you, Luc."

She tilts her head, giving him a tight-lipped, sarcastic smirk.

Eyes narrowing further, he finally speaks.

"One, I don't care if you're not happy to meet me. It's not my job for you to like me, I'm here to train you to become a soldier. Two, back talk will not be tolerated, unless you feel like scrubbing toilets with your personal toothbrush. And three, my name is Luca, don't call me 'Luc' *ever* again. Understood?" He pauses, eyeing her and lifting a light brow.

"Rowan," she beams proudly.

"Rowan," he copies and looks to Sebastian. "You?"

Sebastian eyes him suspiciously before stating his name. Luca looks him up and down before nodding then facing me.

"And you?"

I crack my jaw to the side before answering plainly. "Aurora."

"Aurora. How sweet."

I give him a wide, fake grin. "I'm not very sweet once you get to know me. You might want to hand over a toothbrush in advance."

He raises an eyebrow and jabs, "We'll see about that, sweetheart."

Glaring back at him, I take in a breath through my nose.

This is going to be a *real* fun time.

Chapter 10

Over his shoulder, Luca calls out for someone named Piper.

A young woman with strawberry blonde hair split into two, short french braids peeks out from behind a group of people standing at one of the mats.

She skips forward, a black eye encircling one of her bright green eyes. Light freckles dot her fair cheeks. The smile she wears as she approaches us is kind, genuine. She wears a charcoal vest-like top paired with fitted black pants, all of which hug her curves. Black boots lace up at her feet.

"What's up, *Luc*?" she jokes, slapping a hand against Luca's rigid shoulder.

His look back at her is menacing, and she removes her hand but keeps her grin intact.

"Watch yourself or else when we spar you'll get another one of those to match." He gestures to her eye with a jerk of his head.

"Can't wait," she sing-songs, crossing her arms and looking us over.

Her eyes meet Rowan's first, widening, and a light pink starts to cover her cheeks. Her grin turns to a beam.

Peering at Rowan out of the corner of my eye, I notice her own face light up.

Her gaze trails up and down the woman. After the second time, Rowan catches herself and looks to Luca instead.

I bite my lip to hold in a giggle.

"Can we get out of these things now?" Rowan asks, holding up her bound wrists. I spy my own, considering her question.

"Go ahead." Luca gestures to the guards to unlock them.

I immediately hold out my hands. Griffin sighs, reaching into his pocket, producing the key ring. Unlocking my wrists first, followed by the collar around my neck, he trails down to my feet, finally freeing me completely.

I reach for my abilities, but I feel drained and weak. Panic spreads through my veins.

Rowan is freed next, and the expression on her face once she's released surely matches my own.

"What did you guys do?"

"Chill out. Give it a few hours and you'll feel fine," Griffin says, annoyed.

The unease in my gut slows, but only slightly.

"How long have you guys had those on?" Piper butts in, face full of concern. Rowan and I inspect each other, answering simultaneously.

"Four days."

"Three days."

Piper's eyes nearly bulge out of her head. She gapes at Griffin, opening her mouth then snapping it shut, spearing him with a dirty look instead.

An apologetic look fills her leafy green eyes when they move to us.

"We'll be okay," Rowan reassures her, smirking.

Piper's flush returns.

"Now, we do not take resistance lightly here," Luca interjects, eyeing Piper suspiciously. "So once your powers return, don't even *think* about using them against us. We are not afraid of handing out punishments. Comply with our orders and you'll be fine throughout the duration of your training here."

Is that a... threat?

We've already been forcibly brought here, yet the intimidation tactics continue. I suppose that's what Orellia has turned into under the rule of King Kairos.

"You're dismissed," Luca adds, shooing away Griffin, Mathias, Aiden, and Reid after they've finished uncuffing the three of us.

They turn to leave but Griffin pauses, glaring and pointing at Rowan.

"Careful with this one, she can breathe fire."

Rowan snaps her head around, sneering. "Don't make me do it again."

His eyes narrow at her, but he eventually twists around.

Once the four of them leave and the doors close, I breathe a sigh of relief, hoping to never see the lot of them for the rest of my days.

"Piper, give the newbies a tour, would you?" Luca spins, strutting off without waiting for her answer.

Piper waves a hand for the three of us to follow.

Once she's facing the other direction, I nudge Rowan, giving her a smirk, wiggling my eyebrows up and down. She shushes and elbows me back in response.

A laugh bubbles out of me and Piper turns. She quirks an eyebrow at us then returns to her task at hand.

"This is sort of the main training room, where everyone usually meets," she says, gesturing around.

The sound of activity at the mats begins anew, with Luca handing out orders.

We maneuver through the space, approaching the furthest of four doors on the left hand side of the huge room. Piper pushes it in to reveal a long room with six metal bunk beds lining either wall. Two rows of five of the uncomfortable looking beds run down the center of the room. Only a few feet of space sits between each row.

"Welcome to your new home! This is one of our bunk rooms. There's three more identical ones but this has the most empty beds." She gazes over the space and waves her hand, showcasing the room.

How very… industrial. The opposite of the warm and cozy home I'm used to.

She walks to the right, pointing in the far corner. "Back there are the bathrooms and showers. And before you ask, yes, it's all coed."

"This is my bed. My friend Jade is up top," she continues, flopping down on a bed touching the wall. "Go ahead and pick any that don't have trunks under them, those are the empty ones."

The bunk to her right is free, so I claim it. Rowan plops down next to me, resting back on her hands.

"I'll take the one up top. I figured we could continue to be roommates," she says with a grin.

Warmth fills me at her words.

Sebastian climbs up onto the top bed on the bunk across from us, silently, as usual.

It dawns on me then that we hadn't properly introduced ourselves to Piper.

"Hey, by the way, I'm Aurora."

"Nice to meet you," Piper replies from her bed.

Rowan reaches across me, stretching her hand over my lap, introducing herself.

"I'm Rowan. You've been a great tour guide so far," she beams.

Her obvious flirting has me biting back a giggle.

"It's very nice to meet you, Rowan. Thank you," Piper says, meeting the woman's hand, a sly grin sprouting on her lips. They stare at each other, hands clasped, with color spreading to both of their cheeks.

Oh, boy. I can see it already.

I clear my throat, getting their attention to their locked hands blocking me in. At the same time, they mumble apologies, their faces flushing further.

I gesture over to the bunk next to us. "And this is Sebastian."

Piper waves up to him. "Hello!"

He dips his chin to her, sending the dark curls atop his head bouncing.

"I'm sure you all want to do some cleaning up. Let me get the three of you some clothes so you can shower. And I'll get you your own trunks too, to keep everything in," Piper says, rising and walking off.

As soon as the door shuts behind her, I eyeball Rowan. "A bit obvious much?"

Rowan chuckles admittingly, brushing a handful of braids behind her ear. "Okay, maybe. But she's *so* beautiful."

A handful of minutes later, Piper comes back in, carrying a stack of dark colored clothes and three towels.

"You guys can go ahead and take showers then we'll go get dinner," she explains, handing them out to us.

Rowan and Sebastian in tow, we move to survey the bathing chambers.

To the left is a long row of bathroom stalls, metal walls and doors enclosing each toilet. Across from them are sinks built into metal countertops, with one long mirror hanging above them all.

To the right are the showers. Two rows, one against each wall, a wide walkway between them. Gray tiled walls separate each shower, and a white curtain hangs in front of each stall.

Everything is so gray and bleak here.

Stepping out of my boots and stripping off the disgusting pajamas I've been in for several days, I use the lavender scented soap within the containers attached to the wall underneath the showerhead. I breathe in the smell and am reminded of home.

Closing my eyes, I let the water fall down on me as memories of my aunt and the apothecary flood my head.

I force the thoughts away shortly after they're triggered.

After ridding myself of the journey's filth, I wiggle into a pair of fitted, dark gray pants that hug the curve of my hips, then shrug on a black tank top. I shove my boots on before returning to my bunk shared with Rowan.

Hanging my towel on the peak of the metal structure of the bunk, I peer at an untouched trunk on the ground. Piper must have brought it in.

Crouching in front of it, I go through its contents: an array of pants and tops in various shades of black and gray, undergarments of similar colors, plain pajamas, a pair of black boots not unlike to my own, a light jacket, a dark beanie, and a filled backpack.

I lift the bag out, inspecting it.

"Emergency pack. Has a bunch of crap we may need for when they finally decide to throw us to the wolves– I mean, when they eventually send us on missions," Piper says with a chuckle.

Having placed the trunk and its contents where it belongs under the bed, the four of us now weave through the dozens of mats in the main training room as we cross to the other side.

The once empty tables and chairs of the dining hall are now filled. Tons of people who all seem to be twenty-somethings are scattered at tables or waiting in line for food, conversing loudly.

"How many people are here? I didn't expect there to be so many."

"Last I remember, there were a bit over a hundred of us, not including you three. However, new arrivals come in every week or so and then people leave when they're posted. So, it fluctuates often," Piper says, pausing briefly before continuing.

"The King's Guards have been very efficient at hunting us down in recent years. I heard they receive a bonus for every one of us they bring in. But keep in mind, those loyal to the King turn themselves in when they come of age; not everyone is here by force." She shakes her head at the last of her words, disgust filling her features.

"I knew people willingly joined the King's Guard often, but I hadn't thought many would join the King's Army. It's insane any multiwielder would willingly do this when we're already hunted down and forced into it," I fume as we walk in line to get food.

Piper looks at me with tight lips and furrowed brows. "Believe me, I'm on the same page as you, but there are people who are loyal to that jackass no matter what."

My mind racing, I silently take a plate along the line.

Piper then leads Rowan, Sebastian, and myself to a nearly empty table, a single woman sitting at it.

She looks up from her tray, welcoming us with a bright smile. Her bob of sleek, black hair sways as she waves us over. Dark brown, almond eyes shine as she beams. A small nose and lips, a single freckle sits at the top of her fair cheek. The clothes she wears mimic the same dark-colored getup the rest of us have on.

"This is Jade; the bunkmate I mentioned. Jade, this is Rowan, Aurora, and Sebastian," Piper says, gesturing to the petite woman, then each of us when we plop into chairs.

Rowan and I each give a wave, starting on our food. Sebastian nods as he chews.

"Nice to meet you all. Where are you guys from? How far away do you all come from?" Jade asks, making conversation.

I finish the bite in my mouth before answering about Knothaven.

"I got picked up about a day after her in Willow Springs," Rowan chimes in.

Jade nods her head, understanding, before looking to Sebastian. We all turn to him, waiting to see what he'll say.

He eyeballs each of us as he lifts another morsel to his lips. He chews and swallows it while we, albeit politely, stare him down.

"I'm from everywhere."

My eyes widen, flabbergasted at the record number of words he spoke.

He's yet to reveal anything aside from his name, no matter how small.

Rowan meets my eyes with a bulging pair of her own. We share a matching chuckle.

"Everywhere, huh?" Piper joins in. "We'll get more out of you yet, just you wait." She smirks at Sebastian and his eyes roll.

I swear I see the tiniest glimpse of a smile on his lips before he takes another bite.

We eat our dinner in between conversation. Piper shares she was caught using her powers a few months ago by a pair of King's Guards. Helping her younger brother practice controlling his light abilities, the guards spotted the brightness and came to investigate. Attempting to get away, she used her light, earth, and fire abilities against them. She was dragged away, literally kicking and screaming.

Jade had placed a comforting hand on Piper's shoulder as she spoke of it.

Jade, trying to lighten the mood, commented how they celebrated Piper's twenty-third birthday a few weeks ago.

Eventually, Jade told us how she was apprehended late one night, in the alleyway beside the restaurant she worked at. Her instincts had kicked in when three men came up from behind, attacking her, and she used all four elements—air, earth, fire, and water—to fight them off. Little did she know, a King's Guard was lurking and snatched her up.

My heart shatters, momentarily heals, then breaks all over again at the replay of events they tell.

Wrath burns within me for them. And for every person who was brought here in such unruly ways, myself included.

Openly sharing our own stories with the women, Rowan, Piper, Jade, and I talk until the rest of the soldiers in training are long gone, and the kitchen staff starts cleaning up around us. Sebastian quietly listens in but doesn't say a word.

"We better get back to our bunks. It's almost time for lights out," Piper says, spying a wall clock.

Rowan chuckles. "We have a bedtime?"

"Yeah, and they're strict about it. Guards patrol day and night. An alarm will also wake us up bright and early; six o'clock sharp."

Rowan and I exchange worried glances. What will be in store for us tomorrow?

Chapter 11

As promised, the next morning at six, on the dot, an obnoxious alarm rings.

After jolting awake, I scramble to put a dark ensemble on my body; gray and black fitted clothes being the "dresscode" per Piper's words. I plait my caramel-colored hair down the center of my head while Rowan gathers all of her black braids into a ponytail.

Eggs, sausage, and fruit are for breakfast in the dining hall. Rowan, Sebastian, and I hurry to finish eating when Piper informs us we're to meet in the main training room at seven for line up, where we'll learn our training schedule for the day.

Sprinting onto the mats only seconds after Luca starts his announcement, he immediately calls us out.

"And to you newbies," he says, looking pointedly at the three of us. "Ensure you're on time, *every* day. Now, Prince Killian has an announcement."

Luca turns to the side, gesturing to a nearby door on the back wall, where the mysterious, handsome, chocolate-haired man from the King's throne room enters.

His shoulder-length hair is tied back today, but his face is as stern and cold as yesterday.

He's wearing tight, black pants and boots again, this time accompanied with a deep gray, sleeveless tunic. His hands curl into fists at his sides as he walks to meet Luca, making the muscles in his biceps flex.

I shake the thoughts of him out of my head as I process what Luca said.

Blinded by the presence of King Kairos, I hadn't made the connection. My jaw drops open, but I shut it the moment I realize it's ajar.

He's *the* Prince.

Prince Killian, son of King Kairos. The King who had my parents killed. Because he wanted me, a multiwielder.

My chest tightens. Fire floods my veins. My insides clench and twist. My fingernails dig into the palm of my hands.

Any previous thoughts of his handsomeness disappear in an instant.

The Prince stops beside Luca, looking the three of us over. His gaze meets mine and we exchange cold, hard stares. A flicker of silver brushes across his light blue irises.

He most definitely remembers me, and my actions in his father's throne room.

What feels like years later, he moves on, spying Rowan, then Sebastian. Finally, he addresses the crowd, arms crossed over his chest.

"I've decided to make some changes around here. After consulting with my second-in-command," he pauses, waving a hand to Luca. "I've made the decision to take a more hands-on approach to your training. To get you all into fighting shape, you'll be split up into smaller training groups. A higher ratio of trainers to trainees. And *I* will be one of them."

Gasps bounce across the space.

"*I* will now be the one to decide when each of you are ready. Whether it be weeks, months, or even years, I will not issue anyone a position until I am *sure* you won't get yourself killed over a damn scuffle. Nonsense will not be tolerated in the King's Army."

Ire sparks through me at the King's heir speaking.

He's as bad as his father. He's an extension of the despicable King.

I bite my tongue on every curse I want to spew his way.

He then leans over to Luca, whispering, observing the crowd.

"Who all came in yesterday?" the second-in-command questions us.

Rowan, Sebastian, and I slowly raise our hands, peering around. Three others raise their hand: two standing together off to the right and another towards the back of the group.

"Come forward," Prince Killian commands, his voice deep and husky.

The three of us shuffle forward, followed by the pair, a young man and woman, and a petite woman from deep in the crowd.

"Let's see what you're made of. Follow me."

He turns around, walking to the door he came in from.

"Oh, and don't bother trying to escape. There are guards posted at every exit. You will not succeed," he throws over his shoulder.

The gray, stone stairs we land on beyond the heavy, metal door seem to be never ending, leading down into darkness. Sconces filled with balls of light shine from either wall every so often, barely enough to keep me from stumbling down the steps.

Once the Prince reaches the bottom, far ahead of us, he thrusts open a set of doors. A burst of yellow light shines through, illuminating the end of the staircase.

What lies before me has my eyes widening and stomach plummeting.

An arena. And a vast one at that.

Where we stand after exiting the double doors, amongst the seating, there's a full view of the entire space.

Down below, one side showcases a group of birch trees sprouting from a layer of light green grass. The other is a barren desert made of a yellow, dirt ground. A narrow, cerulean stream lay between the two biomes, dividing them.

Rows of stone seats encircle the massive arena, sitting high up on walls to observe. A metal, chain link fence starts in front of the first seats, stretching up and over the scene, enclosing the huge space in a dome.

"Newbies, let's go," the Prince announces, pulling me out of my observations.

He eventually comes to a halt in front of another door between two sections of seats when we walk the arena's circumference, spinning around on his heel.

"Here we will teach you how to fight both with and without your abilities, but first, we want to see what you're capable of. You will be paired off to spar. Show *all* of your abilities—earth, fire, air, water, light, shadows, the mind—whatever combination you wield. I'll know if you're holding any back."

His muscles flex as he adjusts both hands in his underarms, thumbs sticking out.

"And please don't kill each other. I'll call it off when I've seen enough." His silver and blue eyes twinkle with delight as his lips raise to a smirk. "Or if one of you ends up unconscious."

The petite girl goes to raise her hand, eyes full of concern.

"No questions? Great," he says, then scans our group, considering.

"You, and you. I heard you can breathe fire. Let's see it." He smirks, pointing at the woman who tried raising her hand, then drags his finger to Rowan.

The first girl's eyes bulge before she leans over, vomiting all over the stone seat in front of her.

Prince Killian watches her with a hand on the door's handle, a mix of disgust and amusement on his face.

She wipes her mouth with the back of her hand, head down, and walks through the door after Rowan and the Prince.

The three of them emerge a minute later from a door behind the full trees in the arena, approaching the stream. Rowan stays on the half filled with grass while the other woman takes up the desert-like side.

"Isla versus Rowan," the Prince announces. "You may begin at my word."

He peers down at the women after arriving back in the stands, Luca at his side.

"Go."

Rowan's face morphs into one solely of concentration. Pulling her arm back, she launches a ball of fire at Isla.

The woman dodges, rolling to the ground. She picks up a gust of wind in doing so, creating a tornado of yellow dust around her, hiding within it.

Kneeling, hands outstretched, Rowan lifts two whips of crystal blue water from the stream. She brings them down over Isla and her tornado of dust, scattering it.

Isla stands from her cowered position on the ground, utterly soaked. Her face now in a scowl, she blasts a beam of light from her palm.

A short wall of earth rumbles up in front of Rowan, shielding her at the last moment. She peeks over it and Isla sends more brightness at her face. Rowan ducks, narrowly avoiding it.

From behind her shield of packed dirt, Rowan stretches out her fingers. A thick, obsidian mist crawls into the scene from beyond the nearest trees, spreading over the ground in seconds, rising higher every moment.

Before long, Rowan is hidden within the darkness, and it closes in on her opponent.

Isla springs forward another light beam, but the dark, creeping shadows absorb it.

The pitch black at the front disperses slightly when she follows the attack with a wall of wind, revealing a single boot among the mist.

Isla catches a glimpse of the foot and a small grin plays at her lips.

Her hands flay out before her, twisting as she winds up more of the dull-colored dust.

She creates another tornado, this time building it in front of her. She picks up more and more dirt, forming an opaque cone of wind.

Rowan's shadows edge closer to the spiraling air. Then, the two collide.

My hands fly to cover my mouth.

Rowan's shadows disappear, and she's thrown, landing on her rear in the middle of the stream, hands at her sides, her lower half submerged in the water.

Isla smiles down at her, as if she had won, but the Prince hasn't said a word, and both of them are still very much conscious.

White steam starts to rise out of the water on either side of Rowan. Isla takes a step back, confused.

Rowan rises, the steam a cloud around her. Hazy behind the white, fluffy air, her hands are ablaze.

White brightness flies at her, but she swipes it away with a lit hand.

Then, scarlet and orange flames leave Rowan's palms.

Isla tries blocking the attack with an orb of light, but it doesn't hold up against the blaze and she goes flying from the force.

She lands several paces away, on her side, in the dirt, with an audible thud. She shutters in pain on the ground and I hear a groan leave her lips.

Rowan extinguishes her fire, turning to a silent Prince Killian in the stands, waiting for him to say something.

He remains standing, arms crossed, and quirks an eyebrow at her.

She lets out a huff, curling her hands into fists. Her chest puffs up, as she breathes in deeply. Scowling, she releases a blast of red, orange, and gold from her mouth in his direction.

She holds eye contact with him as she shoots out the bright, flickering flames, the tips nearly reaching the dome barrier. The warmth of her fire hits my cheeks for a moment before she relaxes, dousing her blaze.

Her chest expands and contracts rapidly as she holds the Prince's stare. I peer over to see a devilish grin on his face.

"You're finished. Good job," he finally says, true praise lacking in his words.

Luca disappears into the arena then. When he reaches Isla, he scoops her up in his arms and leaves.

I presume he takes her to an infirmary of some sort, as he doesn't make his way to the stands.

"That was amazing! I knew about the fire but earth, water, and shadows too! It was badass! *You* are badass!" I congratulate Rowan, wrapping her in a hug when she returns to the stands. She squeezes me back fiercely.

"Now you."

The Prince, a stone cold expression once again covering his face, stares down his nose at me.

"Me?" I ask, pointing to my chest.

"Yes, you. And… you," he decides, jerking his head to the one other remaining woman.

A grin covers her face and she dips into a bow. "Of course, Prince Killian. It would be an honor to show you my abilities."

I openly gawk at her, brows shooting to my hairline, uncaring about hiding my feelings. A loyalist? In the flesh?

My suspicion is confirmed when she glares at me nastily, sizing me up.

"You're a disgrace to His Majesty's army," she declares, stomping away.

The Prince smirks at our interaction. I turn a glare at him.

And I can't hold my tongue any longer.

"Fuck you!"

Multiple gasps of horror ring out at my roaring. He only chuckles.

"Sure, whenever you want sweetheart." He winks, retaining his smirk.

I hold my head high and walk right past him, ignoring his presence, entering a spiral stone staircase leading down to the arena.

When I step into the wide, circular space, I spy the loyalist, a blonde woman, who already planted herself on the dirt-covered side.

Good. I'm in my element around flora and fauna anyways.

Stopping at the edge of the stream, the Prince approaches us. He leans over, asking her name.

"Amaya, Your Highness," she replies sweetly.

I nearly double over and vomit just as Isla had.

I force out my own name before he has the chance to speak to me.

"Amaya versus Aurora," he announces. "Don't begin until I say."

The young woman, Amaya, who stands a few inches shorter than me, wears a massive grin on her face.

She is *far* too excited for this.

"You may begin," Prince Killian's voice booms a moment later.

Immediately, she tries to claw into my mind, revealing the first of her powers.

I swiftly pull up my shield the few inches it had slipped, shutting it in her face.

Giving her the same treatment, I yank on the walls she has in place around her mind. I bring them down a hair, slipping a nail inside, but she slams them back up.

We stand there for what feels like hours, staring at each other, playing tug-o-war within our minds, trying to see who can get the others' shield down first.

Sweat beads on my temples. Damn does she have a strong mind.

"We get it, you can wield the mind. Now stop playing with each other and show us something else," a stern voice not belonging to the Prince commands.

Amaya breaks eye contact, whipping her head over to see who had spoken, but I knew it was Luca.

I step into the clear stream and, hands outstretched, raise up two pairs of vines.

Shooting the greenery at her, they grab ahold of all four of her limbs.

Her eyes widen in surprise before dissolving into slits of anger.

Her palms splay open, burning with deep, red flames, frying my vines wrapped around her there. The plants crumble from her arms.

Maintaining my hold on the vines entangled over her ankles with one palm, I gather a wave from the stream with my other.

Before she can burn the bright green pieces of earth at her legs, I spray her with the water, tipping her off balance.

I pull on my vines, dragging her across the dirt.

She twists a split second later, fire shooting from the soles of her feet, scorching the vines just below her boots.

As she rolls to the side, now free of my plants, I form a ball of light in my right hand, behind my back. My left hand swirls, building a wall of water, encircling my body.

She raises to her feet, but stays crouched.

She throws a fireball at my water wall. It disappears into the blue as my barrier holds strong.

My right hand emerges from behind me and I toss the brightness, momentarily blinding her.

I push forward onto her half of the arena, moving and contorting my water wall until it's standing several feet above my head.

Pulling it down, it crashes over her while she's blinded.

As soon as she's drenched, sitting in the dirt now swiftly turning to mud, she kicks a foot towards me, sending out a blast of wind.

The air knocks me back, landing me in the stream.

I sit up, soaked from head to toe, to see her standing, rubbing my light from her eyes.

Throwing my fingers forward, picking up a ribbon of water in the process, I send it into her stomach.

She hunches over at the impact, but doesn't fall to the ground.

She spins then, collecting a gust of wind with her arms, and sends it sailing at me when I rise from my position in the water.

The blast of air sends me sailing back, landing in the grass.

I land hard on my stomach. A groan escapes my throat.

But I stretch my arm out to the side, sending another thick, green vine at her, this time wrapping it around her torso.

Moving onto my knees, I send a second vine sailing at her, aiming for her neck. As my hands flick and twist, wrapping the plants around her, she kicks her foot, blasting out heat.

I drop and roll to the side, avoiding the blow as I keep my hold on my pieces of crawling, green earth. I tighten my grip around her neck and torso.

Her hands fly up to her throat, igniting them.

I give the vine one final squeeze before she burns it to a crisp.

The greenery around her middle still holds and I yank it, pulling her into the stream. As she falls, I direct an orb of light at her.

But she twists to the side just before her body splashes into the water, the light narrowly missing her, instead landing in the stream and fizzling out.

She makes quick work of burning off the wet vines wrapped over her torso and stands.

Damn her. She's not going down no matter what I do.

A light ball blasts from my palm but she spins, missing my strike again. Mid-spin, she gathers another surge of wind, this time with both hands and a single foot, balancing.

And the air sends me back into a tree trunk.

My spine crunches against the bark, a sharp pain shooting down my back, leading into my thighs.

I fall forward onto my stomach after colliding with the tree.

Throbbing pain spreads over my back as I lie on the ground. I clench my eyes tight, forcing myself to breathe through the ache.

Damn, that *really* hurt.

"You're finished," I hear a deep, rough voice call out.

The Prince's voice.

Fuck.

I slowly push myself up, craning my neck high, only to see him, arms still crossed, looking unimpressed as he peers into the arena at me.

Amaya jumps up and down, pumping her fists as she celebrates her victory.

"Enough," the Prince scolds her before muttering, "It's inappropriate for a soldier to dance over those they've defeated. Try it again and I will see to it that your time here is more unpleasant than you can imagine."

She stops immediately, face reddening before she bows, promptly apologizing. She starts towards the exit, passing me without a second look. I stare daggers into her back as she approaches the door.

I turn my head to the audience once I'm upright again, eyeing Rowan and Sebastian.

Rowan gives me a sympathetic look. Sebastian's face is unreadable.

Returning to the stairs, the sharp pain turning into a dull roar, anger and disappointment wash over me. I force a steadying breath, in through my nose and out my mouth.

I can't believe I let her get the better of me.

Amaya is standing off to the side when I reach the seats, whispering to the man who she seems to stick to like glue. She eyeballs me and giggles to him.

I roll my eyes, approaching Rowan, who waits with open arms. She wraps me in her strong arms before whispering, "You did great. Don't worry about her."

Sheepishly smiling at her, I notice Sebastian over her shoulder. When I pull away, he places a hand on my shoulder, giving it a gentle squeeze.

The Prince surprises me by starting towards us then, arms now behind his back. His eyes, a deep ocean blue fading into a lighter one, mix with a silver ring around his pupil as they take me in.

"I thought you'd do better, and I'm not usually wrong, but I guess there's a first time for everything."

My jaw threatens to drop open. Egotistical much?

In the next moment, he's disappeared, returning to the arena, the two remaining men in tow.

"Casmir versus Sebastian. I'm sure you know the drill by now."

Sebastian's opponent sneers at him in the same second Prince Killian issues their start.

The two of them lock eyes. It becomes apparent Casmir had not paid attention to my sparring with Amaya, beginning by using his mind powers to battle Sebastian.

They must be matched in the ability, as they stare at each other intensely.

Then, a hint of a smirk raises on Sebastian's lips as tears begin to leak from Casmir's eyes. Casmir lowers to the ground, landing on his knees in the grass, more liquid covering his cheeks.

He closes his wet eyes abruptly and flings his arms out. The cerulean water of the stream in front of him rises only a few inches before Sebastian flicks his hand, sending a breeze of wind to knock it down.

All while he maintains his stare at Casmir.

The man on his knees keeps his eyes shut tight. His hands fly to the sides of his head, squeezing it. His fingers curl into his light brown hair and he yanks at it harshly.

One of Sebastian's palms rises and with a snap of his fingers, dark shadows appear all around, covering the entirety of the arena in a split second. Our view of the two men and all of their surroundings, gone.

Gasps erupt from the trainees throughout the arena.

My hand flies to my mouth, and out of the corner of my eye, I spy Rowan's doing the same.

Luca mutters something under his breath. The Prince stands next to him silently, arms folded over his chest, still as a statue, observing the pitch black scene below with furrowed brows.

A high pitched scream explodes from the darkened arena.

As soon as they appeared, the shadows then vanish, leaving a passed out Casmir slumped on the floor and an unmoved Sebastian.

"Am I finished?" Sebastian asks, eyeing Prince Killian.

A grin plays on the Prince's lips before he answers. "Yes. Very well done."

Sebastian dips his head, casually making his way back up to us.

"Everyone, go back to the main training room. We'll be with you all shortly," the Prince adds.

Luca and Killian have an unconscious Casmir between them a minute later, one of his arms over either of their shoulders. They heave him up, dragging him off.

"That was awesome!" Rowan shouts, throwing her arms around Sebastian.

His eyes go wide, dark brows flying high, and he freezes as she hugs his tall, lean frame. She releases him a few seconds later, but not before slapping his shoulder joyfully.

"That was epic!" I add, clapping my hands together excitedly.

His cheeks show a tinge of pink as he scratches the back of his neck and looks down.

Rowan hooks an arm in my own and I turn to see her hooking her other through Sebastian's. She grins up at him proudly. His brows knit together in confusion. She holds firm anyways, and we file out of the arena.

Chapter 12

As we enter the large training room, arms no longer linked much to Sebastian's thanks, Piper and Jade sprint over, finding us.

"Sebastian, that was insane!" Piper hollers as she approaches.

"You are so talented!" Jade says, one step behind.

He stands frozen, shrugging his shoulders.

The entire room stares at him, some in awe, others in confusion, and several in fear. Whispers swiftly fill the space.

Some time later, Prince Killian and Luca arrive, their presence silencing the room. Five others, three men and two women, walk in behind them. The Prince paces in front of his second-in-command and the others.

"These are my top ranking generals; those in order of command, behind me, of course."

He smiles smugly. I roll my eyes.

"We will be your trainers."

He pulls out several sheets of folded paper from his pocket. "Here are the groups. When you are assigned, go stand with them on their designated mat."

The six of them split off, and the Prince places himself on the mat directly in front of us.

He starts reading off names, pointing in different directions to identify each of his officers.

The massive group of trainees dwindles as they approach their respective trainers.

Several minutes go by and my name still has not been called.

Finally, the last of Luca's group has been assembled and all of the generals have their groups, except for the Prince. He grins at those of us who remain: myself, Rowan, Sebastian, Piper, Jade, and a dozen others.

"You lot. Follow me."

What a joy.

We shuffle along after him to the far back corner of the spacious training room, to the last door on the right, which reveals a long set of stairs leading up.

Up? After being led *down* the labyrinth that is the King's palace, this was the last thing I expected.

Through another door at the top, a burst of bright light shines in when the Prince pushes it open.

I'm forced to squint my eyes when I climb the last few stairs.

It's… sunlight? We were just underground.

Sprawling green lies past the doorway, filled with equipment.

More mats like the ones in the training room are placed throughout the field, with open barrels of water spread out between them. Dozens of targets varying in size, some set up with archery equipment, others empty, line the far back of the space.

Lush trees line the sides and back of the grassy area.

Stands piled high with swords and daggers are placed off to the left.

And a winding, multi-leveled agility course stands on the right, taking up the entire length of the space.

I spin around, craning my neck to peer up.

The back of the castle stretches high into the sky. The bottom most windows are just specks, several stories above.

I spin back. On the other side, past the furthest trees in the distance, are the White Mountains.

We're sandwiched on this expansive training field between the backside of the King's palace and the mountainous border we share with Norfell.

To the left and right, beyond the equipment and more trees, are gray, stone walls made of the same material as the castle. They surround us, locking us in a massive rectangle.

"Welcome to one of our newly constructed outside training spaces," the Prince says, taking in the grounds.

"We will be training you to hone your powers. Using them to learn to fight and defend Orellia. If you find your wielding incapacitated for whatever reason, you also need to know how to fight by other means. Archery, hand-to-hand combat, and weapon wielding are all skills you will be learning. To those of you who have been here for some time, the weaponry is a new addition to your training because we felt it imperative you learn other forms of fighting."

Rowan eyes me suspiciously. I share her look as I investigate the Prince.

"Now, pick your choice of weapons, *if* you know how to use them, and then you'll be sparring… against me."

My eyes bulge and my mouth falls open at his remark.

He wants to fight *us*?

"Oh great," Rowan groans, rubbing her temples.

"Wasn't expecting that," Piper chimes in, folding her arms over her chest.

Jade gasps, her sleek black bob swaying as an autumn breeze passes through. Sebastian narrows his eyes, remaining quiet.

"So, who wants to go first?" he asks, a taunting grin playing on his lips.

The Prince surveys the crowd while most, if not all, of us avoid the eye contact.

For a moment, I think his gaze lands on me, and when I see him point straight out, I drag my eyes up in response to the motion.

However, when my stare reaches the tip of his finger, I find it's pointed a hair to my left. At Sebastian.

The Prince flips his finger over, curling it towards himself, beckoning Sebastian forward.

We all watch, impatiently, to see what happens next.

His powers were impressive, but how will they hold up to Prince Killian's? He's the leader of the King's Army, and the training he must have had is surely extensive. Especially growing up under the watchful eye of the King, and as the first born at that.

I can only wonder about the skills he has to have mastered by now. A well-trained soldier, bred to follow the orders of the King.

I shake my shoulders to snuff out the chill coursing through me at the possibilities.

The pair approaches the racks of weapons. The Prince picks up a thick, heavy sword and slings it over his back into an awaiting sheath.

Sebastian drags his fingers across the blades, making his way down to the smaller tools. He selects two spiral throwing stars, tucking them into the pockets of his pants.

As they walk on to the mat together, Piper yells, "Kick his ass, Bash!"

Rowan and Jade chuckle.

I cover my mouth with a hand to hide my own.

Sebastian peers over his shoulder at us and shakes his head, but I swear his lips twitch as he faces the Prince once again.

The two men begin circling each other, neither one looking to make the first move.

The Prince finally strikes first, with a gust of wind thrown at Sebastian's middle.

It does little to knock him off balance.

Sebastian continues to circle, waiting. The Prince attacks again, this time with a stream of water from an awaiting barrel a few paces away.

Sebastian maneuvers to the side, spinning, only a light mist of the liquid hitting him.

After his dodge, he flicks out his wrist, sending a star flying towards Prince Killian's side.

In a flash, the Prince's sword is unsheathed, knocking the spiral weapon out of the way before it meets its target. His lips raise in amusement as the weapon scatters along the ground.

Sebastian's brows furrow, and a bit of his dark curls fall to his forehead as he goes back to circling his opponent.

Prince Killian, sword still in hand, glares intently.

The movement of each man comes to a slow stop, until their bodies are completely still, as they hold one another's stares.

Sweat begins to break out on both men's foreheads and necks, glistening in the morning sun. Their faces redden, and veins pop out on the sides of their throats.

Rowan leans into my ear. "What do you think they're doing in each other's minds?"

"I have a feeling they haven't even gotten in yet. I think they're still trying to get in, past one another's shields," I whisper back, maintaining my view of the match.

Seconds turn into minutes as they continue their mental battle, faces contorting every so often.

Finally, the Prince, in the blink of an eye, forms a fireball in his hand and chucks it.

Sebastian catches the movement, throwing up a wall of wind, blocking the oncoming heat. He then pushes the air forward, but the Prince holds steady, the wind only loosening a few strands of his tied back waves.

The Prince bends, lifting his arms out to each side. Two large rocks crack the earth, lifting up from under the grassy floor around the raised mat.

Those of us surrounding the sparring skitter back, the ground beneath our feet shaking as the boulders rise.

As the massive stones come to the Prince's sides, Sebastian flicks the other star out of his hand, one I hadn't noticed he removed from his pocket.

One now aimed for the Prince's throat.

The Prince slams his hands together in a clap. The boulders follow suit, and crush the flying weapon between them before they drop to the ground, revealing the small, crunched piece of metal.

Sebastian's dark eyebrows raise ever so slightly before regaining his composure and whipping out a dozen ribbons of shadows.

Prince Killian grins, wide and toothy. His own pitch black, rippling shadows join Sebastian's, twisting together.

The Prince's brows narrow at his opponent, sweat dripping between his eyes. The onyx strands suspended in air expand rapidly, forming a cloud, before completely enclosing the entire sparring mat.

I gasp. Noises of surprise from Rowan, Piper, and Jade sound simultaneously. And just as the air has entered our lungs from the inhalation, the cloud is gone.

Before us lies Sebastian, on his knees.

Prince Killian stands above him, the tip of his sword under his chin.

"You're finished," Killian commands, grinning. "Not *too* horrible for a newbie."

He pulls his sword away, without leaving a mark on Sebastian, and resheaths it against his back.

The Prince holds out his hand, and Sebastian cautiously accepts. Once standing, he nods and rejoins us on the sidelines.

I stare past Sebastian, examining the Prince in surprise.

My mind races at his display. I had assumed he would be powerful, but not wielding-*six*-abilities powerful.

Chapter 13

Prince Killian meets my eyes, questioning my stare at him with lifted brows before turning to those clapping Sebastian on the back next to me.

"Piper, you've been here a while now, haven't you? Let's see what you can do," he calls out, unfazed by his sparring with Sebastian only seconds ago.

"Sure thing!"

Piper plasters a grin on her face, skipping over to him, confidence oozing off of her. Hair braided in two, the ends fly behind her when she moves.

Piper takes up a fighting stance upon arrival. He looks down at her significantly shorter frame and lets out a sigh before taking up his own.

She moves first, throwing herself into a spin kick as she blasts a bolt of fire from the bottom of her foot.

She lands in a crouch on the ground, one foot out to the side, her grin never having left her face.

Her assertiveness and speed are breathtaking.

I peer over at Rowan, who's smiling impressively. Sebastian's face remains passive, but investigative. Jade grins knowingly.

Resuming my survey of the sparring, I notice the Prince smiling as wide as Piper.

He throws himself into a roll, kicking his leg out in the process. His own foot shoots out a ribbon of shadows, aiming to wrap around her outstretched leg.

Her reflexes are lightning fast, and a massive beam of brightness sprays from her fingertips, enveloping the darkness approaching her.

The stream of obsidian vanishes wholly within the colossal ray of light.

My eyes squint at the brightness, nearly closing completely, and my hand reaches up to cover them instinctively.

The Prince completes his rotation, slamming his lids closed, landing blindly in a kneel.

He punches out gusts of wind in her direction while regaining his sight.

Piper carefully dodges the rush of wind, her nimble movements making her float across the mat. She sends another intense beam of illumination at him as he rises to his feet.

He spins out of the way, creating a cloud of darkness to rival the oncoming light.

The shadows envelope her yellow-white brightness, sending her flying backwards.

She lands, sitting upright on her butt. A huff reverberates out her throat at the contact with the mat.

I bite down on my lip, grimacing at her rough landing.

Narrowing her gaze at him, she picks herself up. Tendrils of light leave her fingertips, spreading over the space like an intricate spiderweb.

Prince Killian meets it with more crawling, pitch black threads.

The light and shadows meet, intertwining with one another as their owners fight for their ability to win. The Prince and Piper each twist and contort their hands as they control the battle.

The size of the interlaced brightness and darkness slowly expands, taller and wider.

Then, the shadows begin creeping over more of the light, steadily winning.

I step backwards as the battle wages on, spreading off the sparring mat. Around me, other trainees back away in the same instant.

The inky strands cover a hair more of the golden rays every second and before long, the once bright radiance is dulled.

Piper lets her attack go, twisting away. A whip of fire swirls over her fingertip, then spirals at the Prince.

He catches the fiery blaze, taking ahold of it, pulling her forward.

She lands on her stomach with a grunt, sweat dripping down her neck.

Another punch of flames releases from her knuckles when she rolls to the west.

She maneuvers out of the eruption of the battling oranges and reds when the Prince meets her attack tenfold, rolling off the mat and onto the ground, forming a cocoon of earth around her curled up body in a flash.

The rocks, dirt, and grass peel away from her limbs when the fire dissipates, revealing a now filthy Piper.

Her strawberry blonde hair is a new shade of light brown, with pieces of green sticking out of it.

She remains in her spot amongst the grass and dirt, angrily peering up through her eyebrows at the Prince, who stands with his arms crossed, still on the raised mat.

"Since you've left the mat, you forfeit. You're finished," he declares, eyes fixed on her sitting position.

Piper rolls her eyes then sneers. Raising to her feet, she wipes some of the dirt off her dark gray pants.

Prince Killian's lip twitches, smirking at her as she stands.

"For someone who's been here for quite some time, you sure do have a lot to learn. Your light may be strong but that attitude of yours, you let it control you. Don't let your emotions overtake your brain."

"Yeah, yeah, fuck off," she snarls, waving him off with one of her freckled hands.

She reaches Jade, who pats her back while beginning to pick out the grass from her braids. Rowan nods, her lips tilting upward at Piper.

Pink flushes on the woman's dirt-covered cheeks before she stares down to investigate her suddenly interesting grimy clothes.

Hands still tucked into his underarms, thumbs peaking out, Prince Killian observes the group he's chosen, silently weighing his options for his next opponent.

"How about your friend? Jade, come on up." He beckons her over with a jerk of his head.

Jade walks up to him, head held high. Her short, black hair is now tied out of the way into two low pigtails, barely hitting the tops of her shoulders.

As she stops a few feet from him, she brings her hands up, covering her face and bending her knees in an agile position.

He considers her size, glancing at her form.

The top of her head only comes up to his chest. Her smaller frame may be thin, but her calm face sits uncaring by the difference in height.

He steps into his own lowered stance, locking his silver-flecked eyes on her chocolate brown ones.

They move towards one another and back again, energy building between them before either of them even strike. Circle after circle, the two form a dance.

The Prince finally attacks first, punching a fist of fire at her.

She ducks under his arm then spins, grabbing his extended wrist and shoving it. Her unoccupied hand punches a puff of air into his face.

Her maneuvers don't distract him and he twists his head away from her wind.

"It's nice to see some hand-to-hand combat," he says as he shuffles a few steps back.

She only responds with a devious smirk.

With one hand, she gathers water from a barrel, flowing it through the air to her awaiting fingertips. In the other, she ignites a flame, having it hover in her palm.

She carefully steps forward, and they begin circling each other once again.

He mimics her, palming clear liquid in one hand and yellow fire in the other, footsteps in time with each of her own.

His steps are heavy and solid, while hers are light as a feather, as if she floats over the surface of the mat.

Their gazes attach once more, studying each other.

Then, Jade strikes first, releasing her blaze in the form of a whip.

Prince Killian takes hold of the attack, combining it with the fire in his palm, snatching it from her control.

He snuffs out the heat with a fist, then flings his water at her, but she blocks it with a stream of her own, all of it crashing to the mat with a splash.

As the liquid lands at their feet, she spins, sending a squall at his torso.

The Prince swipes down, gathering the approaching air, combining it into one spiraling cone, then dispersing the breeze altogether.

Jade swoops her arms around, gathering several scattered rocks from the grassy field into a storm of wind, and sends the flurry sailing.

The Prince meets the rush with a wall of shadows in front of his body, a darkness that embraces the air and earth, and the attack is sucked into his void.

He collapses the barrier of darkness in the next second and throws a sizzling fireball at her in exchange.

Jade flicks her fingers out, picking up one of the massive, discarded rocks from the Prince's sparring with Sebastian. She brings it in front of her, acting as a shield.

His fire reaches the makeshift defense, burning the front side of the boulder.

Maintaining her cover behind the piece of earth, she sends out a burst of air from over the top, quickly ducking back down to send another one out from her left, followed by her right.

Blast after blast, she randomly alternates between the positions from which she sends the wind at him.

He twirls and darts away from the attacks with ease, as if he can anticipate any moves before they occur.

He slings out shadow or fire in return, switching back and forth between the two. Their elements collide, meeting in a swirl.

Smoke rises over the mat as the wind repeatedly smacks against the flames and darkness. Thick, white puffs hide their figures.

Then, the sound of a booming crack spreads over the training field.

I do my best to contain my body's jolt at the thunderous noise but I doubt I'm successful.

The boulder blocking Jade splits in half down the middle, the impact throwing her onto her back. Her pale face contorts but she rolls onto her stomach, pushing up.

He peers at her, waiting.

Jade gathers air from around the mat, slowly contorting it into a tornado, herself and the Prince at its center. The wind picks up fallen pebbles and bits of water as it whips around and around.

She carefully stands, moving towards him, closing the storm in on the two of them. The wind picks up so many pieces of debris that my view of them is distorted.

A *shwing* of metal meets my ears then and in an instant, the monstrous tornado vanishes.

Left behind is a stunned Jade, eyes wide and mouth ajar.

The tip of the Prince's glistening, black sword sits pressed to the middle of her throat as he holds the weapon outstretched straight in front of him.

"Impressive winds, but there's still much room for improvement amongst your other three elements. You're finished," he says, pulling his sword away and placing it in its sheath.

Jade lets out a heavy breath, panting, then nods when she steps off the sparring mat.

Prince Killian calls out another member of the training class, making quick work of the egotistical redhead man he selects.

One after the other he spars with the rest of the group.

Some choose weapons before they begin, others stick to a bit of hand to hand combat. All use their multiple powers against the Prince.

Not that any of them hold long against him.

I can only imagine the amount of training he went through over the years to perfect his abilities. Air, earth, fire, water, light, shadow, and mind wielding from the trainees doesn't even come close to the strength of the Prince's powers.

He occasionally breaks a sweat when a few of them put up a good fight. But he always wins in the end. Every. Single. Time.

And he isn't ready to give up any time soon.

It finally comes down to only myself and Rowan, of which he calls her name first.

She struts over to the rack of weapons and grabs two daggers, placing one in each of her boots. Stepping up onto the mat, she lights a crimson flame in the palm of her hand, waiting for the Prince's response.

His lips tilt up on one side and he raises his own palm up, forming a black, swirling sphere there.

But after only a few, short minutes, Rowan lands on her back, swiftly defeated, with Killian's sword pointing loosely at her throat.

"And… you're finished," the Prince says, reaching out to help her up, but she swats his hand away, raising on her own.

She stomps over to us and I wrap my arm around her shoulders when she reaches me, squeezing her.

"You did a good job," I encourage her but she gently shrugs me off, her ego snuffed. She mumbles a thanks a moment later when she plops to the ground.

She lets out a sigh, circling her toned arms around bent knees before pulling the unused dagger from her left boot and twirling it between her fingers.

"Aurora."

The Prince doesn't want to waste a moment, does he?

I squint up to the sun, now high in the sky, and let out a breath before making my way to him.

"Saving the best for last?" I sneer at him.

He rolls his eyes then deadpans in answer.

Well, *technically* he didn't deny it.

Heat flares to life in my stomach, my body being reminded of the actions of his despicable father. And how he bends to the bastard's every whim.

In a flash, he reaches a claw into my mind. My walls are firmly up but he pulls and tugs, trying to find a way in.

I let him do the work, not bothering to try and get his own walls down, knowing they are next to, if not entirely, impenetrable.

After several minutes, a single bead of sweat drips down his dark brow, next to an ombre-colored eye. He brings down my shield the tiniest bit, reaching in the tip of a finger.

My heart plummets into my gut.

I've trained this power since I was ten, the same age as when I discovered my earth abilities and a year before my light, two before my water. Worry courses down my arms in the form of bumps, as if a freezing cold breeze has swept across my skin.

Breathing deeply, I slam the miniscule opening shut, locking him out for good.

"I'll get in there one day," he whispers in my head, just outside my shield, dragging his ghostly hand against my fortress of a mind before finally backing off.

He flicks out strips of shadows with his fingertips, propelling them my way.

I spread my arms outward, reaching for the earth, asking for its guidance, and pull up half a dozen vines, sending them to battle the oncoming darkness.

Half of them tangle and fight with his attack, the other half weave together, forming a wall in front of me.

His inky strands start creeping along my outstretched vines, covering them. I attempt to pull my plants back, but they yank, resisting my action.

Damn. His shadows have ahold of them.

I release them, having no choice but to allow them to drop lifelessly.

I bite back a frustrated huff, and focus on the earth I still control.

Keeping one hand controlling the vine shield, I grow a light ball in my other, chucking it.

Only one dark, misty, ribbon vanishes at the touch of my brightness, but the rest remain, making their way towards me, slithering through the air and along the ground like snakes.

I shove my shield of vines outward, crashing it into the darkness. Some of my greenery unweaves as it intertwines with the mist.

His shadows then evaporate.

He brings together cupped hands and fire erupts. He sprays my pieces of earth with orange flames, frying them to a crisp.

The impact against my vines forces me to skid backwards. I dig my heels into the mat and slide to a stop when my knees touch down.

This time, I don't hold back the irritation building within me. I glare at him, baring my teeth.

I splay my palms out, grabbing ahold of water from the barrels. The clearness spreads up my arms before I shoot short, quick bursts of the liquid from alternating hands.

He meets each wave with a flash of his now unsheathed sword. His face is one of disinterest as he blocks each strike with ease.

Once all the water I've collected is gone, I grow two new vines behind him, having them crawl to his legs. One is only able to briefly caress his calf before he slices it with his sword.

I leave the fallen vine and with my newly freed hand, I form a ball of light, aiming it at his eyes.

He shields the illumination, twisting to the side.

I grow my remaining greenery up his other leg, wrapping it around his ankle.

Without looking, he swoops his sword down again, chopping off the piece of earth.

Of course he destroyed my attack without having to glance at it.

He continues the swing of his sword, creating black, winding ribbons in the process. They whip out from his weapon in a flash, circling my head, blocking my vision.

A yelp instantly threatens to crawl up my throat at my lack of eyesight.

In the next second, a cold, smooth surface stops against my jugular and I freeze.

The shadows disintegrate, and I feel a presence behind me. Prince Killian, and he's paused the motion of his sword.

To have it resting against the flesh of my throat.

How did he get behind me so quickly?

"You're finished," his husky voice whispers in my ear.

He digs his weapon into my throat ever so slightly before bringing it down.

I spin to face him, the toes of our boots meeting, a scowl covering my face. I glare up into his moonlight eyes several inches above my own.

He smirks down at me lazily, showing a hint of his teeth.

"You're an ass," I snarl.

"Maybe, but I do have a great one." He winks, then matches the distaste on my face.

"You will *never* know a moment of peace when I'm around."

"I look forward to it." His lips tilt up into a smirk.

"You disgust me."

"And your technique disgusts me. I can see we have quite a bit to work on."

He searches my eyes before taking a step back, gaining distance between us. Immediately spinning around, he faces his class of trainees and dismisses us for lunch.

Then, he makes his way to where we entered the field from.

The group turns in silence to stare at his back as he reaches the door and enters, letting it slam shut behind him.

Only once he's out of sight do people finally start trudging towards the same entrance. Mumbles of annoyance and worry spit from mouths along the way.

"He is an absolute machine," Piper comments with a shake of her head.

"You got that right," Rowan agrees from her place beside the dirt-covered woman.

"I don't disagree," I sigh, out of breath, before we make our way to what I believe is a *very* well-deserved lunch break.

Chapter 14

I wake up more sore than I've ever been in my entire life.

After being released for lunch yesterday, we were ordered back out onto the same training field.

We sparred for a few more hours, this time against our fellow trainees. All the while, Prince Killian would stop us mid-strike, correcting our forms and attack strategies.

I hated every second of it.

My vexation towards the Prince grew stronger the longer I was around him.

And the sparring my body isn't used to made me ache in places I didn't even *know* could ache.

Today, our second official day of training, Rowan, Piper, Jade, Sebastian, and I sit on a sparring mat in the outside training area, along with the rest of the trainees attempting to stretch out our sore muscles before we start the day.

The air is still cold and misty in the early morning hour.

I shiver, goosebumps forming on my limbs as I roll my ankles around in my boots and pull either arm across my chest.

"My thighs are still burning," Rowan complains as she reaches to touch her toes.

Piper sits next to her, stretching out her biceps, and giggles at her comment.

"After a while, you'll get used to it. Just make sure to stretch every day," Jade advises.

To my left, Sebastian grunts as he attempts to touch his fingertips to the tips of his boots, but comes up short, barely halfway down his shins.

I crack my neck side to side and rotate my shoulder blades one at a time, cursing. The stiff beds we sleep on are of no help to the aches in my joints.

The sound of a door slamming open so roughly it bangs against the castle's outer wall pulls me from my stretching.

Luca marches towards us, fuming. Why is he here rather than the Prince?

His long, light braid swings as he makes his way onto the field.

My eyes roam down him, and land at his waist.

Cuffs and a collar sit attached to his belt loop.

I thought I had seen the last of those. I suppose I was very much wrong.

"You," the second-in-command grumbles as he points past where I sit to another mat.

He marches up to a man whose name I have yet to learn. The man's face goes white and his pupils bulge.

The moment Luca arrives in front of him, he hauls the man to his feet.

"You broke the rules. You're to be seen by the King," Luca says as he roughly places cuffs on the man's wrists, then his ankles, and finally secures the collar around his neck.

The man stands there, stunned, unmoving.

Whispers fill the field, questions floating in the air.

"What's going on?" I turn to Piper, wondering with her time here if she's seen something like this before.

"He must have been caught doing something he wasn't supposed to. Trying to escape, being out of bed after hours, or something. And obviously Luca found out, so he's going to take him to the King for punishment," she says, eyes still on the scene.

"And what kind of punishment is that?"

She only answers my question with a shrug of her shoulders.

"Usually Luca hands out punishments, but if it's bad enough, the King wants to see the person in trouble," Jade whispers. "It doesn't happen often, but no one ever speaks of what happens to them after they've been taken to see the King."

My jaw threatens to drop open but I squeeze it tightly shut.

Silently, I watch, as my mind spins with possibilities.

Luca, one hand gripping the man's bicep so hard it turns white, drags him along, sneering at the rest of us.

"Mind your business," he snarls loudly, causing several pairs of eyes to look away.

Soon enough, he swings open the door to the castle again and disappears from sight.

Muttering ensues once more, and slowly but surely people continue their stretching as we wait for our *proper* trainer to join us.

Several minutes later, he finally does.

"Let's get a move on people. We're first going to practice your aim. Line up in front of the targets and practice aiming your abilities," the Prince shouts at us as he steps out onto the field, pointing to the back right side of the grassy space.

I grunt, easing to my feet and trudge my way to the circular targets at the far edge of the field.

Most of the group is also slow moving from our harsh sparring sessions yesterday.

I stare at the massive circles placed far away from where we all stand. Ten rings circle the targets, spaced out evenly before reaching the bullseye in the center.

We line up in a row, each at our own target and fire away at the Prince's "go."

Wiggling my fingers, I build up my powers in the palm of my hand.

I push my arm outward, shooting out a ball of light. It lands a handful of inches to the right of the center.

"You can do better than that," the Prince immediately jests.

I peek over my shoulder, glaring at him before fully turning my body to face him.

"Excuse me? Can you even wield light? I didn't see you use any yesterday. And I *definitely* don't think you can, considering no one has ever wielded all seven abilities before."

I fold my arms over my chest, waiting.

His lips tilt up as he takes a step toward me. "Oh, so you've been paying attention to me?"

His arrogance is absolutely *astounding*.

A haughty laugh bubbles up my throat, and pointing at his chest, I sneer. "You wish."

He takes another step forward, running into my outstretched finger.

I may be taller than average for a woman, but he towers over me, something I hadn't considered until he closed in on my space.

He cranes his neck down to peer into my eyes, investigating me.

A piece of his silky, dark hair falls onto his face, over his tan forehead, partially covering a light eye. He blocks the morning sun from my view, sending a shadow cascading over me.

"Trust me, if I wished for something, you'd be the *first* to know," he says snarkily in a lowered voice before raising back to his full height.

My breath catches, not expecting such a response from him.

He spins around, effectively ending the conversation and starts to walk down the line of trainees, observing the other's abilities.

"He's so picky. And arrogant," I mumble aloud, releasing a huff, turning back to my target. "That was only my first throw, and my light ball almost hit the center."

"Don't let him get you down. I believe in you," Piper says with a smile from where she stands to my right. Tilting her head, her green eyes glow bright as the sun peeks through the morning mist.

I thank her before returning my gaze to my target, this time aiming a dark green vine. The piece of earth strikes the center of the target, leaving a small cavity in the soft hay of which it's made.

I grin at my perfect shot and instinctively look over to the Prince's place further down the field.

I stare at the side of his face. His bright eyes are intense with focus on the skills taking place in front of him, his lips pulled in concentration as he holds a fist under his chin. I catch myself and shake my head of the thoughts, glancing away.

On my left, Sebastian alternates between throwing gusts of wind and ribbons of shadows, every one striking the dead center.

He's *remarkable*.

I gape at his magnificent aim and the deep indentation he's leaving with his perfectly aimed attacks.

His deep brown eyes don't stray from his target. His tawny face is flat, unmoving, as he repeatedly attacks his mark and his curly, black hair swishes against his forehead.

I ogle at the ease of his strikes, and his disinterest, curious at his disposition, wondering what led him to have an aura of such quiet darkness.

Then I scan the spaces beside Piper.

Rowan is to her immediate right, and I bite back a chuckle at her convenient placement.

My dungeon-on-wheels companion practices her earth and water abilities. Splashes and pebbles land on the outermost circles.

The dark braids she wears hit against her upper arms and back as she puts her whole body into the movements.

Frustration shows on her face as the elements don't reach anywhere near the middle. Lips curling back, she grunts, squinting at the target.

I bite the inside of my cheek as her irritation becomes palpable.

Piper watches Rowan's irritation take over and immediately places a hand on her shoulder.

Her body relaxes at the touch and she turns to face Piper.

I can't make out what Piper says, but her hands wave with some type of movement, twisting them toward the target and Rowan locks an intense stare on her.

I let out a giggle. Rowan being more focused now than she was on her attacks only a moment ago is more comical than it should be.

On the other side of their conversation, Jade strikes the target with air, water, earth, and fire, in that order, repeatedly.

Her short, black hair tied back in two ponytails again reveals a relatively calm, leveled face, with a tiny scrunch of her nose being the only sign she's thinking hard about landing her blasts.

She seems to be testing her skills in order of strength, as she starts off with strong, powerful gusts of wind hitting the center and ends with short bursts of gold flames leaving small scorch marks on the outskirts, or off the target altogether.

Her discipline is commendable, and I watch her practice attack after attack. Her movements are nimble, and she glides around like a feather on the wind.

My gaze only roams back to Piper when I hear a thunderous applause.

She claps wildly as Rowan points to a gray pebble in the dead center of her target.

Rowan faces Piper, wearing a massive grin. Thanking her for the help, she returns to blasting off more rocks.

Piper's cheeks flare with pink as she shies away, turning to her own practice.

I smirk, my eyes roaming back and forth between the two of them.

Piper first fires off a beam of light, hitting a bullseye. Her two, strawberry blonde, french braids hanging on her shoulders whip with the force of her blast.

She pauses then, staring at the circles in concentration and breathes in deeply. Her left palm flies forward, releasing a quick blast of fire.

A blast that hits below the target, in the grass, leaving a smudge of charcoal gray.

Yikes.

I have yet to practice my own water abilities because I'm sure the results will be similar.

Piper licks her lips before trying again.

Two more strikes later, and a small triangle of dark smudges is made… on the ground.

She curls her hands into fists and puffs air out of her nose. Rowan notices, and takes the opportunity to help Piper with her fire, just as she had been helped by her.

I blink back to my target, pushing the distractions of others away and steadying myself to take my own shots at the outlined circles.

I suppose now is as good of a time as any to practice with water.

Lunging into my throw, I swirl a ribbon of clear liquid from a barrel at my back straight towards my target. The liquid splashes against the very bottom of the outermost ring.

Well, this is going exactly as I thought it would.

Flinging my fist forward, I shoot another ripple of water, this one hitting below the first spot, missing the target completely.

"I see you're still not doing better. In fact, you're actually doing worse," Killian says, appearing out of nowhere. I jump at the sound of his voice, not expecting his presence.

But when I still, I whip to face the Prince, ogling him, flabbergasted.

He is so rude. All. The. Time.

As soon as my eyes meet his, he marches up and spins me right back around. Catching my breath at the sudden, unexpected twist, I realize his hands are on my hips.

What the…

A shiver runs down my spine, the width of my hips now an extremely active thought in my mind. My shoulders tense as my head swirls for only a moment, because the warmth of his hands leave just as swiftly as they had landed on me.

Leaning over me, one of his hands makes a fist and points it in the direction of my target. His arm then droops a few inches and rotates to the side.

"*This* is what you're doing. When you finish the movement, your arm is pointed down and to the left. Make sure it's straight out the entire time," he explains, demonstrating the proper movement with his arm.

He takes a step back before gesturing with a flick of his wrist, gesturing for me to try again.

Seriously? He can't say it to me? He didn't have a problem verbalizing his orders earlier.

His tanned, unfortunately not unattractive, face sits passive, waiting.

My nails bite into my hands.

His presence is utterly infuriating.

I stare at the target once again, breathing in through my nose and out my mouth, attempting to relax after trying to grasp his instructions. I rotate my shoulders forward in circles. Then backwards, focusing on where I should end the movement of my throw.

"Any day now."

I fight the urge to roll my eyes.

More rudeness from him.

I wish I could say I can't believe it, but that wouldn't be true; his ego is ridiculously massive.

I lunge into the punch again. My arm is steady this time, the muscles straining as I keep it held higher and straighter.

This time, the stream of water I contort lands on the second most outer ring.

The corner of my lips pull up but drop when I face the Prince behind me.

"That wasn't as incredibly terrible." He shrugs, then strides away, his stare now on Piper.

I gape in disbelief at his version of a compliment.

I'm sure I would only need a single guess to figure out who taught him to act in such a way.

Giving up on understanding him, I continue aiming the water, honing in on my arm's position.

We practice on our targets for hours, soon forgoing our best abilities, at the Prince's word. Instead, we work on the ones we struggle with.

His perpetual pacing up and down the line eventually becomes almost easy to ignore. *Almost.*

He, at one point, orders us to practice using only our non-dominant hand, a command met with several groans.

Sweat drips down everyone's foreheads and necks, hair sticking to our faces as the sun rises to the highest point in the sky. Autumn feels nonexistent in the unfathomably warm weather.

My shoulder and elbow joints ache from the repeated movements.

"I think Killian's a masochist," Piper comments.

"I think you're right," I agree, rubbing a sore shoulder.

"My arms feel like jelly. I can barely hold them up any more," Rowan whines.

"Mine too. And shoulder blades feel like they're going to fall off."

"I swear, this target practice will be playing on repeat in my nightmares tonight," Jade adds, humming along in agreement, massaging her arms.

I sigh. "I would rather do anything else but stare at this target right now."

Well, maybe not *anything*. When we arrive back outside after eating a fueling lunch, the Prince stands on a sparring mat at the front of the field.

The October sun remains beating down, unseasonably so, as I hold a hand to my brow, blocking out the brightness while he begins instructing us.

Of course it's more sparring.

We're split up, tasked with sparring in groups, rotating through each of the people we're batched with.

Sebastian stands amongst a group of three women. Jade and a blonde girl stride over to two tall, dark-haired men. Piper and Rowan waltz away, head high, to two men ogling them as they approach.

My nose crinkles at the faces they make towards the women.

I'm placed with a curly-haired woman and two men, a dirty blonde and a cocky redhead who had his ass handed to him by the Prince yesterday. Silas, if my memory serves me correctly.

He had gracefully greeted "His Royal Highness, Prince Killian" with a polite, sincere bow.

My eyes could not have rolled further back into my head at the loyalist's greeting.

However, he had been arrogant, all bark and no bite, only worrying about showing off his skills offensively and forwent his defense. While he was able to wield air, earth, fire, shadows, and the mind, Killian promptly took him down.

So, when he and I step onto the mat, he strikes first, punching a wave of red-orange searing heat right at my face.

I lean to the side, dodging the hot blast.

After my swerve, I check the stability of my mind shields, ensuring they're in place.

They are, and he hasn't attempted to penetrate them. He must believe he can win by solely using brute force.

He hasn't been paying very close attention.

I mindlessly toss a ball of light in his direction, purely as a distraction in order to slip into his mind.

I practically walk right in.

Projecting an image of me into his brain, I multiply it, so he views not only one, but a dozen of me.

His confusion is apparent when he swings his arms wildly, and punches out three more flames, aimed at the copies of me.

But he then abruptly shakes his head.

I feel him checking his mind, and shock rumbles from him before he slams his walls up, forcing me out.

A grunt of frustration escapes me. My illusion didn't last nearly as long as I hoped.

His gaze focuses back on the single, real version of me.

His fingers flatten downward, and the earth rumbles. A gigantic boulder lifts up from under the grass, cracking the ground wide open. The colossal rock shifts as he hovers it in front of his person.

Before he can move it further, I shine a beam of light into his eyes, blinding him.

He reaches to cover his face, unsuccessfully blocking my illumination, and forgetting about the massive rock.

The boulder slams to the ground, and onto his right foot.

Oops.

He lets out a howl of pain as he blindly pushes the rock out of the way to get to his foot.

Silas grabs ahold of his foot with his eyes shut, whining loudly while hopping up and down on his other leg. He stumbles, falling to the ground, butt hitting the edge of the mat, causing him to simultaneously slip off and land in the grass.

He huffs out angrily through his nose when he pries open his eyes and notices where he's ended up.

I try to hide my lips raising to a grin as he stands up and stomps back to the sidelines.

Serves him right.

As I finally let out a giggle at the grown man's temper tantrum, the hair on the back of my neck stands up, as if I'm being watched.

I spin around. Completing my rotation, my eyes connect with the Prince's. Eyes that are lit with a mix of interest and surprise.

It only lasts a moment before he briskly struts off, spying another group of trainees.

After sparring with Silas, and winning, we continue taking turns facing one another.

By the time Prince Killian makes an announcement following the completion of our group training, I'm thoroughly exhausted.

"I have some things I need to attend to, so we'll call it a day here." He immediately spins on his heels, striding off to who knows where to do who knows what.

Piper sprints her way to me, throwing an arm up around my shoulders.

"I saw you get Silas to smash that rock onto his own foot earlier. That was genius!"

I chuckle, shrugging.

I suppose it was funny, seeing his ego smashed, *literally*.

"Now I can show you guys around some more before dinner starts!"

She points to a clock I hadn't noticed hung on the side of the huge obstacle course running the length of the training field. "We still have almost two hours until they dish out food."

Rowan reaches her opposite side and Piper slings her other arm around the woman's tall frame. A smile splits Rowan's face.

Jade waltzes up to me, grinning, and loops her arm through my free one.

"Come on Bash! You're joining us," Piper adds, throwing him a toothy grin.

Reaching out a hand, Rowan gently pulls Sebastian along.

Piper and Jade, but primarily Piper, who talks the majority of the time, show us to the three other bunk rooms, all identical to the one we sleep in. She then leads us to more spaces used for training exercises, including a weight room filled with various heavy objects.

She takes us to a massive lecture hall where seats climb up a wall, similar to those in the arena we were thrown into yesterday. Here, she says, they share updates on laws, rules, or declarations from the King, or even news of Norfell, Mistivas, and Evenend.

The mention of King Kairos sends my stomach churning.

I hate the fact that I'm under the same roof as the bastard.

After the hall, Piper and Jade take us to a library.

My jaw drops at the hundreds of shelves stuffed full of books, and spiral staircases leading to the upper levels. Disbelief courses through me at the sheer number of books, all in varying shades, ranging from sunset oranges to bright blues to deep browns, lining the cherry-red, wooden bookcases built into the walls.

I run a finger along the edge of the shelves in admiration.

Excitement at the endless number of stories to read bubbles up inside of me.

Jade stands a few paces away, plucking a book off the shelf, in her element like never before. The feeling of a smirk glides along my lips.

I knew I liked her.

Sebastian has made his way up the first set of spiral stairs. I peer up at him over a banister to see him investigating a thin book.

Piper and Rowan crowd around a short bookshelf standing alone in a space between the wall shelves. Rowan leans against it casually, one arm propped on top, the shelves reaching halfway up her torso. Her other hand moves around while she talks and her face lights up.

Piper stands on the other side, both elbows resting atop, her face sitting in her hands as she stares up at Rowan with big, green eyes. They giggle to one another and I turn away, hiding my growing smirk.

I suppose I really should do my best not to spy on their obvious flirting.

Jade plops down at a nearby table, one of several between the shelves, with the book she had selected and I follow her over.

"What did you pick out?" I ask, peering over to the book resting in front of her.

"A romance novel. I'm a sucker for them." She giggles sheepishly.

"So am I! What's this one about?"

"It's about a man and woman from warring kingdoms, who accidentally meet when he's spying in her territory, and they fall in love not knowing they're on opposite sides. However, once she discovers the truth, she leaves him. He returns to his kingdom to give up his place as a spy and intends to return to her, but by the time he comes back, she's long gone. He searches for her all over and finally, years later, he stumbles upon her in a marketplace. He confesses his love and explains how he's been looking for her, she forgives him, and they live happily ever after."

Jade stares off in the distance, a dream dancing behind her eyes.

"So, I take it, you've read that one before?"

"Yes, it's my favorite! It's been a while since I've read it but the story will live in my mind forever!" She laughs, and I join in.

Sebastian walks down the nearby stairs, fingering his dark brown curls, and joins us, silently sitting down in a chair.

I inspect the book he's brought with him. A poetry book.

I poke him in the arm. "Poetry! That's fun."

He shrugs and pushes up the sleeves of his black, three-quarter length shirt. He crosses his arms over his chest while leaning back in his chair, sliding down a bit.

"A man of many interests," Rowan exclaims as she walks over, slapping her hands on his shoulders, surprising him. "That's our Bash."

He lets out a soft breath and shakes his head, his dark hair swishing against his forehead in the process. Rowan smirks and drops her hands, moving to sit on his left.

"Oh don't be coy," Piper adds, taking the last chair at the square table.

She props her head up on fists, grinning ear to ear before glancing at Rowan.

Discussions of literature, poetry, and the library in general pass between us for a long time.

It's a conversation Jade jumps at, and one that Sebastian actually says a few words during. The latter surprises me, even if it's only one-worded agreements, but it fills me with a pang of joy.

I note several stolen glances between Rowan and Piper amidst the talking, and have to reel in the smirk trying to appear on my lips.

Piper eventually peeks up and gasps.

"Dinner's about to start. We better go because I am *not* wrestling anyone for a piece of carrot cake," she rants, wagging a finger. "Not again. Silas fought me over the last piece a few nights ago and snatched it up first. So, I'm determined to get a piece tonight."

"I suppose he'll be slower today after having that boulder dropped on his foot," I say with a chuckle.

"You are *so* right. But I will still wrestle him for it if he gets there before me, so let's go!"

I giggle at her determination. She never fails to make me laugh.

She huffs out a breath, standing to lead the way. I follow, assuring her we will get her a piece tonight, no matter what.

Chapter 15

Jade was right. Stretching may be painful but I swear it's the only thing not keeping my body from completely freezing up.

Everything hurts. Every joint. Every muscle. Every ligament.

Even my brain aches.

The five of us sit on the training field again, and I look at the other trainees spread out on the field of sparring mats.

My eyes land on the man Luca took yesterday.

While I can't seem to find any visible marks of punishment, his face is lined with distraught. He half-heartedly reaches for the tips of his boots to stretch his legs, but his mind seems to wander elsewhere.

Deep bags lay under each eye, and his light brown hair is tousled in a way that makes it look like he got little to no sleep last night.

He already has fair skin, but he looks especially pale, sickly even.

My mind spirals with the possibilities of what could have happened to him yesterday. Luca was so vague when he came to snatch the man away, no one even knew what he had done wrong. Punishment at the hand of the King could mean anything.

Nausea turns in my stomach.

We really are stuck here under the King's control with no way out.

I do my best to shove the feeling in my gut away, continuing to contort my arms and legs.

As we extend our aching bodies this way and that, the Prince struts onto the grass, gracing us with his presence.

My eyes go rolling before I can stop them.

"Before we begin, I've been discussing some ideas with my generals," he explains, lips lifting into an arrogant smile. Dimples appear on each of his cheeks.

Well, this can't be good.

I scoff and eye Rowan to the east. Her mouth is twisted up in annoyance. Piper and Jade stand on her other side, letting out frustrated sighs of their own. At the end of the line is Sebastian, who I catch silently glowering.

Glad to see we're all on the same page right now.

"We've decided, in order to work on your discipline, to assign you chores. Isn't that wonderful?" The Prince's smirk turns into a full blown grin, splitting his face in two.

My lips curl back in disgust.

With my luck, I'll end up scrubbing toilets, or something equally as gross. Especially if Prince Killian has anything to do about it.

I have a feeling he's still pissed about my spitting on him three days ago.

I hold in a chuckle at the memory, biting down on my lip.

Him and his tyrannical father deserve nothing but the worst, and *nothing* will make me change my mind.

Rowan, Jade, and a handful of others are assigned kitchen duty, where they will help prepare food. Piper and a few more trainees are given the chore of cleaning up the outside fields, the others of which we learn lie beyond either side wall of our training space.

Finally, the Prince tells the remainder of us that we're responsible for laundry.

It may not be toilets but cleaning other people's stinky clothes after sparring? It's definitely a close second.

To my thanks, which I keep hidden, he adds that the chores will only be completed once a week, albeit on our single day off, as the workload is split evenly across the seven training groups.

Grumbles of irritation sound across the crowd as he finishes handing out assignments, regardless of how often he says we must complete them.

"Now, today we'll be working on your aim again, this time with weapons. In order to be well-rounded soldiers, you can't rely solely on your powers," the Prince states, pacing in front of us, his tan hands clasped behind his back.

"I'm shocked we're not sparring again. Since he seems to enjoy watching us beat each other up so much," I lean over to whisper to Rowan. I snicker while she tries to hold in a laugh.

A quiet spreads over the field. I pull my eyes back to Killian to notice he's stopped talking.

His eyes narrow on me. I gulp, and my spine stiffens, forcing me to stand up straighter.

He's heard me.

The Prince pauses his pacing and strides toward me, reaching me in only three steps.

My chest rises and falls rapidly as he closes in on my space. He glares down at me, his face so close his warm breath brushes over my cheeks.

"Would you like to say that a little louder so I can hear you more clearly? Since apparently you're the one in charge now."

I stare up at him, knowing he heard exactly what I said. My hands ball into fists.

Tired of his attitude, I close the space between us, and smile sweetly up at him.

"Gladly. I said I'm shocked we're not sparring again, since you seem to *love* watching us beat each other up."

His eyes fill with an icy silver, overtaking the gem-colored blue. They narrow into slits, searching my own. "You're a handful, aren't you?"

My sickly sweet grin stretches further over my face.

"Undeniably."

His eyes flick back and forth, pondering his next words carefully.

"Why don't you stay after training today for a bit, hm? So we can do more of that sparring you seem to love so much. Private lessons, if you will."

He shrugs nonchalantly. But his lips turn up and he whips around, hands never leaving their place at his back. He resumes his pacing as if nothing ever happened.

My fists clench even tighter.

I *loathe* him.

Faces of astonishment turn my way. I refuse to acknowledge them, my gaze staying forward, although ignoring the Prince's instructions depicting today's plans.

Before I know it, I stand at a target with a dagger in my hand.

I blink rapidly in an attempt to focus my vision and clear my mind.

I twist the weapon, feeling the weight of it, and chuck it across the field. It clatters to the ground when its handle hits the outermost ring.

At my side, Sebastian flings his own dagger. It spins end over end until it meets the center of his target, a perfect bullseye.

My mouth falls open.

Where did he learn his skills? Is he this good at *everything?*

I shake out my hand and try to copy his stance, widening my feet and bending my knees. I bring the sharp edge of the weapon a hair above my shoulder as I pull my arm back, eyeing the red dot in the middle of my target. I throw my hand forward, releasing the dagger from my grip.

And the blunt end of the weapon hits the bottom of the circles before dropping into the grass with a clang. Again.

This is impossible.

My shoulders slump in frustration. With a grunt of irritation, I pick up another dagger and send it flying.

This one barely scrapes the right-hand side. And it falls. Just as the ones before had.

I huff out a breath through my nose and grab a fourth dagger from the pile next to me. I reach my arm up next to my head, readying my throw, but hand wraps around my wrist, halting my movement.

I whip my head to find Rowan staring at me with soft eyes. I relax my limb to my side when she releases her grip.

"You're going to hurt yourself or someone else if you keep throwing like that," she tells me calmly, placing a hand on my shoulder.

Closing my lids, I take a deep breath in through my nose, releasing it out my mouth.

"Don't let *him* and his *private lessons* freak you out, okay?"

I crack my eyes open and find Rowan's gold ringed ones piercing me with concern.

"Okay."

Her lips tilt up briefly before her features pull into a narrowed focus.

She comes around me, positioning my body in a different angle. She maneuvers my throwing arm inward, closer to my ear, as she gives me tips on throwing the weapon.

Taking her advice, I let the dagger loose, and it lands, lodging itself into the outermost ring.

A small flame of hope lights within me and grin plays at my lips when I turn to thank her.

She nods her head in pride, a beam growing on her face. Swiftly, she motions for me to try again.

As Rowan helps me, Sebastian lets dagger after dagger rip through the air, spinning until they all meet, stacked on top of one another, in the center of his target.

My jaw drops again. Every single one has hit perfectly.

"Nice."

The Prince appears behind us, arms crossed over his broad chest. His light eyes widen with investigation at Sebastian's throws. He nods, continuing down the line of trainees without another word.

"You're amazing! And you got a real compliment from him," I tell Sebastian, nudging his side. A chuckle releases from my throat after I return my focus to my own target.

"Maybe if you did something impressive, you'd get one too."

I spin to the grumbling voice. His Royal Highness glares at me several paces away, mouth turned up on one side.

"You have an awfully bad habit of listening in on other's conversations," I spit.

"Perhaps you're just louder than you think."

"Perhaps you're more of an *ass* than you think."

I scoff, giving him a cold glare and turning away.

Rowan places a palm on my shoulder once again, a gentle reminder of her previous words about not letting him get to me.

I take a breath in and out, then toss another dagger, this one landing an inch closer to the middle than my last.

Several hours later, we've moved on from daggers, and onto archery. I never came close to achieving a bullseye with the first weapon so relief springs within me at the change.

Piper picks up the bow as if it's a long-lost best friend and fires three arrows into the bullseye.

Jade, Rowan, and I simultaneously clap in awe at her precision.

She's amazing at this. I don't doubt that she's had many years of practice with a bow.

A crash of objects dropping to the ground sounds then, interrupting our cheering.

The three of us spin to find Sebastian fumbling with the bow and arrows, now laying in an ungraceful pile at his feet.

It seems this form of weaponry may not be his forte.

I head over to the mess and begin picking up the arrows while he untangles an arrow from the bow's string.

"I think Piper may have to give us all a few tips," I holler over my shoulder at her.

Collected arrows back in the stand beside Sebastian, I pat his shoulder.

I move to pick up a bow with my left hand, and an arrow with my right, placing it along the string as the Prince had demonstrated earlier. I pull the string back with my fingertips, all the way to my cheek, and close an eye, releasing the arrow.

And it lands within the ring right outside the bullseye.

A gasp escapes me. I had no idea I could do that.

"Woo hoo! Nice job! I don't need to give you any pointers; you're a natural," Piper whoops from her spot two places down.

I turn, giving her a massive grin.

Jade picks up her own bow and lands an arrow a couple inches to the right of the center. She shrugs her shoulders, assessing the shot, and tries again.

Rowan fires an arrow next. It flies up, up, up… and lands in the grass in front of the target.

Piper steps in to help, guiding her hand, locking it out straight.

As the two of them work on Rowan's aim, Sebastian finally lets an arrow loose. It lands on the edge of the target, then droops, dangling off, barely held in.

He huffs a breath and shakes out his hands, trying again.

The next arrow lands a hair to the side of the first, further within the target.

"You have unnaturally good aim. You'll get it soon." My mouth quirks up at him.

"It's… awkward. Big and bulky," he says, examining the long bow gripped in his hand. Even with his tall, lanky build, the bow takes up more than half of his height.

"I believe in you."

He shrugs his shoulders, picking up another arrow to continue his practice.

It lands an inch closer to the bullseye once again.

I smirk at his target and return to my own, breathing in as I pull back the string of my bow, then out as I release it.

This one lands on the bottom edge of the bullseye.

"I've seen enough weapons hit the ground for the day. Get out. I'll see you all tomorrow."

I groan, placing down my bow with aching arms at Killian's dismissal.

Turning to Rowan, my face crumbles as she gives me a withered look, nodding towards the Prince. He glares, reminding me of our "private lessons."

He is *such* a joy.

Rowan whispers good luck to me while Piper, Jade, and Sebastian each give me a small, unsure nod before following Rowan off the field.

I fold my arms over my chest, awaiting the Prince's instructions.

Without giving me a second glance, he passes by, waving his muscled arm at me to join him on a sparring mat.

"I see you watching the other trainees for their strategies, how they move, any of their weaknesses."

"Oh, so you've been paying attention to *me*," I say, copying his words from yesterday.

He lets out a chuckle through a tight-lipped smirk. "Don't flatter yourself."

My eyes roll before turning a glare at him.

Good to see his ever-persistent ego is intact.

"Now, that may be of use in training, but it won't always be helpful when you face new enemies. Act as if every person you go against, you've never seen them before."

"Fine, stranger. Do your worst," I tell him, unfolding my arms, placing my hands on my hips.

"Oh, I plan to."

The feeling of cold wraps around my legs, and my bottom half is ripped out from under me, landing me on my ass with a thud.

Fuck, that hurt.

As I try to catch the breath he knocked out of me, I scowl up at him.

"Always expect the unexpected." He stretches out a hand, surprising me, but I hold firm in my fury.

Ignoring his palm, I push myself up.

My face heats with embarrassment as I stand. I try to calm the color rising in my cheeks, of course to no avail.

He chooses not to remark on the color in my face, of which I'm thankful for, as he continues to explain his methods.

"Stay light on your feet, even when wielding earth. It takes some practice but it'll help you avoid getting swept off your feet, even by me."

A coy smile plays at his lips, proud of his quip.

"You did *not* sweep me off my feet. You merely caught me off guard."

I reach out, feeling for nearby water molecules, and whip a strand of liquid at him from one of the barrels placed in between the sparring mats.

The water splashes the side of his face, and his mouth drops open. Silver flashes in his gaze.

I don't stifle the laugh that bubbles up my throat at the mix of shock and rage on his face.

"Maybe you should take your own advice, *Prince*."

He slowly nods his head as he musters up a small gust of wind to dry his damp skin.

"You're going to regret that."

His eyes sparkle in the early evening sun before turning his wind on me. I anticipate his move, and dodge the blast of air, letting it slide past my face.

"Missed."

I grin at his failed maneuver and swipe my arm forward, throwing out a blast of light.

He matches me, tilting his lips upward knowingly. He opens a ring of shadows before my brightness can reach him, enveloping my light inside and swiftly closing the circle of darkness.

I stretch my arm down, snapping a vine up from the earth, shooting it at his ankle.

A bright orange flame burns the rope to a crisp before it can reach him.

A storm of shadows flies into my chest then, pushing me into a stumble, and I fall onto my back.

"Bring your arms in. Protect your body," he instructs, sending out more shadows.

I do as he says, rising to my feet in a crouch, blocking most of the darkness from hitting me, and instead forcing it to slam into my awaiting forearms.

"Not *entirely* bad."

He pauses his attacks and strides over. Placing a hand around either of my wrists when I stand to my full height, he pulls my bent arms inward, shielding my chest more.

"Don't leave such a wide gap between your arms. Elements can still seep through."

The calluses on his warm hands are rough against the skin of my wrists. His hands are so much more like ones of a warrior than ones of a prince. But nearly as soon as his hands had grabbed ahold of me, they were gone, the warmth along with it.

I shudder at the sudden cold and drop my arms, rubbing my hands against my wrists and forearms to recreate the heat.

"And make sure your shields are up, don't let anyone get into your mind," he adds.

I whip my head up to look at him, not noticing my gaze had wandered down to my hands.

"No, before you ask, I'm not going to enter your mind. But I could feel your shield slipping. Stay focused, and keep it up at all times. You never know who may be able to use your mind against you. Don't ever let it come to that."

I gulp and nod my head in understanding. However, I can't help but wonder if he is truly being honest about not entering my mind.

"Practice using your abilities with your hands closer to your body. Then you'll have smaller, more controlled movements," he continues.

"It doesn't feel natural to do that."

"Hence why I said 'practice.' It will take time, but it helps during oncoming attacks. Especially in close combat."

I take in his words, considering them.

I suppose he may know about what to do in combat, but he will never hear a word of it from me. His ego doesn't need any more reassurance.

He backs away, and in the next moment, a flame shoots at me.

I twist, ungracefully, to the left and fall to my knees to avoid the fire. I point a scowl his way.

That was *not* necessary.

I brush off my knees as I stand, still glaring at him.

"I hope this taught you a lesson not to talk back to me in front of everyone," he says smugly as he assumes his usual position, with his tan, massive arms crossing over his chest.

His lips tilt up in amusement when I copy him, puffing my chest out and folding my arms in order to mock his stance.

"You know, I'm not sure if your methods worked," I tap my chin in fake consideration. "Maybe I'll have to try again some time."

Sarcastically, I grin widely and drop my arms.

Spinning, I stomp off the field, unconcerned with the fact he has yet to dismiss me.

And I ensure my mind shields are up the entire way.

When I finally make it back inside, my gaze instinctively searches for my bunk mates.

The dining hall is filling up with hungry trainees who line the counter filled with food. I investigate those standing before roaming my eyes over to the tables. Rowan's hand flies into the air, beckoning me over.

After filling my tray full of roasted meat and an array of vegetables, I approach the table.

Rowan and Jade lift their brows in silent question. But Piper's the one who voices their collective inquiry.

"So, how was your *private lesson* with the Prince?" Her light brows waggle around teasingly.

"Ridiculous. He's obnoxious and big-headed."

She snickers, covering her mouth with a hand.

"I can't say I'm entirely surprised," Rowan says, biting back a chuckle.

I notice Sebastian's eyes bouncing between the rest of us before his head shakes side to side and he continues feasting on his dinner.

"His ego is out of control, I swear," I add, poking my fork into my meal and shoving a morsel into my mouth.

"Hopefully he was just in a mood today, and he won't make you do any more," Jade says optimistically.

"I think he's *always* in some sort of mood," Piper tells her. Jade's head tilts to the side in consideration before she nods in agreement.

"Anyways, enough about him," Rowan starts. "This food is *delicious*. The meat is perfectly tender and I think I may have to go back for seconds."

She shoves a piece of it in her mouth and hums with excitement.

"They marinated it well. I can taste some rosemary and thyme in here too," I say over a bite of my own.

"It's nice and warm," Sebastian mumbles.

Piper opens her mouth to speak, but shouting echoes into the dining hall from the wide, main training room behind me.

Our table goes silent and we twist towards the noise.

King's Guards pull a flailing body through the room, the person's body thumping against the raised sparring mats.

The dining hall empties, everyone having rushed to the massive doorframe to peer into the main room.

I'm on my feet in the next second, squeezing my way through the crowd to view the commotion.

Two bulky, male guards haul a young, curly-haired man towards the double doors Rowan, Sebastian, and I were dragged through only a few days ago.

A pair of doors I have yet to even approach since my arrival here.

A chill courses through me as the young man kicks his legs that can't seem to find purchase under his body. His shoulders nearly touch his ears as the guards yank on the upper part of his arms.

"Please, I'm sorry!" He wails. Tears streak down his face.

"There's no excuse for trying to escape. The King will deal with you now." The guard's booming voice sends my gut flipping.

He tried to escape. The exact thing the Prince said *not* to do just three days ago.

My mind wanders, searching for what this man could have done, or at least tried to do, to get out of this place unnoticed.

Between how far we are underground, the security of the training yards outside, and the labyrinth that is the palace, I have no idea what he could have thought was a good escape plan.

The pair of large doors scrape against the floor as they open, and in the next moment, the King's Guards and the young man are gone.

And my thoughts spiral yet again, this time to what punishment awaits the man. Another punishment at the hands of the King.

What is it King Kairos does to those who disobey him here?

A second batch of icy cold sprints down my back. Whatever it is, I do *not* want to find out.

Chapter 16

The Prince stares us down. I can only wonder what he's planning behind those vicious, investigative eyes.

After having us practice archery again this morning, which worsened the burning already in my arms, I expect whatever comes next will only increase the soreness radiating throughout my body.

"I've been able to see what your natural instincts will do while sparring *with* your powers, but what do they look like when you don't use them?" His arms cross over his chest.

The afternoon sun isn't as unbearable today but in our black and gray ensembles, it's as if the heat is attracted to us.

I fan my face with a hand. Jade does the same. Piper rolls up her dark, short sleeves so they sit at the top of her shoulders.

I'm ready for the true autumn weather to hit.

Killian is seemingly unaffected by the warmth. Not a bead of sweat in sight.

I swear, the list of infuriating things he does grows daily.

"You. And you." The prince points to a petite blonde woman, then swings his finger over to Silas. He moves his finger to the sparring mat he stands on. A silent instruction.

Damn is he bossy.

"Take up a fighting stance. Let's see what we're working with," the Prince states, backing off a handful of steps.

The blonde woman nervously bends her knees, digging her heels into the floor and bringing fists up in front of her face. Silas creates a similar stance, but confidence rolls off of him.

"Keep your feet planted, but loose. Don't let someone knock you over but be ready to weave and bob when necessary." Killian approaches her, lightly tapping her boots with one of his. She shuffles her feet, softer against the ground.

"And *don't*, under any circumstances, do this." He strides over to Silas and grabs his fists, pulling them apart. "Your thumb does *not* go on the inside of your fist."

The Prince's face is one of twisted, displeased shock as he adjusts the redhead man's hands. He shakes his head, sending his half tied-back, brown waves swinging.

Silas's pale, freckled face turns beet red while his hands are moved around by the Prince he looks up to so highly.

I bite down on my lip to hold in a snicker.

I don't have much good to say about my fighting capabilities but I at least know how not to get a broken thumb during a fight.

"Now remember, no powers," Killian begins, eyeing the trainees, stepping back. "Go."

The woman bounces on her feet, high ponytail swishing, peeking at Silas from behind her fists.

She waits, anticipating that he will strike first. She's right.

Silas punches out, straight for the middle of her face. She slides to the left, his fist hitting air.

He pulls his arm back in tight. His face screws up.

She circles him, forcing him to maneuver backwards. He throws out another swift jab.

She lowers, spinning, kicking out a leg.

Silas jumps. Then glowers at her.

He edges closer, invading her space and punches out again, two consecutive bursts. She leans to the side, dodging his short, swift attacks.

"Stop," the Prince chides, approaching the redheaded man. "When you practice punching and flinging your abilities at a stationary target, many of you have no problem following through. It's your aim that sucks."

He peers over his shoulder to the rest of us surrounding the sparring mat at his last statement.

"So why aren't you following through with your punches? It's as if you're afraid of them."

Silas stares at him, baffled. "I- I don't know Your Highness."

Here he goes with the title again.

Killian narrows his sapphire, swirling gaze. "Do as you would when using your powers. Follow through. Don't stop your movements short."

The man's bright, orange curls sway as he nods to the Prince. He heeds the command, lining up across from the blonde woman once more.

The two of them round each other, peering into one another's eyes. Silas moves first, again.

This time, he listened to the Prince's words a little too closely.

His fist flies forward. Followed by the rest of his body.

He nearly falls into the woman, but she swerves right. Stumbling, he catches himself. And upon standing upright, a fist collides with his Adam's apple.

Silas grabs ahold of his throat, sputtering a cough. The woman chuckles as her limb is brought back in towards her body.

A feminine voice somewhere in the crowd behind me whoops, "Nice one Faye!"

Kicking out a boot, Silas strikes, hitting the edge of her thigh when she doesn't move away fast enough.

Faye lets her own foot fly. It slams into his shin.

He drops to a knee with a howl. The glare he sends her way is one of pure murder.

He rises with a limp, sauntering to her as briskly as possible, and punches again. She ducks down, his hand only brushing the tip of her ponytail.

She side steps, lurching to the left.

A right hook swings from him then, crashing into her shoulder. She clutches the joint, staggering.

A victorious grin spreads over his face.

Faye's deep blonde brows furrow and she kicks. The heel of her black boot connects with his groin.

My palm flies over my mouth as I watch.

It looks like it hurts. But it's also not unfunny.

His eyes roll back, and he falls with a grunt, cupping his crotch.

"Alright, I've seen enough," the Prince butts in. Arms still folded over his broad chest, he gives them a short nod. He grimaces as Silas hunches over the side of the mat and vomits into the grass.

"Why don't you take a break, you look like you may need it."

A chuckle bursts out of me, and I press my hands harder over my mouth. Rowan leans into my side, biting her knuckle to conceal her own laughter. A fit of giggles take over Jade and Piper too.

"Break off into pairs, let's see what you do," Killian calls, his glare spreading over the crowd.

Rowan immediately pulls me to an empty sparring mat, throwing up fists, and a grin grows on her face. I copy her, staying light, bouncing on the balls of my feet. Matching laughs escape us as we set up across from each other.

We exchange punches, weaving and dodging hits. She twists, and kicking out, she scrapes the side of my knee with her boot.

Shit.

I'm thrown off balance. I shift right, catching myself before I stumble completely. Backing away, I regain my balance.

She follows me, kicking out again.

I jerk left, barely missing her attack. My fist flies forward, and as her foot hits the ground, my strike smacks into the top of her bicep.

She moves a hand to cover her arm, pressing into the injury briefly.

Jumping backwards, she shakes out her limbs. She wiggles her fingers and lunges forward again.

Her fist nearly slams into my stomach but I curl inward, pushing my body away.

I swing out a punch. And I only hit air.

She slides to the right, missing my hand.

"Stop." The booming command has my body freezing. Killian steps up onto the mat. His ocean and ice eyes make their way to me.

In the next moment, his palms land on my hips. My spine straightens. What in the…

"Stop twisting your hips." His stare narrows on my torso. His fingers dig into the soft flesh of my curves. Heat flares up my middle.

"What are you talking about?"

"You're moving your whole body when you throw your punches. Control them into your upper body only. Don't let your hips sway with your hits," he explains, inspecting my body then dragging his gaze up to mine.

I don't even know what to say to his critique. Any quick comebacks have run, if not sprinted, out of my brain.

A nod of my head is all I can come up with, and it's enough for him to release his grip on my curves.

Utterly and completely taken aback. That's all I feel as a shudder comes over me while I reposition myself in front of Rowan.

We throw more punches, kicks, and slide to avoid as many as possible. Only a handful of times do we strike one another, and it's not without a wince. It's not the easiest, striking her.

I'm also more aware of my body than ever before. My torso tight, I keep it straight, not allowing it to sway with my arm movements.

By the end of my sparring with Rowan, my entire body burns. Sweat drips down my forehead and neck from the sun beating down. Muscles strain throughout me.

And a combination of irritation, confusion, and shock fill my brain. All brought on by His Royal Highness, Prince Killian.

My eyes scan the main training room inside, where I sit on a sparring mat with the rest of the Prince's trainees waiting for dinner to be served.

The other general's trainees soon sprinkle in, most collapsing onto sparring mats to take a breather after a long day of training.

All but Luca's trainees.

Several more minutes pass and still there's no sign of them. Whispers fill the space, mostly about their whereabouts. We're usually all dismissed around the same time, and sometimes even early.

"What do you think Luca's doing to them?"

I look to Piper, who gives me a shrug. "Who knows? He's got an ego comparable to the size of Killian's."

I bite down on my lip to contain a chuckle at her comment.

She's not exactly wrong.

Relaxing back onto the mat, my stomach rumbles, sending my thoughts running. Meals in the dining hall with Rowan, Piper, Jade, and Sebastian have been fun, but I also miss the quiet of my home.

I miss spending time with my aunt. I miss her funny vegetable remarks, or when she comes home bursting with ideas for new elixirs and creams.

I just wish I could let her know I'm alright. At least, as alright one can be after being forcibly taken to join the King's Army.

More time passes before the second-in-command's trainees finally show their faces.

I sit up when I notice Luca strutting in behind them. I spring to my feet, letting them propel me towards him, even if a hint of nerves builds in my stomach.

"When can we see our families? Write them letters? Anything?" The questions leave my lips without a second thought.

"Letters are fine. The post goes out at the end of every week. As for seeing them," he pauses, looking me up and down, assessing me. "You will serve in the King's Army until you die, or are too old to be of use any longer, whichever comes first."

Dread mixes with the nerves in my gut. Chills run across my skin.

"So, you forced us here and will never allow us to see them again unless we what? Happen to run into them wherever we're posted? Or when we're discharged in thirty or forty years? *If* they're all still alive and well by then. Or perhaps when they view our lifeless body? If they're even given the chance to see it."

The chills spin, twisting, morphing into heat that ignites in my chest.

"Essentially, yes," he snarls out. "It's the law that all multiwielders are to serve the King, and there's nothing to be done about it. Unless you're trying to somehow get out of your duty to serve Orellia."

He gives me a questioning look, narrowing his light blonde brows as he closes in on my space. He folds his arms over his chest, brooding over me.

I stand up taller, matching his energy.

He laughs when he catches my movement.

"Sit down, shut up, and learn your place here, *or else*. The King doesn't take kindly to rebels, and neither do I. He's always watching. We *both* are," Luca adds before flicking his head to the side, dismissing me completely.

The warmth spreading through me simmers, then is swiftly snuffed out when I step away from him.

He really is a piece of work, just like the Prince.

I saunter back to the sparring mat I left, defeated.

I suppose I'll have to go about writing a letter soon. I don't want her to stress about me, although I know she's a chronic worrier.

"What'd Luca have to say?" Rowan asks when I plop down beside her.

She dips her chin in understanding as I relay the context of why I approached him in the first place.

"Every part of this place is discouraging," I tell her with a sigh. "But I can't let it overtake me."

A wide grin grows on her face. "That's the spirit. We'll all get through it together."

I peer into the dining hall, and notice trays of food being carried to their places along the buffet-style countertop.

I spring to my feet, reaching for Rowan. "Look! Dinner's ready, let's go!"

Our hands clasp together, then she reaches for one of Piper's, and the strawberry blonde takes hold of Jade's palm too. In the next second, we're all linked together, Sebastian gently tugged along at the end by Jade.

And we're first in line for the feast being laid out before us.

Chapter 17

The door leading to the training field slams shut, the reverberation spreading across the grass. Killian strides over to us, nearly thirty minutes late, but he's not alone.

I pull my gaze from the Prince to investigate the man walking at his side.

He's tall, the same height as the Prince, with shaggy, dirty blonde hair kept short on the sides but left full on top. Arm muscles, on full display with the black cut-off he's wearing, flex as he walks. His bronzed skin stands out in the morning mist, as if he's spent so much time in the sun he absorbed the light, and is glowing from the inside out.

I investigate his baby blue eyes, and notice bruising around his left one. Similar to that of Piper's eye when we first met, but has now nearly disappeared. More bruising lines his jaw and a still-healing split sits in his lower lip.

Even despite his injuries, his face is rather handsome.

My stare wanders downwards, to his hands, where fading purple lingers on his knuckles. I would assume from fighting back against whoever gave him his injuries.

All eyes are on the new guy as the pair finally reach us at the grouping of sparring mats.

"It seems we've had some new trainees join us," Killian says, looking the blonde man up and down. "This one is ours. I suppose I've been graced with his presence due to my ability to handle the stubborn ones."

His eyes make their way to mine, finishing his sentence at me.

My jaw aches as I grind my teeth together to keep from making a smart remark back, one that would have likely ended me up with more "private lessons."

His stare doesn't stay on me for long before he spins to face the other man, who scoffs at his comment.

"Time to see what you're made of…" Prince Killian waits, raising a dark brow.

"Asher," the blonde man fills in.

"Asher. Perfect."

The Prince flicks his hand at the rest of us. We scatter onto the grass, leaving him and Asher on the mat alone.

"Damn, he's a good looking dude. Even with the black eye," Piper whispers to Jade and me.

I dip my chin in agreement. She's not wrong.

Jade's fair face reddens slightly as she nods her head, her considering gaze never leaving him.

I smirk over her head to Piper and she laughs, elbowing the shorter woman's side.

"You totally think he's cute!"

"Shush, they're about to spar," Jade snaps, nudging Piper back, a smile playing at her lips. Piper throws me a wink before facing the men in front of us.

I stifle a giggle and do the same.

The two men slowly circle each other on the slightly raised platform, equidistant from one another.

Several drawn out moments later, neither man has attempted to strike the other.

The Prince lets out a sigh. Deciding to move things along, he lazily throws a string of shadows at Asher's chest.

With lightning fast speed, Asher's hand splays out in front of him, surrounding the oncoming darkness with a blinding white light.

His stony face doesn't move an inch as he effortlessly sends the brightness at his opponent.

Prince Killian smirks ever so slightly as he casually spins to the side, dodging the light.

"Finally. What else do you wield?"

Asher's eyes narrow at his question. He swiftly raises a hand, palm up, in front of him. A stream of water flies out of a nearby barrel, liquid that proceeds to rain down on top of the Prince's head.

His eyes close and brows furrow, allowing the water to soak him, making his dark, tied-back hair stick to his head and neck.

Nearly every trainee on the sideline, myself included, tries to stifle a laugh as he takes the beating.

I have a feeling Asher and I will get along *swimmingly*.

When the shower finally finishes, Killian's hands raise on either side of him, and rapid, swirling air surrounds his body.

The breeze from his tornado is so strong I dig my feet in place and shield my face with my forearms.

A few moments later, the wind slows and I unblock my face to peer at the scene.

The Prince stands in the same spot, now completely dry.

"Not bad." He shrugs and punches out a series of fireballs from alternating fists.

Asher hurriedly builds a wall of water in front of his body, right in time for the first scarlet flame to reach the liquid, and immediately be extinguished.

His muscular arms begin to shake as the Prince pounds the shield with his strikes.

Asher finally drops the clear liquid and rolls, avoiding the oncoming blasts. He lands on his knees, off the mat, into awaiting grass, and swiftly brings a wall of earth up from the ground.

"I knew there was another power in there somewhere. I can't say I'm surprised it's earth, considering how stubborn you seem to be," Killian says with a taunting grin.

Asher's hidden position hides any physical reaction but I swear I hear a curse come from behind the mass of dirt.

I bite down on my lip to reel in a reaction, knowing I heard correctly when a chorus of giggles sounds from Rowan, Piper, and Jade.

A fist comes up from behind the wall, punching a beam of light in the Prince's direction. As the strike approaches him, he forms a pit of darkness, swallowing up the illumination.

In the same moment, snakes of water slither along the ground. They rapidly entrap Prince Killian's ankles and climb up either leg, reaching his waist in an instant.

Rather than fighting the liquid surrounding his lower body, Killian rolls his eyes, ignoring it, and instead crumbles the packed earth Asher hides behind.

The blonde man's eyes go wide at the unexpected attack and he freezes the water around the Prince's lower half before spinning away from the rubble of his former shield.

Killian peers down in surprise at the ice trapping his legs in place and shakes his head in an impressive nod. "Nice. Rare."

Placing his tan hands on either of his muscular thighs, he slowly melts the ice away.

Face stony, Asher stares down his opponent, chest heaving, as his attack is thawed. His injured lower lip twitches while spying the Prince.

A moment later, once Killian can move his lower body again, he questions his new trainee.

"Is that it? Three?"

Asher only nods his head in response.

"Good. I've only met a handful of water wielders who can form ice before."

He brings a hand up to his chin in thought. He dips his chin, looking away for a moment, but eventually returns eye contact, investigating the blonde man.

"Make sure your defense is as good as your offense. Both of your shields should be able to hold for longer. It can use some work."

"Anything else, *teach*?" Asher questions, throwing his arms out in annoyance.

"That's the closest thing you'll get to a compliment from him, trust me." The words dripping in sarcasm leave my lips without a second thought.

I nearly consider cowering, the statement having taken on a mind of its own, but hold my head high.

Prince Killian glares at him before spitting out a no and spinning on his heels, peering at me. He tilts his head, scanning my features.

I probably shouldn't have said anything. But I don't care.

Heat radiates down my spine at the reign of terror his father has cast over Orellia. And how he, being the dutiful son, has assisted in amassing the King's Army at his father's order.

He doesn't deserve me holding back.

The Prince's survey of my face silences the crowd, lasting what feels like hours.

"See me after training. Again."

With that, he crosses his arms over his broad chest in what we've come to know as his usual stance.

"We will be doing more of everyone's favorite activity today: sparring."

He narrows his gaze at me and gives me a toothy smirk.

I match his glare before rolling my eyes.

"Because clearly, some of you need the practice," he adds, peering pointedly over his shoulder at Asher, whose arms mimic the Prince's, crossed over his chest.

"Get into three groups of six, and spar until you've matched with everyone in your group. And try not to kill each other. Or don't. I no longer care," he says with a shrug.

Sighs and grumbles spread across the crowd as we form ourselves into groups.

Piper links arms with Rowan before hauling her forward so she's placed in front of Jade and me.

After seemingly dropping her off, she spins around and grabs Sebastian from where he's standing alone at the back of the crowd, dragging him over to our group.

I chuckle.

The shocked, uneasy look covering his tawny face as they make their way to us *is* slightly amusing. I'm not sure I've seen his eyebrows brought so close to his hairline.

Jade and Rowan cover their own mouths, stifling laughs.

"Okay, one more," she says, releasing his arm when he's placed with us. She brings a hand over her brow as she peers around, looking for her next victim.

"Hey! New guy! Over here!" she yells at Asher, who stands on the other side of the mat he once sparred on, arms still crossed.

Limbs relaxing to his sides, he makes his way to us, a shining smile blooming.

Piper grins and sticks a palm out to greet him. He takes it and with a twist, he brings the back of her hand to his lips.

"Asher. Nice to meet you," he says after the kiss.

Piper lets out a chuckle, her jaw dropping open.

"Piper. Nice to meet you too, flirt." Her freckled nose scrunches up in amusement.

He grins at her knowingly then shifts to me, taking my hand from its place at my side and gently raising it to his lips, just as he did before.

After repeating his name and asking mine, I answer, a giggle similar to Piper's expelling from my throat. He moves on to Jade after giving me a toothy smile.

"What's your name, beautiful?" he asks, beaming as he lightly grasps her pale hand in his and brings it to awaiting lips.

"Jade." She squeaks out her response more than speaking it as her eyes widen. She clears her throat and looks away, searching for anything to lock her vision on to.

His confident grin turns into a flirty smirk as his hand lingers in hers for a moment longer before gently releasing it.

"What a lovely name. A pleasure to meet you, Jade."

He makes his way to Rowan, who swiftly places her hands behind her back, clasping them together. She dips her chin and beats him to his own introduction.

"Rowan. Pleasure to meet you."

He repeats the sentiment and struts over to Sebastian, hand outstretched.

"Hey man. What's yours?"

"Sebastian."

He sticks a palm out to meet Asher's, and his eyes nearly pop out of his skull as the blonde man grabs his forearm, pulling him into a manly hug. Asher claps his back, then lets him go.

I cover another laugh with my fist. The three women at my sides follow suit.

Sebastian's face being covered in more emotion than I've ever seen from him before is a sight to see.

Piper makes her way to the shocked man, throwing an arm over his shoulder, stretching up in order to reach him.

"Or 'Bash' as we like to call him," she tells Asher.

Sebastian rolls his eyes at her comment, but what appears to be a tiny smirk climbs to the corner of his lips.

"C'mon, tough guy. Let's see how you hold up against me," Piper jokes at Asher, grabbing on one of his sunkissed arms and pulling him to the closest empty mat.

She chuckles as she throws a few punches into the air, mimicking the beginning of a fight.

He shakes his head, copying her stance and tilting his mouth upwards.

After far too much sparring, in my opinion, followed by a short stint of dagger throwing, which murdered my shoulders, Killian shoos everyone away for the day.

Except for me, that is.

A snarl from him hits me the moment the space is clear. He stares at me from the field on the opposite side of a sparring mat. "Your attitude is unbelievable."

"Have you looked in the mirror recently, Your Highness?"

He steps onto the mat, inching closer. "It just so happens that I peer into one often enough to distinguish confidence from arrogance, the latter of which seems rather difficult to find."

I advance further, boots shuffling in the grass. My toes touch the edge of the thick surface we use to practice. "Looks like you might need to buy a new mirror then."

"I'll let you know when my birthday is. Perhaps you can gift me one."

My feet glide onto the mat, vexation propelling me onward.

"Why me? Why don't you ask your *father* for one?"

A smirk tugs on his lips as he strides forward. "Oh, you don't think we'll still be friends by the time my birthday rolls around? It's in May, in case you were curious."

"Not a chance."

"What a pity. I could've invited you to my party, where you could meet my family, have a drink or two…"

I move again, nearly meeting him in the middle of the mat.

"Now why on earth would I want to do that? Your father is an ass and a coward. And so are you!"

Every inch of my torso flames with fury. My nails dig into the palms of my hands. Images of the King flash through my racing mind, only increasing my feelings.

His eyes narrow, his smirk falling. "Believe what you wish, but you don't know the truth of anything."

"I know more than you think. I've *seen* more than you think."

My arms go to fold over my chest but in the same moment, my ankles are forced together and yanked to the side. I fall ungracefully, arms flailing, to the ground.

"Bet you didn't see that coming."

I balk at the shadows wrapped around my legs.

He seriously pulled my feet out from under me *again*? He is *so* infuriating.

"I told you to always expect the unexpected," he says in a sing-songy voice, releasing his grip on the darkness.

"You're absurd!"

"And you're unprepared. Never drop your guard. It could get you killed one day." His voice is stern, and before I realize what he's doing, he stands behind me, lifting me off the mat, planting me upright.

My body goes rigid at his touch. And I fight against warmth that threatens to spread over my face.

"I have business to attend to so please, don't go pissing off the wrong people in my absence." His eyes swirl with icy tones of blue and silver as he gives the command.

"Wouldn't dream of it."

And on a spin, he leaves me there, on the grassy field darkening with the setting sun, bewildered.

Chapter 18

Achingly, I make my way to the cafeteria. I scarf down dinner, Rowan and Jade at my sides, flinging forward questions about what the Prince had said after they left. Sebastian remains silent, but listening.

Piper and Asher leave early to hunt down a trunk for his belongings, promising to meet us in our bunk room.

I yank my shoes off of sore feet and head straight for the showers upon arrival. The cleanse gives me time to mull over the Prince's earlier words.

He truly is the most conceited man I have ever met.

Finally, I'm able to flop onto my own bed, relieved to be officially sweat-free and able to relax.

Asher trudges over a few minutes later, hair dripping wet from his own shower, and plops himself on the empty bottom bunk below Sebastian.

"Bed's a little hard but I guess it could be worse." He wiggles around before lifting his head off the pillow, placing his hands behind his mop of sopping wet hair.

Sebastian appears then. With a shrug, he climbs to his bunk above, swinging his legs over the side, letting them dangle in the air.

The girls eventually join us at our bunks, each going to their own bed, besides Rowan, who sits next to Piper on hers.

"How do y'all know each other?" Asher questions. "Did you all arrive here together?"

"No, we met here. Although Aurora, Bash, and Rowan here were brought in at the same time. They had the pleasure of sharing a four by six cell on wheels," Piper blurts out for us as she bumps shoulders with Rowan, giving her a playful smirk.

The woman rolls her eyes while fixing her dozens of braids into a single, collective one, but not before her lips tug up as well.

The corners of my own lips begin to rise. I suppress it with a bite to the inside of my cheek.

As if a bolt of lightning had struck her, Piper's eyes go wide, and her mouth forms a toothy grin. "I have an idea: we should play truth or dare! I think it will help us to get to know your new bunkmate."

She wiggles her eyebrows, then with a squeal of delight, she places her thumb and pointer finger on either side of her chin.

"Asher, you first. Truth or dare?"

He releases a deep belly laugh. The sound rings bright and clear.

"I'm already laying down, so I'm going with truth." He gestures to his horizontal position.

"Fair enough. How did you end up here? And what's with the battle scars?" Piper flares her fingers in the direction of his face.

"That's two questions. But since I like you, I suppose I'll answer them both." He gives her a look, raising a single blonde brow.

She responds with a bat of her eyelashes.

I snort at her.

"I was working late on my family's farm, using my water wielding on the crops. I wanted to take advantage of the last bit of sun before it went down over the horizon…"

He pauses, shaking his head.

"I didn't know anyone was around. My family was already inside for the night, and we live in the middle of nowhere. But they saw me, drawing in some of the setting sun and aiming at a particularly stubborn group of root vegetables. Three King's Guards came rushing out of the nearby woods and attacked me. I couldn't fend them off after working in the fields all day. I had so little energy left at that point… Anyways, they got a hold of my wrists first and clamped those damned cuffs on me. Next thing I knew, I was being hauled into the woods and thrown in a horse drawn carriage."

He laughs then. "I swear I got in a hit or two before they dragged me away." He brings his knuckles up for inspection.

"They weren't as sadistic as the interrogators though..."

"Interrogators?" Piper questions, butting in.

My heart plummets into my stomach.

The things King's Guards do... From what I've experienced to the things I've only heard of, I can only imagine what he must have gone through.

"After they brought me here, I was led down an unbelievable amount of stairs and passageways. I didn't know where they were taking me until I saw the iron bars. And heard the screaming." A puff of air releases from his mouth in a sigh.

"They pushed me into the closest open cell and I sat there for hours until *he* came in. He questioned me over and over again, but every time I met him with silence or a simple 'no' I received a punch to wherever he fancied in that moment."

He lifts a palm to his mouth, feeling the split there.

Oh my... Killian did that to him?

"How awful. I'm so sorry," Jade speaks softly from her top bunk.

A similar apology leave my lips in the same moment.

Piper gently places a hand on Rowan's thigh, a question building behind bit lips.

Asher notices. "Out with it."

"I'm so sorry, and I hate to ask but, what were they questioning you about?"

"My family."

He blows out a longer sigh than before, cracking his neck. "I didn't get to say goodbye to them before they snatched me up. I guess that's for the best though."

He surveys the room with caution as he sits up in bed, throwing his bare feet over the side, and placing his elbows on his knees.

I sit up straighter in bed, his look worrying.

The room is nearly empty, aside from two women on the other side of the expansive space who seem to be getting ready for bed.

He checks our surroundings once more, then lowers his voice to a soft whisper. "Because I'm not the only multiwielder in my family."

"How many of you are there?" I ask, curious.

"I'm the oldest of six, and we all have more than one ability."

Piper and I gasp in sync.

"I've never heard of every child in one family being a multiwielder," Piper comments, eyes narrowing in thought.

I investigate his downturned eyes. "Are your parents, too?"

"My father is, but not my mother. I assume we all have him to thank." He chuckles while cracking his still-healing knuckles.

We all sit in silence, contemplating what he's shared with us. Several beats go by until Piper cautiously asks him how long he was questioned for.

He stares up in thought, flicking at Sebastian's dangling, socked foot a few inches from his face.

Sebastian jerks at the touch and brings up his legs, placing them crossed in front of him.

Asher lets out a breathy laugh but squints at Piper through his twisted brows.

"It felt like several days, or a week. Maybe even two. I'm not entirely sure. It was so dark down there. And with no windows, I had no real way of telling time."

My chest starts to hurt, starts to burn. I can feel the pain of my own capture trying to creep its way into my mind and body. The destruction of the apothecary. The knife at my aunt's throat. The threat of the King's Guards going back for her.

I push against the building feelings with all my might. I can't let it take me over right now, or ever again.

I bend forward, reaching out my palm, briefly placing it on his knee. He moves his sky blue eyes to me and puts a hand over mine, giving it a gentle squeeze in thanks.

"Well, that's me. So, is it my turn now?" A small laugh bubbles from his throat, lightning the mood. He grins at Piper.

"Turn? Oh, right! Truth or dare! Yes, of course! Go right ahead." Her face morphs from confusion to elation in seconds.

Asher releases a true belly laugh at her contorted facial expressions.

"I get to choose now… and I choose Aurora," he says, glancing at me with a smirk, revealing a dimple on his left cheek. "Truth or dare?"

I wet my lips, licking them in thought, and shrug.

"I suppose I'll go with dare." It comes out more of a question than a statement.

Seemingly, he doesn't care, as he smacks his hands together abruptly, rubbing them back and forth.

Oh no.

"Alrighty, let me think of a good one!"

He tilts his head up. His hair dark with wetness falls to the side. Bringing a hand to his chin in deep thought, he taps a forefinger on the bone there.

I hold back a retort to his dramatic enactment.

A gasp then leaves his lips and a finger goes pointing to the sky in realization.

What in the world is he going to have me do?

"I got it! I dare you to do your very best impersonation of *His Highness* Prince Killian."

My mouth pops open unintentionally but I force my lips back together at lightning speed.

That's... ridiculous. He's ridiculous.

"Really? That's the best you could come up with?" I attempt to sound unimpressed.

"I heard a little something about you getting some *private time* with him. Plus, he called you out today. I figured you could do it justice." He smirks at the bed to my left.

I whip my head to Piper and Rowan, the latter of whom already has her hands raised in innocence.

Piper moves both freckled hands to her face, stifling a snort.

Rowan's golden-rimmed eyes cast downward to linger on the spot where the hand was once resting on her thigh, then brings her own palm to cover the spot.

I rise, mumbling "fine" under my breath.

I shake out my limbs and try to bite back a chuckle, but fail.

Spreading my feet several inches farther than shoulder width apart, I drastically imitate the Prince's stance.

I cross my arms over my chest, puffing out my breasts like a male bird searching for a mate. I stretch my neck up and force my chin out, glaring at them with pointed eyes.

Piper and Jade attempt to cover up matching giggles while Rowan bites her lip to keep from smiling. Asher slaps his hands on his thighs, and even stoic Sebastian has a minor tilt to his normally flat lips.

"You are all going to spar some more today, because what else would I have you guys do?" A deep, gruff and raspy voice emerges from the back of my throat. "I'm just a sadistic asshole who loves to see you all beat each other up."

I dip my chin and shrug my shoulders, keeping my arms firmly crossed. I tighten my stare and spy each of them individually, moving from one bunk to the next.

Piper and Asher burst out into laughter only a second later. Jade covers her blushing face and shakes her head while giggling from her criss-crossed position on her bed. Rowan closes her eyes, bringing a hand to her forehead in disbelief. Her lips widen into a full, toothy grin as she chuckles.

Even Bash's lips quirk a few degrees higher as he places a fist under his chin.

Satisfied, I bow dramatically, hands flayed out, and flop back down onto my bed, kicking my feet off the side.

Over the following hour we take turns, laughing as embarrassing moments are shared and made as we have each other complete one hilarious task after the next.

Eventually, the few other trainees who sleep in the near-empty bunk room trickle in, eyeing us suspiciously but ultimately decide to keep to themselves.

Our movements collectively start to slow and one by one we relax, laying in our beds. We share some yawns before the overhead lights flick off, signaling our forcibly imposed bedtime, and the official end of our game.

Chapter 19

"Fuck! Again?" Piper yells.

I glance to her target three down from my own, and spot the burnt grass in front of it. Several feet in front of it. And the nearly dozen other spots around it.

I wince as she curses again, throwing her arms up in the air in frustration. Her usual french braids are a mess with sweat and frizz, probably due to the force at which she's practicing.

Pausing my own practice, I jog over to her.

She stares down her target, eyes squinting against the midday sun. She brings a hand up, yellow flames forming in her palm, but before it can be released, I grab her wrist.

The blaze instantly fades, and she whips her head around to see who has a hold of her. As soon as she sees me, her shoulders relax, the fighting form she was beginning to muster, gone.

"Would you like some help?"

She loses a breath, nodding, and I let go of her arm.

"Relax a little bit. Shake it off. Here," I explain as I gently grab each of her freckled shoulders and shake her side to side.

A laugh bubbles up and out of my throat as we sway back and forth in attempt to loosen up our muscles. Her mouth slowly creeps up as I repeatedly jerk us in the funny motion.

I may not be an expert in all seven abilities but the least I can do is help take her mind off of practice for a moment.

"Are you feeling more relaxed now?" I jest, dropping my hands from her and shake out my limbs on my own.

"Yes. Thank you for the 'loosening up.' I guess I needed it." She scratches at the back of her neck and breathes out a chuckle.

I bow to her, flailing my arms out to either side. "A pleasure to be at your service."

I stand back up when I hear a giggle and ask her, "What do you think is the problem?"

She twists to peer back at the blackened patches of grass nowhere near her target.

"I don't know. I just can't get the fire to where I want it to go. It's so different from my other abilities."

"How so?"

"The light and fire, they feel so different. I hadn't noticed it before. Light has always come most naturally to me. The light just comes from within me, filling me up, or I can use the help of the sun if I need to." She gestures to the sky.

"And the earth I can feel. It's right there, always beneath my feet." She stares at the ground. "But fire? I don't know where to pull it from. I can't maneuver it and handle it the way I can with the others."

I process her words, thinking back to lessons my aunt taught me when I struggled with my own powers.

"I don't know what it's like to wield fire, but I remember what my aunt said to me when I had a rough time with water wielding. Sometimes elements are tricky, because they're stubborn. You can't always force them to do what you want, sometimes you have to gently guide them in the direction you want them to go."

Eyes closed, bringing my hands together in front of me, and I pull from a nearby barrel. Soon, the water reaches my palms, filling up the space in between my cupped hands.

I blink open one eye, then the other, as the liquid reaches the top, spilling over briefly before I cut the connection with the water in the awaiting barrel, releasing it from my grasp.

"See? Sometimes you have to… ask it nicely, I guess?" I shrug my shoulders, water still in my palms.

I study her face.

She contemplates my hands inquisitively then she sucks on her teeth, nodding at my explanation.

My lips tremble slightly as I refocus on the liquid in my hands, bringing one hand over the other, shaping the clearness into a ball.

It wobbles, contorting. As the water starts to spin, I carefully bring my arms up and out in front of my chest. Crossing my hands together, I set my aim for the center of her target.

With a breath and a jerk of my shoulders, I shoot the sphere forward.

A split second later it hits its mark, not the dead center, but within the fourth ring.

Damn, not too shabby.

A hand clamps around my shoulder and a squeak leaves Piper's mouth as she shakes me.

"That was really good! Okay, okay, I'll try again." She releases me then and widens her stance, planting her feet firmly, stare homing in on her target once again.

"You got this!" I clap my hands excitedly, taking a few steps back.

I know she can do this, she just has to get out of her head. I've been there. I know what it's like to be in your head so much you can't focus on the task in front of you.

I shake my head and the thoughts away, bringing my focus back to Piper.

With her eyes closed, she takes a deep breath, letting it out as she brings lightly gripped fists up towards her chin. Her lids open, and in a flash, she punches first with her right hand, pushing out a small, yellow flame before she punches harder with her left, releasing a sizable orange blaze.

The first miniature yellow warmth spirals, nearly fizzling out, but it hits the bottom of the outermost ring.

Then the second, bright sunset of an inferno slams into the target, bordering the line between the fifth and sixth rings.

"Yes! Yes! Yes! I did it!" She jumps up and down. She spins round and rushes me, throwing her arms around my neck, squeezing tight.

"Thank you! That totally helped!"

I squeeze her back, giggling. "Of course."

She unfolds her arms from around me and pointedly peeks over my shoulder.

"Someone's keeping an eye on you," she tells me with a smirk, followed by a wink.

I peer over my shoulder in the direction she nods her head in. A frown creeps its way onto my face.

Killian stands on the opposite end of the field, clearly staring us down.

"Oh please, he's only looking to see if he needs to pull me aside after training. *Again*," I say, rolling my eyes at the very thought of him.

There's no other reason why he would be looking over here. He's purely searching for an excuse to be an ass again.

"I don't think so. It's not the back of my head he's actively investigating right now," she whispers.

My hand reaches back, brushing my hair, flattening down any fly aways that may be sticking out from my french braid.

I don't realize what I'm doing until a giggle escapes Piper's lips and I pull my hand away.

I feel my face begin to heat with frustration and I place the backs of my hands there, trying to prematurely cool the burning.

His incessant survey of us is driving me mad. I swear, his scrutinization of my every move will be the death of me. Why should I care if he's looking at me?

I gulp down the question and remove my hands from my face, opting to fan away the visible irritation on my cheeks instead.

Thankfully, Rowan interrupts by slinging her arm around Piper's shoulders, taking her attention away from me. "I saw what you did. You did amazing!"

"You were watching me?" The blonde raises her brows at the tall, dark-haired woman while crossing her arms, leaning into the touch.

A minor blush creeps into Rowan's deep brown cheeks before she looks away. "I don't know what you're talking about."

"I suppose we both have spectators," Piper teases us, nudging the woman's side and nodding her head in the direction of the Prince.

"Spectators you say?" Jade chimes in, striding over. "I hope no one is watching me right now. I'm doing horribly." She laughs to herself at the latter part of her statement, eyes cast downward.

"I'm sure it's not going that bad– Oh, I stand corrected," Rowan says as she peers around me to view where Jade had practiced.

I follow her gaze and bite back on a gasp.

The ground is littered with dozens of pebbles and small rocks no bigger than my fist.

And her target is unscathed.

Jade looks back at her failed earth wielding attempts sheepishly, biting on her lower lip.

"Need some help?"

Training has been rough. All of our bodies are sore. Our abilities have, truthfully, been worsening. But I suppose things are bound to go downhill before they go up.

"Aurora's a beast! Her earth abilities are top notch," Rowan says.

I scoff, then chuckle, at her praise.

"Thanks, Rowan. I'll make sure to add 'top notch earth abilities' to my list of skills."

Jade beams, nodding her head to my original question.

Rowan begins helping Piper, as she is the "resident fire wielding expert" as the latter has now decided to title her, while Jade and I make our way to the spot across from her target.

"So… any suggestions?" She looks at me hopefully.

Wiggling my fingers towards the earth, I reach towards my favorite ability.

"The first thing I would suggest is to make sure you're grounded. Feel your connection to the earth. Concentrate on your feet being firmly planted on the ground. Close your eyes and picture yourself working *with* the earth."

She nods her head and closes her eyes, inhaling a deep breath and letting it out slowly.

"Now, picture yourself gently grabbing ahold of the piece of nature you want to wield. A rock, a leaf, a blade of grass, whatever it may be."

A pebble a few feet away begins trembling.

"Good. Now ask it to work with you. Tell it of your goal. Of what you would like to do with it."

Her mouth twists with urgency. Her hands shake as she raises them out in front of her. Her fingers twitch, then her elbows lock.

The rock slowly lifts, hovering a few inches off of the bright green grass.

"Picture yourself hitting the center of your target. Guide it to where you would like it to go. Imagine it hitting the target with force."

The pebble raises higher into the air, steadier than before. Jade's hands stop shaking and her face relaxes.

"Now, hit the target!"

I watch with heightened hope as she draws her palms back and pushes forward.

The small, gray rock goes flying at the target.

And hits the center of the bullseye with so much force that it lodges itself into the structure.

"Perfect!" I jump up and down, clapping at her newfound skills. "You're a natural!"

Jade faces me, a grin spread wide over her fair face, and her chocolate eyes full of hope. She sprints the few steps it takes to reach me and clasps our hands together.

"Thank you so much! Picturing exactly what I wanted to do helped so much. You're a great teacher!"

I bite back a bashful grin. "Of course."

"If you ever need some help with anything, you better let me know! I may not be as good a teacher as you but I've worked a lot of odd jobs. Potions and elixirs are my specialty." She sends me a wink.

"I'll keep that in mind."

"Nice," someone adds.

Turning to my left, my eyes make contact with Sebastian nodding his head.

A glimpse of what I would consider a full-blown smile from him appears: a tiny tilt of the corner of his mouth rising from its usually flat position.

"Thanks," Jade and I say in unison before snickering at our unexpected twinned response.

Not even a moment later, a loud whoop sounds, and I see our new, shaggy blonde groupmate making his way to us.

"Good work, slick," Asher winks, a dimple on his left cheek visible from the smirk on his face.

His straight, white teeth nearly shine in the sunlight behind what I can tell is normally a pair of perfectly round lips. When one of them isn't split in two that is.

Jade's mouth briefly goes slack. She tucks some loose strands of black hair behind her ear then tugs to tighten her short pigtails.

She finally regains enough composure to thank him, eyes barely meeting his intense blue gaze.

Her eyes then widen when she looks off in the distance behind him, even though she immediately tries to hide her reaction.

My line of sight swiftly follows.

Oh my.

I wasn't expecting that sight after witnessing his sparring with Killian yesterday.

"Looks like maybe you could benefit from some help too," she giggles, nodding to Asher's practice, where only a few scuff marks are visible along the edge of his target.

The rest of it remains unscathed.

Burn marks from his light scatter the ground, and the pieces of earth laying haphazardly all in front of his target are turning muddy from the use of his water wielding.

He grunts, then lets out a surprised gasp.

"You wound me," he says, dramatically falling to his knees, clutching his chest with both of his sun-tanned hands.

Jade's cheeks go pink at his position by her feet and she looks away to shake her head.

My own gasp leaves my throat. Then, I cover my mouth to conceal a burst of laughter.

Jade's mouth opens and shuts a few times, trying to find the right words.

"You might want to follow Killian's orders before he notices," she stutters out, eyeing Asher again.

"I don't care what he wants us to do. I just throw a few rocks any time he passes by. I don't want to be dragged back to that hellhole. I will not be answering their questions, regardless of *any* amount of torture they throw my way," he states, raising from his knees.

His gaze sharpens, then his lip curls in a snarl. He points the angry face at the Prince's profile.

My chest aches at the thought of Asher being smacked around while they interrogated him for information on his family.

My hand goes to the base of my throat in an attempt to quell the rising burn there. I shouldn't be surprised by the actions of those in power in Orellia but nonetheless, I remain stunned.

"I can't even fathom… I'm sorry you went through that," Jade says on a sigh, peering down at her black boots as she twists her fingers together.

Asher whips his head back to us, face cheery once again. "Don't apologize. Please. It's not your fault."

He reaches for her clasped hands with one of his. Her gaze climbs up high to meet his eyes. His dimple shows once more as he squeezes her smaller hands within his own large one.

After forcing his eyes away from Jade, he gives me a quick nod when he sees a sympathetic smile upon my face.

His bare, muscular arms cross over his chest. A look of disdain appears as he glances towards the Prince. "I'm sick and tired of the King. And all of his minions who do his bidding. Who follow his every order. They've turned this kingdom into a shithole."

Chapter 20

It was worse than I thought.

Doing the laundry of over a hundred and twenty trainees who are sparring or training their various skills for several hours a day is atrocious.

The socks especially.

It's definitely not my favorite way to spend my first day off from training.

Separating the loads, keeping each person's belongings organized, tossing them into the largest, swirling, metal machines full of soap and water I have ever seen, hanging them to dry. Repeat.

The couple of others the Prince assigned this chore move about the long, rectangular space, repetitive motions of cleaning, drying, and folding laundry.

Sebastian's face is littered with disgust as he picks up another handful of filthy, smelly clothes. He tosses them into a bin to await the next load.

My shoulders ache as I lift up a pile of sopping wet clothes and place them on a metal counter running the length of the space.

Raising each piece to hang and clip onto the line drawn overhead has my sore biceps burning. I can't help as a groan finds its way up and out my throat.

I loathe this place in its entirety.

It's breaking me down, physically.

Every moment of every day, at least a single part of my body aches. The training regiment is difficult at best, torturous at worst. Sparring, with and without our powers, honing our craft, perfecting our aim, learning to wield weapons I never dreamed of having any control over.

And mentally. My thoughts are constantly spiraling.

Of the King. His creation of this army in the first place. The power he craves, how it was palpable in his presence.

Of my aunt. How she's doing. How I hope she's safe. How I can only hope she is able to handle the load of running the shop alone.

The emotions wash over me and my shoulders feel heavy, like a thousand boulders lie on top of me. I can't shake the helplessness paired with it. It's devouring, all consuming.

It shifts slightly, and my blood verges on boiling. King Kairos has fucked me over in every way possible. Why must I be tested by him over and over again?

A true weight lands on my shoulder then.

Sebastian rounds me, a warm, tawny hand on my shoulder. He lifts a single brow in question.

"It's nothing. Just thinking." I wave him off.

He gives me a skeptical look, not letting up. His brown eyes glint as the fire sconces along the stone wall hit them, revealing a hint of hazel hues.

So, I give in.

"I'm thinking about my aunt. And how the King has completely uprooted my life, more than once."

He dips his chin at my confession. Staring away, he clears his throat. "I understand."

With a squeeze to my shoulder, he drops his hand.

"It's exhausting. All of it," I laugh out.

I stretch my neck side to side, cracking it. I reach for another wet tunic, moving to hang and clip it to the line.

Sebastian comes up next to me, mirroring my movements. "It is."

"I-," I start, wanting to ask him about himself but the guilt of being intrusive creeps over me.

"Go ahead."

My gaze shoots over to him. I open my mouth but shut it again.

He truly gave me the go ahead. And he's openly conversing with me, about life.

The shock of it courses through me. He's always been so quiet, so the go ahead is giving me whiplash.

I sling another shirt over the long, horizontally hanging rope. "You don't seem too shabby. Your powers. Your use of a dagger. You're good, really. Where did you learn everything?"

He sighs, clipping a pair of black pants up onto the thick line. "Taught myself."

"Really? That's impressive."

He shrugs, hanging up a dark gray top. "I had to. Had to fight a lot."

His words spear me through my middle. I don't know what I expected him to say, but it wasn't that.

I continue placing clothes on the line, ruminating on the meaning of his words. I lick my lips, muttering, "That's terrible. And unfair."

"That's life in Orellia."

I shake my head, staring into the pile of soaked clothes. "Only because of Kairos."

A snarl comes out when the King's name leaves my lips.

Even the mention of the bastard infuriates me. The ire filling me is tiring. I push it aside, forbidding it to overcome me once again. I can't allow the feeling to keep crawling its way up inside me.

I spy Sebastian nodding along to my words, lips twisting up.

The smell of dirty and clean clothes waft through the air, combining with one another.

Soon, the pile of clothes in front of us disappears, our working in tandem taking over, effectively ending our conversation.

Time slips by, faster than before.

With all of us working together, we're able to finish in time for lunch, only leaving the clothes to dry.

Sebastian at my side, we trudge into the main training room, free from the shackles of our disgusting chore.

"Oh, I almost forgot. I have a letter to send to my aunt. The post goes out today and I want her to get it as soon as possible," I tell him, the interaction with Luca a few days ago replaying in my head.

"Let's go get it," he says, nodding towards our bunk room.

I swiftly retrieve it from my trunk and we step back into the spacious main room.

My eyes then land on a King's Guard posted at the double doors we were brought through our first day.

After asking around, I learned that the guards handle any mail coming in and out of here, so I have no choice but to approach one of them with my letter.

"I have a letter I'd like to send to my family," I say, stretching out the envelope when I approach the tall, muscular King's Guard.

His gaze narrows at me, then at the letter. With a sigh, he snatches it from my hand and jerks his head as a way of dismissal.

Damn, alright sassy man.

I roll my eyes once my back is to him as Sebastian and I move into the dining hall.

While in line for food, Rowan and Jade wait behind the counter, serving each person as they come along.

A beam sprawls across my face when I spot them. I see them nearly every moment of every day so any time without them has felt odd.

"How was cleaning everyone's stinky socks?" Rowan smirks as she giggles out her question.

"Unbelievably horrific."

Jade chuckles and hands me a bowl of chili.

I may have been grossed out earlier but I think a nice warm meal is exactly what's needed right about now.

"We made it with love. And lots of beans," Jade says before pointing. "Piper's already sitting and we'll come join you when we finish serving everyone."

Food in hand, Sebastian and I weave our way past chattering trainees to an empty table, save for the strawberry blonde woman.

"I thought Asher ended up being assigned to clean the training fields with you. Where is he?" I ask her upon arrival. Swiftly taking my seat, I dig into my meal while I await her answer.

She finishes chewing the bite in her mouth, swallowing before telling me, "We got split into two groups to cover all the fields. Apparently, my group was faster." She smirks and spoons another mouthful of chili.

Bowls more than halfway finished, the blonde man in question finally joins us.

A look of irritation and something like resentment sits in his tanned features. Dirty blonde brows drawn together, it's visible he's thinking hard.

Beside Piper, he sets down his food in silence.

"What's wrong?"

He glances at me from across the table. Hard lines press in around his eyes. "*He's* what's wrong."

I turn when he jerks his head in the direction behind Sebastian and me.

Leaning against the wide doorframe leading into the massive main room covered with sparring mats is Luca.

His fair arms cross over his chest as he surveys the room. His snow-colored hair is tied in a braid again, leading down the middle of his head, past the shaved sides.

Those eyes of his, a pale green, slice this way and that, as if he's hunting for prey.

"Hey, sorry it took us a while to get over here, we had to take some dishes to the back first. What'd we miss?" Jade chimes in, sitting beside Asher, her face cheery.

It drops when she sees the glare the man next to her emits.

"Who's the look for?" Rowan asks, taking up a place beside me. She spins, anything but nonchalantly, peering around the room.

"What happened with Luca?" I study his face as he takes in my question.

His jaw works. Shifts side to side, popping.

"He's the one who did this," he says, pointing a finger to his face.

His black eye has barely faded, and the split in his lower lip remains scabbed over.

"I didn't even know that was his name until you said it. All I know is what his fists look like when they come into contact with my face after I don't answer his questions," he adds with a snarl.

My jaw hangs open. Gasps circle our table.

But I thought…

So it wasn't the Prince who covered Asher in bruises.

Shivers cover my body at the realization.

"I think he's still riding the high of his power trip. With the look he gave me as I passed by, you'd have thought he won the keys to the kingdom from me," Asher sneers, but eventually rips his eyes from the second-in-command.

"He's always been an ass. He thinks because he's essentially the Prince's best friend, he can do whatever he wants. I swear he thinks he's a prince too. Kairos might as well make him one at this point," Piper throws in, scooping more beans onto her spoon.

I can't help but laugh. "They're best friends?"

She shrugs. "As good as, I suppose. I don't know who else would want to be friends with him."

Chuckles fill our table.

I fake surprise, a hand clutching at my chest. "I can't believe you would say such a thing. His warm and fuzzy nature must attract him a plethora of friends!"

At that, full-blown belly laughs spread over the space.

I release my own giggle but my mind fades elsewhere. I still can't help but think, it *wasn't* Killian who interrogated Asher.

Which leads me to the question: Have I gotten anything *else* wrong?

Chapter 21

And another one bites the dust.

Silas steps off of a sparring mat, the Prince standing beyond him, arms crossed over his chest. His eyes, seeping with shocked disappointment, stare at the back of the man's flaming red hair.

Silas is now the third trainee in a row to get his ass absolutely whooped by the Prince. Even worse than the first time too, when we all sparred against him.

Apparently, Killian assumed we would have greatly improved over the past ten days.

He was abysmally wrong.

After even more target practice with both our abilities and weapons, my body is tired. Everyone's bodies seem to be.

"Rowan. Let's see if you've learned anything so far," he calls, tipping his chin up at her.

She rotates a shoulder and moves to face him, the worried look she wore on the sidelines now replaced with one of shaky confidence. The closer she gets to him, the taller she stands. She shakes out her long, toned limbs, her self-assurance growing.

Staying light on her feet, she strikes first with a roaring flame.

The burst of red and orange heat surges forward, and past the Prince's head when he maneuvers away.

He turns a whip of water on her, flinging it around with his fingertips.

More liquid flies, forming an oval of blurred clearness in front of her. It catches Killian's attack, morphing into the rest of the shield, growing it wider.

She shrinks the water, creating two swirling balls, one in either palm.

In a blink, she sends them at the Prince. Her single braid combining all of the smaller ones swings with the force of her strike.

The Prince wears a hint of a smirk as he drops to the ground and rolls to the side, allowing the liquid to slam into the grass behind him.

He swiftly kicks out a boot, sending fire shooting from the bottom of it.

Rowan jumps, avoiding the flames.

When she lands, shadows waft from her palms. She circles her arms, spiraling the strips of darkness.

They twist together, drilling towards the Prince. He meets them with open arms, greeting the obsidian strands.

But only a breath from striking him, the shadows halt, splitting in two. They crawl gently over his outstretched biceps instead. And creep their way down his forearms.

Completely under his control.

He yanks on the shadows, and pulls Rowan with them. She belly flops onto the mat. The sound of air leaving her lungs rings out in the form of an aching huff.

I wince at her fall. My hand moves to my stomach instinctively.

That must've hurt.

Killian disperses of the dark masses along his limbs, keeping his fingers stretched out wide. Grass on the east and west of the sparring mat crawls up, slithering its way to Rowan.

She stretches out a hand from her place on the floor. The thin, green ropes pause their movement momentarily.

However, only a second later do her efforts fail.

The lime-colored strands continue onward, and wrap around her legs.

She takes a dagger from its place at her thigh, cutting the grass on one side. With her other hand, she burns the ties holding her down.

She then goes completely still. The weapon at her side drops from her grip.

"It seems like I might need to include some instruction on how to create and maintain shields over the mind. It was all too easy slipping into yours," Killian says with a tilt of his head.

A tiny, strangled groan leaves Rowan's throat, as if she's fighting back against his hold on her mind.

Then her body relaxes, shifting on the mat. She lifts her head, snarling at the Prince.

His dark brows raise and he shrugs.

"You're finished. I'm surprised though, I thought you would last longer." He spies her with investigative eyes.

She narrows her own gaze. "I'm sore. We've been training hard. Because of *you*."

"I'm well aware. But I see what you all *can* and *cannot* handle. I watch you all. Every day."

She releases a defeated huff and stands, balling her hands into fists on her way to the rest of us on the sidelines. She slumps into the grass at our feet and begins massaging her calves, a grumpy look on her face, directed at the Prince.

Asher is called up next, immediately swinging his palms out to sling water from a nearby barrel at the Prince.

After punching out a few beams of light, throwing discarded boulders, and attempting to drench the Prince in a colossal wave, Killian sweeps him off his feet with a stream of shadows.

He slams into the mat on his back, his straw-colored hair flying into his eyes on impact.

I clamp my teeth together tight, as if I can feel the reverberation of him hitting the ground in my own body.

He went down even faster than Rowan.

Asher brushes his hair back and stands, achingly. The pained look on his face is one he tries to hide, but isn't entirely successful.

He falls in place beside Rowan, laying flat on his back with a groan. She pats his elbow encouragingly.

The Prince spars with two more trainees after Asher, both of whom swiftly end up on the ground. Both in more pain than they started with from our several days of practice.

When Sebastian is called up, the air, shadows, and mind wielding he uses gives the Prince a run for his money.

But not before Prince Killian overtakes the darkness spewed at him and flips it on Sebastian.

Bash ends up on his stomach, hands wrapped in strands of onyx at his lower back. The star-shaped daggers he picked up from a weapons stand hadn't even been put to use yet.

Four more trainees spar with the Prince then, and he selects Piper after wiping the floor with them.

She complained about being sore this morning, so it hurts to watch as she flings light that soars past Killian's head.

The small pieces of earth as well as the few flames she tosses the Prince's way don't do her any good either. She glares at him with an intensity that has me biting down on my lower lip.

She is fierce, but he dodges every attack she throws at him.

She eventually ends up in a spiral of water, rushing liquid surrounding her, and the Prince's sword pointed at her. A displeased frown is all she receives from him as a dismissal.

When she sits down beside Rowan in the grass, she grunts, chucking off her soaked boots and ringing out her braids.

A trio of trainees are called after her, each of which are taken down in a matter of minutes.

The pile of people lounging in the grass, wallowing in their defeat, eventually amasses to everyone except Jade and me.

And of course Jade is picked first.

Why does he always leave me for last? It's as if he purposely does it to infuriate me.

She steps up to him, whipping the air around them.

She told me yesterday it was the favorite of all her abilities. How it made her feel light and free.

The sentiment reminded me of Mrs. Cromwell. How she had once said the same.

Jade twists the air with a strand of water, shooting it at the Prince.

He takes a hold of both, separating them, tossing either element to the side.

She springs forward with short bursts of earth and fire too, but he weaves around her attacks with ease. And pleasure.

He wears a grin through every sparring match. As if he can tell what move each trainee will make next.

Jade is no exception.

A fiery blast from Killian so large it rivals a bonfire sprays at her, and she slides off the mat in a roll. Thudding onto her shoulder on the ground, she releases a huff.

I shiver at the sound.

She begrudgingly makes her way to the pile of trainees, bringing her knees into her chest and resting her chin there.

My eyes move to roam over the Prince then.

His fitted black pants have a matching tunic today, the sleeves nowhere to be found. Again.

His arms cross over his chest, like he knows of no other way to stand.

Chocolate waves are tied half up once more, hardly a fly away in sight, even after sparring *seventeen* trainees.

"I assume you wanted to save the best for last again. Am I right?" I ask him as I step onto the mat without waiting for his command to.

My legs in particular ache as I move, but he'll never hear a word of it from me. He doesn't need to know.

"That mouth of yours sure does get you into quite a bit of trouble. Are you missing our private lessons? Shall we arrange for more?" Confidence oozes off of him as he speaks.

I narrow my gaze at him. "If you missed me so, you could have just said as much."

He tilts his head, then flicks out his tongue, wetting his bottom lip. "I never said such a thing."

He follows his comment with a wink.

A low roar begins in my stomach. "Why must you always try to provoke me?"

"Because I love getting a rise out of you."

A roar of fire spirals my way in the next second.

I duck, hitting the floor in surprise. He had me distracted.

And I will have no more of that.

My palm pushes out, a ray of light shining from it. I angle it up, attempting to momentarily blind him.

A wave of darkness emits from his own hands, scooping up the brightness before it can reach him.

I break chunks from the massive pieces of scattered rocks surrounding the mat, slinging them at him.

His sword is drawn from its sheath in an instant. He slices through the rocks, sending them shattering through the air.

I cover my face, splaying a palm at the same time, forming a ball of light in it. Only once the rain of tiny pebbles disappears do I dim the yellow brightness in my hand.

Killian creates tendrils of water then, creeping them towards me.

One of them ties around my wrist. I jerk my arm, reaching for the feeling of the liquid's molecules with my free limb.

Grabbing onto the water, I tug on it, fighting for its control.

Sweat drips down my neck. I use as much strength as I can muster from my aching body.

Finally, he releases full control of the liquid, and with my pulling on it, I go soaring backwards.

I land on my side, my hip taking most of the fall. A strangled yelp leaves my throat when I crash down.

Damn. There is sure to be a bruise tomorrow.

Then, something sharp scratches along the wall around my mind.

I freeze, focusing on my mind's shield. It's firmly in place. Thankfully.

All my years of practice keeping the barrier up subconsciously has seemingly paid off. This time, at least.

"You kept your mind's shield in place. Not bad," Killian forces out, as if he struggles giving even the slightest compliment. "Perhaps you can give some pointers to your friends."

His stare briefly points to Rowan before returning to me.

"Of course *Your Highness*. Prince. Killian. *Whatever* it is I'm supposed to call you." The words come out on a snarl.

He sends me another wink. "You can call me whatever you wish, sweetheart."

The gasp leaving my lips surprises me. He *cannot* be serious.

I'm beginning to believe this man will say or do anything to piss me off further.

"We're done for today," he announces, peering behind me at his slumped over trainees. "Go eat, drink, and rest."

With that, he spins on his heels and leaves the training field.

The pain ebbs and flows throughout me, but localizes in my hip as I move to stand.

A light brown hand appears in front of me then, and I peek up to find Sebastian standing above me.

"Thanks," I say with a small smile, accepting his offer. He pulls me up, dipping his chin in acknowledgement.

Asher and Piper emit groans as they push up off the ground. A grumble comes from under Rowan's breath when she follows. Jade remains silent, but contemplation covers her fair face, and her downcast eyes.

Bash and I step over to them.

"What a shitshow," Piper says, arms folding over herself.

"Right?" I add.

"You could say that again," Rowan agrees.

Piper glances at her, a grin slowly spreading over her freckled face. "Hey, can I show you that thing I was talking about before we get dinner?"

I watch as their eyes connect. My hand comes to my mouth, hiding a smirk.

Rowan eagerly nods her head and they take off. Well, as fast as they can move right now, after we were all swiftly taken down by Killian.

My stare moves to Jade then, and we share a knowing look.

I doubt they will be arriving on time for dinner.

Chapter 22

The silence eats away at me as the Prince's eyes scan over the crowd.

I rub up and down my arms as bumps form when a cool morning breeze rips through the training field.

"Over the past few days, I've come to notice some of you are lacking in a certain area. Protecting your mind from invaders is an essential skill. One we will be working on today."

Killian's eyes land on Rowan, then sprint to a few other trainees.

His tongue sticks out to wet his lips as he considers his next words. "Most, if not all of you, with abilities of the mind should have this mastered by now. However, let this lesson be a reminder for you all to never let the shield around your mind drop."

His gaze flicks to Rowan again and a jerk of his head is all he does to summon her onto the mat he waits on. A sigh releases from her nose and she begrudgingly makes her way to him.

"Imagine building sturdy, impenetrable walls around your mind. Construct them however you wish, with whatever material you deem strongest. Focus on holding them there. Concentrate on keeping them in place."

She nods, and a serious, focused twist of her face springs to life.

The golden rings around her pupils widen, overwhelming the soft brown tones of her irises.

"Good. I can feel it growing, encasing your mind."

The Prince paces back and forth in front of her as he speaks. "Relax as you focus. Don't tense up."

Her shoulders inching closer to her ears drop. The tips of her boots raise off the ground, then flatten again, as if she's wiggling her toes.

He stops in front of her then. "Exactly. Now I'm going to try to tear down the shield you've put in place. Don't let me."

Latching onto her stare with his own, he begins.

Sweat almost immediately begins dripping down Rowan's temples and along her neck. Her breathing becomes labored, but only for a moment before she reels it in.

Her long lashes flutter as she blinks rapidly, then she reignites her narrowed gaze on the Prince.

The muscles along her bare arms flex, only the tops of her shoulders not visible in the sleeveless tunic she wears. Her hands briefly ball into fists but his words must ring through her mind as she relaxes them in the next second.

"Not bad," he says, tilting his head to the side and stepping back, seemingly ending his attempt to enter her mind.

The breath she inhales is colossal. She immediately hunches over, placing her palms on her knees.

"Crap, that was hard," she sputters in between breaths.

"It will get easier with time. And more practice." His words are assuring, but his tone is filled with boredom.

Rowan maneuvers her way off the mat at a snail's pace, flopping into the morning dew-tipped grass near my feet. The stark contrast to her usual spitfire attitude is a bit mind boggling.

I squat down, resting my fingertips on her shoulder. "I'll help you practice."

She turns to me with an exhausted smile. "Thanks."

Killian singles out others, calling them up one at a time, teaching them the same as he did Rowan. Amongst them are Jade and Asher.

They end up on either side of Rowan, sitting down as they catch their breath and wipe sweat from their brow.

"Wow, that was no joke," Jade says on an exhale.

Asher runs his fingers through his sandy hair. "Definitely."

I bend down behind them, placing reassuring hands on their arms, promising them the same help I did Rowan.

When the Prince runs out of names to call, he struts up to Piper. His eyes investigate her closely, tipping down to her shorter frame.

"Can I help you with something, boss?" She folds her arms over her chest, returning his intense stare.

He copies her movements, tucking his hands into his armpits, sticking his thumbs out. "Are you holding out on one of your abilities? I have you down as light, earth, and fire. Light being your favored one, but you're the only one without mind wielding who doesn't seem to have a problem maintaining a shield."

She smirks up at him. "So you're saying I'm *special?*"

The look he gives her is more than displeased. "No."

"Well, I'm not hiding anything," she says, spreading her arms wide. "I'm an open book, Your Highness."

"For some reason, I don't doubt that. I presume it's your stubbornness which guides you and keeps your mind locked up tight."

Her smirk flips into a beam. "Why thank you."

He rolls his eyes, then spins on his heels and strides away.

"Break into groups of three, one mind wielder per group. Those of you with the ability, practice entering minds. Those of you without, practice building and maintaining your shields."

Jade and Rowan follow me onto an empty sparring mat while Bash takes Piper and Asher to the next one over.

"I think the hardest part of working your mind's shield is ensuring that it stays up at all times. Learning to keep it there subconsciously, without having to focus on it." I bite down on my lip, trying to conjure up any more tips or tricks to help them out.

"Try to shift the thought to the back of your mind, rather than keeping it at the forefront. Imagine it literally sliding to the back, like it's a small, written reminder you left yourself for later."

The pair of them dip their chins in understanding and I start with Rowan, creeping a claw of sharp fingernails across her mind.

I tug and pull, increasing the roughness when I notice she's relaxed into the mind battle.

Sweat begins gathering on my forehead as I fight for entrance into her head.

She grunts when I yank particularly hard, and she winces.

A part of me feels awful, but another part wants to push her a little further. Because I know how horrible it can be when someone forces their way into your mind, making you do or see things against your will.

Several years ago, I went on a date with a man who at the end of the evening slipped into my mind, trying to force me home with him. Thankfully, I thwarted his attempt, attacking him with my vines without revealing I had powers of the mind as well.

And then there was the first day we arrived here, with King Kairos.

The memory of my face against his throne room's floor nearly distracts me, but I shove it away.

Eventually, I'm able to pull down her wall a hair, slipping my hand in. Her face goes slack, paling as I do.

But as swiftly as I enter, I leave, only letting her know I was able to get in.

Color begins spreading over her face once more when we slump onto the mat, tired.

"This is going to take a lot of practice, isn't it?" She eyes me warily, her usual confidence nowhere in sight.

"Yes, but you're doing well so far. You put up quite the fight."

I rest for a few minutes, calming my mind and freeing myself of sweat before beginning practice with Jade.

When joining me on the mat, she closes her eyes and breathes in deeply, centering herself.

Her deep brown eyes lock with mine and we start.

I scratch nails sideways over the barrier over her mind. I sling them left, then right, searching for a way to sneak in.

Jade's jaw works, and she screws up her small mouth.

I reach the top, and pluck at her wall.

It sits feather light compared to the thickness of Rowan's, but it's sturdy all the same. My hand clamps down on it, tugging harder. A heavy breath puffs from her mouth when I do.

She forces her airy walls to tighten, and I pull again.

With another few creeping fingers pushing and shoving, I bring down her shield. One at a time, I slip a fingertip in, then the rest of my hand.

But the same as before, I swoop my fingers back, immediately leaving.

I stumble away and sit, not wanting to make a fool of myself.

Jade's eyes water and she quickly wipes them away. She rubs at either temple, looking down. "That was rough. I will *absolutely* be needing more practice."

"We'll get you there. Both of you," I say, slightly out of breath, eyeing both of them.

Four more times do I use my mind wielding to try to enter each of their heads. And I'm successful.

They work hard, fight back, and sweat pours off all three of us by the end. My brain feels like mush, and all I want to do now is take an incredibly luxurious, several-hour-long nap.

"Let's see what your agility looks like." Sure, Killian. Because we all know how to sprint across beams as narrow as one of our boots and climb up metal pegs sticking out of a near-vertical wall.

The bruises bound to bloom on my knees and elbows from crashing into parts of the elaborate, mostly metal agility course will be fun to discover later tonight.

For the past two hours we've been running in circles, restarting at the beginning of the course if we fail anywhere along the way.

And after practicing dagger throwing and archery this morning, along with Killian's mind shielding lesson yesterday, my body *and* my brain are tired.

Raised on a platform nearly as high as my hips, I wait again to cross the thin metal beam that is the beginning of this torture.

After is the wall of pegs. The one many of us continue to slip on.

Only as wide as my palm, the shining gray prongs are placed sporadically. Some of which are spread so far apart they're difficult to maneuver to as we make our way up the massive wall.

A wall which stretches up at least four times my height.

At the top is another flat platform. Then, a completely vertical wall drops down the other side. Two thick ropes connect to the edge of the metal. The remainder of the tan, scratchy material hangs off the side, and is the only thing to grip as we lower ourselves onto a third platform halfway down.

A wide net we must scramble on top of without it tipping in either direction stretches high over the grass afterwards. It's seemingly as long as our target practice range elsewhere on the training field.

Two sets of stairs lead to the ground when the net comes to an end at yet another charcoal gray platform.

A pair of tall, overhead ladders held up by thick pillars crosses the space next. There, we have to hope our hands aren't too sweaty to hold on to the bars while we dangle from them.

If we're lucky enough to have the grip strength to swing ourselves across the dozen metal bars without dropping, we step up several more stairs to where two ropes hang from either side of a T-shaped structure.

We then get the joy of swinging across a wide expanse of water on the long ropes.

I predict many of us will end up soaked by the end of the day from it.

The last part of the course is a towering, metal wall a hair more than twice my height. No ropes, no prongs, nothing to help assist anyone over it.

Except other trainees.

Not that we've been successful enough to help each other out. And even if we were, cracks of division split the group. The handful of loyalists Killian acquired when selecting his trainees consistently eye the rest of us with a mix of wariness and disgust.

Piper creeps across the beam in front of me, and I follow once she reaches the other side.

I've been over this damn thing so many times now I learned to angle my boots to the left, because with my feet pointed straight, my balance suffered.

I trudge along the slick metal, even as the Prince yells at us to hurry up.

"Your yelling isn't as helpful as you believe it is," I grumble to him as I near the edge of the beam.

"I beg to differ."

"You beg to differ from *everything* I say."

I glare at him where he remains on the ground when I step onto the platform. One part down, six to go.

He shrugs, then jerks his head. "You're the one who loves to argue. Keep it moving."

"You don't have to be so demanding, you know," I say, grabbing the closest peg on the wall.

"I find it rather enjoyable. I can see how you don't though." A smirk appears on his lips.

He is *so* insufferable.

A huff releases from my lungs as I reach higher for the next peg.

"Yes, because you know exactly what it's like to be in my shoes," I say, shifting my boot onto a new piece of metal.

"I think I can take a good guess."

Irritation crawls up my spine. "You have no idea what my life is like. What I've been through."

"I know what you're about to go through if you don't pay attention to the task at hand. You'll be plummeting to the ground as long as your boot continues slipping to the edge of the peg you're standing on."

I peer down at my right foot. I twist it, bringing it closer to the wall. My big toe presses into the metal as I put pressure onto it, reaching for another peg above my head.

I hate it when he's right.

Not that I'll ever give him the satisfaction of telling him he is.

"I'm fine." The words come out on a snarl as I lift myself up again. My shoulders strain at the movement.

"You sure do have some fire in you."

I keep my gaze high, pointed at the platform I can now nearly reach, but I picture him as he says it. Growing smirk, eyes creasing as the joy of annoying me spreads over his face. Arms are surely crossed over his broad chest, as usual.

"Funny, considering I don't wield fire," I tell him on a grunt, taking hold of the last peg at the top and hoisting myself up.

My legs burn as I push myself onto the platform, belly first. It may not be entirely graceful, but it works.

"I'm well aware."

My stare turns to him as I perch on the edge of the sky-high platform.

On instinct, I grip the smallest of lips that runs along the rim before the wall drops below my dangling feet.

Damn this is high up.

This is *not* a part of the course I've gotten used to yet.

I narrow my gaze on his far below, homing in on the tiny specks that are his eyes.

He is so arrogant. Why is he like this? He doesn't *have* to be this way in order to train us.

I'm positive his father is the answer to my question, though.

My thoughts are pulled from my head when Piper shouts up at me to pay attention.

She plants her feet on the next metal platform below, quirking an eyebrow at me while a smirk plays on her lips.

I roll my eyes and grab onto the thick rope.

This part hasn't gotten any easier either. Even though this will be my third time doing it.

Bending my knees, I scoot off of my seat, sticking the bottoms of my boots against the wall as I face it. My heart soars into my throat at the movement.

I wrap a wrist through the rope and lean back ever so slightly. Slowly, I take steps backwards, walking down the wall below me.

My fingertips burn as the scratchy material digs into my flesh.

I gulp, trying to suffocate the pain and focus on my feet along the shining metal.

Piper calls out encouraging words from below, but I can't make them out over noise in my brain.

Don't fall, don't fall, don't fall. Don't move your feet too fast. Slow down. Don't get distracted. Slow down. Slow is fast because steady is fast. Don't fall. Don't lose your footing and slam into the wall, again. The rope burn from that will be living into next week. Don't fall, don't fall.

I finally brave a peek down and spot the landing only a few feet away. I let out a breath of relief. I step down the wall a few more times then push off, dropping to my feet.

Halfway across the netting now, on her hands and knees, is Piper.

At this point, I've lost everyone else. After everyone dropped so many times, the line to start the course became shuffled, even though I started with Rowan, Jade, Sebastian, and Asher too.

I crawl onto the net, staying in the middle, as it swings in the cool autumn breeze. It already isn't the most stable, and the wind that comes and goes only makes it worse.

Piper finishes far ahead of me, sliding her body onto the next platform.

I grip the thin, interlinked ropes, my fingers cramping from how tight I hold on.

The netting then swings to the side wildly.

I freeze, holding on with all my might. I peer over my shoulder to find Silas stepping on, throwing his body forward and moving as fast as lightning.

What an idiot.

As he closes in on me, I notice a flare of heat behind his eyes.

Oh crap.

I guess he's still pissed about the boulder dropping on his foot the other day.

I didn't do it on purpose. *He* was the one controlling it after all. I only shined the light at him.

One of his hands wraps around my ankle when he reaches me. What in the world?

He tugs on my leg, trying to force me out of the way.

Then, he slings a burst of air at me, and the net sways even harder.

"What the fuck are you doing?" I shout.

He only answers with a glare.

A string of shadow stretches from his palm then, wrapping around my middle.

He yanks on my ankle again, in time with the darkness. My body jolts back, but I keep my grip firm on the net. My arms stretch out in front of me, the muscles aching as he pulls me backwards. A yelp escapes me without permission.

"What did I say about no powers?" Killian's voice booms.

I look to the other side of the net, on the platform where Piper exited this stage of the course.

Killian stands on the metal landing, waiting, arms folded over his chest, a scowl on his face as he repeats the rule he explained before we began.

"She was in my way. And she deserves it," Silas spits.

I feel the shadows around my torso squeeze tighter, not letting up.

"Drop them. Now." The Prince's eyes narrow on the redheaded man.

A sigh sounds behind me, and the darkness slowly slithers away.

"Back to the beginning. You don't follow my rules, you begin again," Killian says, stare remaining on Silas as the man shuffles along the net beside me.

An elbow conveniently lands in my side along the way.

I stay unmoving, waiting until he passes by. When he comes to the platform, he peers up. Killian doesn't move.

"Did I say you could take the stairs?" The Prince gestures to the two flights of steps directly behind him.

Silas balks at him, mouth opening and closing like a fish on land.

"I didn't. Now, off the side of the net." He jerks his head to the ground far below.

Silas scoots back, peering at the grass at least a dozen feet below. "But, how?" His eyes move, roaming over the Prince.

"Hang and drop down," Killian answers nonchalantly.

"But… it's so far."

"No, it's not."

An audible gulp sounds from the redhead man, but he eventually listens to the command.

He shifts and shimmies to the edge, gripping onto the netting. One leg over, then the next, he slowly drops his body, hands remaining tight on the interlocking rope of the net. His boots dangle several feet off the ground. A whimper escapes his throat.

I hold back a chuckle at his swift change in demeanor.

"Bend your knees," Killian instructs, but his tone is laced with boredom.

More whimpers sound from Silas until his hands finally let go of the netting.

A yelp rings out as he falls. He does as the Prince said, bending his knees as he lands on the flat of his boots. The force has him sway, and he stumbles, landing on his rear. But seemingly injury free.

He stands a moment later, wiping his hands on his pants and heading back to the beginning of the course.

I finish crawling across the net, but a replay of what occurred flashes through my mind.

When I reach the platform, Killian's boots come into view. And I peer up to find an outstretched hand.

Killian's outstretched hand.

A cool wave of disbelief crashes over me, but without my permission, my palm collides with his, and he helps raise me to my feet.

"Thanks," I say shakily, my voice barely above a whisper.

It had been more confident in my head, but the nerves from Silas and his actions still coursed throughout me.

The silver in his irises swirls, and before my eyes, a cerulean blue begins to overtake the icy tone.

A minor dip of his chin is the only response I get before the Prince strides down the stairs without another word.

Shaking out my limbs, I pause, calming my breathing I hadn't realized turned heavy.

Ahead of me, Piper struggles with hanging on the metal prongs above her head. She swings her body, latching onto the next one, but not without a grunt leaving her.

"You okay?" a feminine voice asks behind me.

I turn, finding Jade. Her thin brows crease together as she investigates me.

"Yeah. Just catching my breath."

And trying to figure out why Killian helped me.

She places a hand on my arm, dipping her chin as her face relaxes, believing my words.

"Shit!" Piper yells. I watch as her hand slips when she goes to reach for another rung over her head. She falls, unceremoniously, to the grass, landing on her butt.

I wince when she stands and rubs her hip.

I fear my fate may soon be similar.

I step up to the set of metal rungs on the right, jumping to grab onto the first bar.

The past two times I've made it this far, I fell before making it all the way across.

I pump my legs, building as much momentum as possible. I reach, and my hand lands on the next one. Swinging again, I grab the third, then the fourth.

Bringing my hips forward and back, I sway more, and grip onto the fifth. Then the sixth and the seventh. My body begins to slow but I push on, throwing myself to the eighth bar. My shoulders ache as I adjust my grip.

Almost there.

I reach for the next one, my fingers wrapping around the metal. I keep my hold on the bar before pumping my body and bending my elbows to help with the swing.

I fly forward, grabbing the tenth, then eleventh. I stretch out one last time and my hand lands.

Jumping off, I soar to the ground, bending my knees when my feet hit the grass.

My arms feel weak, like limp, dead leaves hanging off a tree. My fingers ache. I extend them out straight, wiggling them.

I have no idea how I'll be able to swing across the water on a rope.

Bringing one arm across me, then the other, I stretch to the best of my ability.

A dark-haired man who I've seen hanging around Silas is in the midst of flying across the water on the rope to the left. Brennan, I think his name is.

The tips of his boots hit the other side and he lets go. But his arms flail, and he shoots backwards, falling into the water with a splash.

He sits in the liquid, angrily slapping it with a hand.

Yikes.

I step up to the rope on the right when he climbs out, grabbing as high as possible. Taking in a breath, I tighten my grasp and leap.

The force of the swing has my hands sliding down the rope. And in the next second, I lose my grip completely.

The rope slips from my fingers and I hit the freezing water.

It seeps through my pants, entirely soaking my legs and butt. The lower half of my loose gray shirt turns dark, sticking to my stomach.

I push myself up, water dripping from my limbs.

Back to the beginning I go. Today is going to be a *long* day.

Chapter 23

Both my body and my mind are grateful when I wake up and remember we finally have another day off from training.

I'm especially excited to not have to spar today. I loathe sparring.

In the morning, Sebastian and I work in laundry once more. I'm still not used to the stench. I wonder if I ever will be.

I start with folding dry clothes and returning them into their proper sacks, placing them out of the way. Bash begins new loads, a barely visible grimace on his face while doing so.

The machines do the majority of the work, and when the clothes have been thoroughly washed, I hang them to dry. My shoulders ache once again in protest. But as the movement becomes repetitive, numbness begins to seep in.

The small talk I make with my fellow trainees doesn't do much to pass the time.

Sebastian remains his typically quiet self today. Although I swear I catch moments of him deep in thought.

I don't blame him, my mind slips away into thoughts of my aunt, as well as the shop, my friends back in Knothaven, my place in this army, and even what's to come after this training.

I try pushing them away, but they always come rushing back in.

Being in the King's Army was never a part of the plan. Being *caught* was never a part of the plan. Yet here I am, another multiwielder as a cog in the King's machine. But I will not let this be the end of me. Not now, not *ever.*

A sigh so good it makes me physically slump over releases from my lungs when we finally finish the work for the day.

We all flee the smelly, humid room barely in time for lunch.

Piper and Asher await at a table in the dining hall, grinning at Sebastian and me when we make our way to them, meal in hand.

The four of us then decide to wander, exploring the library before we move on to any other area we stumble upon.

"It's too bad Rowan and Jade had to stay late in the kitchen, I know how much Jade loves this place," Piper says thoughtfully as she runs her hand across the spine of a book.

"And you wish Rowan were here so you two could sneak off again," I tease.

"Shut your mouth!"

A laugh bubbles up my throat as she playfully smacks my arm.

"I have a feeling I know where you'd like your mouth right about now," I add.

She smacks my other arm, her jaw hanging ajar. "You— You know nothing!"

But a blush rises onto her freckled cheeks, giving her away.

My laughter only grows stronger at her insistence on the subject.

Asher shakes his head and lounges in a chair. Leaning on the back two legs of the chair, he props his feet up on a table, a smirk on his face and a new book in his hands.

Sebastian sits across from him, a single dark eyebrow raised at the dirty blonde's boots on the surface.

I approach the square table and sit between the two of them.

"Do you think they have any books on *His Royal Highness Prince Killian?* I'm sure Aurora would enjoy a read on her favorite sparring partner," Piper teases from a few aisles away, peeking her head out from behind the shelves with a smirk.

My eyes roll so far back I swear I view my brain momentarily.

"You know I not only hate sparring, but I can't stand him as well. He's an egotistical control freak who gets off on telling us what to do." I cross my arms over my chest.

My forehead begins to ache. I relax my face when I realize I've been scowling at the mention of the Prince.

"You've been thinking about what he gets off to?" Her smirk grows as she approaches, a thick book in her hands.

My mouth drops open without my permission.

"I-," I begin, but I don't even know what to say.

I've been intrigued with his motives as of late but my distaste for him grows every day.

I swear it does.

Asher bursts out a deep belly laugh, bringing his feet off the table to hunch over in his chair. He slaps his knee and nearly drops his book.

To my other side, Sebastian's brown eyes widen. A noise catches in his throat, releasing on a cough as he hits his chest with a bronzed fist.

I regain what I hope is some semblance of composure before finally answering Piper, "No, no I have not. And I would never think of such a thing. He's an ass. The same as his father."

I'm only interested in why he's insistent on being such a jerk.

What have any of us ever done to him? He's only another pawn in his father's game. Admittedly, an extremely important and influential pawn, but still. Training us for his unruly father's army doesn't have to be so gruesome, especially when nearly half of the trainees are here voluntarily.

Damn loyalists. I will never understand why people would volunteer for such a horrendous man.

I'm knocked out of my thoughts when I hear Piper gasp loudly. "Here's a section on his *Princelyness* himself!"

I roll my eyes at her made-up nickname for him and lean forward, uncrossing my arms to place my forearms on the table when she places the book down.

She reads the passage out loud. Most of the information she mentions is already known to the public: He's the eldest child of King Kairos and his wife, Queen Aura, he has two younger sisters, Princess Octavia and Princess Stella, he's the general of the King's Army, et cetera.

She reads the next line to herself, and I squint at her. She's been reading out loud thus far, why stop now?

"What is it?"

"It says here he can wield air, earth, fire, water, shadows, and the mind. I've never heard of someone wielding so many abilities. I mean, I'm sure we've seen him use them all but, I never put it together."

She peers up curiously. "I know no one has ever wielded all seven abilities but six is quite impressive. Regardless of how much I can't stand him. However, it explains why his ego is the size of the damn moon."

I knew he had all but light. I noticed it the first day of training, after sparring with Sebastian. But I never knew others hadn't realized the same.

"I wonder why he's missing light, cause he sure is a ray of fucking sunshine," Asher adds on a huff, sarcasm dripping from his tone.

Piper busts out laughing, her pair of braids swinging as she throws her head back.

I cover my mouth as a snort leaves my nose behind a chuckle and out of the corner of my eye, I see Bash shaking his head.

"Anything else interesting?" I ask after our laughter has ceased.

She wipes away a tear, peering at the text. "Not really. There's not a whole lot here."

She scrunches up her freckled nose and flips the book around, facing me, sliding it across the table.

I grab the leather bound book and follow the lines to where she had been reading from. She's right. I guess he enjoys being a mysterious pain in my ass in person *and* in text.

The four of us leave the library a short while later, heading down the passageways that brought us to the expansive space of books.

Rather than turning left to go back in the direction of our bunks and the main indoor training room, we turn right. Peering casually down halls breaking off on either side from our main path, nothing catches our attention, and we continue straight forward.

"I haven't ventured very far in this direction since arriving here. I hope we find something interesting," Piper squeals with excitement, clasping her hands together.

"Nothing too interesting, I hope. There's definitely too many secrets within these walls I don't think I'm ready to learn yet," Asher says, brows furrowing as he eyes the stone wall stretching up beside us.

Sebastian lets out a humph, nodding.

Piper rolls her eyes and brushes her light-colored braids off both shoulders. "Oh lighten up, we probably won't find anything in this labyrinth of a castle."

"I hope not. I don't disagree with Asher," I add, suspicious of the vast number of halls I've already been dragged through once before.

When we eventually reach the end of the hallway, after going neither left nor right anywhere along the way, we face each direction before turning and looking at each other.

"Left," Piper, Asher, and I say in unison.

Sebastian tilts his head to the side, pointing the same way and I chuckle to myself.

We follow the long corridor that seems to lead nowhere but straight.

The light tiled floors we walk on are striking against the significantly darker charcoal walls. Torches are placed evenly apart on the walls, same as they were on the way to the arena we entered my first day here.

We turn left when we're given no other choice, and a right not long after.

The light from the torches here don't seem to reach as far as in the previous corridors. Shadows become larger, looming over more and more of the space.

There's still enough to manage for now, but the hair on the back of my neck stands up a little straighter at my assessment.

After following the ever growing darkness to the right at a Y-shaped intersection, purely out of curiosity, soft clinks begin to sound. Like pebbles hitting against a stone wall.

My feet stop in their tracks. I turn to Piper, blazing with curiosity.

"What's that noise? Do you hear it?"

Piper cranes her neck at my questioning, a crease forming between her brows, attempting to listen closer.

"I think I hear it. It sounds like soft pitter-patter noise?" Asher tries to explain.

I whip around to face him and Sebastian behind me.

I nod. "Yes! That's it!"

Piper turns around too. "I hear something, but I don't know what it is," she says, hand raised to her mouth.

Bash nods, his thumb and forefinger on his chin in thought.

With a shared look of agreement, we take off, our steps picking up speed as we follow the strange noise.

We weave our way through the labyrinth of hallways, turning left and right as the sound grows more clear.

The closer we get, the more it starts to sound like… sparring?

But… we've never trained this far away from our dorms before. Could it be other trainees? With one of the other trainers?

What started as one, soft plinking sound has now grown into a cacophony of noises: authoritative figures yelling commands, the smashing of earth hitting other objects, whooshing of air and water flying in different directions, the crackling of fire and light striking their targets.

And crying. There were people crying.

It hits me like a wall of bricks and my breath catches on instinct.

My feet screech to a halt, my boots sliding along the floor. Asher almost crashes into me from behind but he stops in time to gently place his hands on my back to brace himself. Piper stops, turning to face me a few paces ahead when she realizes I'm not beside her. Sebastian eyes me closely.

My throat aches as I peer at the three of them.

"It's kids. There's kids crying."

The look Sebastian shoots my way lets me know he's heard it too, and he has the same suspicions I do. A chill goes down my spine as I dip my chin at him knowingly.

"There's kids being trained," I say aloud, my gaze solely on him.

His eyes darken, pupils blowing wide and brows coming together, a scowl building on his face as he slowly nods.

Asher's energy shifts behind me. I can only imagine what's written on his face right now.

Piper's jaw drops open in realization. The strawberry blonde then whips her head in the direction of the sounds and takes off in a sprint.

Without another thought, I run after her.

The vibrations of footsteps thud against the solid floor as we chase after her, and the scene that awaits us.

We turn another corner and I see it.

There's a break in the side of the hallway, nearly at the end of the expansive length. A large, gaping entry way with lights flashing, creating shadows along the opposite stone wall.

I pick up my pace, breathing heavily from the speed. A knot forms in my throat next.

Piper comes sliding to a halt barely within the entrance to the space. I catch up to her a moment later, forcing my feet to stop even when a part of me wants to keep on running. To run away from this, to run back to my life from before I was taken by the King's Guard.

My eyes burn as I take in the sight before me.

Dozens of children are spread out, sparring with fully grown adults.

More lie crying off to the side or against the wall, some nursing injuries, some seemingly unharmed.

My mouth dries out and my tongue goes numb at the sight.

Rocks, fire, and water go flying at sparring mats closest to us. Most of the kids duck out of the way, missing the strike from their trainers.

A few of the older ones, who are probably ten years younger than myself, fight back. They throw light, air, and shadows in the direction of the adults sparring against them.

The anger in the air is palpable as Piper steps forward, entering the vast training space that looks nothing unlike our own.

"What the fuck is this?" she yells, fists clenched, venom dripping from her rhetorical question.

The room quiets as the trainers spot us in the massive doorway. Most of their faces pale, and many sets of eyes widen at our presence.

I scream, stepping up next to her. "Who the hell do you think you are? Sparring against children! What are they doing here?"

I know the answers, but I ask anyway.

They succeeded.

They succeeded in capturing children. Like they attempted with me eleven years ago.

My brain feels fuzzy, and my jaw hurts from clenching my teeth.

"Get out of here. This is none of your business. Forget what you saw and leave," a burly, dark-haired man with a full beard threatens, folding his arms across his chest. He slowly approaches us, eyeing the four of us down.

"Why don't you pick on someone your own size?" Asher growls.

He runs forward, knocking over the closest barrel of water. His hand glides above the spilled liquid, swiftly picking it up and spiraling it into a conical shape.

The liquid instantly freezes and goes flying at the man, who had been sparring against a little girl probably only a third my age.

The bearded man dodges the ice, landing in a crouched position, letting it shatter against the floor behind him. He looks up from his low position, eyeing Asher, snarling.

"You're going to regret that."

And then all hell breaks loose.

Rocks fly towards Asher's head. Shadows stretch out, grabbing Piper's ankle, yanking her away. A wave of clear water crashes into Sebastian. And a blaze of bright orange soars at me.

I duck and spin, throwing myself behind a nearby boulder. I hear shouting, and more crying, as elements go flying.

I peek above the ginormous rock to see the children dispersing, running out of the way, trying to reach the outskirts of the room.

A whip of water releases from a black-haired woman's hand, directed at me.

I jump to my feet, stretching my hands out before me, taking control of the oncoming liquid and steering it away, crashing it down.

We're too far underground and surrounded by too many stone walls to grow any vines up through the ground, so I opt for cracking the boulder in half, sending a piece flying at the woman.

She forms a barrier of water in front of her, but my earth is stronger, breaking through the liquid and slamming into her stomach.

Before I can see her hit the ground, something twists around my leg.

I peer down to find a pitch black shadow winding over my calf.

I hit the floor with a gasp as my leg is pulled out from under me.

The wind is knocked from my lungs. My hands fly to my chest, as if it will help me catch my breath.

My back aches. Pain shoots down my spine.

I'm yanked several paces away. My shirt catches on the floor as I'm pulled.

A lanky, brown-haired man with a pointy features appears above me then, a disgusting smirk on his face.

My throat tightens, squeezed. My eyes go wide at the sensation.

He's wrapped his shadows around my neck.

I feel the wisps of darkness on the skin at my throat and a breath puffs out involuntarily as it gets tighter.

My hands move up to my neck, and the little light I can conjure in this state tries to burn through the shadows, but is unsuccessful.

My vision goes hazy, the image of his pointed face becoming blurry around the edges.

I try inhaling. I can't.

I attempt to work at the void around my throat with my light.

Burn dammit!

The man's teeth get bigger, his grin widening as his face comes closer to my own. "Wouldn't you like a piece of this? Huh, you pig?"

Gasping, I try to take in more air.

A gurgle is all that leaves my mouth.

The choking worsens. My head feels like a balloon about to explode.

Now, parts of his face aren't visible. Only the white of his smile and the pockets of darkness on either side of his nose.

I focus on those two concaved pieces of his face, trying to find the whites of his eyes. I push through the fuzziness in my head, forcing clarity into my brain.

Finally, a hint of white appears in the darkness.

I lock onto those small, light bits, and with all my might, I force my way into his head.

A moment later, my neck is released, free of shadows.

The breath I inhale is dizzying.

I fill my lungs to the brim with air, even though it burns, and blink rapidly, the darkness slowly slipping away. I cough, rubbing at the blooming bruising on my throat.

I'm still locked into his head, and I scrape fingernails along his mind.

Forcing his vision dark and his body limp, I watch him fall to the floor. At the sound of the thud, I release my control on his mind.

Taking in another deep breath, I sit up and shake my head, trying to rid it of any lingering fuzziness.

I wiggle my fingers and my toes, regaining movement as blood freely flows through my body once more.

The thin man lies passed out only inches away. I scoot back to gain some distance. He's out like a light but I won't risk staying close to him in case he wakes.

My back hits the closest wall. I sit, regaining my composure, regulating my breathing.

I take in my surroundings and peer up to find Piper flinging light at a short, curly-haired woman. Sebastian snakes shadows around a pale, bald man. Asher remains drenching the bearded man in water.

Fewer trainers seem to take up the space. Some must have ran off.

I spy movement to my left and flick my eyes over. A young boy and girl are sat huddled together, knees to their chests and arms covering their heads. My eyes follow along the wall past them.

More children line the space, some curled up small, some trying to hide behind any object able to conceal them.

A few paces away, a preteen girl cowers behind the unused half of the boulder I had split in two.

That could've been me. I could have been her, or any one of these kids.

This would have been my fate if they had caught me the night my parents were killed.

The King's Guard would have brought me here to train, to become a part of the King's Army. And my parents sacrificed themselves so I could get away. So I wouldn't end up here.

A pang hits me square in the chest.

My hand reaches for my mouth. I choke back a sob rising without my permission. I blink. A tear rolls out and down my cheek. I use my other hand to swiftly wipe it away.

This would have been my fate. Being forced to spar against adults at least twice my age and size. Tossed around as they used their powers against me. Abilities they practiced and skills they honed for years and years.

How could he do this? How could the King do such a thing? I know he's deplorable, ordering his guards to capture adult multiwielders and convincing those loyal to him to turn themselves in all just to build up his army. But children?

It's still unbelievable.

He truly was successful in doing such a heinous thing.

Shouting pulls me out of my thoughts. Luca and at least a dozen King's Guards enter from a door somewhere in the back of the wide room.

He points, ordering the guards in the direction of Sebastian, then Asher, and finally Piper. Then his eyes land on me.

I scramble to my feet, but before I can make it to him, I'm grabbed from behind.

"Get off of me!"

Someone has their arms around my torso, locking my arms at my sides. I throw my head back, aiming for the person's nose, but it doesn't connect. Pain shoots through my neck at the movement and a hiss escapes me.

I'm shoved down, my knees slamming into the concrete. My hands are forced to the small of my back. Cuffs are clamped onto my wrists.

My muscles ache at the familiar position.

Luca then steps into view, blocking most of my vision of the others also being subdued, forced to the ground, and handcuffed.

I glare up at him.

What a vile, hateful man.

He roughly grabs my chin. With his other hand, he pushes a collar onto my neck, briefly choking me before snapping it shut.

"You guys are a piece of work," he snarls, eyeing me with disgust. He pushes hard against my chin, forcing my face to the side, releasing me. His hands cross over his chest as he surveys the others.

Asher and Sebastian lie face down, hands behind them, cuffed. Collars circle their necks. Three male guards hold them down, each. They shove the men's faces into the ground, refusing to let them move even an inch.

Piper is on her knees like me, cuffed and collared too. One guard has a hold of her shoulders, and another has her braids wrapped around his fist, forcing her head to tilt awkwardly.

The second-in-command peers at us with interest, sighing.

"You four shouldn't be in here."

Chapter 24

We're dragged back to the main sparring room, down the series of hallways and corridors. Upon arrival, the four of us are thrown on our knees to the ground.

Pain shoots up my thighs and into my stomach.

I'm positive bruises will form there later.

The trainees sprinkled about the room become silent, and dozens of pairs of eyes land on us.

Luca stalks ahead, his back facing us, his voice booming, *"Don't* go wandering around the castle. You are all to stay within your assigned wing. Do you understand?"

The guards who pushed and pulled us through the endless corridors then kick me in the back.

I land on the ground with a grunt, the air being knocked from my lungs, not for the first time today. My lungs ache from all they've been through in such a short time period.

I spy Piper to my left. Similar noises emerge from her, as well as Asher and Bash, who are on her opposite side.

I may have not had to spar today but man is my body going to hurt tomorrow.

A booming voice stops my thoughts of my aching body.

"What happened?"

Killian storms in from beyond the gathered trainees. The room splits in two as they clear a much wider path than necessary to let the Prince through.

His dark, shoulder length hair is fully pulled back at the base of his skull. And he's in one of his typical all black ensembles: black boots, black cargo pants, and a black cut off shirt.

Knees still on the ground, I'm yanked upright by the guard behind me. He tugs on my collar, choking me, and a cough sputters up from my throat.

"These four were in a part of the palace they shouldn't have been in," Luca answers, standing up a bit taller in the Prince's presence. He pushes his one, long braid over his shoulder and cracks his neck side to side. His knuckles are cracked next.

The Prince reaches his second-in-command and eyes his movements suspiciously.

"What did they do?"

Luca's eye twitches, and he looks off in the distance before staring at Killian again.

"They got into it with some guards."

Oh yeah, leave out most of the damn story you ass. The most important parts too.

Killian looks over at the four of us, suspicion still covering his features.

Another cough escapes me when my collar is yanked again.

"I'm taking them to the King. But first... I'm going to make an example out of them," Luca grumbles, turning to stare at me.

His gaze is cold and full of rage. It buries into me as he leaves the Prince and struts over to me.

In the next second, his hand is raised, ready to strike.

Time crawls, as if it all happens in slow motion.

My stomach drops.

I freeze. Every part of me goes icy as chills spread across my skin.

His palm shifts, moving towards my face.

I brace myself, awaiting his punishment, but his hand never reaches me.

"I don't think so."

Killian is beside him in an instant. His hand grips Luca's wrist, halting his movement.

The Prince's command leaves no room for doubt. The second-in-command flicks his gaze to Killian and slowly lowers his outstretched palm.

"I'll handle them. Thank you," Killian booms, then releases Luca's wrist. His eyes turn to me, searching.

"Release them. Now." His stare remains on me as his command is followed.

The collars are first to go. Then the cuffs are removed.

I slowly push myself up, rubbing my aching wrists first, then my neck, the flesh there sensitive from the shadows which choked me only minutes ago.

With a twist, I face the male guard who still holds the metal pieces. I snarl at him, prepared to lunge.

"Leave. Now," the Prince's voice echoes around the room.

Luca and the guards leave, shuffling out of the room, but not before glaring at us one more time.

Once they're gone, my gaze goes back to Killian.

He's still spying me, silver flecks spinning in his deep ocean eyes. He snaps out of it and twists to view the gathered trainees. "Don't you all have dinner to get to?"

Within an instant, people make their way into the dining hall behind me and my now visibly injured friends. They look awful. Bruises are beginning to form on their faces. Asher's barely-healed face is torn up once again.

The three of them follow behind the crowd, but my feet stay planted where they are.

Burning surges through my veins. My fists ball at my sides. My eyes lock onto the Prince. The glare I point at him is unlike any other.

He doesn't have *anything* to say to us?

The heat rising within me takes over and before I know it, I'm flying towards him.

"You knew about it! You fucking bastard! You asshole! They're just kids!" I stomp up to him, hitting him in the chest with my fists.

Damn, that felt good.

He grabs my wrists as I move to pull them away, before I can hit him again.

"What are you talking about?"

"Don't act like a fool! I know you're not stupid," I spit at him, ripping my hands out of his grasp.

I know he could have held on tighter. He let me take my hands back.

His shining blue eyes narrow, staring into my green ones. "I don't know what you're talking about."

I huff and roll my eyes. He is *truly* exhausting.

Stepping in even closer, I feel his breath fan across my face. I clench my teeth as I tighten my glare at him, biting back the slew of insults forming in my throat.

"I can't believe you and your father are building an army of multiwielding children. It's despicable. Disgusting. But fine, keep playing dumb."

His face blanches at my remark and he steps back, looking at me like I've grown a second head. Brows pulled together, he stares down at me. He studies my face, then my neck.

His silence is deafening.

He must believe me to be a moron. This quiet act; I don't believe it for a second. He is his father's son.

He looks down at his boots. His toned arms flex, hands making their way into fists. His stubbled jaw works, shifting back and forth.

He must be concocting a suitable lie for the things we witnessed.

I fold my arms over my chest, tapping my foot in impatience, waiting for an excuse to come.

But one never does.

The Prince's gaze finally flings up to mine, filled to the brim with something I'm unable to read.

He only stares at me for a moment. Then, he sets his sight behind me and takes off, his bicep brushing the top of my shoulder as he exits the room, slamming the doors behind him.

My gaze stays on the set of doors, waiting. A buzzing noise fills my ears as I replay the kids, and their faces, in my mind. I shake my head, pushing the thoughts away for now.

Once I follow everyone in the dining hall, I find Piper's hand shooting up, signaling me over. She sits, gathered at a table with Asher, Sebastian, Rowan, and Jade, talking in hushed voices.

"Oh my- your neck," Jade stutters out when she sees me. Her dark eyes gloss over.

My hands go to cover my throat but as I sit down, Rowan reaches over, grabbing my hands and slowly removing them. Her mouth opens and shuts a handful of times before she finally speaks. "Woah."

I let out an uncomfortable, strangled chuckle. "Tell me about it."

"They told us what you guys saw," Jade says gently.

I nod my head and finally take in my friend's appearances.

Asher's lip, which was mostly healed, has split open again and is an angry red. His dirty blonde hair stands in every direction.

Jade takes notice and tries fixing it. She bites her lip and does her best before inspecting his lip, worry covering her small features. He winks at her in response.

Hair has come out of Piper's braids. Her pale green eyes sit full of rage, accompanied by dark bags underneath. But the anger slips away when Rowan throws an arm around her shoulders and they begin talking amongst themselves.

To my left, Bash rotates his elbow, wincing ever so slightly when it straightens out fully. The dark curls on the top of his head are mostly uniform, but a fresh burn runs along his light brown skin just behind his ear, stretching down his neck.

I nudge him softly. "You okay? Your elbow? That burn?" I point to the deep red mark.

He stops stretching out his arm to find the burn along the upper side of his neck. He pulls his fingers away, eyeing me. "I'll be okay. Are you?"

He scans my face, then examines my own neck. His brows pull together as he studies what I'm sure are some gnarly bruises.

"I'll be fine. But I'm afraid what we saw today is only the beginning. I suspect there's much more to come, being a part of the King's Army."

He nods solemnly.

"I think you're right, Aurora. There is a lot more to come."

Chapter 25

Repercussions never came for what we had stumbled upon.

Well, at least true ones.

Killian had been in a mood the past several days since the incident, glaring and being more tense than usual. He was shouting more commands at us in training, particularly during target practice. Harsh words were spewed when skills were hitting anywhere but a bullseye, which happened frequently.

He was pushing us harder than ever before. However, regardless of his attitude, his words were working.

Apparently, there *is* a method to his madness.

Everyone's been making improvements. Those who weren't even hitting the target before were now at least grazing the outer rings. Those who were hitting the outer rings were now making bullseyes with some of their shots.

He also forbade us once again from using our strongest ability, the one we would most typically lean towards.

Rowan, Piper, and I are most upset over the temporary new rule.

And we haven't stayed particularly quiet about it.

The past few days have felt like weeks. I miss connecting with the earth, feeling the nature all around me and working with it to achieve my goals.

Piper says the same about her light, but that she's glad to at least feel the slightest bit of warmth from the sun against her skin as we spend time outside on the training field. Even if the days have become significantly cooler, and more clouds hang in the sky.

And I can feel the fire building up within Rowan, her frustration with not being allowed to use the explosive ability grows every day.

I suspect Sebastian also isn't thrilled. His hands had curled into tight fists at the order. He was also the first to vanish from the field that day, walking faster than I had ever seen a human move before without their legs picking up into a jog.

It felt unnatural, not seeing him surrounded by shadows the past few days in practice. It was so odd seeing only his air or mind at work. So invisible in contrast to his typical dark, mysterious demeanor.

Most of the others, however, were seemingly used to the new rule after a day or two, even though there was a ripple of grumbles at the announcement.

Asher mentioned while he favors the coolness of water, he used earth and light nearly as much, with his work on his family's farm.

And Jade said she always could rely on air because it was constantly around her, regardless of where she was, so this would be a good way to push herself to truly perfect her earth, fire, and water abilities.

"Alright, that's enough for today," the Prince grunts out, his moodiness clearly still intact.

I huff and bend over, placing my hands on my knees. My hands tingle from switching back and forth between light and water earlier. My elbows ache from the repeated movements.

I close my eyes and let my mind go blank. My head pounds from the overuse of creating hallucinations within other minds, forcing people to bend at my will.

Those of us with mind powers had been paired off, fighting against one another through manipulation of the brain.

I would argue that mind wielding is the most challenging of the seven abilities. Its use weakens me unlike any of my other powers.

Eventually, I reopen my eyes and begin to follow the rest of the trainees off the field.

I can't *wait* for dinner.

I fully believe mind wielding makes one the most hungry after prolonged use.

"Wait."

My shoulders slump at the voice calling out to me when I'm only a few paces from the door leading inside.

Of course it's *him*.

I look up at the fading sky, hoping whatever he has to say doesn't take long.

Spinning around, I stare at Killian, a bored expression plastered on.

His gaze roams over my face. "Been doing any more sneaking around?"

A haughty laugh escapes me. "Wouldn't you like to know."

I haven't been, but he doesn't need to know about every moment of my free time.

He shakes his head. "What the four of you did was stupid. You guys shouldn't have gotten involved."

"I'm done listening to you. I'm tired and hungry," I snarl, facing my exit once more, desperate to leave his presence.

I will *never* forgive him for being on board with his father's wishes of building an army of child multiwielders.

Just before my palm reaches the door's handle, he catches me, spinning me around to face him. My back hits the outer stone wall of the castle with a light thump.

Only a few inches from my face is his own tanned one. His breath mingles with mine when I gasp in surprise.

He did *not* just do that.

"How dare you?" My voice raises higher, and louder, than I expect.

"You and I both know I didn't hurt you," he says, one dark eyebrow arching as he towers over me.

It didn't hurt, but still, I'm exhausted, and frankly, I want to sit down and stuff my face with whatever is on the menu tonight.

His hand stretches out, putting a barrier between my head and the awaiting door that I so desperately want to leave through.

I glare up at him, paying far too much attention to those intense eyes of his, trying to find the exact name of the color to perfectly describe them.

I struggle to find one.

They're blue, but change depending on the light. Lighter, sky-colored shades in the sun, but darker, like a sapphire, in the shadows. Swirls of silver, icy tones peek through in some moments too.

Right now they look like an ocean made of steel, so pastel the color is nearly leached from his irises.

Warm breath slides across my face and I come back into myself, shaking off the thoughts of his eyes.

But I still peruse over the rest of his face that takes up the majority of my vision.

A few deep chocolate strands frame both sides of his face, loose from the tie at the back of his head. Below his strong, straight nose lies those damned lips. Perfectly created lips from which bullshit spews at us all day long.

His normally clean-shaved jaw is heavy with scruff, as if he's been too busy to care about it lately.

I snap my gaze back to his, words falling from my mouth in a rush of anger.

"What do you want? Aside from trying to feed me more lies about the child army you and your father are forming. How could you sick people be alright with that?"

"Lower your voice. Trainees could be just on the other side of that door," he growls out.

"Sure, they are," I say sarcastically, too afraid to roll my eyes with him invading my space.

At least when I've done it before, he was several paces away from me.

His left hand comes to the other side of my head, palm pressed flush against the wall, fully caging me in. His gaze intensifies as he speaks.

"What makes you think I knew about it? Or that I had any say in the forming of such a deplorable thing."

My jaw drops, leaving my mouth slightly ajar. *Deplorable.*

He referred to it as *deplorable*. A shudder runs through me.

"Be- because I would think the Prince would know about a child army that his father, the King, was creating," I stutter out.

Right? He would have known about such a thing. Is he lying to me?

But, he called it what it is. Deplorable.

My mind spins, a bout of dizziness taking over.

"Well, sweetheart. You thought wrong."

He rips his hands away from the wall, snatching the door handle, and stalks inside without another word.

Twenty-four hours after my encounter with Killian, I still think about what he said.

I was wrong about him. In at least one way.

If I were to believe him.

Should I? Do I? I'm unsure about it all. He *had* acted odd when I first confronted him about the children, so maybe he is telling the truth.

I stalk amongst the dozens of shelves of books in the library, my mind wandering in every possible direction while I wait for Rowan, Piper, and Bash to join me.

He confuses me.

Anger seeped off of him yesterday. But I'm not entirely sure it was directed at me.

I shake my head.

I *need* to think of something else.

Much needed reprieve from my incessant thoughts comes when the sound of footsteps echo nearby.

"Oh thank goodness you're finally here. I–"

My words halt in my throat when I round the corner and come face to face with the Prince himself.

"I have a feeling I'm not the one you're looking for," he says, a smirk tilting his lips upward.

"No, you're not," I speak frankly, crossing my arms over my chest. "What are you doing here anyways?"

"Can't a man visit his own castle's library?" He lifts a brow at me, leaning against the side of the shelf to his left.

His hair is loose today, rather than it being fully or partially tied up like it usually is during training. And it sways ever so slightly to the side as he rests on the shelf.

Why did I ask him that? Of course he can go wherever he pleases in his own home.

I shake my head, looking down. "You're right. I don't know why I asked."

He chuckles. A *genuine* chuckle.

"I'm here to find a particular book but, you're standing in the way of the aisle I need to go down." He tilts his head to the side.

It's only then do I notice where I'm standing: right smack in the middle of the entrance to the aisle.

I bite down on my lip and shuffle out of the way, embarrassment bubbling in my gut.

"What are you doing here?"

He slides past me as he asks the question, his hands in his pockets, peering at the spines of books.

He's so… *casual* right now.

It's throwing me off guard.

"Well, I like to read. And I'm meeting some others here."

"I never would have guessed," he drawls sarcastically. But he faces me briefly, and his lips twitch up again. "What do you like to read?"

He faces the bookshelves once more, tipping his head to the side as he reads the titles on the spines.

"Mostly tales of fiction. Romance, primarily. What about you?"

He shrugs. "I don't have much time to read for pleasure anymore. But when I did, it was most often fiction."

"Right, I assume being in charge of the King's Army and heir to the throne takes up a lot of your time."

His eyes move away from the books, finding mine. He considers me for several moments, his pupils growing as they take me in, covering the ocean tones.

"Something like that."

Resuming his inspection of the books, he slowly begins moving down the aisle. And I don't know why, but I follow him.

"What are you looking for?"

"A specific piece of historical text."

"That's not exactly helpful if you'd like me to be a second pair of eyes."

He dips his chin, and chuckles once more. "I suppose you're right. It's about the landscape of Orellia throughout our history. It features maps, old and new."

I investigate the side of his head as he moves further away.

His attitude is so different today, I think it's giving me whiplash.

Slowly, I move my gaze away from him and begin reading the titles of books.

"What do you need it for?" I finally decide to ask after several minutes of searching through the shelves.

I feel him still beside me. Then, he sighs, and continues moving along the shelves.

"The children were moved. I'm trying to figure out where they might have been taken."

His confession stops me in my tracks.

"What do you mean?"

"I mean, my father moved them," he says, a mix of frustration and fury lacing his voice.

"Why? When you're in charge of the King's Army."

"Like I told you yesterday: I would never have helped form such a deplorable thing. And I am *certainly* not in charge of it. My father doesn't exactly tell me everything."

He *didn't* know.

His father built a child army right under his nose and never told him about it.

My jaw falls without my consent.

I've always known King Kairos is the worst thing to ever happen to Orellia, but this is more maddening than I ever thought possible.

"I- I don't know what to say," I confess.

Killian turns to face me, a stony yet somber expression on his face.

A moment passes, then another. His eyes soften just a hair before he speaks again.

"I'll figure it out. Just forget I said anything."

It isn't a command; his voice is… gentle.

I barely have another moment to process his words when I hear the library doors swing open, followed by Rowan and Piper's laughter filtering through the stacks of books.

"I'll come back later and search," he says, eyes cast downward then bouncing up to me. With a nod of his head, he spins on his heels and silently exits the library, slipping past Rowan, Piper, and Sebastian without them ever noticing.

Several hours later, after spending as much time as possible between the rows of books, the four of us finally leave the library and start towards the dining hall.

But my interaction with the Prince has yet to stop replaying in my head all this time, even with the distraction of Rowan, Piper, and Bash.

However, my thoughts on the subject are interrupted when a limb flies into my chest.

Ouch.

My view lands on one of Rowan's dark brown, toned arms. She's stopped me, Piper, and Sebastian from walking forward any further.

Piper leans closer to the long, black braids hanging near the woman's ear, whispering, "What–"

But she's swiftly cut off by Rowan's other hand reaching up, slamming over her mouth.

Rowan removes her hand, bringing it to her own mouth a moment later, her index finger standing vertically in front of her lips.

Then, I hear hushed voices.

She stopped us just before we met a hallway intersection, and there are people talking around the corner on our right.

"I don't want to hear anymore of your bullshit, Luca."

I'd recognize that voice anywhere. I've heard it yelling at me every day in practice.

And it was replaying in my head only moments ago.

"Your father swore me to secrecy. There was nothing I could do. He said you weren't particularly fond of the idea but it's his kingdom and his rules," the voice that must belong to Luca breathes out. He sighs, awaiting the Prince's response.

"So you'll do *anything* he tells you to do now? Grow a damn backbone Luca."

I can picture Killian's face as he makes the remark. Dark eyebrows pinched together, upper lip tweaked up in a snarl. He probably threw in a jerk of his chin at the end.

"I'm sorry. I don't know what else to tell you."

"Fuck," Killian whispers angrily, more to himself than to his second-in-command.

"Look, I'm not here to argue with you. There was another reason why I came to find you."

"What now?"

I can once again picture the Prince in this moment, his arms crossing over his chest into his typical stance.

"There was an attack at one of our border stations up in the White Mountains."

"On which one?"

"Mount Jasper."

A heavy sigh releases from who I assume is the Prince.

Jasper Mountain. One of the main three peaks sitting between us and Norfell.

Why would they be attacking us?

Footsteps begin receding down the hallway, and the next reply is too hushed for me to hear.

Rowan faces us, whispering so softly I have to read her lips to understand her. "I didn't know we were at such odds with Norfell."

I shrug my shoulders. I thought relations between the four kingdoms were good. Great, even. Perhaps that's untrue. Perhaps we were only led to believe as such.

Who knows with King Kairos?

"I've heard about a scuffle or two when they've accidentally patrolled into the other's land but nothing *truly* bad has ever happened," Piper adds in a whisper.

"I can't hear them anymore. They're moving down the hallway," Rowan states, disappointed.

"I'll follow them," Sebastian says.

We whip our heads at his declaration.

"Are you crazy?" Piper whisper-shouts.

Before any of us can say another word, Bash peers around the corner and dashes down the corridor.

The three of us peek after him. His booted feet move silently across the ground, and he spins into an alcove a quarter of the way down the hall.

I hold my breath as he makes his way to the next one, and one further after that.

The sound of a gulp comes from Piper. I glance at her with nervous eyes, then bite my lip and face the long corridor once more.

This is such a bad idea. The thought of the last time Luca caught us spirals through my mind.

I can no longer see which cavity Bash hides in and I assume he must have moved into one on our side.

Luca and Killian stop walking, and begin twisting in the direction they came from.

My eyes nearly pop out of my skull at their movement. I throw myself back around the corner, out of view. The two women move in sync with me, our backs now against the cool, stone wall.

The hushed voices continue but, after a few minutes, completely disappear. And we don't dare peek around the corner again.

My foot begins to tap impatiently. Where is Bash?

I cross my fingers on either hand, hoping he didn't get caught listening in on their seemingly private conversation.

Then, not a moment too soon, the dark haired, mystery man himself comes waltzing around the corner.

I let out a breath, finally relaxing.

Piper's the first to question him. "What did they say?"

His hands slide into the front pockets of his loose, black pants. He leans a shoulder against the wall before answering, "The King's pissed about the attack. He wants to retaliate."

"What? Why?" I ask, intrigued.

He eyes Rowan, Piper, and then me, taking in a breath before speaking.

"Because two multiwielders were killed."

Chapter 26

From going to the library to strolling through the never ending halls of this castle in the hopes of stumbling upon more hushed conversations, we've been doing everything we can to find out more information on Norfell.

And to find out why they may have attacked.

I've also kept a decidedly closer eye on Prince Killian.

I didn't mean to at first, I only caught myself in the act. After what happened in the library, I suppose I couldn't help myself. He intrigued me. Eventually, I leaned into it.

At some point, I started to believe he was watching me too.

There were times where I could feel eyes boring into the back of my head, and once in a while, when I did get the urge to turn around, I saw him. He was always there.

But I only actually caught Killian staring once.

The other times he had been quick enough to look in another direction, or turn his body a different way completely. However, I knew it was him every time.

He never did publicly announce there was an attack at Orellia's mountainous border, which has caused more and more questions, and theories, to build up in my head.

I'm thrilled we don't have to train today, and while I'm finally starting to become used to the rigorous schedule, I have yet to *not* be excited for our weekly day off.

Even if it means working in laundry with Sebastian. And an array of smelly socks.

My abilities are becoming stronger with the near-constant use, and my aim has improved, but my body still aches at the end of each day.

The four of us who listened in on the Prince's conversation now sit in the library, along with Jade and Asher, who joined us the second we told them what we overheard.

"Can you grab that one for me, too?"

I turn my attention to the feminine voice asking the question.

Piper stands with one arm above her head, pointer finger out, identifying a book on a shelf.

Asher eyes her, slightly annoyed, but a smirk lingers on his face. He places a stack of at least a dozen books in his arms down, reaching up, easily taking the book off the shelf.

The strawberry blonde woman beams up at him, snatching the book from his hand.

"Thank you," Piper says before waltzing back to the rectangular wooden table a few of us occupy. She plops down in the seat across from me, and beside Rowan, the thick book thudding onto the tabletop.

Rowan's eyes stay on her own book as her arm immediately comes down in between their chairs. In the next moment, Piper's chair slides towards Rowan's, only stopping once it can't come any closer.

I cover my mouth with a fist, hiding my growing grin, and peer back down at my book when Piper lets out a shocked noise.

My eyes find the line I left off at, and I continue reading about *The History of Modern Times*.

Who even named this book? I acknowledged it was a vague title when I picked it up, but I figured it was worth giving a shot. Especially considering we have collectively read through nearly a hundred books by now.

Every free moment we could spare over the past week has been spent in this place. The stack of books we've deemed utterly worthless grows as each day passes.

I tilt my head side to side, stretching out my stiff neck.

We have found such little information on Norfell, I'm beginning to believe we're never going to figure out what may have caused the attack on Mount Jasper.

We truly only learned three things thus far. The first was that the King of Norfell is named Tidus Bane. The second was he had been crowned King only three months after King Kairos. And the third was he has only visited Orellia once since being crowned, a little over seven years ago, to meet with King Kairos.

That was it. No information on what he was like, what he believed, how he ruled his kingdom, how he came to be crowned, nothing. Not even a general description of what he looked like.

I'm beginning to think we aren't going to find anything on this man. And that we'll never find out why he had his men attack and kill two of our multiwielders posted at the border.

What could he possibly want? What is worth risking retaliation from another kingdom? Retaliation that could lead to an all out war. It would throw the world into complete chaos. Both Mistivas and Evenend would end up getting involved too. So, why?

My thoughts on the subject are halted when I hear an earth-shattering gasp.

My head flies up to find Piper jolting out of her chair, pushing the book she's reading flat onto the table, and pointing to a passage amongst the text.

"Look! Here's information on him and his family!"

I lean forward, as far as I can across the table, to view the lines she's identifying.

Rowan puts her elbows up on the table, getting closer. Asher, Jade, and Bash circle around us, leaving their table beside ours to peer at the book's contents.

"He's middle-aged, about as old as King Kairos. He's described as having a head of white hair under a silver and green crown. He was married to his queen, Lucinda, but she died in childbirth when delivering their only child. A daughter named Callista. She is the sole heir to the throne of Norfell, as he never remarried," Piper reads aloud.

"Does it say anything about his powers? What does he wield?" Jade asks from my right.

Piper scans the page further, then shakes her head.

"No, it doesn't say what abilities were passed down to him. We don't even know if he is a wielder, or a multiwielder. He could have no powers at all."

"What about his rulings? Is he fair and just? Or is he more like our own *beloved* King Kairos?" I ask, my voice laced heavily with sarcasm.

Asher snickers, nudging me a second later.

"No. It doesn't say anything about how he runs his kingdom. Only a brief mention that his father's funeral had the largest attendance of any of their kings. So, I guess his father was well liked by the people," she says, shrugging.

"Damn. So nothing about what he's like as a king?" Rowan asks, tucking a few of her small, dark braids behind an ear. She leans back in her chair, crossing her arms.

The strawberry blonde woman flicks her own pair of braids behind her. She places her palms back on the table to keep reading from the book. A few moments later, she shakes her head back and forth once more.

"After the mention of his father, it goes further back into the ancestry of the ruling family. There's no more mention of King Tidus," she states with a huff and descends into her chair.

One of Rowan's toned arms comes uncrossed and folds around Piper's freckled shoulders. The latter leans into the touch, resting her head on the lean, bronze bicep.

"Don't worry. We'll find something useful soon enough," Jade says, ever the optimist.

She briefly rests a pale hand on Piper's forearm in reassurance. She only pulls away when leaving the table, heading to the one her, Asher, and Sebastian occupy.

"We'll keep looking," Bash promises, dipping his chin.

The smile I give him is small.

The hope I once had is dwindling fast, and I know it's starting to show. Why was it so hard to find any information on this kingdom?

Asher cups his hand around my shoulder, giving it a light squeeze. He accompanies the gesture with a perfect, gleaming smile.

"C'mon, let's get back to it," Asher says, moving to sling an arm around Sebastian.

Asher then brings his other hand up to ruffle the dark curls atop Bash's head. The coffee-colored curls fall forward, into his eyes, and Bash swats at him.

Asher laughs, like an older brother after teasing a younger one.

I stifle a laugh of my own, biting on the inside of my lips.

Asher lets up and Sebastian runs his fingers through his hair to fix the mess before the two of them make it over to their shared table with Jade. The former stops in front of the huge stack of books he was carrying around earlier. His golden, muscled arms flex as he brings his hands to his hips, eyeing the collection.

"Let me help you read through some of those," Jade says, gesturing to the pile. She takes a handful of books, forming a stack of her own.

Asher beams one of his usual pearly white smiles at her. "Thank you, love."

Her face reddens at the comment and she peers down, letting her sleek, black bob hang forward on her face in an attempt to conceal the color in her cheeks.

My eyes rapidly swing back and forth between them, fighting a grin that threatens to take over my face.

"Of course. You're welcome," she replies, biting her lower lip. She whips open a book, forcing her attention on reading.

Asher's stare lingers on her before picking up a book of his own and sitting down.

His concentration barely begins moving away from the petite woman, who now pulls out the closest chair, intended to plop onto it. The chair wobbles, and she nearly misses her seat. But before she or it could fall, Asher's arm reaches out, steadying the wooden furniture.

Her eyes go wide as she grips onto the chair, regaining her balance.

He holds onto the piece of furniture as she adjusts, her face blooming even more scarlet. She brushes her hair down and clears her throat.

"Thank you," she says softly, not looking him in the eyes.

"Anytime," he answers, matching her quiet voice. A conversation meant solely for the two of them.

He only releases her chair after she wiggles once more, leaning forward to study the text.

I attempt to reel in my own focus, to study the words before me.

The table Rowan, Piper, and I occupy is covered in stacks of books both read and unread. I look them over again and begin to feel overwhelmed.

There's so many we've read. And there's still so many to look through. Not to mention the sheer size of this library. Aisles and aisles of books we still haven't gone through. To find even a scrap of information on why Norfell would attack at the border.

I push the thought of the vast number of books out of my head before it completely consumes me.

I just need to focus on the one in front of me for right now. One at a time.

A while later, after finally finishing the piece of text, I peer up to find Piper stretching.

Her arms fling wide, out on both sides of her.

Her hand outstretched behind Rowan flexes, flipping up and down a few times, like a wave. She turns her head, looking over her shoulder.

Then, she winks at Jade. And the woman dips her head in response.

My face twists up at the exchange.

What secret is being passed between those two? They *absolutely* have something up their sleeves.

A moment later, Jade gets up, closing her current read and placing it at the top of a stack of what appears to be finished books.

She makes her way over to us and taps Rowan on the shoulder.

"Hey, would you be able to help me put some books away? Some of their places are too high for me to reach."

While I know that second part is true, considering she's the shortest amongst the group, my gut says there's another reason for her to pull Rowan away.

"Sure thing," Rowan says, standing up to help.

After they reach the first shelf beyond the group of tables, Piper whips her head to me. A massive grin covers her face. She nearly jumps up and over the table as she leans in as close as possible to me.

"Tomorrow's Rowan's birthday," she whispers, her freckled nose wrinkling with her smile.

"Wait, really?"

I'm going to kill her for not telling me.

"Yes. She's only told me about it. She said she hasn't had the best experience on her birthday the past few years, but I want this year to be different!"

"Alright. What's the plan?"

Of course I want to celebrate her birthday. She deserves to have a special day. And I know the woman in front of me has already concocted a, probably elaborate, plan.

"I talked with Jade, because she has kitchen duty and she knows where everything is. I wanted us to bake a cake for her. A chocolate one. It's her favorite."

"That's perfect!"

"The only problem is, someone needs to distract her while the cake is being made. I was going to take her wandering around the castle for a few hours, far away from the kitchen. Would you, Bash, and Asher help Jade make the cake while I do that?" She searches my eyes hopefully, biting her lower lip.

"Of course I will."

"Great! After dinner tonight, once the kitchen is cleared out, Jade will take you all there."

"Sounds like a plan."

"Don't beat the eggs so hard. They're going to fly out of the bowl!" I scold Asher, who holds the bowl in the crook of his arm, whisking the eggs with his other hand like he's locked in a battle with the yellow yolks.

This man makes me nervous in the kitchen.

So far he has spilt flour on the floor, hit his head against the pans hanging from the ceiling, and got more than half an eggshell in the bowl while cracking it.

He is seriously starting to make me jumpy.

Finally, he places the bowl down on the counter, and Jade snatches it away as politely as possible.

I know he was making her anxious too, but she's too nice to say anything.

She mixes everything together, and I finish greasing the two circular pans for the batter to be baked in.

Behind us, I hear the guys going through cabinets, taking out ingredients for frosting.

Thankfully, Sebastian seems to know his way around a kitchen. Or perhaps he's just good at being light on his feet and taking in his surroundings. My money is on the latter, considering the way he had eavesdropped on Killian and Luca's conversation.

Once the pans are in the oven, Jade and I start on the frosting.

Asher happily hands her the bag of sugar we previously used.

"Oh. Thank you, but we actually need *powdered* sugar. Not regular sugar," she explains gently, squeezing her eyes shut and taking it anyways.

The honey-haired man's palm flies to his forehead. "Ugh. Yeah, you're right."

She chuckles, and I join.

At least he has the spirit.

Powdered sugar found, we whip up a large bowl of white frosting.

Only a few minutes later does the timer for the cake ding, and as Bash takes both pans out of the oven, I wash my hands.

"Time to let it cool and then we can decorate," I chime, excited. I haven't been able to stand in a kitchen and make food in several weeks. I've missed it dearly.

"This is fun. We should sneak in here more often," Asher says, drying his also freshly scrubbed hands. He then proceeds to jump up to sit on the counter, and hits his head once more on the dangling cookware.

Bash chuckles, clapping him on the shoulder as he scoots off, setting his feet on the floor.

I don't think I've heard that man let out more than a huff of amusement before now, and it fills me with pride, knowing he's opening up more and more to us. I smile to myself at the thought.

To my left, Jade stifles a giggle and peeks into the bowl.

"This looks great," she says about the mountain of white fluff.

"It does," I add, leaning in, scooping up a finger full of it.

I flip around to lean against the counter, ready to taste the deliciousness but stop when I realize my hand has collided with something.

I've smacked someone. Someone I didn't know was behind me.

Sebastian.

A smear of the light frosting lies across his cheek, contrasting rather beautifully with his tawny skin.

My frosting-free hand flies to my mouth.

"I am so sorry, Bash," I say, trying to conceal a giggle.

He stares at me, but I can't read the expression on his face. He reaches up, wiping it off with one of his own fingers, and tastes it.

"Yum," he states, cracking a grin.

Then, we all burst out laughing. Full blown belly laughs coming from each one of us, even the hard-shelled frosting face himself.

"I want a taste," Asher hums, making his way to the bowl and sticking in his pointer finger. "And *you* should try some too," he continues, plopping a dot of the fluff onto Jade's nose.

The woman's eyes go wide at the action, then they cross, viewing the food on her face. Her mouth pops open.

His tongue sweeps out then, cleaning his finger of the frosting, and pink creeps into her cheeks.

Another chuckle releases from my throat, and I cover it with the back of my non-frosted hand. A cacophony of laughter fills the room once more, returning to its full, booming volume.

Jade's reddened face glows as she giggles, delighted.

I bend over, clutching my stomach to try and control the continuous chuckles spilling out of me. Tears stream out the corner of my eyes and I stand up, wiping them.

I stare up at the ceiling, blinking more tears away as the laughs bubble up again.

I don't think I've laughed this hard in weeks. Not since the King's Guards took me from my home, from my aunt, from my life before.

My chuckle finally begins to die down, and only then do I hear that the rest of the room had gone silent.

I return my gaze forward, and I see what made everyone quiet.

Not a what, but a who.

Killian.

"I'm so sorry. We were–," Jade starts. She stops when the Prince holds up a hand.

"Who's the cake for?" He crosses over to the circular pans. "It looks good."

My hand, on my stomach to curb the laughter, drops to my side, but I keep the other one pointed up, the top of my finger still covered with some frosting that didn't make it onto Sebastian's face. I peer at the fluff, realizing I still haven't tasted it.

My stare moves back to Killian as he makes his way towards the frosting bowl at Jade's side, leaning over it ever so slightly.

Then, his eyes land on me.

"Rowan. It's her birthday tomorrow."

Not even a moment later, he's standing only boot length away, right in front of me.

"What kind is it?"

"Wha-," I begin. But before I can ask what he means, he grabs ahold of my outstretched hand. And frosting still on my finger, he bends down, opening his mouth to stick out his tongue, and licks it clean off.

Oh. My.

I go still, holding my breath. My eyes widen so big I swear they actually pop out of my skull. My mind completely goes blank.

"Hmm. Buttercream," he says, pulling his head back and releasing my hand. He nods his head as he returns to his full height.

"Alright. Carry on. Remember, lights out is in less than an hour."

And with that, he spins around and strolls out of the kitchen.

Once he disappears beyond the door, I stand there, peering at my freshly licked finger in shock. Or perhaps even in awe.

What. The. Hell.

Chapter 27

"Surprise!" we shout in unison at a sleepy Rowan. She sits on Piper's bed, rubbing her eyes.

"It's your favorite! Chocolate!" Piper sing-songs.

The five of us had woken up nearly an hour early this morning in order to finish any last minute touches to the cake.

And to search for candles. Which we couldn't find.

I hold the cake a bit closer to Rowan, showing her the swirls of buttercream along the edges.

Buttercream that I have not been able to stop thinking about.

Because of Killian.

What *was* that last night?

Insane, that's what it was.

I still can't believe rather than using a spoon or even his own finger, he decided to lick the frosting off of my finger.

My face starts to warm as the memory of the interaction floods my mind. I force myself to think of what's in front of me instead. I'll be damned if I drop this cake we worked so hard on.

"We couldn't find any candles but Piper had an idea," Jade explains.

"Here, you can blow this out after we sing to you," Piper says, holding up her pointer finger, a small orange flame rising out of the top.

"Your fire wielding's gotten better," Rowan comments.

Piper smirks at her. "Well, I have a great teacher who's helped me out a lot lately."

"I wonder who that could be…" A thumb and forefinger raise to Rowan's chin as she taps them against her face.

"Time to sing! And then time to dig in!" Asher chimes in, rubbing his hands together as he stares at the cake, licking his lips. On his other side, Sebastian rolls his eyes.

My eyes follow suit and I count off to start the song.

Rowan covers her face as we sing, but I can see her lips tilting up behind her hands.

When we finish, Piper brings her pointer finger in front of the birthday girl's lips, allowing her to blow the flame out.

"So… cake for breakfast?" Rowan asks, peering at each of us.

"Of course, it's the most important meal of the day!" Piper shouts.

The rest of us chuckle before a trunk gets pulled up. I place the cake on it, and we dig into our celebratory breakfast.

Stomachs full, we make our way to the icy training field nearly an hour later.

These early mornings are freezing compared to those nearly a month ago when I first arrived.

Winter is nearly here. Frost fully covers the tips of the grass, and a thin layer of ice covers the sparring mats, along with the targets lined up on the far end of the field. The agility course running down the right side of the field is also slick with frost.

Being this close to the mountains means it gets colder here faster than at home in Knothaven, and I have yet to adapt to the rapidly dropping temperature.

My breath is visible in front of me as I rub my hands up and down my arms. I wear two layers, but without having warmed up yet, I'm still cold. Once we start moving, I'll eventually warm up. But the beginning of training is always the worst.

We all face Killian, who stands upon one of the icy mats with ease.

"I heard it's someone's birthday today, so I have a special treat for you all," he glances at Rowan, a growing smirk on his face.

Then, his eyes land on me.

The air between us is frozen, like the ground beneath our feet, and I don't know what else to do besides stare back at him.

I still don't know what to think of last night.

Before I can attempt to read the thoughts behind his eyes, they move once more, surveying the rest of the trainees.

"Tomorrow you will all be fighting in the arena against Luca's trainees. We want to see how far you all have come. What still needs work. Who needs more work."

His breath puffs a hint of white as he speaks.

"We have paired you all up; one on one matches. We'll be preparing for these fights today."

Groans sweep across the group. His arrogant smirk widens.

"And we will be preparing for these matches… indoors."

At that, the groans turn into sighs of relief and a few whoops of excitement.

Thank goodness.

"I know there's no earth inside, so those of you with the ability will have to go without. However, I had some barrels brought in, so you'll have access to water," the Prince explains when we arrive in the main room we pass through every day.

Another trainer congregates with their trainees on one half of the room, a burly man about ten to fifteen years my senior. Killian leads us past him, to the far side, pointing to an array of sparring mats we can use.

"Pair up. We'll rotate throughout the day. And don't hold back, Luca's trainees won't." He waves his hands, ushering us to start.

Jade and Piper spring onto a mat, with Rowan and Bash on the one to their side. I face Asher at a mat on the women's other side.

We may both be down an ability but we circle one another, ready to strike at a moment's notice regardless.

The sound of boots shuffling fills my ears as we look the other up and down.

Our bottom halves match: slightly baggy, black cargo pants breathable for training and the standard black boots every trainee sports. My loose, dark gray, cap-sleeved tunic and his black top with long sleeves that reach his elbows are the only differences in our clothes.

He attacks first, flicking a sun-kissed arm forward, ripping a lick of water from a barrel and spiraling it at me.

I weave to the right, missing the element. In the same moment, I wave my fingers up, shooting out a flash of light.

He ducks, dodging it. A bright beam of his own flies at me next.

I slide further right, bobbing out of the way.

Feeling for the liquid, I stretch a hand out, and maneuver a wisp of water. It only strikes the top of his bicep as he swerves to avoid the rest.

He runs a hand through hair that had fallen into his eyes at the movement.

We lock gazes, his blue one spearing me as his next move formulates behind his eyes.

But I reach into his mind, grabbing at the top of his shield.

He tries to fight back but it's too late, I slip my hand inside, forcing his body still.

I hold him in my grasp and slowly push him to the ground. He's strong, and fighting to slam his mind's wall up.

My neck aches as I tense up, focusing on bending him to his knees.

He pushes and shoves, his shield of crystal blue ocean waves collides with my palms.

My fingers slip backwards, releasing a hair of control over his mind.

Heavy and powerful, the walls within his head force me out. Just enough to where he can use an arm again.

Crap.

As soon as I spot his wrist moving, a wave of ice cold water crashes into me. The second the liquid hits me, the power I have over his mind disappears.

I slam to the ground, landing on the curve of my hip with a crunching thud.

I yelp with the impact.

Damn that hurt.

I rub at my side, peering up at Asher who winces at my position, his sky blue eyes immediately full of apology.

My hope of winning my match tomorrow dwindles.

I am *not* looking forward to this fight.

I bite my lip as I watch a fireball barrel towards Rowan's head. She easily takes hold of the approaching flame and uses it against her opponent, hurling it back.

I let out a sigh of relief as she catches the attack.

The woman from Luca's group of trainees matched against Rowan is the same blonde-headed bitch I fought on my first day here, before we were split into groups.

Amaya.

Her ego has only seemed to grow after her time spent training with the second-in-command.

She's putting up one hell of a fight against Rowan.

She's sneaky, trying to trick my friend in the arena. But Rowan's smarter.

Yesterday, Killian warned us that other trainees may try to sneak in tricks here and there. He was right so far, and Rowan is only the first to go.

The Prince called it a "belated birthday gift" for her when he selected her to begin.

I had rolled my eyes at the comment.

When they stepped into the ring, Amaya had immediately tried using mind wielding on her, just as she did with me those few weeks ago. But Rowan's strong, even though she doesn't share the power.

Rowan had wrapped her shadows so tightly around Amaya's head, she screamed and began flailing her arms around wildly, shooting blasts of air and fire in every direction.

And now, Amaya was pissed.

She's lobbing fireball after fireball across the arena. But Rowan easily takes control of every one thrown her way.

Rowan's dark braids are tied back into a single, larger one, in her usual fighting style. It whips to the side as she spins around, twisting and growing the sphere of flames launched at her into one three times the original size.

A grin grows on my face.

She's about to kick Amaya's ass. *Atta girl.*

Rowan is the strongest fire wielder I have ever seen, and her opponent has no idea what she's gotten herself into.

The orange and red sphere releases from Rowan's control, heading straight towards the blonde.

Amaya stretches out her arms, in an attempt to grab ahold of the element, but the flame is flying at her too quickly.

At the last moment, her eyes widen and she attempts to duck out of the way. The heat scorches her shoulder, and singes the tips of her straw-colored bob.

The scream coming out of her an instant later makes me clamp my hands over my ears.

She falls to the floor on her knees, gripping her shoulder tightly as choked sobs release from her mouth.

Rowan stills for a moment, her own eyes of golden rings blowing wide, then jogs over to the woman on the sandy side of the arena. However, she's met with a gaze full of rage.

She ignores the look Amaya gives her and picks up a sphere of water from the stream running through the middle of the space. The globe of liquid levitates through the air, to their position on the ground.

I see Rowan's lips move but I can't make out what she says. Her voice seems to be a hushed whisper as she speaks to the woman still glaring at her.

Just before the glob of water is placed onto the burn to cool it, something makes Amaya's face twist up.

The next thing I know, her fist connects with Rowan's jaw.

The liquid under Rowan's control drops to the floor in a splash as she flies backward by the force. She lands propped up on her side, an arm outstretched underneath her for balance. The shocked look on Rowan's face rapidly morphs to one of fury.

The blonde, now with a crooked bob from the singed section of her hair, sits in the same place, a wide smirk on her face.

My jaw drops before I can control the movement.

Woah. What's her problem?

Rowan is up in an instant, not bothering to even touch her face to assess the damage.

Black swirls of smoke fill the floor of the arena in seconds, and a copy of Amaya's disgraceful smirk grows on Rowan's face.

The thick darkness rises instantaneously, covering them whole in the next second.

And then, Amaya lets out a blood curdling scream.

A few feet down from my spot in the balcony overlooking the arena, I hear movement, and twist my head to the sound.

Killian is up on his feet, heading towards the door that hides the staircase leading to the arena. Luca stays in his seat, next to where the Prince had been sitting, arms folded and a scowl on his pale face.

Before Killian can grab ahold of the door's handle, the entrance swings open, revealing a smug Rowan.

My open mouth closes, twisting into a grin.

He lets her pass by him as she heads straight for the five of us clumped together in the first row. His lips tilt up in amusement while watching her, then faces away to finally descend the stairs.

We all stand at the same time to greet Rowan when she approaches. When her golden-ringed brown eyes land on us, her grin grows wider.

And out of the corner of my vision, I notice the shadows dissipate in the arena.

"I didn't even do anything. She just seems to be scared of the dark," Rowan laughs, shrugging her shoulders.

Laughter echoes all around as we join her.

Piper is the first to wrap her up in a hug, swaying side to side, and I hear the strawberry blonde call her a "badass bitch."

As soon as they release, I sneak in for an embrace of my own. I squeeze her tightly and my eyes float behind her, to the opposite side of the arena, to the nearly empty seats aside from a small clump of King's Guards.

I couldn't look over there when we first entered the arena. I couldn't let it be a distraction. But now, as I hug Rowan, I have nowhere else to look. Nowhere else but the half dozen guards surrounding the vile man himself, King Kairos.

Killian told us only moments before we arrived that the King would be in attendance.

I swore to myself I wouldn't acknowledge the bastard. But here I am.

Heated fury spirals in my gut as I glare at him.

The arena's lighting hits the gold of his crown, making it shine, and irresistible to stare at, no matter how much I hate him.

Upon letting go, a beaming smile blooms on my face as I refocus on my friend, my eyes purposely averting the opposite side of the arena.

"You did amazing. Shame on her for hitting you when all you were trying to do was help cool her burn. She'll get what's coming to her in the end," I say, briefly inspecting her jaw.

Her deep bronze skin is mostly unscathed, aside from a small, growing bit of purple just to the right of her chin.

"She absolutely will," Rowan agrees, bringing me in for another quick squeeze.

We let go and I spy Asher grinning from ear to ear at my side.

"She was scared shitless in those shadows. It was hilarious! And totally deserved," he says excitedly, wrapping an arm around her shoulders, talking with his other hand.

I peer down at the arena while Asher talks with Rowan, and I hear Jade, and even Sebastian, chime in too.

Amaya is being helped by Killian to the exit, his hand covered in a lumpy ball of flowing water pressed to her burnt shoulder. Her head is hung low, avoiding eye contact.

But the Prince's face is stoic, unmoving as they leave the expansive space.

Chapter 28

Killian hadn't returned yet by the time Luca abruptly stands up, calling for the next match to begin. He turns to face our still-standing group. His barely-there blonde eyebrows that match his long braid come together, inspecting us.

"You," he says, pointing. "Freckled blondie. You're up."

Piper shoots him a pointed look then rolls her eyes.

Luca faces away from us, signaling to one of his male trainees. He must be her opponent.

The selected dark-haired man rubs his hands together menacingly as he stares at Piper, wiggling his eyebrows. Her eyes roll once again.

Piper approaches the door but before she can enter, the man, whose black hair is gathered in a low ponytail, snatches the handle first, pushing his way in front of her.

As I briefly inspect him, I notice he stands perhaps an inch above her. And she's only a bit taller than the average woman.

I chuckle. His attitude aligns *perfectly* with that of an insecure man who is compensating for what he lacks.

In the arena, his attitude doesn't do him any favors.

He throws wildly uncontrolled blasts of water at her. Blasts mainly aimed for her head.

Piper's movements are fluid, avoiding the anger-fueled attacks with ease.

Her typically spirited attacks are contained as she lets him tire himself out, only sending a beam of light his way a few times, compared to his dozens of attacks.

She then swirls her finger in a figure-eight motion, and a ring of burning flames surrounds his feet.

A smirk plays at her lips as he peers down, his head springing back up with ferocity. He glares daggers at her, and promptly sprays the fire with water from the stream.

His arm stretches out in her direction, and a trail of darkness leaves his fingertips, forming the shape of a whip. He draws his hand back, preparing to crack it.

The two strawberry blonde french braids fly behind Piper's head as she spins her hands in a giant, circular motion in front of her, creating a shield of blinding light.

The dark whip flies toward her, hitting the bright shield, the defense mechanism holding.

And before he can use the shadow whip again, she pushes the shield, launching it at him.

His face goes slack, and the light collides with him, sending him through the air.

The darkness stretching from his hand instantly disappears and he crashes onto his side so far away he could touch the wall of the arena if he were to reach out for it.

He sits up slowly, with a grunt. His left arm hangs uselessly at his side, like an overcooked noodle.

Yikes. That one's definitely got to hurt.

The moment he spots it himself, he shrieks, piercing the entire colosseum's ears.

A huff of annoyance releases from someone nearby, and I turn to see Killian. He must've returned at some point during the fight.

His sharp, stubbled jaw works from side to side as he appears to assess the man's injury. And a few moments later, he sighs, heading for the arena's door once more.

I face the pitch below when I hear curses and insults being spewed.

Oh damn, he's not just in pain, he's pissed.

My friend's opponent is on his feet, clutching his injured arm with the other one.

His once neat ponytail is a mess. He's seemingly yelling any insult or curse word coming to mind at Piper, who backs away from him as he tries to approach her.

She narrows her light green eyes on him, watching his every move, waiting to see if he'll take a strike of revenge.

I don't blame her. His words are swiftly turning into threats.

She reaches the exit the same moment Killian enters the wide space. She flicks a single braid over a shoulder then waves to her opponent, her eyes now relaxed and a sugary sweet smile upon her freckled face.

After a round of hugs and high fives with our group's newest champion, I notice Luca staring at us once more. His eyes flick back and forth.

And with Killian gone to help the dark-haired man to wherever the infirmary is, the second-in-command points in our direction, again.

He summons Sebastian next, pairing him with a muscular, bulky man who wears a buzz cut, and a scar through his eyebrow.

Physically, the man is Bash's opposite.

Sebastian may be significantly leaner than his opponent, but he is skilled; naturally talented. He rarely struggles during training, and he put up one hell of a fight his first day here.

Clearly, Luca either didn't notice or he doesn't care.

The match between them is rather short. The bulky man stands too heavy on his feet. Whereas Sebastian is lithe and light-footed.

The man sends huge rocks and boulders flying, but Bash easily dodges the pieces of earth.

He flicks his wrists in return, twisting a wave of pitch black darkness around his opponent, sending the man spinning.

He's able to whirl the man around again and again, the giant man's defense entirely nonexistent. When the man eventually collapses from dizziness, Sebastian stops.

Did Luca even train him at all?

Most people in the stands snicker when the man falls, myself included.

The laughs then turn into groans as he begins vomiting from his place on the ground. And with that, Sebastian swiftly leaves the arena, his tawny face twisting with disgust.

"I'll let *you* get that one."

I hear the words and turn, the Prince speaking to his second-in-command. He must have returned mid-match once again.

I watch as Luca lets out a huff, crossing his arms like a toddler, and stomps into the arena.

Now that it's Killian's turn to pick who follows, he only peers at our group briefly before deciding on others.

A few turns later, Jade is chosen.

She fights against a woman with curly, red hair who wields air at her the moment they step foot in the arena.

Once she discovers Jade wields the same, when a tornado of wind forms around her at the hands of the petite, black-bobbed woman, she switches to her other abilities.

First, she punches a flurry of yellow and orange flames at Jade.

The fire never connects as Jade blocks it with a wave of water.

The redhead tries again, this time with three punches in a row, but Jade bobs and weaves, avoiding the fireballs.

The woman's frustration is seemingly growing, as she then sends six more flames full of fury at my friend.

My jaw goes slack at the sudden aggression, and I sit on the edge of my seat, hoping Jade can dodge them all.

She's light on her feet when gathering her defense. With a swift sweep of her arms, columns of water stretch up into the air on her side of the dividing river. In rapid concession, the half dozen blazes fizzle out, the liquid extinguishing them all.

Jade spins, dropping the water and kicking her foot out, blasting the woman with a gust of wind from the bottom of her boot.

The curly redhead flies through the air, but lands crouched on the ground.

She stands to her full height and changes to using light, shooting a beam in the direction of Jade's face.

Lifting her hand up straight in front of her, Jade lets the shining light smack against another raised, wide column of water.

In the next moment, Jade pushes off the ground, jumping into the air with a twirl, and kicks each leg out, one at a time, propelling two massive gusts of wind at her opponent.

The woman soars backwards, landing hard on her back in the grassy part of the space. She doesn't get up from her spot.

Oh no.

I squint my eyes to investigate closer.

Her chest rises and falls. She's still breathing, but she's knocked out cold.

Killian and Luca both move towards the arena, after Jade runs over to her. Jade carefully brushes curls out of the woman's face, watching her inhale and exhale in her sleep-like position.

A few minutes later, the redhead sits up, catching her breath. She slowly but surely follows the rest of them back into the colosseum's stands. She must have refused to go to the infirmary.

Two more matches go by, and then Asher is picked, matched with a man of similar stature who has short, black hair.

The fight seems to be never ending between them.

Their match has been going for at least twenty minutes now, and while they're equally covered in sweat and dirt, neither one looks to be giving up any time soon.

The two men were not only alike in build, but also in powers. Both wield water, earth, and light.

Where the Prince and his second-in-command sit a few seats down, Luca has his hands on his knees, intensely staring at the pair in the arena. Killian sits with his arms crossed over his broad chest, his usual position. His tanned face remains flat and calm.

Luca's appearing more and more on edge with each fight that passes.

Because his trainees keep losing. And he seems to be counting on this one to be a win for him.

My attention returns to the pit below, and I spy a sneaky trick from my friend's opponent.

The large man builds a wave of river water with one hand, and with his other, he tosses in countless rocks and pebbles, discreetly mixing them into the liquid.

As the wave comes crashing down, Asher is able to avoid most of it, but the wall of earth he conjures in front of him isn't high enough to stop all of the water from reaching him.

Several pieces of the earth rain down on him, along with the liquid. His sun-tanned face scrunches up as he takes the beating.

Asher then rises to his feet, arms stretched out wide. Water swells up in front of him. The rising water spans nearly the entire stream along the middle of the arena's massive space.

Before Asher's opponent can react, the liquid, now nearly three times the man's height, circles around him, encasing him within.

He thrashes around in the sphere of clear liquid, or at least as fast as one can move while being fully submerged underwater.

The whooshing of the water grows louder as it spins around and around. Asher works his arms in circles in front of him, his body swaying, moving with the motion of the water he controls.

Asher's face is sweaty but calm as he lifts the ball off the ground, his opponents feet now several inches away from the muddy surface he once stood on. The man's eyes go wide, panic covering his face.

I have to force myself to bite back a giggle at his predicament.

Once the sphere is higher off the ground than Asher is tall does he finally drop his control of the water, and his opponent.

The man crashes to the ground, and it becomes clear Asher is the winner of this match when the black-haired man stays on the floor, hacking up water for several minutes straight.

Trainee after trainee is then chosen to fight in the arena.

I force my eyes on the sparring the entire time, refusing to let myself acknowledge the King once more.

I wait for my turn, my hands fidgeting more and more as I continue to not be called.

I knew it. He's going to leave me for last. Again.

I swear, I'm going to kill him for making me wait until the end.

Eventually, I'm the only one left from Killian's group, unsurprising to me. And a woman with light brown curls sits down the way, the lone one from Luca's group of trainees who hasn't been matched yet either.

The second-in-command is fuming from his place beside the Prince. Only three of his trainees have won their fights, and it clearly has him riled up.

Killian's face remained mostly neutral throughout all of the matches, but a small smirk arose on his lips once in a while, each time one of his trainees won a fight.

"You know who's up next! Get down there!" Luca shouts over his shoulder to us.

I'm on my feet in an instant. The irritation seeping through his tone is not to be argued with.

"Good luck," Piper says, grabbing and squeezing my hand.

"You got this," Rowan whispers encouragingly, patting my arm as I leave.

I reach for the door's handle but a cough sounds behind me. I twist to find Killian staring down at me.

"Don't let the presence of my father distract you. Ignore him, and focus on the task at hand," he says at a near-whisper. His brows relax, flattening from their scrunched up position as he takes me in.

I meet his soft blue eyes for only a moment before I look down, nodding my head. I bite back on the words that want to fall from my lips.

You can be a bit of a distraction too.

Especially after our run-in at the library.

I nod once more and turn to the door. My hand collides with the metal handle, ready to pull it open.

At the same time, his palm slides atop my hand, his fingers brushing against my own.

I pull my arm away, allowing him to open the door for me. And I don't dare to look back before stepping onto the staircase.

My heart beats faster with each step I descend. My pulse races throughout my body, the soles of my feet pounding, the top of my head throbbing. My stomach twists, then plummets.

I wasn't even this nervous on my first day here.

But I can't let any of this get to me. I *have* to focus. I'm not planning on finding out where the infirmary is today.

I push open the heavy door, the light momentarily blinding me when I step onto the dusty surface of one half of the arena.

My opponent, Carmen, as I hear from the shouts of encouragement for her, is already there, standing on the grassy side of the space.

The sounds of crunching dirt beneath my boots and the soft rippling of the creek washes over me as I take up my own side, and I instantly feel calmer. I focus on the sounds of nature, reaching for the feel of the flora and fauna throughout the arena. And I focus on the task at hand.

I stop a few paces from the stream and take in Carmen's stance. Her knees are already bent, hands up to cover her face.

Her gaze narrows on me. Her hand swoops out to the side, and I throw an arm out, letting light splay from my palm, hoping my attack beats hers.

My bright beam collides with a wisp of pitch black shadows, the two nearly bouncing off each other.

I bring my other hand out, reaching for the earth beneath her feet. Vines crash up from out of the ground, wrapping around her calves and thighs.

She tries to rip at them with one hand. With the other, she flicks her fingers, swirling a gust of sand-filled wind my way.

I duck, pulling a wall of earth up from the dirt in front of me for cover.

Her strike slams against my makeshift shield.

I peek around the barricade when I hear the wind cease its attack and lock my gaze with hers as she rips off the last vine.

I try to push into her mind and her brown eyes widen. Her mind locks up almost instantly, the shields I yank on not budging.

Damn.

I tug harder, and harder, trying to pry into her mind. My breathing deepens with my focus. Come on, come on, come on.

Sweat begins dripping from my forehead, running down my temples, then my cheeks.

While I pull on her frustratingly solid shield, I twist my foot on the ground, springing up the earth from underneath one of her own booted feet, throwing her off balance.

She stumbles to the side, her focus on her mind's wall faltering.

And I take my opportunity.

I stretch my fingers into her mind, clawing at it, flooding it with images of spiders and bugs, insects covering her body.

She lets out a yelp, smacking her legs, then her arms. Another cry releases from her and she spins, wiping at her back.

A chuckle escapes my lips as I hold on tight to her mind. I slowly make my way towards her, my control growing stronger as I close in on her.

Her yelling increases in volume, and the sound starts to hurt my ears.

She hits herself again and again in a frenzied panic. She brushes her hair out of the way frantically. She itches any spot she can reach, her fingernails leaving marks on her bare arms.

I twist a finger, barely flicking it out from my hand, waving growing vines around her boots, then her legs, and up her torso, the green plants locking around her tight.

Her eyes find mine again and she snaps out of the hallucination.

Ugh. I didn't pay enough attention to it as I grew the pieces of earth over her body.

She slams her mind's shield most of the way up but I fight to keep it at least a hair ajar, my claws digging in.

Prying the wall down as much as I can, I create the itchy feeling of the insects crawling on her again.

A muscle in her neck quivers as she twitches left, then right. Her movements become harder, jerking to either side, as if she's trying to shake the bothersome feeling away.

A bead of sweat drips down my lips, the saltiness reaching my tongue, the struggle to hold onto her mind becoming more apparent the longer I hold on.

She releases a battle cry, closing her eyes and crunching her fingers into her curls, pulling at her scalp.

Then, her mind's shield slams closed.

I step back with the force of my power coming back into my body. My lungs burn as I take a deep inhale, gasping for air.

My palms reach out straight when I refocus on the plant creeping up more than half of her body.

I yank on the vines, pulling her forward, and into the river at the toes of my boots. The splash sprays the bottom of my dark pants.

She comes up soaking wet a moment later, liquid dripping from her once bouncy curls. Before she can move to throw out an attack, I jerk the vines once more, removing her from the water.

I circle my arms outward, forcing the greenery backwards, towards the awaiting trees several paces away.

With her arms still loose at her sides, she sends a tendril of darkness at my feet.

I don't allow it to reach me, shifting to the side while twisting the vines, spinning her along the ground.

She releases the shadows as she's dragged further back. A series of frustrated grunts and yelps escape her at the movement.

My boots hit the water of the creek, and I walk through it, meeting the green, grassy half of the expansive space.

Carmen twists on her own, and folds her hands together, creating a spinning ball of air. She launches the wind at me but I dodge it, sliding to the side while I have the vines tug her towards the closest, towering, thick tree.

One hand holds onto the plants circling her and with my other, I throw an orb of water, soaking her even more after her short time in the river.

Her feet reach the trunk of the tree and I drag the vines up the bark. The rest of her body follows, sliding up and up until she dangles upside down, fully off the ground.

She screams, flailing her arms as she starts to swing side to side.

I wrap my greenery around the lowest hanging branch, a few feet higher than my head. I draw them tight, raising her feet until the soles nearly touch the underside of the branch.

After securing the vines, I finally release my hold on the crawling plant and let out a breath.

My palms go to my hips as I observe my opponent, drawing air deep into my lungs. I can finally relax now, and focus on my breathing.

Wow. I did it. A smile cracks on my face, hurting my cheeks.

Carmen's swaying has stopped and now she spins slowly in a circle, hardly moving aside from her mouth gaping open and then closing.

I think it's safe to say she's a bit surprised at her predicament.

Satisfied, I make my way to the exit, and to my awaiting friends in the stands. Friends who I can hear going wild before I make it even a few paces away from my opponent.

The five of them greet me at the top of the stairs and I'm immediately sandwiched between Rowan and Piper, where a laugh is squished out of me.

The two of them, Jade, and Asher all talk at once as they release me from the hug. Bash beams at me, which for him means the smile he points my way actually shows off his teeth. Compared to the small, closed-mouth smirks we all typically get from him, I'll take this as a major win.

The sentiment of it fills my heart and my own smile widens impossibly further.

"Alright, alright, settle down," Killian booms, an impressed grin on his face.

The genuine smile has me going still, intrigued.

He then surveys his entire group of eighteen trainees.

Out of the corner of my eye, I spot Luca's trainees filing out of the stands, and the trainer himself is in the arena, cutting Carmen down from the tree.

"Since *most* of you won your matches today," Killian says, staring down the few who didn't. "You all get the rest of the day off."

Celebratory cheers erupt through the gathered crowd.

"However, those of you who didn't win will be getting a private lesson from me tomorrow, after our regularly scheduled training."

Most of us go silent as the three who lost groan to themselves.

Killian nods, officially releasing us for the day. Then his eyes move to me.

I step away from my still-celebrating friends when I notice he starts towards me.

"Impressive finale," he comments, folding his arms over his chest.

"Why thank you. I didn't let *anything* or *anyone* distract me. And I think I really tapped into what you taught me during *our* private lessons. I'm sure those who have one tomorrow will learn a lot," I joke.

I dip my head to the opposite side of the arena, where I spy movement out of the corner of my eye. But I don't dare turn my gaze in the direction of the King.

He nods his head, lips tilting up in one corner. "I can see that. Just be careful when holding on to a person's mind for an extended period of time. It will drain you quickly in battle."

Ah, there it is. Always the teacher, the trainer.

The sky blue tones in his irises swirl with silver as he investigates me.

"Sir, yes sir," I respond with a salute. Then a chuckle escapes me. And this time, he's the one to roll his eyes.

Chapter 29

Whispers fill the dining hall once more when a few others from Killian's training group walk in. The six of us had been first to experience all the voices hushing into soft tones nearly twenty minutes ago when we came in.

Apparently, word had gotten around fast that the vast majority of us from the Prince's batch of trainees kicked ass yesterday against Luca's group.

Our matches were first, in the early morning. Then, the rest of the trainers had paired up, matching their trainees against one another throughout the late morning and afternoon.

Come to find out, most of the training groups walked away with only half of their match's wins; we were the only ones to have won nearly every fight.

And while many seemed impressed, some were not very happy about our achievement. Rumors were being spread, based on the belief that we received special treatment from Killian, but they couldn't be more wrong.

Dirty, wary glares were pointed our way as we feasted on our breakfast.

Asher even had his shoulder slammed into in the serving line. He blazed with rage at the man. Jade and I were forced to convince him to brush it off, unless he wanted it to escalate into a fight. Which then would have all of us facing disciplinary action. And with what he faced before he was brought to join Killian's group, he wasn't too hard to persuade.

However, the Prince is not amongst those unhappy with our new status. He actually wears a convincing grin on his face when we meet him outside after our meal.

Thankfully, the temperature today is more tolerable than as of late. My breath is still fogging, but only slightly. My lungs aren't burning cold with every single breath I inhale.

Killian's grin widens, unbelievably so, as we settle into place in front of him, waiting for today's schedule.

His toothy smile shows off his perfect, straight, white teeth. A pair of dimples show in his tan skin, one on either side of his mouth.

Surprise settles under my skin. I never expected those.

With his usual grumpy or stoic features, his face remains mostly flat aside from sly smirks he points my way once in a while when his ego shines through.

They suit him.

"I appreciate that the majority of you didn't embarrass me yesterday."

I stifle a giggle threatening to bubble up. He sure does have a way with words.

"Those who did, know your extra time spent with me will be time well spent."

I hear a loud gulp from someone behind me, someone who must be awaiting that extra time later today.

"I remember those days, I'm glad they're behind me," I say sarcastically, under my breath, to Rowan. She shakes her head, but her lips raise at my comment.

"Now," he continues. "I don't enjoy telling you this, but there have recently been attacks at our border with Norfell. In the White Mountains."

His face drops, going somber yet stony at the delivery of this news.

Attacks. He said *attacks*. Plural.

So there must have been more since the one we overheard him and Luca discussing.

"There have been three attacks from our northern neighbor. And while two may have been a coincidence, we've decided three is most definitely a pattern."

My mouth gapes at the information but I shut it when I notice a light cloud of mist form in front of my face.

"In light of these recent events, today I will start having you spar in teams of two. When you are eventually sent out on patrol, or one day even into battle if the time comes, it can be vital, even a means of life or death, to work with one another against attackers."

Chills run down my arms, the hair there standing on edge.

Battle. My stomach rolls. Nausea spreads up my esophagus.

Battle.

With these attacks on the border, it's now a real possibility. Even after having over a century of peace across the world. No two kingdoms have been at odds in well over one hundred years.

I focus on my breathing, in and out. Allowing the cold to fill up my lungs more purposefully, letting myself be distracted by the coolness, pushing the thought from my mind.

Battle is a possibility I will think about at a later time.

"Aurora and Sebastian."

My head raises to the sound of my name being called, pulling me from my concentrated breathing. Killian jerks his head to the side, eyeing us.

Oh, we've been partnered.

Bash gently places a hand on my shoulder, guiding me forward, onto a nearby mat.

Over the following several hours, we rotate as pairs.

Rowan and Asher were paired together, and when it's Bash's and my turn to spar them, we have to fight against the urge to go far too easy on one another.

We face off against Jade and her partner, a tall woman with a blonde pixie cut who is light on her feet, much like my dark-haired friend who she's teamed up with.

Some time later we're matched against Piper, who had been paired with a young, lanky man with dreadlocks.

We repeat the same order of matches again after Killian sends us to lunch, eventually sparring every team twice.

I plop down on the edge of the mat when we finish sparring. The edge digs into the curve of my ass, so I adjust slightly, my body sore enough already.

The last thing I need is another part of me hurting. Muscles in my arms and legs ache with the sheer amount of fighting we've done today.

Bash joins me as I wiggle into a more comfortable position.

Sweat drips down the side of my face, and every other crevice of my body, even in the chilly afternoon.

I am horribly glad to be finished. My powers are also feeling drained.

In the first round of matches, Killian told us to solely use our abilities. But for the second, weapons, fists, and whatever else one could come up with, was fair play too.

I stare blankly at my booted feet stretched out in front of me in the dying winter grass.

Exhaustion is hitting harder after this second round of sparring. Getting used to fighting with weapons wasn't nearly as easy as honing my powers and using those.

Sebastian however, is the opposite. Not only are his abilities strong, but his usage of weaponry is admirable. The way he so confidently uses blades of all shapes and sizes, even though he leans towards the star-shaped throwing blades laying at his feet.

He inspects them each closely, wiping them as necessary with the backs of fingerless gloves he's started sporting in the cooler weather. Once each blade seems clear of debris, he places them in a neat pile to the side.

"I know what you said about having to fight but, where'd you learn to be so good with blades?"

Without turning to face me, he replies, "My father was a blacksmith and we lived above the shop. When my mother died after giving birth to my brother, we practically lived in the shop with him."

My eyebrows nearly met my hairline at the disclosure. And the sheer number of words that left his mouth at once.

I can't believe he's confiding in me about something so personal. A mixture of shock and honor sift through me.

I right my face before replying, "I'm sorry about your mother."

His lips pull tight, and a quick nod of his head follows.

"It was a long time ago. It's been a long time since all of them."

"Since all of wha-" My question is cut off by Killian gathering our attention.

I'm too tired to stand but Bash reaches his hands down after he rises, and pulls me to my feet.

I truly loathe sparring.

"Your teamwork is coming along nicely," Killian remarks. "But let's see how you do against me."

"What?" Piper instinctively responds, annoyed.

My gaze snaps to her.

She slaps a freckled hand over her mouth when she realizes she hadn't meant to say the word aloud.

"Thank you for volunteering your team to go first Piper," the Prince says, smirking at her, then her partner, and gesturing for them to follow him onto the mat in the center of all of the others.

Her partner, whose name I've since learned is Iver, glares at her. Piper groans, squeezing her eyes shut momentarily, then opens them, walking behind Killian and her partner to the space.

Iver attacks first, sending a wave of cool, clear liquid flying at Killian.

The Prince's face still holds a smirk, like he expected one of them to start the fight.

Killian takes hold of the water, throwing it back at the lanky man.

Piper uses the opportunity of her partner being drenched to fire off a ball of blinding light at Killian.

But his hand shoots up, covering his face, and a sphere of shadows springs from his palm. The void captures the brightness, enveloping it in its entirety.

Fire then releases out of Killian's opposite hand, just in time to meet a whip of water hurling his way from Iver.

The two elements clash, slamming together to create an explosion of steam.

Clouds of white push up and outward. Several of us beside the mat step back as it wafts towards us.

I briefly cover my face, blocking the steam. When I pull my hands down, I try viewing the mat. I can barely make out the three figures amongst the thick mist. My eyes squinting, I attempt to see what attacks are thrown next.

A few moments later, a gust of wind blows the haze away, clearing the image. The air blows the fog outwards, towards us, from inside the commotion.

Waving the mist from my face, I focus on the picture in front of me.

Piper and Iver sit back to back, strips of shadows wrapped around their torsos, tying them together.

The ribbons of darkness swirl over their bodies, their arms locked down in place. Their legs are stretched out before them, with more of the long pieces of obsidian bandaging their limbs to one another. Even their mouths are covered by a thick strip of the swirling darkness.

They tug at their restraints, to no avail. Killian stands behind them, looking down at the two. He shakes his head and crosses his arms over his chest, as if it was all too easy beating them. Then, he peers up at the rest of us.

"Who's next?"

One after the other, pairs are called to spar against Killian.

Some of the teams put up a rather good fight, but no one even comes close to beating him. The years of training he has been through far outweigh the month we've had.

Not that I'm surprised, even in the slightest. He may push my buttons, and irritate the living hell out of me, but he's a machine.

My mind wonders. When did he start honing his skills? Was it when his father was crowned king? It couldn't have been much longer after he took the throne, since the decree declaring all multiwielders must submit themselves to the King's Army at eighteen came only a week after King Kairos's father, King Amos, passed away.

Although, the King clearly doesn't abide by his own adult-only army rules, as we've learned.

My mind spins at the discovery still.

Killian swears he never knew of it, and as much as I'm inclined to not believe a word he says, I do. I do believe him. Something in my very bones tells me it's the truth.

My stomach flips and flutters as I think of his words. How he caged me in against the wall of the palace.

I push that thought away instantly, allowing other questions to fill my head.

When did Killian become in charge of the King's Army anyways? When did his father decide to have his only son run his military? I would assume the Prince must have been practicing for years ahead of his being appointed to the position.

The running list of questions come to a screeching halt when someone nudges my shoulder.

My eyes fly up from where they had been locked onto the ground, glazed over in thought. Focusing my vision, I see Sebastian and Killian giving me pointed looks.

"It's our turn already?" I whisper, leaning towards Bash.

"Everyone else has gone."

Oops.

I follow his lead, stepping up onto the slightly raised, charcoal gray sparring mat.

Blinking, I focus on the task at hand. I lower my center of gravity, bending my knees enough to where I can be ready to move in a split second. I twist my boots and bounce on the balls of my feet.

Killian launches the first attack, blasting the two of us with a gust of wind, forcing us to skid to the back of the mat.

Feeling the earth beneath the mat and the expansive space around it, I reach out, calling for it to assist me.

I stretch my arms downward, wiggling my fingers. Pulling up, the blades of grass to the east and west thicken instantly, twisting together to form six stretching vines.

The greenery from the left fly at him first, attempting to grab ahold of him.

Without even looking, the Prince hits them with a wave of fire, burning them to a crisp.

His attention is on Bash, who spins shadows from his fingertips.

Darkness flings back and forth, spiraling all around.

I take this as my chance to creep my plants in, slowly this time.

I flick my wrist, gathering a tendril of water from an awaiting barrel, and send it soaring at Killian.

My other hand holds tight to the crawling pieces of earth, pushing them closer to the far side of the mat.

The liquid I release weaves and warps around the shadows, splashing the lower half of his body when another flame from his palm doesn't reach it in time.

My first vine swipes across the toe of one of his boots, stretching for his laces.

Before the slithering greenery can go any further, I feel claws yank at my mind's shields.

A yelp springs from my throat at the sharpness, and the earth under my control flops to the ground as I focus on my mind.

I push against him, but he's so strong.

Then, my vision goes dark, and my body tenses. I can't move. And it's not of my own doing.

Killian's taken hold of my mind.

Shit.

He slides in with ease, fingertips pushing past the edge of my shield, gripping claws around the entirety of my head.

The muscles in my neck and shoulders burn as I try to fight him, shoving the wall of my mind upward.

I'm forced to a kneel on the ground, my sight still gone, and I push harder to seal the gap in my mind's shield.

The opening starts to close, but it's going too slow.

I relax my body, letting him fully control my muscles, rather than fight back, and focus solely on my mind.

My breathing shutters when I pull in a new, deep breath to concentrate. I shove and yank the wall up some more. With all my might I push. And push. And push even harder.

I feel sweat dripping from my forehead with the force I use.

I'm almost there. Only a sliver of a gap remains.

I feel my vision returning when flashes of orange and yellow appear through my closed eyelids.

Just a little bit more now.

My neck strains and my head begins to throb with effort as I finish closing the shield, locking it airtight.

I open my eyes. My vision is blurry, only vague shapes and colors.

I fall forward onto my hands, panting. My brain hurts, and my head pounds even harder.

Damn Killian and his powers.

In the next moment, Bash lands on his stomach in front of me with an "oof" followed by a grunt. His hands are behind his back, wrapped together with long tendrils of greenery.

Peering up, Killian stands only a pace away, fingers swiping through strands of chocolate waves that came undone from his typical half-up style.

"So, you like my vines after all?" I ask, my question heavy with sarcasm when I lift my chin in Bash's direction.

"I guess you could say they're *growing* on me," he responds, a tilt of his lips going up, along with a shoulder.

I sit back on my knees, shaking my head. I use the little strength I have left to hold back a chuckle that threatens to bubble out my throat.

I can't believe he just used an earth wielding pun on me.

Instead of replying to the terrible pun, I lean forward to untie a grumpy, defeated Sebastian. He mumbles a "thanks" after he sits up, rubbing his wrists.

Killian's voice rumbles across the field then. "You're all dismissed."

Bash stands, but before he can extend his hand out for mine, another one appears in my vision.

Killian's.

Bash's eyes widen momentarily, and he withdraws his limb, taking several steps back.

I eye the slightly calloused, tan hand.

Oh what the hell.

I grab it, allowing him to help me up.

Only when I stand, he doesn't let go. He keeps my hand in his own, leaning closer, bringing himself into my space.

"Don't let your shield down even an inch. You never know who may want to enter that pretty little mind of yours at any given time."

I- What?

My head involuntarily jerks back, and I stare at him with wide eyes, my heart picking up speed.

The braid I have in fails me, and a piece of my caramel hair falls forward into my line of sight.

His other hand reaches up, tucking the loose strand behind my ear.

My insides twist and sink at the motion.

My mouth opens to say something, but I don't know what.

I close it to think of what to say. But not a single word comes to me. I don't know how to respond to such a genuine, gentle act from a usually stony man.

I blink, holding my gaze with his own sapphire and silver one. A gaze that forces me to crane my neck up with his proximity.

I'm still unable to formulate a reply when he continues.

"I guess we'll have to keep working on your training, perhaps your private lesson days *aren't* behind you." He winks, then releases his grip on my limb.

I stand there on the sparring mat, dumbfounded, as he turns and walks away across an empty training yard.

Chapter 30

"Come on Jade, you can do it!"

I peer up at her as she climbs the near vertical wall, stretching to reach the next metal peg high above her head.

A strong, early winter breeze passes through when she grabs ahold of the rung she reaches for. She pauses, waiting for the wind to pass.

Biting my lip, I watch her extend an arm again, searching for a new peg.

This course has been difficult on all of us, but this wall is what Jade tends to struggle with the most. The grip on the metal rungs is already poor, and her petite limbs are making it difficult for her to climb.

She nears the top of the wall, where Asher waits. He cheers down words of encouragement I can't fully make out when another breeze crosses through.

"Just go already," Silas grumbles behind me, urging me to climb behind Jade.

"Shut *up*."

I don't turn to face him when I speak. Instead, I shift closer, blocking his way if he were to try and sneak past me to ascend the wall.

The team sparring we've been doing the past few days has yet to make Silas much less of an asshole.

Asher sticks an arm down, and Jade takes it. He pulls her the rest of the way up, a proud, wide grin on his face.

"Finally," Silas huffs, exasperated. I bite my tongue, literally, and focus on beginning my climb.

An early morning frost remains covering parts of the course, even as the sun has begun rising higher into the sky. I pull my long, black sleeve over my hand, wiping away the wetness before gripping a peg.

More annoyed noises come from Silas as I slowly make my way up. Thankfully, the nearby trees, almost free of leaves as we enter winter, rustle in the wind and block out whatever he says.

I finally near the top and Asher reaches down again, helping me ease my way up onto the platform he kneels on.

Killian never said anything about not helping each other. And I'm beginning to believe that was intentional; he wanted us to figure out how to work together on our own.

Jade thumps onto the next platform below, not the most gracefully but on her feet at least. She releases the rope and nods up to me as I look over the edge I sit on.

"You got it," Asher beams. "Just be careful of the dew."

He points along the wall I place the bottoms of my boots against while grabbing the rope.

I bend my knees, lowering my body as I walk backwards down the wall.

My foot slips when I'm halfway down and I spin, banging into the sheet of metal. My grip on the rope slips, rubbing against my hand, burning my skin.

A hiss leaves my lips and I painfully slide the rest of the way down, crashing into the platform.

"You good?" Asher calls from above, his voice laced with concern.

I view my scraped hands. Scratches line my palms, blood starting to bead in a few places.

"I'll be fine," I yell up to him, wiping my hands on my pants. The bleeding will stop eventually, hopefully.

I ignore the stinging and move onto the net stretching in front of me now. I bite down on the inside of my cheeks as I shimmy across the rough rope. Red continues to seep from my hands. I dig my elbows into the net to propel me forward, and so I don't smear the blood on the ropes.

A grunt creeps out of me as the burning on my hands worsens.

When I finally push myself onto the metal platform on the other side of the net, I sigh. My hands ache.

I investigate them again and they've only worsened. The scrapes on my palms have opened, widening, and more crimson leaks out.

I stare at them while I step down the stairs off of the platform. My gaze roams over the grass, and to the next obstacle. The bars Jade holds onto, above her head, swinging from one to another.

"You're not going to be able to cross those with your hands looking like that."

I spin to the voice. Killian stands with his arms crossed, but he drops them as he approaches me.

I press my palms into my pants again so he can't view them any closer. "Yes, I can. It's not that bad."

He lifts a brow at me, like he knows all the better. Smart ass.

I brush off the look, ignoring the way his eyes glint as he tries to silently tell me to back down.

Digging my palms into my black jeans one last time in an attempt to curb the bleeding, I step up to the bars, and jump. My grip isn't strong with the cuts in my hands so I swing, moving my grasp to the next one as fast as possible.

"You're going to hurt yourself," he chides.

I'm *already* hurt. It can't get much worse now. And I'll bandage them later.

"I'm fine," I grunt out, swinging to the next bar.

"I don't believe you."

"I'm—" My words are cut off as my grip slips and I fall.

The few feet to the ground feels like a hundred when my back slams into it.

I gasp at the pain shooting down my spine when I sit up.

Damn, that hurt.

My heart beats faster, frustration building within me. I turn my glare at Killian from my place in the cold grass.

He peers down at me with a look that is the epitome of "I told you so."

So, with more force than I thought I had in me, I shove myself to my feet and stomp over to him.

"You made me flustered! I never usually feel that way, you know!" I point at him, poking a finger into the leather vest covering his chest.

"I guess I just have that effect on you." He grins, a dimple popping up on the right side of his lopsided smile.

My rapidly beating heart pauses for the briefest of moments, his words shocking me like a bolt of lightning.

A response fails me, and he continues, his face dropping into a serious stare.

"You need to clean those up, and bandage them."

He pushes the long sleeves of the tunic he wears underneath his vest up to his elbows, and grabs the wrist of my hand still pointing at his chest. He pulls it close, analyzing the wounds there.

My heart stops again, then flutters, speeding up, the rhythm at odds with the normal, steady beat it typically thumps at. His warm breath snakes over my palm, then my wrist.

I gently take my hand away, his sea blue eyes moving up to mine as I do so.

"I have some gauze and bandages. Follow me."

He spins on his heels and leads me across the field to the racks of weapons. He reaches under one of the stands holding an array of daggers and retrieves a black box I'd never noticed before.

He kneels to the ground, popping open the lid, and immediately begins rummaging through supplies.

Stacking a few things to the side, he shuts the box and begins unrolling bandages.

I reach down for the supplies to patch myself up but his knuckles gently brush against my wrist, guiding me away.

Words momentarily fail me and I choke down a gasp. His change in attitude is giving me whiplash again.

And I don't know how I feel about it.

When my gaze meets his, the silver is leeched from his irises, and a soft ocean blue fills the space. Calm concentration has washed over his face.

"I'm a big girl, I can do it," I say, cracking a brief smile.

He blinks, spying the supplies, and nods silently, standing.

I assure him once again that I can do it on my own, shooing him away, and he strides back to watch the other trainees bounding through the course.

A few minutes later, the blood is cleaned from my wounds and I wrap them in bandages. But my mind continues to wander back to the way he instantly jumped in to help.

I shake away the thought, carefully placing the box of supplies away and return to the first of the obstacles, where Rowan waits to cross the thin beam of metal.

I make my way through the course again after she begins.

I cross the beam with significantly more ease than the first several times I crossed it, up the pegs on the wall with a pattern I've mapped out of ones easy for me to reach, down the rope on the other side while keeping my knees bent, over the extremely long, stretched out netting, and when I get to the overhead bars again, I swing from one to the other with success.

Rowan latches onto one of the two ropes hanging from the metal T several paces in front of me, and sways over the water, like she's been flying all her life.

I beam at the ease of her movements, and spy the solid wall beyond.

Asher, Iver, Silas, and now Rowan, stand by it, arguing.

I eye them for a moment and then focus on the task ahead. I take the same rope Rowan used and twist it around my forearm, securing my grip. With a jump, I bring my knees up, and swing across the surely freezing water.

"I don't need your help," Silas sneers at Asher when I approach the four of them.

Asher rolls his eyes. "You've tried running and jumping onto the wall several times now. What do you think is going to change?"

Rowan taps her foot impatiently, crossing her arms over her chest.

I lift a brow at her, blinking back and forth between her and Silas.

"He's being stubborn. He won't let Asher and Iver help boost him over the wall," she leans over, whispering.

Silas runs a hand through his fiery orange hair, arguing with the men further. He then waves a hand, and takes several steps back.

Rowan and I move to the side as he runs, and throws himself at the wall. He stretches his arms high but comes up several inches short of reaching the top.

"Alright, while you keep trying whatever *that* was, I'm going to get some help," Rowan says, wide-eyeing Silas.

She walks up to Asher and Iver, placing her feet into their awaiting, clasped hands. They boost her up and she grabs onto the top of the wall. She pulls herself to the top and straddles the thick, metal wall, releasing a whoop of victory.

Her arms extend up in triumph and she grins down at me. She grips the wall once more as she slowly lowers herself down the other side.

Cheers erupt when I hear her boots thud as she drops to the ground.

The redheaded man grumbles while watching the wall. He has *got* to get over this.

"Silas, I think the whole point is to help each other out. There's no way to get over it without helping each other or using our powers. And Killian explicitly said 'no powers' so, what other choice do you have?"

I use my most calm, reasonable voice as I approach him, as if I'm luring a scared animal out of its hiding spot.

His face twists up momentarily, frustration filling his features, then it falls, and he lets out a sigh. "Fine, I guess."

A grin grows on my face when he begrudgingly makes his way to Asher and Iver, who silently let him use their bent knees and folded hands as steps to reach the top of the wall. More cheers sound when Silas swings his legs over and drops down the other side.

"Next in line," Asher jokingly hollers. A toothy smile springs to his face as I step up to him and Iver.

For a moment, I panic about being lifted, but I don't let it consume me. My overthinking is one of my worst enemies, and it's got the better of me too often.

They hold out their palms, fingers tightly interlocked, and one at a time, I place a boot into them, stretching for the top.

My fingers connect with the lip of the wall and I pull with all my strength. I slide onto the top, belly first. Only a foot wide, I lift my legs up and out of Asher and Iver's grip, straddling the wall as Rowan did.

Claps sound from both sides of the wall. From my vantage point, I count those who've completed the course, then spy the only two that remain aside from the men who helped me up, one working their way over the netting and the other on the swinging rope.

Piper holds the rope in her grasp as she swings over the water successfully, and another woman, who I can't make out at this distance, climbs down the stairs after leaving the edge of the net.

I drop down to the ground on the opposite side of the wall, with the thirteen trainees who successfully completed the course.

Rowan and Jade beam, each placing a hand on my shoulder. Bash nods, his lips barely tilting up.

Piper's over the wall next, shouting with excitement.

The last woman follows a minute later, grunting while maneuvering her body to the top. She swipes some of her curly brown hair out of her face then lowers herself to our side.

"Come on Asher! Come on Iver! You got this!" I start the cheer for them, and the rest of the trainees follow. Yells of motivation and clapping fill my ears as Iver latches onto the top of the wall.

He pauses at the top, straddling the metal, and reaches an arm down. In the next moment, he helps hoist Asher up.

Asher's shaggy blonde hair falls into his eyes as he pulls himself up with one arm on the wall and the other in Iver's grip.

Both of them raise their fists into the air, cheering as they straddle the wall. When they drop to the ground, comradery like I've never felt before fills the space.

We did it.

We *all* finally finished the course. For the first time.

I release a massive sigh of relief and squeeze Piper, Rowan, and Jade into a hug, which spirals into a group hug. Everyone joins in, whether they want to or not, including Bash, whose eyes nearly pop out of his head, and Silas, who grumbles again as he's pulled into it.

We collectively turn to Killian when we unravel from one another's arms. He eyes us carefully, but a grin pulls his lips upward in a matter of seconds.

"Nice. Your teamwork was impressive," he says, looking over our crowd. "Now, do it again."

Chapter 31

Over the course of the next two and a half weeks, at sporadic times throughout our training, Killian announces the news of four more attacks along our border in the White Mountains, which is startling to say the least.

Each time we're notified of another attack by Killian, the air gets tense, and whispers spread throughout the trainees.

We aren't exactly sure what each new strike from Norfell means, or what their true intentions behind them are. All we know is they're getting more aggressive.

So far, they haven't invaded Orellia, nor did it look like that was their intention.

Patrols consisting of both the King's Guards and the King's Army have fought Norfell soldiers off every time, but that didn't mean there were no deaths.

In addition to those who we learned were killed in the trifecta of first attacks, six King's Guards and fifteen multiwielders from the King's Army were murdered. The latter piece of information had everyone on edge.

It begged the question—What does this mean for us?

However, we still haven't discovered the answer.

Killian has continued to drill us on paired sparring, and while I loathe it, a feeling has blossomed inside me. A feeling of preparedness for whatever may come next.

We've switched partners too many times to count since I was initially paired with Sebastian. At one time or another, I've been teamed up with every other trainee in our group.

"Listen up!"

My attention is pulled at the command. My head whips up to the voice.

Killian's.

I stand with the rest of our group of trainees inside, amongst the dozens of sparring mats littering the floor of the main training area. Ever since snow started falling in more than a flurry about a week ago, we've been training indoors.

Being free of the cold has been nice, but using my abilities inside has never felt the same.

I miss feeling the earth beneath my feet. It's difficult not having easy access to it.

"In a few days, we will be facing Luca and his trainees once more. This time, in pairs. And now that you've all had more time to practice your skills, they won't be as easy to fight as last time," Killian explains, his tone too serious for my liking.

I groan at his announcement.

I don't want to deal with them again.

The last time, when the majority of us kicked their asses, we paid for it, majorly.

Their attitudes lasted for at least a week. The dirty looks, the bumping shoulders. It was childish.

However, I don't believe they'll best us this time around either.

We've become a well-oiled machine, thanks to Killian's consistent paired training.

I've learned the skills and quirks of all seventeen other members of our group. We've figured out when to strike in tandem, or when to hit attacks back to back.

The stony Prince has even taught us what to look for in our opponent's movements, in order to predict their next moves.

That teaching moment explained *a lot*.

How he was always staring us down during sparring matches, watching us closely, and hardly ever striking first. How he would take so many of our attacks we threw at him and spin them back on us.

He may be harsh at times, but I don't think he's *entirely* evil.

At least not anymore.

The past several weeks have revealed more than I ever could have imagined.

He's truly taught us how to defend ourselves. How to align our bodies and minds.

At times, his coy comments have confused me, but they have made one thing clear: There is more to Prince Killian than what meets the eye.

And he's making me feel more than I ever thought possible.

"Now, I want to warn you all, with this pattern of recent attacks in the White Mountains, you may start receiving assignments soon. We're preparing for anything. We don't know what will be next from Norfell," he says, eyebrows knitting together.

A wave of uncertainty spreads throughout the group, the feeling palpable in the air.

My own stomach flips and flops at his words.

"These assignments will require us to leave the castle, most likely to head to our shared border with Norfell. To the White Mountains."

I swear I feel a shutter unfurl over the crowd. My chest aches in the same moment.

"Steady your minds, and hope for the best, but prepare for the worst."

I gulp. My hands fidget together.

"That being said, I'm ending practice early today. Go prepare, mentally."

And without another word, Killian relaxes his muscular arms from their notable position across his chest, dropping them to his sides, and spins on his heels, walking away.

It takes longer than usual for everyone to disperse, his comments seeming to weigh heavily on everyone's minds.

My own included.

The precariousness of an attack from Norfell has my mind racing. His mention of being prepared mentally makes my throat tighten and sends nausea turning in my gut.

I steel myself straight, clearing my brain of the what ifs. We will face whatever happens next when it comes to us. Preemptive panic won't help anyone.

Rowan nudges my arm, eyeing me questioningly. I give her a nod and a small smile.

"Just in my head a bit," I say.

She nods back then loops her arm through mine.

Peering around Rowan, I spy Piper winding her arm through Jade's.

Without discussion, those of us with our arms linked head towards the library, Asher and Bash not far behind.

The library has truly become our sanctuary, where we talk about anything and everything, as well as hunt for any scrap of information on the neighboring kingdom.

But alas, it has resulted in dead end after dead end.

We're nearly to the expanse of books when I hear a booming voice, an angry one.

I stop dead in my tracks before we stumble upon whoever the upset voice belongs to.

Rowan comes to a halt at the same time I do, her head tilting to the side as she listens. She must hear it too.

I can feel the rest of our friends pause behind us, their conversations ceasing. The six of us swiftly fall in line against the stone wall. Slowly but surely we make our way towards where the raging voice is coming from.

When the voice is clear enough to understand, we pause. I look to Rowan, who leads the way, with concerned eyes.

It sounds like… Luca.

He's seething, screaming and yelling at someone. About… not telling him something?

It's like we walked into the middle of a conversation, and the context has already been said and done.

Stomping closes in on us, and we start to shuffle away. But we don't have anywhere to go in the lengthy hallway behind us. Straight for a long while, there's nowhere to hide.

We pick up speed, attempting to make it all the way back down the hall with as little noise possible.

But we only make it a quarter of the way there before the second-in-command comes fuming around the corner, forcing us to stop in our tracks, doing our best to not look suspicious.

"What the *hell* do you all think you're doing here?" he yells at us, his typically pale face now cherry red with fury.

Rowan answers for us first, her chin held high.

"Going to the library. Where we are, in fact, allowed to go."

Oh boy.

I don't think he likes that answer.

The light blonde man's braid swings to the side as he marches up to her, closing in on her space.

"What did you just say to me?" His tone is full of rage. A piece of spittle flies from his mouth as he speaks.

I take a step closer to Rowan, my shoulder brushing against hers. I copy her confident stance as I butt in. "You heard her. We're in a part of the castle we're allowed to be in."

At my comment, I feel the presence of my friends closing in behind me, the warmth of bodies hitting my back.

I smile internally, suddenly grateful for our time here, regardless of how we were each brought here against our will.

Luca's towering frame moves from in front of Rowan to me. He's obviously trying to intimidate me with his size, but I've been up against bigger than him.

Killian immediately comes to mind. And now that I think of it, I don't know if I've even seen Killian this angry before. Especially not at one of his trainees.

He's been irritated sure, frustrated definitely, but never filled with genuine, terrible fury at us, like his second-in-command is now.

"You better watch yourself. I know you seem to be Killian's little pet and all but don't think you can speak to me that way." He leans in so close to say this, spittle lands on my cheek.

What is he even saying?

I keep my mixture of shock and confusion in check, not daring to let it show on my face. My features stay stony. I suppose I channel my inner Killian, keeping my face cold.

"Back. Off."

I hear Asher bite out the command from behind me. Heat ripples off of him in waves.

I peek over my shoulder when Luca's attention turns to the honey blonde man.

The second-in-command stands to his full height, and while Asher may have two or so inches on him, he looks down his nose at Luca.

"Move along. Or else you'll get a repeat of your time in the cell. That black eye took quite some time to heal, didn't it?" He glares at Asher, tilting his head to the side, inspecting my friend's fully healed face.

"Don't threaten me with a good time," Asher claps back, a smirk tugging at his lips.

"From what I remember, your punches may leave a nasty mark, but my bite left a worse one on you," Piper chimes in, revealing herself on Rowan's other side.

She chomps her teeth at him, then pulls her mouth into a grin. She bats her lashes at him while she waits for a response.

Luca's glare whips to her, and his face screws up with vexation, his skin growing more visibly red. He stares her down for several seconds, and the air is still as we wait for him to snap at her.

To my surprise, he doesn't.

He only narrows his pale green eyes at each one of us. Even at Bash and Jade behind me, who haven't said a word, but whose glares I can imagine bore into him all the same.

In his fiery state, he only squeezes his hands at his sides.

I move my gaze down to his balled up fists then, and find a cream colored piece of paper sticking out.

He notices my line of sight and swiftly sticks the hand into his pocket. And not even a moment later, he flings himself past us and stomps down the hall.

I spin, watching him disappear at the end when the pathway turns.

"Here I was, excited to get an early start on our day off tomorrow and then asshat has to go and ruin the mood," Piper says, folding her arms across her chest.

"What was his problem anyways? Is he really that pissy about us kicking his trainees asses last time? Is he afraid we'll do it again?" Rowan questions, hands going to her hips as she glares down the corridor.

My mind flashes to what I had seen in his fist.

"Did you guys see the paper he was holding in his hand?" I ask, looking between the five of them.

A chorus of "no's" follow my question.

"Whatever it was, I wonder if it had something to do with his temper tantrum," I think out loud.

Giggles follow my comment.

"I hope his trainees don't have the same temper as their trainer. Although if we learned anything from last time, I doubt it. I'm already not looking forward to facing them again," Jade adds.

"I don't disagree with you for a second."

I have a feeling his sour mood will definitely come back to haunt us sooner or later, probably in the arena, and I'm dreading the moment it does.

Chapter 32

"Wake up!" Someone loudly whispers in my ear. "Wake up!"

My arm jerks when whoever it is the voice belongs to shakes my limb with force.

Startled, I open my eyes, blinking them rapidly to try and rid the sleep from them.

My opposite arm comes up to brush the loose strands of hair from my nightly braid out of my face. I finally sit up when my arm is shook again.

My eyes focus when I see who it is waking me up.

Killian.

"What are you doing?" I question him.

"Good, you're awake. You all sleep like the dead. Help me wake the rest of them up," he orders, heading over to Asher and Sebastian's bunk.

I'm still sleepy and frankly, confused, but the look on his face is full of uncertainty. And it's enough to get me to jump out of bed to wake up Rowan above me.

I stand on the edge of my bed, reaching up to tap her awake.

The room around us is still dark, aside from a fire-lit lantern sitting on the floor between all of our bunks. A lantern Killian must have placed there. It was pitch black when the lights went out last night.

The light casts a shadow on Rowan's bewildered face as I nudge her arm and whisper her name.

"What's going on?" she asks, rubbing at her eyes.

"I don't know, but Killian's here and telling us to get up. Something's wrong."

The latter part of my answer has her sitting upright. Distress covers her features as I jump down from the edge of my bed and she follows me to the ground.

Wordlessly, she goes to Piper's lower bunk, rousing the strawberry blonde from her sleep. I climb up the built-in ladder at the end of her bed to shake Jade's leg, hoping it's enough to wake her.

She flips to the side, groaning what sounds like a refusal. I jiggle her calf a bit harder and softly shout her name.

She groans again, rotating to her other side, and tries shooing me away.

Damn, he was right. We do sleep like the dead.

"Jade, wake up! Something's going on!"

Her face scrunches up so I know she's heard what I said. She sits up, leaning on an elbow to stare at me.

"What do you mean 'something's going on'?"

"I mean, Killian's here. And I have no other information."

I jerk my head in his direction. He has Asher and Bash awake now, and is rushing to tell them something as they scramble to get dressed.

Jade's eyes widen at the sight of him and she climbs down after I step off her ladder.

Rowan and Piper are halfway dressed when I approach my trunk to pull out clothes. But before I can even flip open the latch, a shadow looms over me.

"Dress warmly. We're heading up the lower side of Mount Jasper. There's been another attack."

Worry shows in the shape of Killian's dark brows, and the downward tilt of his lips as he speaks. But there's a hint of a fire in those lunar-blue eyes.

I nod at him, and he spins to tell the other women the same. Before I can even finish grabbing the warmest clothes out of my trunk, he sprints out of our bunk room.

Any semblance of modesty was thrown out the window nearly two months ago when I learned the bunks were all coed, so I dress in my warmest layers and tug on my boots as swiftly as possible.

I grab my emergency pack from my trunk, which we have yet to use, and follow my friends out of the room in a matter of minutes.

I suppose this is us being thrown to the wolves.

Killian's warning from yesterday has become a reality more quickly than I could have ever prepared for.

Another trainer, who I've seen in passing, stands outside in the common area when we exit. He waves us over.

"We've just received word that there's been another attack on our border with Norfell. You all are being sent with Prince Killian to investigate what went wrong, and to help the King's Guards and King's Army that are stationed there. Good luck," he states, then leaves, making his way to the rest of Killian's trainees who are spilling out of other bunk rooms.

Only a split second after the trainer exits, Killian walks in. His purposeful stride fills the room with orders unspoken. The hushed conversations immediately halt, and everyone, myself included, stands with complete attention on the force of a man before us.

My stomach plummets to my feet as I wait for him to speak.

"I don't know the details yet, but we will be heading to a border station on Mount Jasper. We'll find out more upon arrival. Go select a jacket and a pair of gloves off the tables in the dining hall. Quickly."

I march to the tables where we eat our meals but pause when I view the clothing.

The jackets are all black, aside from the symbol sewn onto its shoulder. A golden crown, sitting atop two crossed swords, shining blade tips pointed skyward, all encapsulated in the shape of a deep red shield.

The symbol of the King's Army.

It's real. It's finally real.

I'm a part of the King's Army.

A knot forms in my throat as I reach for a jacket, running my fingers over the patch. I swallow it down forcefully.

It's... so official now.

I stuff my arms through the sleeves, yanking my gaze from the hideous symbol I now wear. I push my hands into a pair of gloves next, casting my gaze down, away from the other trainees who shove on the clothing.

Winter gear for our trek up the snowy mountain on, I return to Killian, and the nineteen of us make our way through the labyrinth that is the castle. We follow Killian in near silence, turning left and right more times than I can count.

A case of stairs lies ahead, and realization hits me.

This is the first time since arriving here I've climbed *up* stairs outside of our designated areas. Not the stairs to our training field. Not the stairs leading from the arena. Or even the spiral staircases in the library. But stairs that will actually lead us out of this place.

The feeling of freedom is so close, yet still so far. I may be leaving this palace, but it won't be for good.

The tiny flame of excitement building within me at the thought of leaving is swiftly snuffed out.

I nearly run into Rowan then, but I brace myself before slamming into her. The rest of the group has stopped walking too.

I peek over her shoulder to see Killian paused up front.

Because Luca has stopped him.

He has a hold of Killian's arm, and is giving him a questioning look.

"What's going on? I know you don't sleep well, but why are all of your trainees out of bed at this hour?" His eyes narrow at Killian.

I can't see Killian's face from this angle but I can only imagine what it looks like when he rips his arm out of Luca's grasp.

"There's been another attack. We're being sent on an assignment, *if* you must know," Killian forces out.

Luca's hands fidget as he speaks. "What's the assignment? Why didn't you come get me?"

"You know assignments are classified to everyone not going on it, aside from myself and the King. What's your issue?" Killian's voice might have been bordering on irritation before, but now it's the full-fledged wrath of the Prince of Orellia coming out of him.

I shutter at his booming voice, the authority in it unlike what he even uses with us in training.

"I just think I should be informed. What if you need help out there?"

Luca's face is flushed, paler than I've ever seen it.

"Why should you be informed? *You* have nothing to do with it. *You* were not put on this assignment," Killian thunders.

Luca's hands grab onto each of Killian's biceps, gripping them.

"But I can help! I-," Luca cuts off as Killian seizes the man's hands, throwing them off of where they held tightly onto his arms.

"*What* is wrong with you?"

Killian's voice booms so loudly, it echoes off the corridor's walls.

I move to cover my ears at the sound but take my palms away to hear his next words.

"*I* am your superior. And my team and *I* have been put on assignment. I will see you when we get back." His voice once again reverberates off of the stone surrounding us.

"I… b-be safe out there," Luca stutters several moments later.

His face is as pale as the moon, his eyes as wide as saucers, and sweat drips down his temple.

He moves to the side when Killian starts forward again, not giving his second-in-command another word. And the rest of us follow behind him, in complete and utter silence.

We watch the sun rise and see it move directly overhead before we finally reach the border station on Mount Jasper.

Pines surround the building, the dark wood walls matching the dark bark of the trees. The roofing tiles sit slanted on the peaked roof of the single story building, a deeper brown than the sides.

Snow leads right up to the front door, white fluff beginning to pile up on both sides of the entryway.

My body aches, both stiff from the cold and warm from the maneuvering through the snow up the mountain.

All of us shuffle inside, shaking off the snow on our clothes at the door before shedding our warm layers.

I swipe beats of sweat on my forehead away. The jackets kept out some of the cold, but they also kept in the heat from our hike up here.

The large room we enter has six square wooden tables strewn about, a single wooden chair on each of their four sides. I survey those sitting amongst the tables. Half of the seats are already occupied by the King's Guards and King's Army stationed here. I spy the mixture of symbols upon their clothing, the shields on the guard's shoulders, and the swords on the multiwielders.

I take in a steadying breath at the thought of having to work with the same kind of people who took me from my home, away from my life.

We move swiftly then, filling in the empty seats. Those who aren't fast enough slump against the dark, wooden paneled walls.

With people lining the walls, the room feels cramped, but when the man who appears to be the outpost's head guard approaches Killian from a nearby hallway, he maneuvers around easily enough.

"Your Highness," he says, bowing to Killian. The man's salt and pepper beard hangs a few inches off his face. The color matches what's on his head, pulled into a bun at the back.

His tanned face is weathered with battle, rather than age. If I had to guess, he was probably at least a decade younger than my aunt.

I wonder how bad things must have been up here for him to look such a way.

My chest tightens as my eyes move down to the guard symbol upon his shoulder, then the rest of his all black uniform. It's slightly tattered and wrinkled but not in awful shape. Not like a few of the men and women's uniforms, who I spot at the tables towards the back of the room.

"Commander Hastings," Killian addresses him, holding out a hand. The bearded man shakes it, respect flowing off of him in waves.

"I'm so glad to see you, Your Highness. The attack last night was different from those we have experienced before."

"How so?"

Killian's brows knit together as the sky blue of his eyes adjusts to the darkness of the room.

"For starters, they weren't trying to kill us this time." The commander stares off into the distance, as if he's replaying the attack in his head. "They had cuffs with them. I found it strange, considering they hadn't in their previous attack."

He looks back to Killian then. "I didn't even know they had the technology. I thought we only discovered the metal on our side of the mountains."

Killian's eyes narrow at Commander Hastings.

"That was the last I knew, too. My intelligence has told me they've dug their own mines but have been unsuccessful in discovering any of the mineral."

He puts a hand on his chiseled jaw in thought, then nods at the bearded man to continue.

"As I said, they weren't here to murder us this time. They were here to capture. And they didn't want any of us guards. They only wanted those in the army. They only wanted multiwielders."

Another knot forms in my throat.

I peer at Rowan, Piper, and Jade, who all sit at a table with me. Then I turn, eyeing the boys at the next table over. Bash's dark brows come together in thought, while Asher's skyrocket to his blonde hairline.

Facing forward once again, I give Rowan a confused look.

Norfell has discovered how to make the cuffs too? I've never heard of any other kingdom but Orellia using them. But then again, none of them have a king who forces multiwielders to be a part of his army.

She shakes her head back at me, letting me know she doesn't have a clue either.

At my sides, Jade and Piper stare at the table, eyes glazed over as they rack their own brains.

Why would Norfell want to capture Orellian multiwielders? Every kingdom has non-wielders, single wielders, and multiwielders; it's not like we're the only one.

"Three Army members were captured, Your Highness," Commander Hastings states mournfully.

Silence fills the room, and it's overpowering. Killian's subsequent silence is even more so.

He waits several moments, eyes pointed downward in consideration, and crosses his arms over his chest. "We'll go get them. We will rescue them, and find out why Norfell captured them."

He states it with such certainty that the tightness in my throat disappears, and I sit up straighter.

"We'll devise a plan to rescue them. Do you know where they are being held?"

Shock covers the commander's face, but he rights it as Killian raises a single brow at him.

"Y-Yes, Your Highness. I had one of my few guards who was uninjured follow them. Discreetly, of course. They took them to the closest Norfell border station a few hours away, and to my knowledge, they have not been moved yet."

"Good. We will cross the border tonight, and rescue them under the cover of darkness," Killian says matter-of-factly.

The rest of the afternoon is spent discussing strategies and devising a multitude of plans with the woman guard who followed the Norfell soldiers. She described the layout of their outpost, and where they had people posted. Her attention to detail was impressive, and we had a map drawn out by the time the sun set.

Over a dinner consisting of plain soup and stale bread, we have the specifics of the primary plan drilled into us again. Along with half a dozen backup options.

"I believe in you. This is what you've been training for. I know you all can handle *anything* those Norfell soldiers throw at you." Killian's pep talk has the tiniest glimmer of hope forming in my chest.

The hope shines bright, shoving down any uncertainty threatening to bubble up.

His eyes are a bright cerulean as he speaks to us. His face is calm, relaxed even. He leans against a wall, spine slouched. And his hands move as he talks. All so opposite of his typical composure.

His faith in us is what I keep picturing, keep feeling, as we pack up and head out to see what lies in wait for us in the darkness of the wintry night.

Chapter 33

One. Two. Three. Four.

I count the Norfell soldiers in their forest green uniforms who circle the chain link fence wrapping around the perimeter of their log cabin-style border station.

The trek here took some time, going up and over the mountain to cross into Norfell, but thankfully no more snow fell tonight.

The thin layer of white crunches softly beneath my boots as I shift in my position. Some of us crouch behind a gathering of boulders while others hide behind the wide pine trees covering the wooded area surrounding the outpost.

As I peer at the building laying downhill from us, I search for any sign of how many may be inside. The curtains are drawn, covering every window. But twice now, through a window on the second floor, I've spotted a figure moving, light beyond the person casting a silhouette on the drapes.

Off to the left of the log cabin-like building lies a single guard tower made of the same wood. The four dark wooden posts of the tower connect with a series of rods, each in an X shape, leading all the way up to the platform.

Two soldiers stand on it, the short wall around the edge of the platform coming up to their waist. The two men's heads atop the tower are on a constant swivel.

Yet they don't pay enough attention when Killian throws a rock into the branches of a nearby tree, causing a raven to squawk and fly away. The soldier's eyes go to the bird, and stay there, as Bash and two women from our team sneak up to the tower, beginning to climb.

Asher flicks a hand out after them, clearing the icy snow of any footprints.

My heart beats rapidly in my chest as I watch the initial step of our plan take place. Every muscle in my body is tense, hoping they aren't seen.

When Bash reaches the top first, he wields the Norfellen's minds, forcing them still and silent.

The two women who follow behind him climb over the raised edge and knock the unmoving soldiers out. Once their bodies hit the floor, Bash starts down the tower as the women duck down to bind the Norfell soldiers' wrists and ankles.

Sebastian sprints his way back to the treeline before the next soldier struts around the perimeter of the fence near the guard tower.

Asher once again swiftly manipulates the tiny bits of ice making up the snow-covered ground, covering Bash's bootprints in time for a lanky man of a soldier to appear.

The women peer over the edge of the tower's wall, watching as the man below passes by the base. And as he approaches the far corner, with his back to them, they silently crawl back down. Their footprints too disappear, just as soon as they create them.

My heart rate settles and my muscles relax when the Norfell soldiers continue their rounds outside of the fence, oblivious to our plan.

To my right, Rowan lets out a sigh, her breath clouding in the frigid air.

Beyond her, Piper and Jade stretch out their bodies, preparing for our second step of the plan. Eight of our team, including the two of them, will rush the soldiers guarding the fence.

The rest of us will wait in hiding for when more of the Norfellens inevitably exit the building, revealing their numbers as they run to help when hearing the sounds of our ambush.

I close my eyes, and focus on the following step. When the remaining eleven of us join the primary attack team, we are to fight our way inside.

Once inside, Killian has assigned himself, Rowan, and me to locate the multiwielders.

I haven't the faintest clue why he chose me.

The pressure of the task builds up in my chest, but rather than weighing heavy, I let it fill me with pride. Rowan and I were chosen to rescue them. And I won't let anyone or anything get in the way of our mission.

Behind a nearby pine, Killian raises both of his arms, gathering the attention of those who will begin the ambush. The moment he waves them down, the selected eight sprint downhill to the building, and the guards that await them.

Blasts of fire and water ring out. Shouts from the Norfell soldiers echo throughout the forest.

I feel the earth rumble from my hiding place behind the boulders and I shutter at the thought of it being an attack from one of their soldiers against my friends.

Leaning to the side, I peek around the rock formation. Piper and Jade are throwing combinations of light and air at a Norfellen man nearly twice their size.

He fires back with a wave of water he pulls from the surrounding snow, drenching them.

The door beyond their fight flies open, revealing half a dozen more soldiers clad in deep green uniforms who race to meet the attack.

They've shown their numbers.

And now, our primary team is outnumbered.

I prepare for my own rush down the side of the snowy hill. Breathing slowly in and out, I focus on the goal ahead.

My crouch behind the massive rocks turns into a stand when Killian whistles, our signal to attack.

I sprint around the curve of the stone, Rowan on my tail.

The layer of snow crunches beneath my boots as I approach the explosive fights.

A woman soldier as tall as myself spots Rowan and me, punching out three rapid bursts of orange flames in our direction.

Rowan beats me to the defensive, capturing the fiery balls and snuffing them out. She then sends out a blanket of darkness from her palms, enveloping the woman's figure as she screams.

Rowan dips her chin at me and I continue forward, down the remainder of the hill as she handles the Norfellen woman.

A scrawny soldier with a patchy beard eyes me when I reach the opening in the fence in front of the building's door.

He blasts a gust of wind at me, trying to force me back.

I dig my heels into the slush, holding my body still.

When the breeze lets up, I fling a ball of light from my fingertips, aiming for his face. The brightness makes contact before he can react and he goes down with a wail, clutching his eyes.

I'm only able to take a single step forward, and something wraps around my ankle, holding me in place. I peer down to find a deep green vine climbing its way up the top of my boot.

Something burns inside of me as the attack registers in my mind.

Spinning, I grab ahold of the earth beneath my feet and two of my own creeping vines spring up from under the white covered ground.

I look up, locking eyes with the soldier who controls the earth around my foot and shoot one of my spiraling pieces of greenery at him, aiming for his throat. The other I use to twist around his own feet, which are far too close together for a proper fighting stance.

Wow, I sound like Killian.

The first vine connects with his neck, circling around the sensitive flesh there.

His dark eyes widen with fear and his hands claw at the plant restricting his airway.

The vine around my own lower limb instantly goes limp at his lack of control over it.

My second dark, leafy vine tugs his feet out from underneath him, sending him crashing to the ground with a thud.

The creeping plants grow up his calves and thighs, holding him firmly to the ground. I squeeze the one around his neck just enough to have him pass out in the next moment.

I finish securing his body to the snow-covered ground with the vines so he can't move a muscle when he does eventually awaken.

I won't have him coming after me again.

When I start towards the entrance once again, Rowan rushes past me in a blur. I'm on her heels in an instant, watching her back for whoever or whatever may be inside.

The interior of the border station looks like a cross between our own and a well lived-in home. Dark wood matches that of the tower outside.

The chaos of the forest outside is also reflected in here.

The place is in shambles, furniture flung in every direction and curtains hanging haphazardly off the walls.

In the midst of the mess, Killian battles with another man who nears his father's age, slinging shadows at the aging soldier.

His face is the stony calm I have come to know he wears while fighting.

Eyes icy blue, jaw strong, and brows only slightly furrowed. Furrowed in concentration rather than concern. His dark brown waves, which often lay on the tops of his broad shoulders, are tied fully back, away from his opponents.

A few paces behind him is Asher, who stands firmly behind a knocked over table, his shaggy, straw blonde hair strewn over his forehead.

A tall, muscular woman with short hair punches a ball of light at him.

His hand flies up, catching it in his grasp, and smothers the brightness as he tightens his fingers into a fist.

I spot movement out of the corner of my eye and whip around to meet an oncoming attack.

A petite woman soldier who reminds me of Piper comes hurling at me from the bottom of the stairs leading to the second floor.

Rather than using any powers, she sticks out her arms, preparing to tackle me.

I lock my eyes with hers as she reaches for me and shove my way into her mind, my nails ripping through with ease.

I feel across her open, empty mind. The only thought of hers I find is to stop us from retrieving the captives.

Gripping onto her senses, I force her vision to go dark and her ears to ring so sharply she might as well have been inside a bell itself.

She collapses to the floor with a screeching sob, pulling at strands of her hair.

I hold my focus on her as I peek at Rowan. It's my turn to give her a nod, and I flick my head towards the stairs where the woman came from, signaling her to see if the multiwielders are being held up there.

Without so much as a glance back at us, Rowan climbs the staircase and out of sight.

Sweat beads at my temples when I face the howling soldier at my feet once more. With one hand, I push the droplets away, then slide my fingers down to the golden caramel braid hanging over my shoulder, pushing it behind me.

I close my eyes and reach deeper into her mind, feeling far past where the non-existent shield should be.

She dropped so easily, I assume no one has taught her how to properly defend herself against mind wielders.

My fingers spread out as I feel around her thoughts, which now consist of fear, uncertainty, and pain.

The last of the three is what bothers me most, and I send images of a deep, peaceful sleep into her brain.

Her body thumps completely to the floor as I release my hold on her mind. A soft snore exits her mouth a second later, letting me know she is indeed out cold.

My head floats for a moment from the use of my mind powers, making me dizzy, and I blink to focus my vision. The sides of my face feel wet, more sweat having poured off of me in buckets.

A hand grabs onto my bicep to steady me and my head turns on instinct. Killian's frosty sapphire gaze meets my own, concern piled up high within them.

"I'm fine," I tell him.

But we both know it's a lie.

He gives me a look as if he's about to call me out on my bullshit but it swiftly leaves when he glances over my head. His head dips and then Asher rushes past us, zooming out the front door.

I tap his hand on my arm, silently letting him know I can stand without his help. He lets out a grunt but removes his fingers from the steadying grip.

Shaking my head, I view the spacious room we're standing in.

Several Norfell soldiers lie scattered in odd positions around the mess; some knocked out, others potentially more than that.

That thought has my mind fully righted, any lingering dizziness gone.

"We should split up to find the multiwielders. I-"

Before the words can fully leave my mouth, Killian cuts me off.

"No."

The look he gives me rivals any I've seen before.

To anyone else, his eyes may look cold, controlling even. But the cobalt flakes dancing around the light silver in his irises tells me it's not. It's something else.

Something I can't fully determine.

I roll my eyes, pushing the thought of his stare out of my mind.

"This way," he declares abruptly, jerking his head to the side.

I follow his gaze to the wall on the far side of the room, where a tall bookshelf sits.

My eyes trail to the hard wood floor beside it, where several horizontal scuff marks lay.

Killian speeds over to the shelving unit, sliding it to the side with ease. I go after him, and we peer down at a hidden staircase. It must lead to some sort of basement.

Urgency fills me and I bound down the stairs first, forming a ball of light in my palm to see in the darkness.

When I reach the bottom, I push open a heavy wooden door.

Dim, yellow light escapes the concealed room and I take in the sight before me.

Three, tall metal cages take up the far side of the room, separated by thick iron bars. And within each of them lies an Orellian multiwielder. The King's Army symbols sitting on each of their shoulders glare at me as I peer over them.

The man and two women on the opposite side of the bars perk up upon my entrance.

Their battered faces seem to spring up as much as possible without pain from the bruises and cuts lining their skin.

One of the women points to the wall on my left. I follow the direction of her outstretched finger.

The keys to their cages.

I sprint over to them, grabbing one of the three rings and tossing another to Killian, now at the bottom of the staircase. About two dozen keys line the ring, but I start attempting to unlock the cage closest to me, trying them one at a time.

But before I can try more than a pair of keys, a shout comes from behind me.

"Aurora, get down!"

The command is loud in my ear as I'm thrown to the ground, a heavy weight on top of me.

Darkness envelopes my surroundings.

The air is crushed from my lungs as my chest is shoved against the floorboards.

I try to take in a new breath but struggle, sputtering.

My eyes squint open, viewing a thick, black mist all around me. Confusion slams into me as hard as the hit did.

The pressure is relieved a few moments later and I take in a dusty breath, the particles from the unclean ground filling my nostrils and lungs.

Shadows gone, the faint lighting from the ceiling spreads around me. I slowly push myself up, coughing out the grime I inhaled, to view whatever it was that slammed into me.

Killian's back is to me, within reaching distance if only I stretched out my fingers, and another man stands in front of him, throwing punches both with and without flames.

Did he… shield me?

Killian catches one of the man's hands in his grasp, yanking the arm attached to it, and flips the man backwards, then over himself, tossing him to the ground.

Something catches my eye on the wall to my right, and I glance over to find a wide, dark scorch mark covering the wooden panelling.

My head whips back to Killian, who's picking the soldier up from the floor by his neck, and slamming him down again.

Woah.

I turn away, shuddering, and spot my key ring on the floor. I swipe it up and push to my knees, reaching for the lock I was transfixed on not so long ago.

After trying a couple more keys, the latch finally clicks open. The pale, dark haired woman inside beams at me.

She heads to the wall to grab the remaining set of keys and I slump to the floor, exhausted from my impact with the ground. An ache runs through my body, and I squeeze my eyes shut.

I feel as if I'm only sitting for a split second when I feel a warm hand on my shoulder.

I know who it belongs to before I turn to face him.

Killian breathes heavily, the air sending loose strands of hair around my face spinning.

Behind him are the three multiwielders. The woman I released and the man hold up the other woman between them.

I move my gaze off of them to find the Norfell soldier who sent the scorching attacks lying unmoving in the corner of the room, his neck at an inhuman angle.

My gaze immediately wanders to Killian.

"Thanks," I breathe out.

I swallow, waiting for a response.

I search his eyes, ones already turning more cerulean than silver before me. Ones I simply cannot look away from, as they pull me in dangerously close the longer I look into them.

His head tilts down, wisps of his deep chocolate hair slide around his temples.

His jaw works side to side, then a light chuckle comes out between his heavy breaths before he looks back at me.

"Anytime."

Chapter 34

I right myself, standing up from my crumpled position on the dusty floor.

Killian's stare remains on me, but movement in the doorway beyond him catches my attention.

A flash of dark braids is the first thing I see, and I let out a sigh of relief.

Rowan's found us.

She peers at the two of us on the far side of the room with curious eyes. Her attention then swings away and she briskly swoops in to replace the dark-haired woman whose cage I opened, taking the weight of the sluggish, beaten woman who now sits strung up between Rowan and the man. The four of them start for the stairs.

My eyes stay on them, refusing to stray away to the direction of Killian. The startling interaction between us still shakes my bones.

What are you supposed to say to someone when they throw their body over yours to protect you?

I need time to think over his actions.

And the way he looked at me after.

I step around him and bound up the stairs, feeling his presence at my back when we approach the front door, stepping past the disarray of the first story.

Shouts of combat ring out from beyond the ajar door we near.

Rowan exits first, the injured woman within her grasp.

A body stretches out horizontally in front of the door, laying in the snow. It's a Norfell soldier.

She steps over it without a second glance.

I follow suit, unable to look at it for longer than I already have.

Outside, our multiwielders fight with Norfell soldiers. Flashes of light, wisps of shadows, and splashes of water echo all around.

Orellians who aren't locked in combat are sprinting towards those who are, and soon the fighting is three or four against one.

Norfell's lost this fight.

My head is on a swivel, eyeing those who are battling, ensuring our escape route is clear as we leave the building and head back to the hill we came from. Reaching halfway up the snowy canvas, my eyes are locked on the dark trees ahead.

Then, I hear Killian send out booming orders from behind me.

"Retreat! For the treeline!"

I turn to face the scene below. Most of the Norfell soldiers are subdued now, a few presumably dead and others lay unconscious on the icy ground. Our people's heads whip towards the sound of Killian's command, and they do as told.

The handful of soldiers who remain standing, fighting members of our team, pause when they finally look at the destruction we caused.

Their numbers have been more than halved.

I finish climbing to the top of the hill, but not without slipping on the cold, wet surface.

I shake the white fluff off of my pant legs then peer down at the rest who follow, counting our people, and hoping they're all making it back alive.

With Rowan already safely behind me, I search for the rest of my friends amongst those retreating up the snowy mound.

I spot Bash first, who's almost to the top of the hill himself. His dark curls, typically in a uniform pattern, sit haphazardly on top of his head. A thin cut lines his cheek, barely missing his right eye. His face droops with despair and exhaustion.

Next are Jade and Piper, who practically carry a limping woman whose ankle is twisted in an unnatural way.

The former's hair sticks up at odd angles, halfway out of her usual short, black pigtails. Her face is unmarred but heavy bags lay under each deep brown eye.

The latter looks more rough than the others. Piper sports a busted lip, blood still dripping from it and down her chin. Cuts slash across her face in different directions, one going through the edge of an eyebrow. And a gnarly gash lies on her forearm, taking up more than half of the skin there.

But you would never be able to tell of her injuries by the determined look on her face as she continues to heave the woman with the broken ankle up to the treeline.

More people swiftly follow behind them, and I keep counting as they approach.

My chest aches as the count stops at seventeen and I still haven't seen Asher.

There's nineteen of us.

Two. We're missing two. And Asher's one of them.

My hands tug at the strands of my braid as I continue searching, looking past the border station below, to the treeline on the opposite side. I eye the watch tower, then the lining of the chain link fence.

I even turn and recount everyone who crouches once more behind the boulders and wide trees.

Still seventeen.

Spinning back, I survey the land again. The few Norfell soldiers who remain conscious tend to those who weren't and pay us no mind, whether or not they see us staying within the treeline.

I rub at my forehead with my fingers, attempting to eradicate an oncoming headache. Gulping, I face the group again and approach Killian.

He doesn't look up from the ankle of the woman Jade and Piper brought to him to treat as he forms a makeshift splint around her injured limb.

"Is everyone back?"

So, he knew I was keeping track of our numbers.

"No. I don't know where they are. I don't see their bodies on the ground. But we have two missing," I tell him, the tiniest bit of hope in me from not finding their bodies withering.

"Not anymore you don't," I hear a deep voice grunt.

Spinning around at a dizzying speed, I face Asher. He looks disheveled, but he's alive, and relief blooms in my chest.

He carries an unconscious woman in his arms, a red head woman whose name I've come to know through training is Penelope.

The other missing member of our team.

Asher strides up to Killian, crouching down beside him and placing Penelope down.

Killian takes in her state, rapidly finishing off the ankle splint he's working on, and begins pointing to our surroundings to items we can use to build a makeshift stretcher.

He pulls a tarp out of the bag he brought with him. The ones we all did but discarded behind our hiding places within the treeline before initiating our rescue plan.

In minutes we have a functional stretcher made from the tarp, two long branches, and twine from someone else's pack. The front of the stretcher is picked up by Killian, the back by Asher.

And on Killian's order, we take off back across the border, into Orellia.

Jade and Piper help up the woman with the twisted ankle they were with previously.

I carry my pack along with all three of theirs. Aches and pains radiate throughout my body as I adjust the bags.

Sebastian walks beside me, carrying Killian, Asher, and Penelope's packs along with his own.

We walk in near silence through the darkness of the night, only the moon's light and a handful of palmed flames to guide us.

We stay quiet for the next few hours it takes us to enter Orellia. Not because we have to, simply because we are too tired to.

Too shocked to. Too amazed to.

Because we just completed our first mission. As members of the King's Army.

And we were successful. We rescued the three multiwielders.

We all made it out.

When we arrive back at the Orellian border outpost we left from, with plenty of time until the sun rises, we slump down in heaps, exhausted.

Killian and Asher take the unconscious Penelope to an infirmary in the back of the building, Jade and Piper close on their tails with the woman whose ankle sits in the makeshift split.

The rest of us sit amongst the tables we were at for dinner only hours earlier.

Oh how so much can change in so little time.

A few of the King's Army and King's Guard bring out supplies to patch up the varying injuries.

Busted lips, forming black eyes, purple bruises, as well as cuts and scrapes mar the faces and bodies around me.

Aside from a handful of bodily bruises I'm sure to find under my clothes in the next twenty-four hours, I'm unscathed. The surprise of it floods my veins.

I wonder what I would look like had Killian not thrown me to the ground, his body over mine.

Asher, Piper, and Jade rejoin us then. Bash stands, pushing together two tables so we can all be together.

Rowan immediately reaches for items to clean and bandage Piper's wounds the moment the blonde plops down into the chair beside her. Hissing and biting down on her split lip, Piper allows Rowan to dab at the laceration on her left arm to clean the wound.

My eyes roam over to Jade, who sits between Asher and Bash.

The first two were tousled in their fights but they thankfully remain unscathed. Sebastian on the other hand, has the mark on his face, nearly jutting into his eye.

He starts cleaning it himself, a mirror in hand, but Jade takes one look at him, twists up her face, and pushes in, taking the cloth from him and washing the long line running diagonally over his skin.

Asher's gaze stays on her the entire time.

Minutes tick by as everyone slowly begins to relax and soft voices stir while wounds are tended to.

Killian eventually steps out from the infirmary, closing the door softly behind himself. The murmurs halt the moment he enters the room, all eyes landing on him.

"Good work everyone," he starts, gaze sweeping the space. "I'm happy we got you guys out in time. We'll discuss more after you've rested." He looks to the three rescued King's Army multiwielders who sit slumped at the table closest to him.

He peers at the rest of us, dipping his chin in a nod. "Get bandaged up and rest. We will head back to the castle later today."

With that, he strides over to an open seat at our table.

The one next to me.

He grabs a clean towel from the stack of supplies on the tabletop and I inspect him with confusion.

Did he get hurt too? He hasn't acted like it.

My eyes roam over him and I spot his right hand flexing on top of his knee. His palm lays open, facing the sky. And then I spy the torn away flesh in the middle of his hand.

I would have never known anything was wrong if he didn't reach for that towel.

A gasp releases from my mouth without permission and I fake a cough to cover it up. Although I fear it was anything but subtle.

He raises a single, dark eyebrow at me, then proceeds to reach for more supplies.

He tries to open a container of fresh water with his uninjured hand, the lid stuck tight. Before he can try a second time, I'm sticking my arm out and grabbing the canister.

A baffled look covers his features at the movement, but I don't meet his eyes as I open it.

Oh what the hell.

I pull my chair closer to him, to where our knees almost touch, taking the cloth sitting loose in the grasp of his uninjured hand, and wet it. I carefully reach out, pulling his marred hand into my lap. I hold onto his wrist while I gently wipe the gash clean.

I don't dare move my eyes up to his as I tend to his raw, deformed flesh. Not even when I glance up each time I need to grab more supplies off of the table.

And he lets me. He doesn't fight me as I help him.

He doesn't say a word either.

I only feel the warmth of his breathing fanning over my face, no doubt from him observing me as I work on his injury. His face, his mouth, his lips, they're so close.

He is so close.

I bite down hard on my lower lip, shoving the thought of his proximity far away.

We sit in silence until I finish tying off a clean, white bandage around his hand.

Then, he's the one to break the quiet.

"Thanks."

"Anytime," I say softly, maintaining my stare on the bandaged hand.

A beat of silence goes by until a voice flows over the room. "If you're all ready now, I can show you to the sleeping quarters."

I seek out the person who spoke and my eyes land on Commander Hastings, who's beginning to usher people down a hallway at the back of the room.

Standing to follow them, I don't make eye contact with Killian's gaze I feel lingering on me.

We're shown the way to sleeping quarters at the end of the hallway. The army and guard members who are lying down vacate their cots to make space for us.

The three multiwielders we rescued sit on the furthest of cots at the far end of the room. And then I swiftly count the number of beds in the rectangular room.

Only thirteen cots remain.

Knowing there aren't enough for us all, I move to the side, allowing those who are more injured to pass through the doorway.

Rowan leads Piper over to a cot on the left. They squeeze onto one of the narrow beds together, Rowan's arm circling around Piper's back with a protective grip when they lay down.

My heart flutters and I bite back a grin as I watch them.

I watch as nearly every bed is taken up. And when the last person passes me, I turn to see Sebastian, Asher, and beyond them, Killian, waiting behind me, having let everyone else pass by them too.

My eyes return to the view of the two rows of cots lining either wood-paneled wall.

One lone bed sits empty only a few feet away.

I turn back to them and Asher peeks out from around Bash, resting an arm on the curly-haired man's shoulder.

"Go ahead. We'll take the floor."

Bash nods in agreement, then jerks his head, as if telling me to go.

Climbing onto the bed tucked against the wall, I spy Asher crawling onto the floor between my cot and the one next to me. Bash does the same across the aisle separating the rows of beds.

Killian leans in the doorframe, muscled arms crossed over his broad chest, taking in the space.

Commander Hastings leans over a moment later, whispering something to him.

He dips his chin in agreement with whatever the man said and eyes us once more before those icy blues land on me for a split second.

A second that feels much longer than it actually is. A second that I swear expands into minutes, hours, days, even weeks.

Then, he slips out of sight, waving his hand freely behind him first, snuffing out the flames lingering in lanterns around the space, leaving us all in the dark.

Chapter 35

The hike back down to the castle almost felt more grueling than the one leading up it.

And my body was still feeling it today.

After arriving at our underground training facility beneath the palace in the late afternoon yesterday, to a combination of odd looks and surprised stares from the rest of the trainees, we all flopped into our beds and didn't move for at least an hour.

Per Killian's orders, we were to rest, hydrate, and until further notice, keep the details of our mission under wraps.

And coming from him, those were probably the easiest of orders to comply with.

Now at breakfast, I sit with a bowl of unappetizing oatmeal in front of me. Although, any food that has laid on a plate or in a bowl in front of me within the past twenty-four hours hasn't been appetizing.

Taking my spoon in hand, I mix in the blueberries I placed on top of the light brown mush, hoping it will help.

To my left, Jade nudges me gently.

"The fruit today is really good. I think you'll like it." She jerks her head at my food, raising her thin brows.

I'm sure she's noticed my lack of food intake, and I appreciate her for keeping an eye on me. But the pit in my stomach has been taking up so much space that I don't have any room for real food.

It was awful seeing those I've grown so close to get hurt.

I almost feel… guilty.

And the questions I have pile up in my brain, with more being added the longer I think over each moment.

Why did Norfell capture multiwielders in the first place? What were they trying to torture out of them? What made them switch from killing to kidnapping? And how are they going to retaliate?

There's no way they won't retaliate after the damage we did to their border's outpost. While we barely outnumbered the Norfell soldiers, the destruction we caused was formidable.

Giggling interrupts the questions spinning in circles in my brain and I face the sound, rather than my sad looking oatmeal in front of me.

Across the cold, metal table where my forearms sit, Piper and Rowan take a seat. The freckled blonde has one fair skinned arm linked through a rich brown elbow belonging to the woman whose fire-ringed eyes spy down at her lovingly.

"So," Piper starts, dragging out the vowel at the end.

She peers at myself and Jade on the opposite side of the table, waggling her eyebrows, then moves her gaze to Sebastian at the head, and finally Asher who sits beside her. The latter of whom is shoveling pieces from a mountain of pancakes into his mouth.

She eyes him questionably before rushing out, "I wanted to tell you all that Rowan and I talked and we decided to make things official! She's my girlfriend! And I'm hers, *obviously*."

Her cheeks redden as her word-vomiting ceases and she grins wider than I've ever seen before.

She wrinkles her nose as she rests her head on Rowan's shoulder and the smile that appears on the latter's face is one of pure, sweet joy.

Piper glows past the cuts along her lip and face, the happiness pushing the battle wounds away instantaneously.

The shield usually built so high around Rowan relaxes; I can see the walls dropping as her head goes to rest on top of Piper's. The fiery blockade she has in place around nearly everyone hasn't seemed to lower this much since, if I remember correctly, the evening we met.

At the same time, Jade and I gush out how happy we are for them and how much we love them. Our hands whip out over our breakfast, colliding with theirs as we squeeze them together in excitement.

"Congratulations," Bash says, his smile showing the tiniest bit of teeth.

I count that as a full-on grin.

"Wait… I thought you already were?" Asher questions on a mouth full of food, a puzzled look on his face.

Piper's lips pull together and she raises her hand not currently tucked through Rowan's arm, and smacks him in the back of his head.

He lets out a small "oof" at the playful hit.

"Yeah, well, we wanted to make it *official* official!" She laughs out, a grin reappearing on her face.

He finishes swallowing his food then continues, "Hey, I've been team 'Rowper' since day one! Or is it 'Pipan'?"

He places a hand on his chin in thought as she swats at him again with a chuckle.

I snicker at their banter and glance down at my breakfast again, the rest of them continuing to eat and talk amongst themselves.

Giving up, I push the bowl away and reach for the glass of water I had set aside. I gulp down the liquid, the only thing I have been able to regularly stomach since we crossed back over into Orellia.

Asher and Piper joke back and forth once more while Jade discusses how training will fare from now on with Rowan.

Only minutes have passed when I feel a presence slide into the seat next to me. When silence falls at the table, I know who it must be.

But I could identify that presence anywhere by now.

A plate full of eggs, pancakes, fruit, and bacon slides in front of me in the same moment. I don't look up to meet the eyes I can feel boring into the side of my head.

My face begins to warm before the words even leave his lips.

He must have been watching me.

"You need to eat something. Not just drink more water," Killian says softly, a gentle command laced in his words.

"I'm not hungry," I tell him defiantly.

My face stays forward and I move my eyes to each of my friends. I meet each of their stares and the pleading flowing from them. They look back and forth between one another, considering, then, slowly start their conversations up once more.

So, they've all noticed? And they think Killian will be the one to get through to me.

I can't help the mixture of emotions in my gut that have me wanting to do anything but consume food.

A sigh bubbles up and out of me when I finally turn to face him.

His sapphire eyes study me, his deep chocolate brows coming together. His matching hair is worn in the half-up style I see most days, with the lower ends resting atop his shoulders.

Along his sharp jaw sits a bit of stubble, the dark hair contrasting his paling skin in the winter months, the tan he wore when I first met him lessened. His lips sit in a flat, unimpressed line, the dimples I've seen on his cheeks nowhere to be found.

"Why?" I eventually ask.

I smooth my face into the best annoyed mask I can muster. The elation I felt such a short time ago for my friends has disappeared.

"Because I don't need you passing out on me," he states simply.

He shrugs his shoulders and brings his still bandaged right hand over to push the plate closer to me.

A shiver crawls down my spine as I consider his words, then view his injured hand.

"My mind is too busy to eat and the sinking in my stomach is keeping me full enough," I retort, staring at the food, accompanying my sarcasm with a laugh.

I don't know why I told him that, but it's out there now.

"And it's never going away unless you eat. Don't let it take you over."

His words remain an order, but a calm one.

I eye him again, questioning his words.

I hate when he's right. I lick my lips and bite the lower one briefly before releasing it.

"I have questions. A lot of them."

A shutter involuntarily runs through me then, when I feel his ghostly hand brushing against my mind. He lets it sit there, not trying to push past my shield but instead allowing me know he's there, waiting.

"I'm sure you do, but I don't have all the answers right now."

His survey of me remains, those damn bright eyes still connecting with my own.

I turn away and investigate the breakfast platter in silence.

"Everyone came back alive and we will learn more of what Norfell wants soon. In the meantime, fuel yourself, please."

My eyes widen at his last word. *Please.*

Then, I swiftly rewind the rest of his words and I'm rendered truly speechless.

Of course he knows exactly what my worries are.

I shake my head and reach for the fork beside the plate. I reluctantly dig into the fruit first, taking one bite, then another.

It is rather good. The berries are tart and sweet all at once.

As food enters my stomach, the unease there dissipates, and I become ravenous.

Beginning on the pancakes next, I finally peer over at Killian.

His plate is untouched and his gaze hasn't moved from me. A satisfied smirk pops up on his face, showing a single dimple, and with a nod of his head, he starts on his own meal.

I roll my eyes and continue eating.

As the time passes, our food is finished and conversation stirs, now between the seven of us, and I feel any lingering uncertainty between us dissolving.

Piper throws her head back in laughter while Rowan covers her face, snickering. Bash shakes his head at Asher as Jade giggles. A belly laugh breaks free from me as Asher tells us about one of what he calls his "farm life escapades" from his years growing up on his family's farm.

I notice Killian joins in when a belly laugh comes from my right. Peering over, I take in his cheery expression.

What a day of firsts from him.

First the word "please" and now a genuine, cheerful laugh from him? Not just a slight chuckle?

The surprise fills me up, and it's not until my cheeks start to ache that I recognize how big of a grin lies on my face.

Asher's story is cut short when a chair slams into the ground somewhere behind me. We all whip towards the sound, discovering it was Luca who had thrown one of the metal dining chairs to the floor.

Killian is up in an instant, marching towards his second-in-command.

"You cancelled the matches?" Luca shouts as he barrels towards Killian, more of a demand than a true question.

My eyebrows knit together. What is he going on about?

The realization of his words dawn on me as I investigate the unfolding situation.

Killian cancelled the matches between us and Luca's trainees. Matches that were supposed to be tomorrow.

He must have done it because of our mission. Maybe he didn't know how long we'd be gone, or what would ensue.

Luca stops in front of Killian, hardly an inch between their faces, a scowl covering his. Rapidly growing rage pours off of Killian, silencing the packed dining hall.

"Why would you cancel them?" Luca spits out. A vein in his pale neck sticks out as he speaks.

"I don't answer to you. You seem to keep forgetting that," Killian states with a lethal calmness that has goosebumps rising on my arms.

Luca laughs maniacally, tipping his chin upwards. His single, ivory braid falls backwards at the movement.

"Get over yourself, *Prince*. I think you're scared. I've been whipping my people into shape and they would kick your trainee's asses."

A ripple of fury spreads over the space and I shrink into my seat, preparing for the worst.

"You need to leave. You're making a fool of yourself."

The Prince's order is defied; Luca stays put, cocking his head and grinning wide.

"I don't think so. I think you're afraid of making a fool of yourself," Luca declares. He starts a slow spin, forcing Killian to turn in time with him as they begin to circle one another.

"You are not acting like the man I thought I knew," Killian says with disgust, his face all hard lines mixed with ire.

Underneath however, I swear I find the slightest bit of shock, but he's doing everything in his power not to let it shine through.

"I suppose if you're too afraid of sending your trainees into the ring, then perhaps you should take their place." Luca ends his orbit with Killian when he issues the challenge, a deadly smirk upon his lips.

He's challenging Killian.

He is truly challenging the Prince of Orellia. The man who he's second-in-command to.

My stomach twists, the food I consumed threatening to expel itself.

A quiver so small and so quick passes over Killian's face, I question if I even saw it.

He has been upset with us before, and there's no doubt he's been pissed off at Luca too, but being opposed like this, and by someone who he thought he could trust, has a new, different type of anger rising within him.

Killian leans in close, his modest height difference with the man seeming to grow tremendously by the second.

His blue eyes morph into a complete icy silver when he responds to Luca's disturbing proposition.

"If that's what it takes, then by all means, have at me."

Chapter 36

Luca immediately takes Killian's words as an invitation to strut out of the crowded dining hall and towards one of the closest sparring mats in the common area.

He stomps his feet in place there, digging in his heels, then proceeds to bow to Killian, throwing his arms out wide, mockingly.

Killian's eyes narrow on his opponent as he takes long strides to meet him at the mat.

Murmurs filling the dining hall shift to the common area as we follow them, careful to keep a distance from the two men.

My heart starts to race at the sight before me, and it dawns on me that I'm nervous.

I'm *nervous* for Killian.

His second-in-command's attitude has been questionable before but to outright challenge the Prince? Is Luca insane?

There must be another reason for his erratic behavior. He can't solely be upset over cancelled matches.

There must be more to it.

A shit-eating grin covers the lower half of the man's face. He pushes his snowy blonde braid over his shoulder, out of the way. He dances across the raised mat, light on excited feet as he takes in Killian.

All muscle and power, Killian faces him, stance wide and waiting. He observes the man who is meant to be one of his most trusted allies with eyes of intense, icy rage. His jaw ticks to the side and I recognize it as a sign he's considering the options of what Luca may throw at him.

Only a split second later does the second-in-command attack. He whips a hand out, sending a tendril of light at his opponent's head.

Killian dodges the move, and I suspect he knew exactly what Luca would do first.

Then, my brain is shocked with a new revelation: I've never seen Luca use his powers before. And I have no idea what kind of attacks will be hurled at Killian.

My rapidly beating heart drops into my stomach and I clutch my hands together.

Light flies at Killian once again, this time in the form of a massive blinding ball. Of course Luca would use the only ability Killian doesn't have, against him.

Darkness erupts in the same moment with a swirl of a bandaged hand.

The one I bandaged.

The brightness fades in an instant, the pitch black folding over it.

Then, with the twist of his non-injured hand, he flings a burst of orange and red at the blonde man.

Luca drops to the ground and rolls, landing in a crouch a handful of paces away. The look he gives Killian up through his eyebrows is downright murderous.

He kicks a foot out, sending another blaze of illumination over the top of the mat. In the next heartbeat, a matching beam is aimed at Killian's head.

The simultaneous attacks cause Killian's eyes to widen ever so slightly and leap through the air, landing with a grunt several paces away, the two of them now having rotated positions on the mat.

I stare daggers into Luca's back now that it faces me.

I know it won't do anything to end the fight, but it makes me feel better on the inside.

A dozen strips of pitch black shadows erupt then, growing from Killian's hands splayed out at his sides.

One after the other, Luca swats at them, releasing rapid blasts of light from his palms to meet the darkness.

A dark thread of Killian's is able to connect with the blonde man's foot, grabbing hold and yanking it to the left.

Luca tumbles to the ground, landing forward on his elbows. From his position on the floor, he releases a guttural growl and glares at his opponent.

And Killian's molten silver eyes return one back.

Unmoving, they stay in their respective stances, leering at one another. Their bodies tremble slightly, with force. It becomes clear then: a battle of the mind has ensued.

Sweat begins to glisten on Killian's temple. Of the little of Luca's profile I can see, I spy the same.

The second-in-command slowly pushes off of the sparring mat, keeping his eyes locked onto the Prince's.

With a twitch of Killian's dark brows, Luca slams back to the floor, his feeble attempt at standing, squashed. A straining sound comes from him, his head cocking to the side, swishing the end of his braid across his back.

He makes another attempt to stand but it's as if a force is shoving him back into the mat.

The force that is Killian.

Heavy breathing bursts out of Luca, his profile entirely shiny with moisture now.

In the next second, he jerks, a vibration spreading over him, then spins on his knees, kicking out a blaze of brightness along the way.

The hold on each other's mind seems to break when Killian uses his shadows to block the attack and dodges, rolling to the side.

Chuckling, Luca finally rises from the ground, stalking his way to the opposite side of the mat where Killian had once been.

Fly aways stick up from the braid trailing down the middle of his skull. Deep bags lay under his light green eyes.

Those eyes move to me and I step back, accidentally bumping into Bash beside me. His hands steady me on instinct.

Luca's crushing gaze tightens on me further and I freeze.

He's trying to enter my mind.

My shields are firmly in place, my learning to subconsciously keep them up at all times coming in handy once again.

But claws scratch at them, more of a tease, a threat, than a real tug to test the wall's strength.

My view of him is cut off barely a moment later.

I blink at the obstruction.

My vision focuses, landing on Killian's back. The black, sleeveless tunic he wears showing rippling muscles underneath.

I glance away, to anywhere else but at him.

Flames then blaze up, tickling the outskirts of the sparring mat. The bright orange, red, and a hint of purple force myself and the crowd back, away from the searing heat.

"Don't look at her. Don't look at *any* of them. Your fight is with me. You caused a problem with *me*. So finish it. With me. Afterall, this is what you wanted, yes?" The words release on a near growl from Killian.

A breathy sigh that must be from Luca follows. Then, a hysterical laugh accompanies it.

"Oh please, pretty Prince. I won't actually do anything to your precious trainees."

"This is *over*. I'm done fighting you."

The command doesn't leave any room for argument when it booms from Killian's lips.

The fire flicks higher around them, crackling with his statement.

"As you wish, *Your Highness*."

Luca folds into another mocking bow, the only indicator of his motion being his outspread hands lowering on each side beyond Killian's massive form in front of me.

"But this isn't over," he adds bitterly before waltzing off the elevated mat, through the flames, and out the room's main set of double doors.

I release a dizzying breath, one which makes my head spin faster than I thought possible.

The blaze disappears and the room suddenly feels dark, like a shadow looms over the entire space, even after the second-in-command's threat is gone.

"Shit," Rowan comments from my side.

All I can do is tip my chin in agreement as the encounter replays in my mind.

Shock fills me up initially but outrage swiftly squashes it.

Luca running a finger over my mind is a threat I am not willing to let go so easily. How dare he? I've never done anything to him.

The rerun of events is promptly pushed away when my arm is shaken by someone.

Piper's fair, freckled hand rests on my bicep, her bright green eyes filled with concern stare into me.

"I guess Luca isn't a very big fan of mine," I say hoarsely. I follow up my sarcasm-filled remark with an uneasy chuckle.

Before she can respond, Killian's voice booms across the spacious area.

"Get to your trainers. As for my own trainees, today's practice is cancelled. Clear out."

The command is followed instantly, people quick on their feet to flee the room.

I start behind my friends who move towards the door leading to our bunk room, but halt when my name is called.

And I don't need more than a single guess to know who it is.

The five of them turn to eye me, then the voice behind me. I wave a hand at them, letting them know I'll catch up with them shortly.

If this goes smoothly.

I don't know what he could possibly have to say now.

I spin to find Killian only inches away from me. His once platinum eyes already transforming into a lighter, softer blue.

"Aurora, I'd like to… apologize for his actions."

That's not what I expected.

At all.

My mouth opens and shuts while I try to find my response.

"You don't need to apologize on behalf of him."

"I don't know what is with his attitude," he says, his eyes falling to the side. He licks his lips before continuing, "He tried to get into your mind, didn't he?"

When his gaze finds mine again, the cobalt in them shines.

"Yes. Not very hard, though. It was to try to scare me more than anything."

I fold my arms over my chest as I consider the motive.

A beat of silence passes between us before I swiftly fill it. "He doesn't scare me. And I can handle myself when it comes to him."

The warmth of wrath begins to fill my chest. His actions will *not* be forgotten.

"I know you can," Killian responds with a coy smile that makes a dimple appear.

I wet my lips then bite my lower one, containing a matching smile.

He looks me up and down once, then his lips drop. "But you don't need to be worrying about him too."

"I won't. He will get what's coming to him." Assurance fills not only my voice, but my body too.

Killian's smirk returns at my comment. And the tilt of his lips makes my heart beat a hair faster.

He copies my stance, folding his arms over his chest, which is really his own typical one, and lets out a huff of a laugh.

"He will," he agrees on a nod.

I don't have a second to respond as he speaks again with a jerk of his head.

"Go join your friends. Enjoy today off."

My arms fall to my sides and I dip my chin. I consider him one last time, peering into those ever-changing eyes.

I scan the rest of his lightly tanned face. His relaxed, dark brows, his straight nose and round lips, the stubble lining his sharp jaw that moves as he thinks.

And unlike Luca, Killian's flowing hair stayed in place. Half of the deep cocoa waves still lay on his shoulders, the other half tied back.

I snap my gaze away from him, remembering his last words.

"Right. I will," I spill out.

Without glancing at him again, I spin, briskly walking to the door my bunk room lies behind.

Closing the door after me ever so softly, and officially putting a true barrier between myself and Killian, I let out a breath.

He... seemed worried. About Luca attempting to enter my mind. And earlier, when he wanted me to eat breakfast.

My hand goes to my forehead, rubbing at the skin between my brows, the dull pain of a headache beginning to bloom as I consider this morning's events.

When I finally remove my fingers from my face, I spy my friends.

Piper lays on her back on Rowan's top bunk. Her head dangles off the side, viewing the world upside down, allowing her pair of strawberry blonde braids to swing around.

Rowan stands next to my bunk below, giggling at her and shaking her head. She carefully grabs ahold of either side of Piper's face and leans in, kissing her.

Bash and Asher sit on the latter's lower bunk, talking. Although it's mostly the blonde man who moves his hands around as he speaks, and the dark-haired man runs a hand through his curls while listening.

Jade sits with her legs crossed on Piper's unoccupied bed, writing in a journal. She taps a pen on her cheek after lifting it from the paper. Her stare lands on me when she picks up her head, attention away from the booklet. A sly grin appears on her lips and she raises her brows at me.

I roll my eyes and peer at the ceiling, wondering how today has already been so eventful, and it's not even seven in the morning.

"Ugh. Ew," I groan, sputtering, waving hands in front of my face to clear the dust flying off the shelf of books I accidentally sneezed on.

Damn these old books.

I know the books we used won't reshelve themselves, and I don't mind putting them away but doesn't anyone ever come in here to clean?

"Not as often as they should."

The silence of the library being interrupted has me whipping around.

I didn't realize I spoke the question aloud.

The break in quiet is what truly startled me so I'm not surprised when I turn around to find Killian. I'd recognize that voice anywhere.

But immediately as I finish my twist to face him, the tower of books in my arms tilts, leaning at an awkward angle before falling to the ground.

Of course they would fall once I finally got to the rows they belong in.

Cursing, I bend down, scrambling to begin picking them up. And in the same second, I find Killian crouching down, stretching his hands out to build a stack of the fallen books around him.

"Did you really do this much reading on your own?" he asks when we each finally have a neat pile of books loaded into our arms.

I chuckle, shaking my head. "No, my friends were here earlier, too. I offered to put them all away. I needed the peace and quiet after... well, everything."

He nods his head, eyeing a book on the top of his stack before placing it on the shelf. And while he didn't say a word of it, I swear I can feel the understanding radiating off of him.

A few beats of silence pass between us as we shelve more books, and it's… comfortable.

It's not awkward or strange, but instead, rather peaceful.

"Thank you for your help," I tell him, peering down at my last two books, contemplating where they belong.

I peek over at him, waiting for a response. My heart picks up a beat when his sea blue gaze lands on me, the weight of it forcing me still.

"You're welcome."

The sincerity in his voice sends heat soaring into my face.

Such a simple exchange with him should *not* have me blushing like a school girl.

I bite down on my lower lip, turning away to read spines once again, and finally find the place for the pair of remaining books in my hands.

When I do eventually face him, after taking my sweet, sweet time shelving the books, he's leaning against the built-in shelf, investigating me, arms crossed now that they're empty from putting his own books away.

"You did exemplary on the mission, you know. You're a natural, caring leader."

"Thanks, I'll make sure to add it to my resume," I chuckle out. But another wave of warmth spreads through my face and up to my cheeks, as much as I try to fight it.

"I'm serious. I mean it."

I wet my lips, glancing down for only a moment before steadying myself and returning my gaze to him.

"Thank you." It comes out softer than I mean it to as I search his face, taking in his features: his strong jaw, appearing even sharper in the shadows of the library, his heavy brow, always so full of emotion, his sapphire eyes, showing his true feelings, no matter what they are.

"You did so well that, I'm not surprised you felt the emotions of it all after. It means you have a heart, and good leaders need those or else we end up with power hungry, selfish people in charge." His eyes tell me everything I need to know, without him saying the exact words.

He means his father.

But for once, I look past the mention of the King, and return to his words about me.

The way he sees so deep into me, how he can tell when something bothers me, and how he just *knows* what I'm thinking or feeling at any given moment.

I never expected him to express such concerns about me. Or be able to read me so well.

We stare at one another for what feels like forever. Fluttering begins in my stomach, a companion to my flittering heartbeats.

In this moment, and I suppose for quite some time now, I realize he's so different from what I originally thought.

He takes a step closer to me, then another. He breaks the eye contact first, peering down and sighing, before looking back to me.

"I also needed to tell you that," he pauses, taking in a breath. "Since our last run-in here, I still haven't been able to find the child army my father moved."

A hint of a snarl comes out at the mention of the King.

"I'm running out of options; I don't know where he's hid them. I have as many of my trusted guards as I can spare searching for them, but so far, no luck. I just... thought you should know."

His eyes turn several shades darker, coming close to the color of midnight.

Without thinking, I reach out, placing a hand on his upper arm. The warmth of his skin collides with my palm, even through his long-sleeved tunic.

"You–" I start, but consider my words.

It's not up to *only* him.

"*We* will find them," I say, my lips tugging up at the corners. "I know you won't give up on them. Just like you haven't given up on me."

"I would never give up on you."

The flitting happening inside me freezes, only for it to restart a second later at twice the previous speed.

He takes another step forward, coming impossibly closer. My hand slides up higher on his arm at the movement.

I don't pull it away.

His breath fans across my face, his features mere inches from mine. "It's alright to let yourself feel the heaviness after the fact, too. To feel the weight of it all loaded on your shoulders, and not immediately brush it off like it's no big deal. You were amazing out there, and good leaders *always* feel the impact of their choices. But *please*, take care of yourself."

The words strike right into my heart, and pierce my soul.

This man has shocked me time and time again but never has he made me feel... like this.

Whatever this may be.

He slowly moves in, his eyes feasting on mine, his nose nearly brushing against mine, his perfectly shaped lips inching towards my own.

A curl falls onto his forehead as he enters my space.

My instincts want to brush it away, but no movement comes from me.

I'm a stone statue when his breath caresses my cheeks, and skitters over my lips.

Is he...

The doors to the library slam open then, several chattering voices filling the room.

I step back, swiftly turning away. I spy him doing the same out of my peripheral.

Was he about to?

No. No, he couldn't have. It's not possible.

My heart thunders in my chest, beating so hard I swear it can be seen protruding past my ribs.

"I'll see you later. Enjoy the rest of your day off," he says, dipping his chin and spinning on his heels. It doesn't take but a second for him to disappear from sight.

But once again I stand, unmoving, and incredibly unsure of what to do next.

Chapter 37

Throwing my foot out, I slide along the ground. I've been trying to trip up Rowan's steady footwork as we spar one on one. But she nearly always sees me coming.

The past three days since Luca's challenge to Killian have been boring, thankfully, because in the beginning, we were waiting for tensions to boil over again.

Aside from sparring, we've been practicing weapon wielding today. The former of which I still very much loathe, so I'm grateful for the reprieve of any other activity.

After spending the morning indoors throwing daggers, we moved outside to our frigid field.

We bundled up in our warmest layers in preparation for the wintry day but as time went on, our jackets were shed, thrown onto the closest empty sparring mat.

Since it isn't snowing and the sun is still fairly high in the sky, the frost on the grass has mostly thawed, and our breath could hardly be seen in the wind.

I let loose a sigh when Rowan hops to the side, missing my outstretched foot.

Today's sparring is restricted again; no abilities allowed.

I twist, pushing myself up onto my feet. A fist comes hurling my way as I stand and I dodge to the right.

Rowan pulls her fist back, covering her upper chest and face with her forearms.

I jump back as I watch her bounce on the balls of her feet, readying her next move.

Bringing my own fists up, I spy her footwork. She always takes a step back before lunging into an attack.

Not a moment too soon, her left foot moves backwards. She kicks a boot out to where my torso would have been but I pivot to the right before she can reach me.

While she's still on one leg, I crouch down. Swinging my own leg out towards her, my right ankle catches on her one foot remaining on the ground.

Her black boot skids along the mat, connected with mine, and out from underneath her. She lands on her back as I bring my foot back under my body and stay in a squat beside her.

Rowan groans from her place on the ground and I wince. "Are you alright?"

She stares up at the sky when she answers me. "Yep. You bruised my ego more than anything."

Matching giggles bubble out of us.

I stand and lean over, stretching my hand out to her. She takes it, and I pull her up off the ground in a swift motion.

"At least now I have one point on the board. You already have three," I chuckle and rub at my hip where a bruise is bound to form from when I landed on it only a few minutes ago.

Rowan tricked me on that one; I thought she was going to strike from the left, but I was very much wrong.

It turns out, flying backwards through the air and landing on your ass is not the most comfortable thing in the world.

She laughs with me and we move off the mat, taking up residence just outside of where Piper and Jade spar a few spaces away. They are both sly in their own right, and have hardly been able to slip one another up.

Piper's arm launches forward, aimed at Jade's gut. But the woman with the sleek, black pigtails is too quick, sliding to the side, then around the back of the blonde.

Twin braids flick through the air as Piper spins to face Jade. With a jump, Jade twists and kicks in Piper's direction.

The freckled woman grins at the maneuver before dropping to the ground, rolling to the side, and swiftly standing to her feet. She's upright again just as Jade's booted feet land back on the ground.

Their spinning and dodging continues for several more minutes. They circle around the mat, like two leaves caught in a breeze spiraling around each other.

As Jade evades another one of Piper's fists, I spy movement out of the corner of my eye.

Someone runs onto the field, letting the castle door slam behind them. My attention stays on the figure as they get closer, heading for Killian, who weaves his way around the sparring mats, watching each fight.

Not that I've been paying attention to him. Much.

"Your Highness! Prince Killian!" the man shouts as he sprints over the wet grass. Short, blonde hair covers his head, and I notice he wears a similar dark ensemble the rest of us trainees do.

Killian whips around to the sound of his title being called. A crease forms between his brows as he takes in the man racing toward him.

Wide eyes bulge on the man's pale face and he leans in close to Killian upon reaching him, out of breath.

He whispers something that has Killian's face narrowing and his jaw tightening. He dips his chin in understanding to the blonde trainee and the man takes off, sprinting back the way he came.

Moving his hand to his chin, Killian considers whatever information he's been given, then folds his muscled arms over his chest.

"Stop your sparring." The command halts those still on the mats immediately.

Jade and Piper stare at him and take in gulps of air now that they've paused.

The energy radiating off of Killian is jarring. He's tense, and his face twists up briefly, then it relaxes into a harsh calm.

Something must be wrong, and it causes my mind to spiral.

"We are being sent to Mount Bear. Norfell has attacked again."

The blue hues in his eyes fade, silver beginning to overtake them.

The retaliation we've been waiting for. This must be it.

Damn, they are fast.

"A rescue mission once again. Five of the King's Army have been taken. A dozen King's Guards have been killed." He states these facts as if reading off a grocery list.

But the icy tones in his eyes are growing.

This is going to be worse than last time, I know it.

My chest tightens. Anticipation and anxiety squeezing it. And I assume my stomach will fall in sync with the ache in my chest, but it hasn't. At least not yet.

"We're leaving now. Gather your things. And this time, select any weapons you may need. I know we didn't have time for any before our last mission." He waves a hand to the weapons rack off to the side of the field.

Bows and arrows, short swords, and daggers of all shapes and sizes are taken.

I only take a single, short dagger just in case, my confidence in my powers stronger than any of my weapon skills. I slip it in my boot, as I've seen Rowan do so many times.

Everyone then scrambles to grab their coats laying around the field.

I swoop my own up, eyeing the King's Army crest on the shoulder of the solid black jacket. But I shake off the uneasy feeling the golden crown atop the pair of swords give me and take off towards my bunk room.

After filing inside behind Piper, Jade, and Rowan, I spy Asher and Bash already there, the former of the two stuffing last minute necessities into his bag.

I shake my head, fighting a giggle, and lift open my trunk, grabbing my own emergency pack that's ready to go.

The last time we were sent out on a mission, the supplies came in handy for building the stretcher for Penelope. Although I still can't believe such a thing was necessary. The guilt of those around me being hurt during the rescue starts to crawl its way up again, but I swiftly stuff it down.

Her first day back at training was yesterday and now here we are, being sent on yet another mission.

When we enter the common area, layers on and bags in hand, I spy Killian glaring daggers across the room. My eyes follow his stare to find the source of his vexation.

Luca stands at the end of his gaze, a mask of severity on his face as he discusses something with a man who I recognize as one of the other trainers.

My investigation moves from the second-in-command to the commotion around him. His trainees close in on him, putting on jackets, beanies, and gloves while others are bent over, messing with their packs.

The realization hits me and I speed over to Killian.

"He's coming with us, isn't he?"

His jaw works back and forth for a beat. But I know what words will fall from his lips before they even do.

"Unfortunately, yes."

He tears his eyes away from the man who challenged him to stare down at me. Light, ocean blue starts to creep its way past the cold silver as they spear into me.

I feel my cheeks start to heat as our gazes remain locked for several moments, neither of us saying a word.

Ending the silence, I speak first. "What are you thinking?"

His eyes narrow ever so slightly before he answers.

"I'm thinking that someone who I thought would never break my trust, has. And the little trust I have remaining now belongs to another."

The intensity in his now fully cerulean eyes grow, boring into every inch of me.

Fluttering starts in my stomach as unspoken words pass between us.

Seconds feel like hours as our stares stay on each other. However, our time is cut short when a cough sounds from beside us.

My head whips to the figure who interrupted. Luca.

I don't have to look back at Killian to know of his displeasure. The irritation flows off of him, making the air all around us tense.

"What?"

He says it curtly, more of a statement than a real question. At the same time, he steps towards his second-in-command.

A hand then reaches out to his side and before I recognize what he's doing, he gently rests his palm on my elbow and guides me behind him.

I stare at his back, astonished.

My stomach forms a knot. And not a moment later does my heartbeat skip.

He just… put himself in front of me, again. In front of Luca.

I hold my breath, waiting for another explosion between the two of them.

"I'm sorry about the other day. I shouldn't have spoken to you like that," Luca begins, his voice rough like gravel.

I lean over, peeking at the man as covertly as possible. He glances my way for a split second but swiftly returns it to Killian.

"I shouldn't have been so angry with you. I would like to put it behind us, if you're willing to accept my apology."

One of Luca's hands fidgets as he speaks, while the other goes into his front pocket. His viridescent eyes turn away solemnly while he awaits a response.

The massive room falls into complete silence, not a whisper or murmur to be heard.

The tension builds thicker. From my place behind him, I notice Killian roll his shoulders, the muscles on his back flexing then relaxing through the black, long sleeve shirt he wears.

"Fine. It's in the past," Killian finally announces.

The breath I let out is dizzying.

The second-in-command eyes his Prince, sticking out his hand to him. Killian grabs Luca's outstretched arm, clapping their forearms together. They stay with one another's arms in their grasp for a moment, then release them on a nod.

Luca heads back to where his trainees wait on the far side of the room, hands behind him, and starts giving them indistinct orders.

Killian turns to face me then, but continues looking at the snowy-haired man warily.

"I thought you knew I could handle him, if need be," I joke, trying to lighten the mood.

His stare flicks to me, eyes softening, and a smirk grows on his lips.

"I do. But it doesn't mean you have to, at least when I'm around."

And there goes my insides again, my stomach filling with butterflies and my heart missing the next beat.

Many hours later, with the sun long gone and the moon having joined us on our journey, we arrive at the desolated border outpost on Mount Bear.

The deep brown of the structure is a stark contrast to the icy white that covers the forest floor.

This building is hardly hidden, unlike the last border station we visited on Mount Jasper. The trees around the structure are far and few between.

Those that do come close match the exterior of the outpost, with no leaves to be found on their branches.

As we round the building sitting on top of a small hill, my jaw drops at the sight revealed before us.

Hundreds of footprints flatten the fluffy crystals, leaving the entire hillside slushy. Stones anywhere between the size of a pebble and a boulder litter the ground. Scorch marks cover the side of the building, turning the mahogany wood a pitch black.

And red stains the once pristine blanket of snow.

My stomach churns, nausea rising up as I take in the color.

Just to the left of the station lie two giant, black tarps.

Large, uneven lumps sit below the crinkly material. Crimson tracks streak over the white forest floor, coming from all directions, leading underneath the coverings.

A lump forms in my throat as I ogle the scene.

A bloodbath. That's what took place here.

My hand flies to my mouth, covering a gasp and the urge to vomit. I tear my eyes away, blinking back forming wetness.

On my right, Rowan and Piper pause. Their hands folded together between them squeeze while they observe, mouths agape.

On their other side stops Bash. He lets out a puff of air, one that shows up white in the frosty wind. He continues on to the building's entrance after shaking his head, eyes pointing downward.

Asher and Jade pass by then, the golden blonde man on her left, with an arm around her shoulders, using his body as a shield, ushering her past the devastation as quickly as possible.

My heart melts for the briefest of moments at the sentiment.

A warm hand on my lower back startles me.

I peer up to find Killian at my side, concern pushing his face inward. Wordlessly, he jerks his head towards the tall, wooden door leading inside the building and gingerly presses me onward.

His hand doesn't leave my back until after we're all inside and the door shuts firmly behind Luca, who trailed at the end of the group.

All thirty-six trainees mingle between the hallway we're immediately led into, a room full of plush couches to the left, or a room with two long, pine dining tables and matching chairs to the right.

"Hello, Your Highness," a young man who must be no older than nineteen greets, walking down the hallway to us.

He wears a King's Guard patch on his shoulder, the sleeve below it ripped down to his elbow.

He swings his hand to the side, directing Killian to the array of sofas. "Please, come with me."

I follow behind them, surveying the room.

In the middle is a large, rectangular coffee table, made of an orange-colored wood. Complementing the longer sides of the low surface sit lengthy couches of a soft beige. In front of the short sides are smaller loveseats, both in a cool, caramel color.

A fireplace is lit behind the long couch the young man sits on. The two corners of the space, on both sides of the brick hearth, are occupied by single wingback chairs. The wall opposite of the fire is covered in bookshelves, aside from a space in the middle, where a window sits with dark curtains drawn over.

Killian rests on the end of the sofa across from the young guard. He places an elbow on the armrest, leaning back against the cushion.

People fill in the empty spaces, piling onto the furniture.

In the corner, I spy Bash in a wingback chair. On the far loveseat are Asher and Jade, the former with his arm laying over the top of the back cushions. Rowan and Piper remain standing, leaning against the wall near Bash, fingers interlaced.

The guard pulls out a map, placing it on the coffee table, smoothing out the edges.

Someone then bumps into me as they enter the room.

I turn to see Luca, who mutters an apology before taking up residence along the wall beside the burning hearth.

When I take in the area again, I notice Killian sitting upright, staring at me. He removes his limb from the arm of the couch and pats the soft surface.

Oh.

Hesitantly making my way through the trainees standing about the room, I reach him.

But before I can perch on the armrest, he stands and plops himself onto it, leaving his seat wide open.

My jaw falls, leaving my mouth hanging wide.

He's giving me his seat?

My mouth slams shut as I shuffle around him.

I feel pairs of eyes landing on me as I take the spot. I cringe internally and fold my shoulders in as I cross my arms in front of me, placing my clasped hands in between my knees.

Licking my lips, I begin to investigate the map, hoping I've made myself small enough to where people stop staring.

The map shows this station, the line between Orellia and Norfell, along with several other buildings on either side of the border.

The young guard, who introduces himself as Declan, states as much a moment later, pointing at the parchment.

One building sticks out on the Norfellen side of the border, being the closest to us.

"This is where they took the captives. Five multiwielders; two men and three women. Asha followed them…" He pauses, gesturing to a tall, dark-skinned woman with a bob leaning in the doorframe. She nods stiffly at the acknowledgment.

"I stayed behind with Stellan, the only other one who made it out alive. He's in the infirmary now." Declan states the last part solemnly, his eyes cast downward.

He shakes his head, then continues, "Asha's also the one who went to the next closest Orellian station and told them of the attack. They must have been the ones who sent word to you. I don't know what we'd do without her, and her help."

Declan stares up at Killian, brown eyes beginning to water before he swiftly blinks the liquid away.

"And you're the one who moved your fellow guard's bodies, covering them, giving them a semblance of dignity in death, aren't you? *That* is important and honorable too. Thank you," Killian tells him.

Killian slides off of the armrest beside me, kneeling on the ground next to the low table, and places a hand on the young man's forearm. "We will get those who were taken, back. I promise."

He pulls his hand away and peers around the room before speaking once more.

"My trainees must rest for a while. Our trek here was long and they need their strength. But in the meantime, I will devise a rescue plan. We will go for them in the morning."

With the final words having left his lips, Killian stands and turns, nodding to Luca.

The second-in-command returns the gesture and leaves his place against the wall.

Asha then has most of the trainees follow her out of the room and to the sleeping quarters.

One look at the swarm of bodies on her tail has me unmoving from the couch. Most of these outposts weren't built to sleep more than twenty people or so, and I am *not* fighting for a bed tonight.

Rowan and Piper join me on my sofa when the crowd exits, sighing as their bodies relax into the cushions.

I can't say I didn't feel the same relief when I sat down in the spot Killian gave me. My body aches from the hike here, and the icy cold didn't help keep my joints or muscles loose.

"I guess this is where we're sleeping tonight," I laugh, peeking around the space.

"The couch sounds good to me. I'm not arguing over a bed tonight. I'm absolutely beat," Rowan chuckles out, smoothing a hand over the tan surface of the sofa. She then rips off her boots, and Piper immediately follows the movement.

Now *that* is something I can get behind.

I unlace my boots and chuck them off with a sigh of relief.

She lays down with her back pushed against the cushions and Piper scoots in front of her, her back to Rowan's chest, snuggling in. With an arm draped over Piper's hip, Rowan stretches her hand out, and the freckled blonde takes it, wrapping their fingers together.

Declan at some point had left, but he walks in now holding a stack of blankets, placing them on the table.

Piper snatches one up, throwing it over her and Rowan. They both bend their knees, curling them towards their chests, folding the end of a plaid quilt under their feet.

Long enough that they only take up half of it, I curl up on the other end of the sofa, my feet only a few inches away from the women's, with a fuzzy, gray blanket from the pile. I tuck my feet under the blanket, just as Piper and Rowan did, hoping to form a warm cocoon after being out in the bitter cold for so long.

Bash then rises from his corner chair and plops onto the loveseat next to me, flat on his back. His calves and feet hang over the armrest closest to the fire.

On the opposite loveseat, Jade's pale face turns pink when eyeing Asher next to her. He whispers in her ear something for only the two of them to hear and when he pulls away, her cheeks glow brighter. She bites down a smile and shakes her head side to side.

Then, I watch as he yanks a deep blue quilt onto their laps and she brings her feet under her body while leaning into his broad chest, his arm going around her petite shoulders.

The fire crackles beyond the couch across from me, where two women from Luca's group of trainees lay.

As I close my eyes, I try to picture what tomorrow may bring.

But the only image conjuring in my mind is one of silver and sapphire eyes that bore through my soul in real life, and now in my dreams.

Chapter 38

Rays of soft yellow sunlight peek through the vibrant green of the pine trees above my head as I only half listen to Killian's whispered commands.

After a night filled to the brim with dreams of him, it was difficult to hang on to every part of the plan he listed off. Instead, over the past few minutes, the details of my boots have become rather fascinating.

"I don't think that's a good idea."

I finally tear my eyes off of my shoes to see Luca stepping towards Killian, interrupting him.

"Excuse me?" Killian's gaze snaps to his second-in-command, eyes lighting with a molten fire.

Luca holds his hands up defensively. "Hear me out. I think it should just be you and me to find out where the multiwielders are being held. We don't know the extent of their numbers. We should have as many trainees as possible hold back and fight off the Norfell soldiers while the two of us slip inside to find them."

"Why?" The question is out of my mouth before I know it.

My palm jerks, wanting to fly up and cover my mouth, but I hold it down, folding my arms across my chest.

The death glare Luca sends at me is formidable.

After several moments, and to my surprise, he answers me. "Because we can take on whatever or whoever comes at us. And remind me again, how many of you were *truly* needed last time to rescue the captives?"

How did he know it was only Killian and I who entered the hidden basement the multiwielders were held in?

It must have been Killian, but I'm surprised he told him anything after the way they've been butting heads.

I run my tongue over my teeth while considering his words. He's infuriating, and I can't place at what point he surpassed Killian on that scale. But I have a feeling it was quite some time ago.

"There are more captives this time," I state plainly.

He scoffs. "I don't foresee that being a problem for us."

I roll my eyes and leave the subject be.

If he wants to play the hero, fine. He is welcome to the limelight.

Killian's icy stare bounces between the two of us before continuing. He points off in the distance with his next words, at the Norfell border station sitting past the clumping of trees we wait behind.

Similar to our station we left from this morning, the area around this building is cleared of any flora and fauna. A blanket of snow covers the forest floor, untouched aside from the path in which the Norfellen soldiers walk. They circle around the perimeter of the two story, dark wood building and the four matching towers placed near the corners of the primary structure.

This outpost may be more grand than the one we ambushed last time but our strategy remains largely the same.

The only problems this time around are the lack of foliage nearby and the amount of guard towers.

To resolve these issues, Killian tweaked his plans for us before we set out this morning when the sun had risen.

Piper and three other trainees who excelled at archery stood holding a bow, and wearing a quiver of arrows strapped across their backs. They would be the ones to silently take out as many of the soldiers within the towers as possible.

The hand not holding Piper's bow was held by Rowan, their attention staying on Killian and the hushed directions he gives out.

At their left is Bash, who spins star-shaped daggers between his fingers. If he can get close enough without being seen, those pretty, onyx blades of his will be sent flying at any soldiers who remain in the towers.

Crouched down beside me is Asher. He's seemingly paying about as much attention as I am while dragging a stick in circles on the fluffy, white ground.

Jade is his opposite, standing at full attention on his other side. Her pair of short pigtails nearly disappear within the dark beanie she adjusts while listening.

Soon enough, Killian finishes the last of his instructions and the silence that falls is eerily quiet. With a nod, everyone disperses, stretching out to hide amongst the trees standing far away from the outpost, ready for when he gives the order.

I press my back against the closest pine and breathe in a steadying breath.

On its release, Killian approaches me.

Our eyes lock and I nearly pause, a question on the tip of my tongue, but decide to speak it aloud anyways.

"Are you sure?"

The look I give him alone speaks for itself; he knows I'm referring to what his second-in-command said.

His frosty blue eyes hold on me, then trail down and back up in a blink. The glance has me momentarily shrinking, but I shake it off when he answers with a small smirk.

"Don't worry. I'll be alright."

A scoff escapes me, then I roll my eyes, a closed mouth grin growing on my face at his haughtiness. When my stare returns to his, he takes a tentative step closer. Then another one.

He's close enough now that the next breath he releases brushes warm air over my chilled cheeks. The upward tilt of his lips slowly drops, his gaze falling from my face.

I gulp, questioning where his eyes are moving to.

His hand reaches up, and my stomach flutters, unsure of where his palm will land.

His fingers stop when they meet the end of my braid hanging over my shoulder. He brushes his thumb over the tips of the caramel strands, wide eyes absorbing the details.

The action is so gentle, so… caring.

After what feels like an eternity, he carefully takes the braid and places it behind me, where it slides until it hits the blade of my shoulder.

Soft navy eyes meet mine for a second before he steps back and whisks off to the next pine tree over.

The fluttering in my stomach finally settles and I peek over at him one last time, but the mask of a warrior is laid over his face. His features reflect a narrow calm as he sets his sight on the archers who lie in wait, arrows already nocked.

I close my eyes and take in another calming breath, my previous one having been ineffective since Killian's approach.

We can do this.

When I reopen my lids, I peer at him again. With the rise of his hand and a swift swipe downwards, the arrows go flying. Soaring through the air, aimed at the pair of towers on the right, three of them meet their mark.

The two guards at the closest tower slump to the ground behind the railing, arrows protruding from their chests.

But only one of the soldiers in the second tower stands for a brief moment with an arrow sticking out of his neck before he follows suit.

The single guard remaining freezes in shock.

The arrow aimed for him sits lodged in the top of the wooden railing.

Another arrow flies at him a split second later, but it's too late. The man drops to the floor behind the siding and blows a horn so loud I swear it can be heard across the border in Orellia.

Shit.

Shouts ring out from the Norfellen soldiers, indistinguishable from our distance.

Four more arrows are spinning through the air towards the second pair of towers on the left, and the soldiers in them peer out into the forest frantically.

With their movements erratic, only two of the targets are hit, and a single guard from each tower falls, impaled.

The door to the border station swings open not even a moment later. Before the first soldier can step foot outside, Killian shouts the order.

"Attack!"

As we all flock out from behind the trees, snow beginning to spray up at the rushed movement, arrows soar overhead one last time.

The remaining two targeted guards in the left towers fall, one over the edge, landing face first in the snow.

Another arrow strikes a patrol guard who has a flame lit in her hand, and when she drops to her knees, the fire goes out as she stares at the wood protruding out of her stomach.

The final arrow hits the side of the building, missing any soldiers entirely.

Sprinting at the building, I feel for the earth beneath my feet. One hand stretches out to connect with the nature buried deep under the frozen carpet, and I use my other to gather a sphere of light.

Soldiers pour out of the building, throwing blasts of orange at trainees in the front of the ambush.

Tendrils of obsidian slither along the white ground, like wicked fingers reaching to grab ahold of their prey.

The race to the outpost takes me longer than expected, even from our great distance behind the far away trees. The snow is thicker than during our previous mission, and it takes more effort to lift my boots with each step.

Halfway across the wide, frozen space, I launch the brightness from my palm at a blonde woman soldier who appears in front of me.

Her forearms cross over her face, a shield of darkness forming around them, deterring my illumination.

The earth under my boots rumbles and I shoot my hands forward, a pair of vines I spring up through the snow airborne in a matter of seconds as they extend towards her.

My deep emerald plants wrap around her wrists just as she pulls her arms down from their protective position blocking her face.

She huffs out an angry, frustrated breath and flicks her fingers, spraying a gust of wind from them.

But it does nothing against my greenery on her limbs.

I yank on the plants, pulling her forward, and she belly flops onto the ground. I sprout two more vines, one on each side of her torso, and wrap them around her, my arms swinging wildly in front of me as I make quick work of tying her up.

She goes to scream but I cut off the sound, pushing my way into her mind easily. Without a shield in place, my claws dig in, shoving in images of a deep sleep.

She's unconscious in the next moment.

Fully secured to the ground with my climbing plants, I leave her, and continue onward.

Only a handful of steps closer to the structure now, a bulky, Norfellen soldier nearly twice my size spots me, and sends a wall of freezing cold air at me.

Unable to plant my feet in place fast enough, the heavy breeze slams into me, knocking me backwards.

My ass hits the hard, wintry ground and the impact reverberates through me. The snow melts into my pants, soaking my bottom half and numbing my legs.

Crap.

Before I can take in a breath, after having my previous one knocked from my lungs, another blast of air hits me.

I slide along the icy ground, leaving tracks in the snow from my boots and hands where I scramble to keep my place.

The man saunters towards me, the grin on his lips telling me he believes he has already won. He towers over me as I gain my bearings, waiting, cocky and arrogant.

I throw my fist at his face, but he catches it in his palm, gripping my hand to the point of pain.

A yelp involuntarily leaves my throat.

He's going to break it if I don't get it loose soon.

I grab his wrist with my free hand in an attempt to rip it off of my now throbbing one.

He snarls down at me. Long, unbound, dark hair droops around the sides of his face as he holds my fist tighter.

My eyes start to water and a whimper falls from my lips.

As soon as the sound leaves me, his grip loosens and he jerks back several paces, as if something has overtaken his body.

I clutch my pulsating hand to my chest the moment his fingers no longer touch my own. Luckily, I don't suspect it's broken, but a sprain may be a possibility.

The hulk of a man drops to his knees, eyes wide at the sky. Then, he slumps into the snow face first.

I peek up to find Bash leveling a look at the motionless man's back. His deep brown eyes find mine and a single brow raises in question.

I nod to him, silently telling him I'm fine after I rise to my feet and shake out my sore hand.

With a dip of his chin, he stalks away, pitching darkness at the closest Norfell soldier battling with one of our own.

My hand aches when I stretch out my fingers, testing their strength. It's, thankfully, still usable. Something tells me my limb is, in fact, most likely sprained, but between my focus on the mission and the icy mountain weather, it starts to numb.

With the pain beginning to dissipate, I take in the fighting before me. What I see nearly pulls the air from my lungs once more.

The door to the outpost swings open. Norfell soldiers pour out of the building like a tidal wave.

Our people are *severely* outnumbered.

The intelligence we have on how their border stations operate is limited, but overall similar to the way Orellian ones are run. But the sheer number of soldiers running out of the outpost to battle our own is more than double what we expected.

My stomach drops.

Out of the corner of my eye, I see a flash of darkness. It's Killian and Luca, sprinting at full speed from where they waited back in the forest coverings.

They dash past Norfellen soldiers, only throwing up defensive shields of light and shadow if any powers are sent their way. The door they aim for still lies open, but I spy movement beyond the threshold.

To hell with the plans.

I keep moving across the crisp, white field, my pace picking up as I acclimate to the thick snow my boots try to stick to with every step.

The men enter the building and instantly, flashes of battle appear through a window on the first floor.

Nearly to the doorway, a flash of heat flies at my head from a soldier.

I duck, throwing myself onto the ground in a roll.

In the next moment, a figure comes from my left, firing off a flame quadruple the size of the one lobbed at me.

The fireball flies over my head, streaking towards the Norfellen who threw the heat at me.

I investigate who tossed the defensive attack for me and find Rowan's back as she slides in front of my body, her black braid of braids swinging against her shoulder blades.

After another inferno leaves her fist, she spins to face me. I grab onto the hand she holds out for me and jump to my feet, now covered in another layer of freezing snow from my time on the ground.

Wordlessly, we lock eyes and move into the doorway in sync.

An incredibly massive beam of golden brightness shines in our eyes the moment we enter.

I splay my hands wide, grabbing onto the light, and fight to shrink it.

Whoever is holding onto the rays of light pushes back against me. I squeeze my eyes tight and feel the warmth seeping between my fingers.

Arms straining, I shove back, and the blinding illumination slowly begins to dim.

Just enough for me to peek open my lids.

I fight back even harder, compressing the light into a smaller and smaller orb.

Finally, I feel the person release their hold on the element. The expansive brightness disappears and I pry open my eyes all the way.

And just a few paces in front of me stands Luca, outstretched hands barely aglow, a wide, toothy grin on his face.

And to his side, on his knees, lies Killian, restrained, with a silver metal collar glinting around his neck and hands stretched behind him, surely enclosed in cuffs.

Half a dozen tall, bulky, Norfell soldiers surround him. One fists his dark waves, yanking his head back. Others at his sides grip his arms.

My chest empties as my heart falls into the pits of my stomach.

"Killian!" I scream as I surge forward.

The floorboards beneath my feet begin to rumble as I reach for vines to sprout up through the cracks between.

Just as soon as they begin to shake, they settle, when my vision goes dark and my knees slam into the ground.

The wood creaks at the harsh landing. My legs ache at the impact.

Dammit. I must have let my mind's shield slip. Even a tiny bit is all it takes.

In the next moment, I regain my sight, but my body is still not mine to control.

My throat burns when I try to speak, my tongue working against me.

"Shh. You speak far too much anyways," Luca quips. He strides towards me, then pats a rough hand against my cheek.

He moves to my side and my eyes follow his movements, even if my head can't. He taps Rowan's face the same as mine, a grin not only upon his lips, but in his eyes too.

Rowan kneels on the floorboards beside me, nearly vibrating as she tries to fight the mind wielding whichever Norfellen soldier is using on us.

With so many of them surrounding us, and glaring at us, I can't pinpoint which soldier it is.

Luca rubs his pale hands together maniacally before folding them together in front of him.

"Dispose of these two. We got what we wanted." His gaze never leaves Rowan and me while he spews the orders to the soldiers spread out around the room.

From somewhere off to the edges of the space, two men in deep green Norfell uniforms grab ahold of my shoulders, yanking me backwards out of the building.

My throat tightens as I try to scream, but my body won't listen to me, my mind remaining someone else's.

I watch a vein in Killian's neck strain when his wide, icy gaze sticks to mine.

And I swear his body jerks forward ever so slightly, pulling against his restraints and whatever hold they also have on his mind.

I feel the cold against my body before I see it.

My ass and legs begin to numb a few seconds later as more wetness seeps into my pants from the icy forest floor.

Two massive men trudge along in front of me, a limp Rowan in their grasp.

Fighting to regain control over my body, I shove at the claws wrapped around my mind.

The fingers curl in tight, placing more pressure in my head, making it pound.

I feel a single tear leak out and run down my frozen cheek when I wince at the pain.

I push again, and again, trying to raise the shield up at the forefront of my mind.

A sharp jolt sprints down the back of my head and straight through my spine in response.

A strangled whimper releases from my throat.

I can't do it.

I can't get them out of my head.

My chest is heavy with the realization that I can't fight off whoever is using their mind wielding on me, and panic seeps in.

I've fought so hard for so long. I'm not ready to give up now. But without the use of my body, I can't use my abilities.

I can't fight back.
Another tear slips out of my eye, my vision blurring.
Black spots fill my sight.
My body is not my own.
The tight grasp on my arms aches.
My shoulders are pulling at the seams, stretching beyond their use.
The force presses deeper into my head.
My brain is on the verge of exploding.
More wetness spills onto my face.
Another garbled whimper crawls up my throat.
And then, my body is dropped to the ground.

Chapter 39

The Norfell soldier to my right falls beside me, like a thick tree being cut down in the forest. An arrow sits in the base of his throat, blood pouring out of the wound.

Screaming breaks out at my other side when brightness flares, and my head turns to see the other soldier clutching at his eyes.

He pulls a palm away for a brief moment and I spy a dark, empty socket where an eyeball once laid. He flops to the snow only a second later.

Wait.

I *turned my head.*

I blink rapidly, and stretch out, wiggling my fingers one at a time, then my toes.

A sob of relief crashes over me and I slowly push myself up.

My body is my own once again.

The first soldier who went down, he must have been the one holding onto my mind.

Piper appears before me, bright green eyes flaring with a touch of turquoise. They sit staring, full of concern. She flings her bow over her back, beside the quiver of arrows.

"Are you alright?"

"I- I'm okay," I muster up.

A contemplative look covering her face says she doesn't believe me, but she helps me to my feet regardless.

Her arm loops through my own when a wobble nearly sends me tumbling.

When I right myself, I peer up at the scene.

A sea of green Norfell uniforms. Orellian trainees, in all black, make up only a fraction of the people on the field. Two or three of their soldiers battle every one of our own.

When I couldn't move, I was dragged by the soldiers off to the side, nearing the treeline, much further than I realized. They must've wanted to "dispose" of me amongst the trees.

A chill runs through me at the thought.

My survey of the massive space stops when I spy two bodies being yanked along the opposite side of the snowy field by Norfell soldiers.

Killian and Rowan.

Piper must spot them in the same moment, because her arm around mine tightens.

"Let's go." The words fly out of my mouth without missing a beat.

My boots find purchase underneath me as the adrenaline kicks in.

We have to save them. No matter what.

A wave of shadows crash down around the soldiers who have Killian and Rowan.

Bash appears a few paces away from them, one hand outstretched, controlling the darkness. The other flings a star-shaped dagger at the throat of a man holding Rowan.

The weapon meets its mark, and the soldier thuds into the white at his feet, staining it crimson.

A dark wagon drawn by a mighty, chestnut Clydesdale emerges from the pines behind the lot of them.

My stomach aches at the sight, and I pick up speed.

A new green-clad soldier replaces the fallen one at Rowan's side and they continue on with my limp friend, heaving her along.

Dammit, the one taken out wasn't the one wielding her mind.

Bash grows his shadows, sending out whips to wrap around arms and legs of the Norfellens.

But four soldiers are on him in a split second, materializing from the forest beyond the wagon.

One blasts a glaring, red blaze at him. Another shakes the ground beneath his boots. A third slams beams of light into his pitch black tendrils. And the fourth whips out a dagger, spinning it in hand.

Only halfway across the expansive, snowy clearing now, I reach underground, feeling for the earth beneath those soldiers.

A singular vine shoots up, and I wrap it around the man who grips the dagger, locking his wrist within my piece of greenery.

I tug on the vine, forcing him to crash onto his side, and the weapon falls from his grasp, sinking into the snow.

He yanks against the deep green tendril but I spring up another, sending it over his neck, further securing him to his place in the snow.

I squeeze it, and he's unconscious only a moment later.

My attention flies to the carriage when, out of the corner of my eye, I notice the double doors to it fly open. More than half a dozen soldiers surround the stilled wagon, forcing Killian inside.

No.

No. No. *No.*

Killian twitches, seeming to fight for the control of his mind, and past the collar ridding him of his powers. He locks eyes with a Norfell soldier, the one I assume who has a hold of his mind.

The soldier's eyes briefly widen, then tighten on Killian.

Is he… breaking through the strength of the collar?

I didn't know it was possible. But… it seems like he may be.

I know he's powerful but, he's truly that strong?

When one had been placed on me, it felt like my abilities drained from me wholly, like the cuffs and the collar stole them right out of my body.

My heart hammers in my chest and I push forward, finally closing in on the chaos.

The soldier beside Killian drops to the floor then.

And Killian rages.

On his sides, the Norfellens grapple with him, grabbing onto wherever they can in order to control him. He jerks and kicks, throwing himself into the men.

Then, the hilt of a dagger slams into his head.

Killian nearly collapses, but the soldiers haul him up. His feet meet the floor of the wagon.

And my heart stops.

No, they can't be taking him away. No!

Killian lifts his limp head, hovering on the brink of unconsciousness.

His sapphire stare bores into me then, pleading with me. A ghost of a hand shakily runs over my mind's shield, barely there.

"Leave."

The side of his head is struck again, and his body crumbles.

No!

My throat burns when a vicious scream escapes me.

The soldiers make quick work of shoving Killian's unconscious body into the wagon.

In an instant, I reach below me, asking for the earth to forgive me for what I'm about to do.

I take control of the ground, forcing it to shake, and a crack forms under one of the soldier's feet. It widens, swallowing his leg. I clamp it shut, squeezing the earth together.

The sound of a shriek rips me out of my intense fury, and the plans I had for the soldiers go with it.

I whip around to find the men who have ahold of Rowan veering away from the treeline.

Now, they stomp towards the carriage.

And a few paces away lies Piper, on her knees, in the snow, stone still.

Luca stands behind her, strawberry blonde braids in his grasp. He leans down, whispering something in her ear.

Tears run down her freckled face while the rest of her remains unmoving.

He's... controlling her.

My eyes roam between Piper, forced not to move under Luca's watchful eye, and Rowan, whose limp body is being dragged through the snow, now only a few paces from the dark wagon Killian lies within.

I'm stunned into an unmoving state, my racing heart the only part of me in motion.

No. Not again.

A flash rips past, in the corner of my vision. The moment I see the person's black pigtails, I know who it is.

Jade.

"Get Rowan! I got Piper!"

Her command recenters me and I rush to Rowan.

The soldiers surrounding the wagon begin to shift towards her while one of them throws open the doors.

Her golden-ringed eyes are closed, and her face droops down. They knocked her out cold.

All at once, a swell of snow topples over me, throwing me to the ground. My head hits a patch of icy, dense snow. The impact sends my vision swimming.

I watch from the ground as Rowan's body is hoisted into the air and shoved into the carriage alongside Killian's.

No! *No!*

A sob climbs out my throat. Wetness that isn't from the snow drips down my face.

A sharp pang of guilt runs through my chest.

I couldn't get to either of them in time. I've… failed.

Hands abruptly reach beneath my arms and raise me up. Soft, heavy breaths sound in my ear and I turn.

Bash stands behind me, tawny face twisted into one of disbelief. The soldiers he battled left blooming bruises along his jaw and temple. His mouth hangs open as he takes in a gulp of air.

Then, a blaze of light burns brightly before us and we cower behind our forearms.

A maniacal laugh booms from beyond the brightness. "Goodbye, Orellians. Do say hello to your king for me. I want him to know who bested his heir to the throne."

The light disintegrates and reveals Luca, smiling ear to ear, with a single foot up on step to the carriage's seat. He pulls himself onto the lifted bench and the wagon takes off, the echo of the Clydesdale's whip reverberating off of the nearby pines.

A handful of tears streak down my face. Hopelessness sinks in my gut simultaneously.

Snow flies past me, pelting the back end of the dungeon-on-wheels.

I twist to see Asher sending ball after ball of the icy flakes at the carriage.

Racing with him is Piper, angry sobs coming from her. Jade isn't far behind the pair.

A hot blaze shoots at the three of them from the soldiers that once surrounded the wagon.

The Norfell soldiers are pushing on with the attack. Another flame whizzes by. Then a gust of wind. And a streak of shadows.

I think back to the word Killian slipped into my head before he was knocked out.

Leave.

He said to *leave*.

We have to retreat.

I spin, viewing the mass of Norfellens battling on with the rest of the trainees. Pieces of earth go flying. Beams of light shine. A whip of snow turns to liquid as it slashes around.

"We have to retreat."

My stare finds Sebastian as the words leave my lips.

His blown pupils shrink, showing more of the cocoa in his eyes as he takes in my words, then he dips his chin in acknowledgement.

He throws up a wall of shadows between us and the soldiers sending out attacks at Piper, Jade, and Asher.

At the top of my lungs I yell it.

"Retreat!"

My friends skid to a stop before the dark shield, faces distraught.

I repeat myself, voice cracking when I shout the order.

Piper runs at me, face red with a mix of cold and misery. "We can't leave them! We have to save them!"

"I know. We will. Look around," I say, trying to hold back more tears as I wave my arm at the battle strewn across the vast field. "We are outnumbered. Severely. Killian said to leave. We will retreat and regroup. We will get them back, but if we stay here, we *will* be slaughtered."

I grab her hands, pleading with her. My vision waters and a tear falls.

She throws my hands off of hers and grabs onto the shoulders of my shirt.

"No! We can't! We can't leave Rowan! We can-," Piper's pleading is cut off as Asher grabs her, hauling her off of me.

"She's right. We have to go." He stares at me with solemn, yet understanding eyes.

Piper screams, clawing at his hands around her middle. Her tears turn to wails as she fights him.

My chest aches and I blink rapidly at the mass of tears threatening to fully escape.

"We have to go," Bash's voice strains behind me. His arm begins to shake as he holds back the soldiers beyond his shadows.

I eye Jade, then Asher. The blonde man swiftly picks up Piper, throwing her over his shoulder.

She yelps, then pounds on his back. Jade rushes to her, consoling her as she hangs upside down.

I can't wait to listen to her words if we want to get everyone out of this alive.

Spinning around, I take off, spreading the word of the retreat.

I yell the command repeatedly, blasting light at the eyes of Norfell soldiers, just as Piper did for me, to help other trainees get away.

One at a time, I aid my fellow trainees in their battles.

Slowly but surely, we escape the soldiers and their abilities, heading to the pine trees we started our ambush from.

I push people forward, hollering at them to go while I linger behind to enter some of the soldier's minds and force them to sleep.

Sweat pours off of me as I work my ability to the brink of burnout, ensuring our people get away.

Asher goes ahead of me into the bush, Piper still slung over his shoulder. Jade leaves their side to help a young blonde woman who walks wobbly with a limp.

Bash finally releases his hold on the huge shadow wall once he's backed away, nearly halfway to the line of trees.

My throat is raw from the yelling when he meets me a bit further back. Loose strands of hair from my braid stick to the dampness on my face. My brain aches from the amount of minds I shoved my way into.

I ensure all our people are amongst the trees behind Bash and me when I crouch down, sinking my hands into the snow.

I finally release the tears I fought back, letting my anguish fill me.

They took Rowan.

And they took Killian.

The guilt erodes every inch of me. It mixes with complete and absolute fury.

I reach into the earth, and it begins to shake.

A screeching, whining sound unrolls across the icy ground. Then with a boom, a crack forms, running horizontally before me.

The ground splits, widening, two paces in front of me.

Reaching deeper into the earth, the fracture extends on both sides.

I allow the earth to feel my pain, and it understands me.

The ground rumbles even harder. The crack opens even wider, stretching further.

By the time I let go of my hold on the earth, it spans dozens and dozens of feet long on each side.

I fall to the icy ground, the tears ceasing. My eyes burn from the sheer amount shed.

I swallow bottomless buckets of air while my head spins.

I don't know how to get them back. I don't know how we'll find Rowan and Killian again.

But I will *not* stop until they are found.

A cool hand rests on my shoulder and Bash lowers himself next to me.

"I'll go. I'll track them through the forest."

My eyes go to the far edge of the clearing, where beyond the branches of the pines, I spot the speck that is the dark wagon, heading further into Norfell territory.

I turn to him, words escaping me.

Bash leaves my side to race to a tree, snatching his pack from behind it. He swiftly pulls out his black cloak, the one he wore the day he was captured, draping it over his shoulders.

"We'll get Rowan back," he begins. With a small tilt of his lips and the raise of a brow, he continues, "Killian too, don't worry."

"Thank you," I whisper, my throat sore.

"You don't need to thank me, just wait for my word."

I give him a weak nod.

And with a squeeze of my shoulder, he sprints off into the trees, like a shadow amongst the pines.

Chapter 40

The silence is deafening.

The quiet of the hike back into Orellia bled into our late lunch, and now our dinner.

The cold shock running all throughout me has lessened, but still holds tight in my chest. My eyes sting from the amount of crying I have done.

The guilt of retreating eats away at my insides, forcing my stomach to flip and roll. My mind spins with every possibility of what they may be going through at this very moment.

Rowan. Killian. Even Bash.

The urge to vomit crawls up my throat. Not for the first, second, or even third time today.

I reach for the glass of water just beyond my untouched bowl to stew and gulp it down, attempting to soothe the sensation.

Faint tapping begins next to me, the thrum gently shaking the stained wooden table.

I move my eyes from my now empty glass to Asher, and his fingers hitting the solid surface. His golden, tanned face is scrunched up, his mouth twisted, eyebrows tilted down, and nose wrinkled. Very much opposite of his usual disposition.

Words don't have time to form on my tongue before he breaks the silence.

"Why Luca? I just don't get it."

His words stretch over the dining room, and Jade, Piper, and a few others look up from their meals.

Jade's shoulders slump as she rests her forearms on the table. Her pale face is flat, tired eyes laying hollow, but a twitch shortly follows in her brows.

Piper's eyes and cheeks have remained red since our retreat.

She first sobbed in Asher's arms, after beating her fists against his chest when he finally removed her from his shoulder; he had stayed still, allowing her to, arms outstretched and ready to hold her for when she inevitably crumbled.

She then moved into Jade's hug and wept when we reached our border station, skipping lunch in the process.

She hadn't dared look at me in all that time.

But shortly before dinner, her puffy gaze met mine across the couch we had slept on only hours ago and her facade fell.

I bawled with her when she rushed into my arms.

My chest aches at the memory from less than an hour ago.

"That fucking bastard!" Piper roars, pushing out her chair and standing from the table.

She begins to pace behind our chairs. The pink on her cheeks blooms to a bright cherry color as she moves.

"He's always been an ass." She crosses her arms over her breasts and huffs. Her light green eyes turn glassy when she spins to stomp back in the direction she came from.

From my place at the head of the table, I listen as she spews more expletives, one after the other, marching back and forth.

Her fury swiftly descends into angry sobs.

"Wha-what does h-he want wi-with them?" she chokes out amidst her tears.

"I don't know but please, sit. Eat," Jade encourages from the seat opposite of Asher's.

"I c-can't! I d-don't want to!" Piper raises her voice, throwing her hands wildly in the air. She turns, strutting the other way again. More cries burst from her when she faces away.

Asher pulls out her chair beside him, trying to usher her into it.

She ignores him.

I fight to find the right words. My own stomach is flipping and flopping in tune with her pacing.

I miss Rowan too. So much.

And Killian. I *really* miss him too.

Although it's hard to admit to myself.

His presence… It reassured me. And I don't know when that feeling started.

Because he used to infuriate me.

It's confusing.

But I feel… something for him.

His frustration had morphed into something like benevolence. I see that now.

And it's made him grow on me, a lot. A lot more.

There is so much more to him. He's so different from who I thought he was when I first met him.

The realization of the change in feelings has me disoriented. I don't know what to do about it all.

Why do I feel this way?

I squeeze my eyes closed and rub at my temples, forcing the matter aside for the time being.

"Rowan wouldn't want you to be like this. She would want you to rest, then think with a clear mind."

The words fly out of my mouth. They feel right, and after everything Rowan and I have been through together, I'd hope I know one of my best friends well enough to think as she would.

I pry open my eyes to view Piper coming to a halt. Her shoulders fall and she glances at the floorboards.

"You're right," she says softly. She slides into her seat beside Asher, nodding. "You're right. Thank you."

I stretch my hand out over the surface, careful to avoid our food, and place a palm over hers.

"We'll devise a plan. We just have to wait for Bash. He'll be back soon."

I don't add "I hope" to the end of my sentence, although it is part of why I worry.

I have no idea when he will be back, *if* he comes back at all. And if he's spotted spying on them…

I shake away the dread that threatens to build.

"In the meantime, let's get some rest and allow people to heal," I continue, eyeing her with as much reassurance I can muster.

The only upside I can find in this moment is that the rest of us all made it out alive. Every person I urged to retreat listened.

Minor wounds covered the faces and bodies of nearly everyone. Some battles landed others with twisted or broken limbs. The handful of those who sustained such injuries now rested in the infirmary.

But, they all got out alive.

I truly have no explanation for it. My mind spirals back, replaying the scene to just before the retreat.

The retreat. It was Killian's idea.

He told me to leave. Leave *him*.

He's the explanation.

Wetness unexpectedly covers my cheeks.

I pull my hand from Piper's and wipe at my face. My throat tightens, like a boulder has lodged itself into my esophagus.

I reach for my water, only to remember the glass is barren. I lean forward and grab a pitcher just past Piper's untouched stew.

Filling my cup once, then twice, I drink the cool liquid rapidly. I only place it down when the boulder has finally shrunk.

The liquid sloshes around in my empty stomach, sending it flipping once more. Then, the compulsion to vomit the water I just consumed fills me up.

This is going to be a long wait for Bash.

Dinner two nights later isn't entirely different from that of our first without Rowan and Killian.

The table is quiet once again. Roasted meat and vegetables lay nearly or completely untouched by us all.

Morale has never been lower.

And no word has come from Bash.

I poke at the root vegetables on my plate, pushing them back and forth for the umpteenth time. The food isn't bad by any means, but the knots in my stomach have only grown larger as time goes on.

Footsteps loudly bounding down the hallway pulls my attention from the meal.

I sit up straighter in my chair when Asha enters the room. Her face bunches together as she surveys the tables. Then, her swirling eyes land on me at the end of it.

She rushes over, placing both hands on the wood next to my plate.

"There's a woman. She came out of the forest," she begins in a hushed voice.

Piper jumps out of her seat next to me, leaning in. "What does she look like? Is it Rowan?"

Asha shakes her head. "No."

Her gaze briefly moves to Piper, but then points to me, her hazel eyes bright and brimming with questions. "But she's asking for you, by name."

Piper returns to her chair, her ever-puffy eyes sinking down to the table. Jade places a gentle hand on her shoulder, whispering into her ear.

I eye Asher, who sits across from them, elbows on the table, fist covering his mouth while his brows knit together. His stare meets mine, a multitude of questions building behind his sky blue eyes.

I look at Asha. "Bring her in."

She nods, and whisks away.

If not Rowan, what woman is asking for me? And how does she know my name?

My fingers move to my chest and I rub at the ache building there. Dread begins to soar through my lungs. And bumps of nerves appear on my arms.

When Asha returns, it's with Declan, whose hands grip a young woman's biceps. On her pale neck sits a metal collar, her wrists, a set of cuffs, and her booted ankles, shackles.

Asher raises to his feet, crossing his arms over his chest, staring her down.

The woman's near-white long hair lies in a braid, draped over her shoulder. A woolen, deep green dress covers her petite frame. A solid black cloak rests atop her attire.

"She agreed to the restraints, as a precaution," Declan states, suspicion lacing his words.

"I mean you all no harm." Her voice is smooth, unwavering.

Her sight bypasses Asher, looking around at the three of us women still seated.

A moment passes before she seemingly makes up her mind, her light green gaze landing on me.

"You are Aurora."

"I am. Who are you? And how do you know my name?"

I mimic Asher's movement without realizing, folding my arms over my breasts. I feel my eyes narrowing at her, inspecting her.

A calm demeanor. Not fighting against the restraints or Declan. She stands straight as a pole, as if an imaginary string is pulling her from above. Her features are soft, still relatively young. Only eighteen or so, if I had to guess.

"The Princess," Jade contemplates out loud.

My head whips in my friend's direction. I study the thoughtful regard she gives the young woman.

"The King of Norfell's only heir. Princess Callista," Jade continues.

"I am Princess Callista. I-"

Before the woman can say another word, Piper lunges. Hitting the table in her swift movement, food flies off of plates. Water sloshes from glasses when they tip.

Asher grabs her around the middle, holding her back, pulling her to the closest corner of the room, as Piper spews vitriol all the while.

"Your people took her! Where is she? You bitch! How dare you!"

Jade and I spring to our feet. Back to back we stand in front of Piper, Jade facing her in an attempt to calm her, me glaring at the Princess.

My voice booms over the commotion, reminiscent of Killian without my knowing until the words leave my mouth.

"What do you want? Why are you here?"

Wide, green eyes aside, her disposition remains peaceful, nearly unfazed by Piper's reaction.

"I was sent here. By your friend."

"Who?" I spit out, my frustration getting the better of me.

"Sebastian."

Chapter 41

My stomach bottoms out. And silence fills the room in an instant.

"What do you mean?"

It's the only question I can come up with.

Callista's lips turn up into a pleasant smile when she speaks.

"Your friend is alright. I can assure you that. We found each other whilst observing one of my father's hidden outposts." Her face notably falls at her last few words.

"What outpost? Where is it?" Piper spits from behind me. From her voice alone I can picture the mirth covering her face.

"Please, let us sit so I may explain." Regality surrounds the Princess's words as she gestures to the chair Asher sprang from earlier.

Slowly, I move to my abandoned seat, eyes never leaving the Princess of Norfell.

Movement shuffling around me lets me know Jade, Piper, and Asher have positioned themselves in chairs on my other side, across from the Princess.

The possibilities of what she may say filter through my mind, shuffling like a deck of cards. Her father, Norfell, Bash, it could be anything.

I lick my lips while waiting for her next words.

Princess Callista places folded, pale, hands on the wood before her, the metal cuffs gently clanking.

"Allow me to start from the beginning," she starts, peering around our end of the table.

"I *am* Princess Callista Bane of Norfell. However, as your friend said earlier…" She nods at my side, and I swing my head to meet Jade's angular face.

"I am technically *not* the sole heir to the throne of Norfell."

That makes my head swivel back to her.

"I am the only *legitimate* one. At least for the time being," she continues. I spy her throat bob as she swallows. Her fingers squeeze together.

"I have an older brother. A half brother from my father. He is a bastard," she tilts her head to the side in thought, green eyes drifting off.

"My mother had trouble conceiving; she spent many years trying. She then died giving birth to me. So, I suppose I was not entirely surprised to find out that at some point, my father impregnated another."

She chokes on emotion before going on.

"I only recently discovered his existence. But my father has known of him his whole life."

I study Callista, her lips red from the cold, hair windblown, but still held well enough together in the long, white plait. Her cheeks are pink, a stark contrast against her porcelain skin. Lime-colored eyes turn glassy as she picks through her mind.

"Why should we care? What does this have to do with us?"

The questions come from Piper. Genuine curiosity laces her tone. Although I'm positive exasperation lies underneath.

"Because you know him. Lucifer. But I'm sure you all have referred to him as Luca."

My eyebrows shoot to my hairline. My mouth gapes.

He's… a prince? The Prince of Norfell?

And then the dots start connecting.

He's the one who took Killian, who had him in restraints while he blasted Rowan and I with light when we stormed into the border station. The Norfell soldiers bent to his will.

And now, we know why.

When my eyes refocus from my train of thought, they narrow on the Princess.

"How?"

She nods, investigating her folded hands before answering.

"You see, when I found out of his existence, it was from a correspondence letter from him to my father. He wrote of detailed movements of the Orellian military. Specifically, the Orellian King's multiwielding army."

I thought my stomach had sunk before, but now it hollows out and nausea bubbles up.

I'm going to be sick.

Luca wrote letters.

And not so long ago, we had caught him in a fit, while holding a piece of paper.

My gut twists more, as if wringing out a soaking wet cloth.

"He once noted that his position gave him influence, as he had worked his way up through the ranks over the years. That was how I learned my father knew of him for a long while. And that he sent Lucifer undercover many years ago," she says solemnly.

Years. Luca had worked his way up for *years*.

All the way to Killian's second-in-command.

My head spins with more questions. It takes me a few moments to land on just one.

"Why would Luca agree to it?"

She dips her chin expectantly.

"My father told him that he could earn his place as a rightful heir. That he would name him the heir and no one would ever know he was a bastard so long as he infiltrated Orellia's military to give him as much knowledge as possible. And also if he…" she pauses, her mouth open, ready for her next words.

She closes her mouth, eyes flittering back and forth before landing on mine.

"And also if he killed the Prince."

The blow feels physical, as if the air rushes from my lungs due to a blast of someone's powers.

My hand lifts from the table to land on my chest. I barely feel it.

Everything in me begins to numb.

Something lays over my other hand still on the wooden surface. Eyes hazy, I look.

It's the Princess's palms.

"He is still alive. For now."

Wind refills my lungs at the words, as if she breathes life into them herself. As if the knowledge that he's alright fills me.

Alive.

Killian's *alive.*

"I believe Luci- *Luca* is attempting to torture any information left out of him," she says softly. Her light sage gaze bores into me, sympathy pouring from the look.

"What about the woman taken with him? Rowan. What about her?" I muster up, the questions as quiet as her previous words.

"Also still alive. For now."

Another wave of relief crashes over me.

They're *both* still alive.

A woosh of a sigh comes from my right and I feel Piper's relief radiating off of her.

Princess Callista gently pulls her hands back, now placing them in her lap, her rigid posture returning.

"We must hurry. My father wants to name his successor relatively... soon." She briefly peeks away but rights her gaze once again, leveling me with an intense stare.

"My father is sick. It's a sickness of the mind. A sickness no one has been able to cure. He has been ill for some time now, but as the years go on, it has worsened."

She releases a huff. "*That* is what started this mess. His delusions began not long before he sent Luca away to infiltrate your ranks; he was barely old enough to join at the time."

She eyes her lap, fingers fiddling with her cuffs.

"I was half his age. I was a child. I could not have done anything back then. But it hurts to know that this has been happening under my nose for so long and I only discovered it a handful of months ago."

"But you're doing something now." I reach out, placing a palm over her hands, just as she did mine.

"Thank you for coming," I whisper, my voice caught in my throat.

She gives me a tight grin when she raises her head to me. "It was your friend who sent me, after all. He is sneaky, that one. Gave me a fright when he flew down from the branches above me and tangled me in his shadows."

Her eyes widen and her brows raise as she recalls the moment.

"But he is a good one. You are lucky to have a friend in him. And he, you," she says, grin broadening when she views my palm.

"Now," her face grows grim. "Luca will be taking the captives to the palace to present them to my father in two days time. If they make it there, we will *never* be able to save them."

"Then let's go get them!" Piper raises her voice, standing to her feet.

Callista's face goes white. "I- I am not versed in rescue plans. I do not have a plan for you all."

I contemplate her.

She has been forthcoming so far, and she was restrained willingly.

Taking my limbs back, I observe her for another several seconds.

And I land on an idea.

"I would like to see into your mind," I state plainly. "I believe you. But if we are to successfully rescue our people, I need to be absolutely sure. I need to see what you have seen."

I surprise myself with the decorum in my voice but I hold still, studying her.

She blinks, nodding. "Of course you may. I understand."

With a steadying breath, I gently reach into her mind.

Closing my eyes, I focus on what she has said, searching for the moment she spoke with Bash, and the truth of Luca's betrayal.

Everything she stated was true.

I see Bash's face as they talk, crouched behind trees similar to those I saw the carriage carrying Rowan and Killian pull away into. Icy wind brushes against my face. I smell smoke from a chimney rising out of a small, dark building in the distance behind them.

I view her father's aging face at the head of a dinner table, babbling on about how his kingdom will fall without a strong leader such as himself. Wetness dampens my cheeks as he speaks.

I read a letter addressed to him, explaining the location of Orellian border patrol stations along Mount Jasper, Bear, and Smokey, signed by Luca.

Coldness runs through my body when another letter appears, with the word "kill" sitting in front of Killian's name.

I pull out of her mind instantly, unable to watch more. I squeeze my eyes, then look at her.

"I saw it. Thank you," I murmur.

My sight begins to blur. I look down, blinking rapidly to clear the building droplets.

Only after ridding my eyes of the stubborn moisture do I view Piper, Jade, and Asher. An undeniable wrath starts to grow in my stomach at their forlorn, defeated faces.

No more of this. No more crying.

I can't take it any longer.

The words leave my lips on instinct; a quiet darkness rising within. And it comes out as a near growl.

"Let's go get them back."

Chapter 42

The pale light of the midnight moon shines through pine trees high above my head.

The several hours it took us to hike here in the near total darkness has my joints freezing, my wrist especially. After holding up a ball of light for hours on end in order to find the way, it's severely sore.

Legs aching as if it were my first day of training all over again, I swipe snow off of the closest boulder I can find and slump onto it.

My anxious foot would tap if I had the strength to spare.

The rest of the trainees follow suit, resting against whatever piece of nature lies nearest. I count them in my head, like a mother hen checking on her chicks.

Excluding the few who had to stay behind due to their more severe injuries, they were all accounted for. Plus our two additions.

Princess Callista plops down beside me, Asha closing in behind her, concern filling her eyes.

"Are you well, Princess?"

The young woman holds up her hand graciously. Although, the rest of her reads more than slightly disheveled.

"I am. Thank you. More walking. Than I've. Ever had to do," she explains, out of breath.

"These mountains are no joke," I tell her, chuckling.

Asha joins in. "You also hiked to us first. I'm not surprised."

Under the cover of darkness we continue to sit, getting a sliver of reprieve before we execute what we came here to do.

I twist my head, staring off at the quaint, dark building in the distance, half blocked by the dense trees. The building I saw in Callista's mind.

Only I wish I could see what lies inside too.

The Princess said earlier she has never dared enter the small, cottage-like house. But she overheard soldiers discussing its secretiveness, and that it wasn't a formal outpost. Instead, it was used for special, private business of the Norfell King.

My stomach dropped when she added that the soldiers said "most people never leave" the hidden building.

With others still holding flames or light to create enough brightness, I drop the orb in my hand.

I rub my freezing hands together after smoothing them down my chilled face.

Finding our way through the mountains, as well as hiking up and down smaller hills full of snow, has taken several hours. Snow began to lightly fall nearly an hour ago, tanking the temperature around us.

A puff of white fogs in front of my face with each breath I let out.

Spying the little cottage in the distance, I try to find any source of life within. The lights are off, curtains drawn, and it seems abandoned. Had it not been for the bit of smoke trailing out of the chimney, I would've thought it empty.

Crunching of the icy ground draws my attention to the left.

And making his way around a pair of pine trees stalks Sebastian. A waft of shadows drifting off of him slowly disintegrates as he approaches.

I spring to my tired feet and throw my arms around his neck, probably choking him. But I don't care.

I'm glad to see him with my own eyes, safe and sound.

"I'm so happy you're okay. I was worried."

I pull away and stare up into his faintly widening brown eyes. He dips his chin, gathering the thoughts I can see dancing behind his eyes.

"What is it?"

Nerves eat away at my insides while I wait for him to respond.

Several beats pass as fearful anticipation builds within me.

"They're all in there. The captives we were searching for. Rowan and Killian. I saw them dragged in. But, I don't know what state they're in now," he says solemnly. He runs a hand through his mess of dark curls beneath the hood of his even darker cloak.

His eyes don't meet mine when he continues. "I've seen more soldiers go in, but none have come out. And it remains dark."

I ponder his words.

A basement.

The hidden basement stairs Killian and I found before, there must be something similar here.

I don't realize I've thought out loud until I hear Bash agree with me.

"I believe so, based on what she said," he states, peering around me and gesturing to the Princess with a flick of his chin.

She shivers, running her hands along her arms.

I reflect on the not-very-structured rescue plan we devised around the dinner table before coming here.

"Do you think they have look outs? How close can we get without being spotted?"

"I've searched the whole forest. There's no one out here. No one's looked out the windows either. I snuck right up to the front door."

I let out a sigh of relief. That's one good thing we have on our side.

"The trees are dense back here. Are they around the building too?"

He nods, pointing. "Yes, they go right up to the front door."

I contemplate our numbers, how many may need to stay back if soldiers flood out and attack like before. How many should search for the captives. For Rowan. Killian.

Orders start flying out when I make my decision.

"You all," I begin, specifying the majority of the trainees with a hand. "Stay hidden when we get closer. Use the trees to your advantage."

Understanding fills the eyes of those around me, followed by a handful who dip their chins in acknowledgment.

I turn, observing those I trust most, those who I want inside with me if the situation takes a turn for the worst.

Piper. Jade. Asher. Bash.

The former three perch on a wide, flat stone.

"We're going inside."

Intent gazes from the four of them tug at my heart. The moisture from my mouth disappears.

I can't allow things to go wrong. Not again.

My stare finds Bash, holding it there. "Thank you."

An upward tilt of his lips forms. "Don't go thanking me yet. We haven't even saved them."

I roll my eyes, nudging him with my elbow. "Let's go."

A couple of hand signals later, we're off, moving in silence from tree to tree towards the small cottage. The only sound coming from the lot of us is the light shuffling of snow.

Minutes later, we stash ourselves behind the closest ring of thick pines surrounding the building. I bend my knees, closing in on the ground and peer around the tree I pause behind, investigating the cottage.

A tap on my shoulder startles me from my focus on the entrance.

Bash is crouched behind me, his gaze intense.

"What?" I whisper as softly as possible.

"I know."

Confusion spins in my mind. "You know what?"

His stare turns into a knowing look, his eyebrows raising. "That you have feelings for him."

I thought I was cold before, but a chill runs down my spine, turning me completely and utterly frozen.

"I- I don't know what you're talking about."

The incredulous look he gives me in return makes me gulp.

"It's nothing. There is nothing," I lie, unsure if I'm ready to speak on the uncertain feelings I only recently admitted to myself.

Bash's light brown eyes soften. "The look you give him is the same one he gives you."

My heart stops.

"Wha- what?"

I can't control the stutter that laces the word.

"I see the way you look at him. I may not know the fate that befell him beyond those walls but I'll do anything you need to help you get him back," he whispers, peeking down before he meets my eyes again.

Tears prick my eyes. I blink rapidly to clear them.

His candor fills my heart, overflowing it, like water bursting open a long beaten-against dam.

"You see everything, don't you?" I chuckle.

His only response is a smile.

"You don't know what that means to me," I say, shutting my eyes briefly, then continue. "I can't thank you enough. You. Rowan. Piper. Jade. Asher. You're family."

"I've got your back. Always," he tells me, and cups a hand around my shoulder.

I glance away when the next words start from my lips.

I can't look at anyone while admitting it. Not just yet.

"You're right. I don't know when it happened. But... I think I do have feelings for him."

His fingers tighten in a gentle squeeze on the start of my arm.

"Then let's go get him for you."

Chapter 43

The crash of the door flying inward echoes, bouncing off the surrounding pines. I pull my vines back from their attack on the entrance, retaining my grip on the pieces of earth, readying for a counter strike.

Rushing forward, Bash at my back, I sprint inside. Wood splinters crack under my boots in the doorway.

Before I can peer into the room's darkness enveloping us, a flash of red streaks in front of me, speeding towards my face.

I fling one of my vines up, knowing it'll most likely burn to a crisp. It does.

But once the blinding heat has dispersed, I see the attackers launching forward.

I duck and spin, drawing the attention of a thin, lanky soldier.

He sends a shadowy tendril to wrap around my arm with a wave of his fingers. It latches onto me. He yanks on it with a sly smirk.

Two can play that game.

I stretch out a thick, green vine through the doorway, twisting it over and under his shoulder.

The end of the greenery creeps up his neck in an instant, slithering over his Adam's apple.

Attempting to take over his movements, I reach into his mind but hit a solid shield.

Ugh.

With my hand enclosed in his darkness, I light a shining, yellow ball. I let it grow brighter, widening over my limb. With my other, I focus on the earth I intend to suffocate him with.

A sense of darkness rises in me as I creep the earth along his neck.

The vine succeeds, and he releases his hold on the shadows when his hands fly to his throat, scraping at it.

I squeeze the vine until he drops.

I look away, turning from his limp body and find Bash standing only paces away, a bearded man kneeling at his feet.

The man fists his eyes, sobbing, begging for forgiveness. Bash's eyes stay locked on him.

I can only imagine the things he's showing the soldier in his mind.

On his other side is Piper, whose hands are now currently gripping a Norfellen man's ponytail. She lights it on fire.

I bite down on a smile attempting to grow.

She's the best.

The man falls into a heap on the ground a moment later.

Jade, close behind, peers at Piper for a moment before her dark eyes widen and she makes a surprised, yet gleeful face. She smothers it swiftly when she begins to investigate a side wall.

I view Asher, who takes up the rear, a deadly stare covering his usually relaxed features.

He surveys the room, and I follow.

Only three soldiers attacked us. Now all incapacitated, fallen to the floor like marionettes cut loose from their strings.

Jogging over to Jade, I push against the wall she starts to feel out.

"It's fake. From outside, the building continues another few feet," Jade explains from my side.

Soon Piper, Bash, and Asher are shoving on the dark, wood paneled wall too. I hear a click, then a section shifts.

"Yes!" Piper grins as she moves the fake segment aside on what appears to be some kind of small wheels. It reveals an unlit set of nearly never-ending stairs, stretching down to a barely visible, wide, dark door.

The dark pit that never leaves my stomach spreads as I view it. Unsettled fury bubbles in the darkness, overflowing into my chest.

I glance at the four of them, unsavory possibilities of what lie ahead filling my mind.

Each of them meet me with intense stares. Unspoken words pass between us. An acknowledgement that no matter what happens, *all* of us are getting out of here *now*.

The steps blur by as I tear down them first, an orb lighting in my hand as I do. The metal handle drops to the ground when my palm touches the door, disintegrating the wood surrounding it.

A kick to the door sends it swinging.

And a swarm of shadows blast us backwards.

I stumble into my friends. The light in my hand pulses, growing larger as I fight off the darkness.

Piper and Asher join me in the next second. I feel their brightness spreading around both sides of mine.

I hear a screech, and the shadows disappear, as if they were never there.

On the floor, a pale, young man clutches his hands.

Hot, red burns blister both of them, leading up his forearms, to his elbows, and even his lower biceps.

His mind is mine in a moment, reaching in my claws without a care.

Pain laces through him. Screaming engulfs his head.

I push him over the edge into unconsciousness easily. His eyes close and he falls forward, completely limp.

Two more soldiers rush us then, my head whipping at the movement out of my peripheral.

Between Bash, Asher, Piper, and Jade, they're on the ground, unmoving only a minute later.

I take in the expansive space we've entered.

Outstretched in front of me, leading off to the right is a sweeping room. Significantly longer than it is wide. Deep, red wood makes up the floors and walls.

Cages line the length of the space. Thick, metal bars make up the barriers of them. And behind them lay the captives.

I count them as I sprint over to the closest one.

Five.

Fuck.

The multiwielders we went for last time. No Rowan or Killian in sight.

Damn it.

Dark rage whips around inside of me.

We *have* to find them.

"Here," Asher throws a ring of keys at me. I barely catch them in time. Then, he does the same to Jade, Piper, and Bash.

The captives blink at us in shock. We work swiftly, trying one key after the next.

But it's not fast enough.

Through a twin hidden door within the far right wall emerges four more Norfell soldiers. All tall, hulking men.

Their faces boil, twisting up. And elements start flying.

A gust of wind immediately threatens to push me but I dig my boots into the wood under my feet. I stretch my fingers down, feeling for where earth would normally be.

None. It's all too far away.

This underground building is too hefty, too sturdy to get through. I can't pull up any vines.

Vexation pulses within me.

I throw a light ball at the air wielding man instead, and try to feel into his mind. A shield as sturdy as this structure is in place.

The air attacking me halts. And I feel a slimy, dirty hand run fingers down my own shield. He tugs at it, striding closer to me.

My nose scrunches at him.

Disgusting man.

I hold my mind's shield strong, glaring into him as he dares to take another step to me. Reaching for his again, I yank.

A sly grin appears on his face. He brushes his fingers through long, blonde waves. He inches closer, towering over me, breathing on me.

I know this game.

He thinks he can best me, intimidate me. He thinks he can force his way into my mind. To try and break me.

But I've already been broken. They already did that to me.

I'm here to pick up the pieces. Again.

Again and again I've picked up the shards of my shattered soul.

When my parents were taken from me.

Their lives stolen *for me*. For a chance that their daughter may escape unscathed.

I did, barely.

And I had to put myself back together again.

Then, I was taken, ripped from the life I built with my aunt. The woman who took me in as I fit each piece of me back into its rightful place.

I was taken from her, forced into a tyrant's army.

Against my will, I had to put myself back together *again*.

And just when I thought I could live this unfortunate life in this forsaken King's Army, and had placed the pieces back together once more, I was broken *again*.

When a woman who I was imprisoned with, cried with, trained with, and laughed with, but also bonded so deeply with, was taken.

And a man who I once swore would never know a moment of peace in my presence, but who I have seemingly fallen for anyways, was taken.

A man who was supposed to be my sworn enemy. Who instead made me falter so completely. He was taken.

I will pick up the pieces of me only once more. *Never* again after this.

Because it's my turn to finally take for myself.

My fist goes flying before I can register my own movement. Blood sprays from the soldier's nose as my hand collides with it.

My knee juts out when I grab his shoulders with my palms. The joint of my leg slams into his groin.

I shove with all my body weight, throwing him backwards.

He wobbles on his way to the ground, falling to the side.

An ear-shattering clang rings out when his skull smacks a metal bar on the cage I had been trying to unlock.

When the rest of him finally hits the ground, he's out cold.

I gaze up from his limp body to see the last of the remaining three soldiers fall at the hands of Jade, who sucks the air from his lungs.

A lock clicks undone and I turn to see Piper opening a middle cage, helping a young woman out.

After searching for and finding the keyring I dropped in the heat of the moment, I open the cage nearest me.

I shift one of the unconscious soldier's legs away to clear space for the metal door to scrape ajar. I wish his stupid ass wouldn't have collapsed right in my way.

The multiwielding man that stumbles out of the cage in the following moment gives me a silent, thankful nod.

My sight then lands on the discrete door in the wall the soldiers came through. It sits slightly ajar on the opposite side of the room.

I hear more clicks and curt instructions given, but my eyes stay locked on the entry.

They must be in there.

They *have* to be.

I'm across the massive room and pushing the door aside before I know it.

A mirror image of the first stairwell sits before me.

I hear four sets of footsteps I've come to know so well approach behind me. Down further we go.

The darkness I step into eats away at me, regardless of the light I form in the palm of my hand.

Same as before, I breach the wooden door with my brightness, shoving my way inside.

This time, instead of immediately being met with an attack, the door swings open to reveal the traitor himself.

Luca.

Flanked by two more soldiers on each side.

"Come for a visit, have you?"

The former second-in-command chuckles. Deranged, green eyes leer at me, threatening me, beckoning me. White hair sticks out in every direction from the messy braid that lines the center of his head.

"Have you missed them? I hope you have, because this will be the last time you ever see them," he snides, turning, motioning behind him.

My eyes flicker to the bodies against the far wall.

On the left, black braids covering her face, is Rowan. A metal collar sits tight around her throat. Bleeding knees show through rips in her pants. Her bare ankles are encased in shackles, rubbed raw. Her wrists are high above her head in matching cuffs anchored to the wall.

Pitch black wrath unlike anything I've ever experienced before builds within me.

My hands shake. No, they vibrate.

I force my eyes to the right.

Face twisted to the side, bloody, torn, and bruised, is Killian. Chocolate curls coated in crimson brush against a silver collar. One arm is stretched up properly into a wall cuff. The other is bent at an inhuman angle, the bone protruding in the wrong direction. His wrists are an angry, irritated red. Restrained ankles match Rowan's. Shirt off, marks mar the light olive skin up and down his toned torso, scarlet dripping off his chest.

The vibration crashes over me like a tidal wave.

Darkness fills me, replacing my insides, my blood, with shadows. My vision goes dark.

And so does the whole room.

Chapter 44

Someone is screaming. Yelling. At the top of their lungs.

Pure ire fills the room.

The emotion is so strong it's palpable, tasteable on one's tongue.

Shadows fill the space, spinning, circling like a whirlpool.

Barely visible through the darkness, the faces of Luca and his soldiers are slack, color drained from them.

My throat burns. I inhale. And the screaming stops.

I didn't realize the sound was coming from me until the breath fills my depleted lungs.

Tingling in my fingertips crawls up my palms, and into my forearms. I peer down at the sensation.

Pitch black tendrils flow from all ten of my fingers.

The shadows… they're coming from me.

I don't wield shadows.

The darkness vanishes and I step back, holding my hands out in front of me as far away as possible. I stare at them, foreign to me.

Before another thought can race through my head, a beam of light blasts at me.

I throw my hands up defensively. More shadows slip from my hands, spreading out to shield me a second before the brightness hits me.

The darkness absorbs the light instantaneously.

I peer out from behind my void of a shield. Luca's harsh glare meets me.

I shove the inky wall away, forcing it into him. He stumbles backwards at the impact.

Bright colors flash past me. Burning red and sunset orange. Soft yellow and blinding gold. All leaving the hands of my friends.

The soldiers at Luca's sides spring into action, throwing attacks back.

So, I close in on Luca.

Bent on a knee from the force of my blast, he snarls at me as he stands once again.

"You've always been a piece of work," he growls.

"You haven't seen *anything* yet."

I send a snaking shadow spiraling from my fingers. A ray of light collides with it.

Pushing and pulling initiates. He propels his brightness forward an inch, I press harder, shooting it back.

His crazed eyes stare into me, into my soul, as he grunts against the movement.

I ram my darkness into him. I let the shadows fill me, use every part of me. As long as it means I stop him, I will do *anything*.

Sweat pours down my temples, dripping down my neck as I shove again. His light is nearly out. If I can just push a little more.

I release a grunt of my own and my shadows overcome his brightness.

The wave of black bangs into him. He goes flying, landing on his back several paces away on the hard, wooden floorboards. A crack sounds when his head hits.

He grumbles, forcing himself up onto his elbows as I stalk forward.

He lobs a ball of light at me with a palm.

I dodge it easily. And shoot out dark whips of my own.

One tangles around his outstretched arm. Another twists around his neck.

His free hand reaches up. Light emanates from it, trying to burn through the restraint that threatens to choke him.

I squeeze the darkness.

"You bitch," he whispers, his airway restricted.

I pick up my shadows, moving his body with them, and slam him up against the wall to my right. My fingers dance around, twisting the tendrils tighter. I step to him, closing in on his space.

"Damn right I am."

He fights against my swirling, inky coils beginning to cover the rest of him. They slither down, locking his arms firmly to his sides. Further down they trap his torso, then his legs that kick wildly.

His movements begin to slow as he becomes fully encased in my darkness. A smirk pulls on my lips when his jerking finally ceases.

I let up on the shadows around his neck, just enough for him to answer my only remaining question.

"What did you want to learn from them?"

There must be secrets Killian knows about the kingdom, military operations, something that Luca tried to torture out of him.

And he used Rowan as a pawn for it too.

"Wouldn't you like to know," he says, a hint of a grin lifting in the corner of his mouth.

Fuck it. I'll find out another way.

I yank the shadows upward, coating the rest of his neck and face. I twist his head up and to the side, using all the force I can muster, and with a swift snap, I feel his body go limp within the darkness.

Dropping the shadows surrounding him, his body falls, nothing holding it up any longer.

I bend, yanking off the pair of key rings attached to his belt. Standing, I view his body as my vision blurs.

My ears ring. The vibration in my fingers begins to fade. Stillness settles in the air.

With a spin, I view the room.

The four soldiers lay unmoving across the floor. Jade, Bash, and Asher stand still, panting.

Piper dashes forward in the same moment I do.

She sprints to Rowan. And I to Killian when my eyes land on his tortured state.

I drop to my knees in front of his crumbled body. My hands shake as they reach towards his bruised face.

My fingers brush ever so lightly against his jaw, then his cheek.

"Killian?" My voice comes out at a near whisper.

He turns slowly, lifting his head off of its resting place against his bicep. His coffee colored waves crusted with crimson graze the back of my hand.

His eyes, a deep, ocean blue, land on me. One has dark purple formed around it, making it sit partially shut.

"I knew you could handle yourself when it came to Luca. I did agree with you that day," he says, choking on a strangled chuckle.

The heaviness weighing down my chest the past few days lightens, just barely.

"Let's get you out of these," I tell him as I reach up with one of the keyrings, grabbing onto his cuffed wrists.

The first key I try, works. A sigh escapes me when his arm falls, then immediately wraps around my waist.

I gasp at the feel of his arm clutching me tightly.

Without a second thought, I chuck the other ring to Piper. She holds Rowan in her arms, tears slipping down her freckled cheeks while she unlocks the restraints.

My chest aches as I view my friend in chains. A tear slips down my cheek at the same time.

As soon as Rowan is free, she closes her palms around Piper's face, kissing her.

I glance away, trying to give them even a bit of privacy, and move to unlock the cuff around Killian's mangled arm.

I'm afraid of hurting him even worse.

I hear the bolt click, and I gently guide his wrist downward, slowly placing it at his side.

Now that his upper body is free, he slumps against me.

I hold back a gasp at his movement. His chin rests on my shoulder while I brush his hair to the side, releasing the collar from around his neck with a new key.

He remains there as I carefully undo the shackles around his ankles.

"You're free," I whisper to him after I push the clanking metal to the side.

He doesn't move. Worry spears through me.

"C-can you move?" I don't mean for my words to come out on a wobble, but they do, regardless of my wishes.

He pulls his head back.

My shoulder feels empty without his warmth.

His eyes rest on mine again. The darker blue swirls, mixing with a stunning aquamarine. His mouth opens, then closes. Then opens again. The split in his lip gets angrier as he moves.

"Thank you. For coming to get us… I don't know what I'd do without you."

Fluttering whirls around in my stomach at his words. The cocoon holding the feeling cracks wide open, sending the butterflies up into my chest and throughout the rest of me.

His breath hits my cheeks. He tips his head down, and rests his forehead against my own.

"You mean more to me than you know," he murmurs, only loud enough for the two of us to hear.

I take in his features. The beautiful eyes that stare into me, into my heart and soul. The bridge of his strong nose, rubbing slightly against mine. The sharp lines of his face, covered in glaring shades of purple and dark blue.

"You do, too," I whisper.

I feel a rush of heat blooming on my face. But I don't back away or try to hide it. As much as a small, nervous part of me may want to.

He leans closer, impossibly closer.

And his lips crash into mine.

My eyes close on impact and a rush surges through me.

I burst into oblivion.

Then I move my mouth in time with his.

I stretch my fingers up, into the hair at the base of his neck, gently tugging him closer. I feel his lips open in a smile, and he tightens his grip on my waist, fusing our bodies together.

A new kind of heat burns within me. Warm and comforting. All consuming.

When the tip of his tongue runs over my bottom lip, I open, allowing him in. He slowly dips his tongue in, letting me taste him. And him, me.

It's agonizingly slow yet lighting fast all at once. It's as if time has stopped and we're the only ones in motion.

Grazing the injury on his lower lip, I pull back, stunned out of my daze.

I narrow my gaze on the split, and lift my thumb up to it. "I don't want to hurt you."

My vision climbs, finally meeting his eyes.

"You could never," he breathes, searching my stare.

A mix between a sigh and a chuckle bubbles up my throat. I lick my lips, pulling on my lower one with my teeth.

"Let's get you out of here," I declare, suddenly eager to be back on our side of Mount Bear.

I haul him to his feet, although I nearly fall in the process.

The moment his feet are flat on the floor, I see movement out of my peripheral.

"We got him," Asher says, swooping in on my left. He takes Killian's uninjured arm, placing it around his shoulders.

Bash comes around on my right, and with delicate hands, sets Killian's broken forearm across his shoulders, letting it lie there limply.

As they take his weight, helping him out of the room and up the stairs, I speedily make my way to Rowan.

Dozens of more tears fall from my eyes when she looks at me. Blooming bruises line her jaw, and dried drips of scarlet cover her chin.

I want to crush her in a hug, but I opt for a much gentler one.

"I'm so sorry."

The sentence comes out in a huff as I struggle to keep my breaths even. I run a hand along the side of her head.

"Don't be. I'm fine," she tells me with a half-hearted smile. But her glassy, brown and gold ringed eyes tell me different.

I shake my head in disbelief, at the strength she's scrounging up.

I admire her beyond words I have the vocabulary for.

Placing my hand under her shoulder, Piper and I help her stand. Jade stays next to Piper, gaze bouncing back and forth between her and Rowan. Concern fills her eyes.

We loop Rowan's arms around us, Piper and I on each side, with Jade at her back when she stumbles briefly.

The way up the flights of stairs and across the rooms seems otherworldly, as if our path down here occurred a lifetime ago. The emotions filling me when we entered the building were so different from the ones coursing through me now.

When we eventually make our way out, after pivoting and shuffling through the narrow then wide spaces, I spy the outlines my fellow trainees faces in the middle-of-the-night darkness. Some covered in shock, some despair, some confusion, some worry.

A handful of them work together on the ground, faces I can't see. But the work they do, I can. They swiftly take supplies from their bags, building two stretchers in a matter of minutes.

A reluctant Rowan and Killian make unsavory faces when the stretchers are complete, both insisting they can walk.

The two of them are so damn stubborn. Too stubborn for their own good.

Jade takes my place under one of Rowan's arms when I give her an exasperated look.

With a brisk stride to Killian, I glare at him, knowing Piper can convince Rowan of nearly, if not, everything.

"You don't have a shirt or shoes," I state, pointing at the tarp held between large, straight sticks on the ground. "Now, lie down."

He grumbles but listens, being lowered by Asher and Bash. Then, the two of them move to grab the end of the long stretcher. Bash pauses before he does, taking off the cloak from around his body, and places it over Killian.

My heart warms at the gesture.

Two more trainees, men from Luca's group whose names I never learned, take hold of the front end, and together the four of them lift Killian up. He begins to grunt at the movement but swiftly hides it.

He stares up at me then, a mischievous look in his eyes. I ogle him with suspicion.

"What?"

"There was once a point in time where I never would have guessed I'd be taking orders from you." A coy smile dances on his lips.

I turn my face away, feeling a flush creeping up my neck and into my cheeks. And I try to convince myself that I would hit him right now, if he weren't already injured.

Chapter 45

"Lie him down here."

I gesture to the large bed centered against the far wall in the captain's quarters. The *old* captain's quarters.

Declan's the one to usher us inside, so I suppose he's the next best thing since our initial arrival at the border station a few days ago.

While lying on the stretcher on our hike back over the mountain, Killian began edging the line of consciousness.

I did my best not to let my emotions show but, it worried me.

Some of the abrasions on his torso didn't stop bleeding for some time, even after I halted our trek to apply pressure as well as clean gauze and bandages from my pack.

We had taken so long to get back that we saw the dark of the night disappear as the sun rose and lifted into the sky.

His arm wasn't much better. I had developed a makeshift splint around the broken bone in his left forearm a couple of hours ago. However, I could see the lines of pain grow deeper and deeper around his eyes.

"Go get whatever pain medicine you have from the infirmary. Whatever you're not using on the others," I tell Declan, who stands in the doorway. Harshness laces my tone but in this moment, I don't care.

Asher and Bash carefully lift Killian off the stretcher and onto the bed. My stomach turns over when Killian's stubbornness doesn't show as they move his body for him.

I *wish* he would be stubborn right now. It would give me hope he's feeling alright. But I know he's not.

Sweat drips from his forehead in buckets. An outline of his body begins to form on the sheet, made of the moisture.

He shouldn't be like this after being out in the icy weather for so long.

I place my hand on his forehead. A fever.

I curse under my breath. Peering up, I spy Rowan now leaning on the doorframe, Piper on her right, with Jade just inside the bedroom on her other side.

"Did they give him or you anything at all? Anything that could be poison? A strange liquid they made you drink? A coating of something on the weapons they used on you?" The questions come out strangled as I realize I don't truly know the extent of the torture the two of them endured.

Rowan shakes her head. "No, I don't think so. Luca mentioned that as much as he wanted to kill us then and there, he was going to keep us alive. To deliver us."

A shutter runs through her. Something I never thought I would see my fearsome friend ever do.

I briskly make my way to her, placing a hand on her cheek, my vision beginning to blur.

"I'm so sorry Rowan. I'm so sorry Luca took you."

"Don't you *ever* apologize for things you didn't do. Never apologize for the actions of a man. Especially one as heinous as he was. *You're* the one who took him out. And I'm proud of that," she tells me, a sternness in her voice so commanding I have no choice but to listen.

She brings her own palm up to my face, mirroring my movement when she continues. "I'll be fine. Now go take care of your Prince, and we'll catch up later."

She winks at me. I squeeze my eyes shut, nodding my head.

When I open them again, I spot Declan approaching behind her, arms full of vials, tinctures, and a variety of other items I can't make out from within his grasp.

Rowan, Piper, and Jade step out of the way, and I start backward to Killian's bedside. Declan sets the haul down on the side table, the glass bottles clinking together.

I rush over to the pile and start digging through its contents, reading labels as quickly as my eyes can move. Another curse falls from my lips when I have to put some aside when I notice their labels are illegible.

Jade places a calming hand on my shoulder a moment later, and with her other, begins to investigate the ones I set away.

"I was a midwife's assistant for a short stint a few years ago. I know my way around quite a lot of medicines," she explains before I get the chance to say anything.

I smile at my brilliant friend, hoping she feels my silent gratitude.

I finally find what I'm looking for, a remedy my aunt and I sold for fevers. It's one most commonly used for children in our village but it will help nonetheless.

I hope I do my math right as I pop open the bottle, eye the amount of elixir, and glance over Killian's size not once but twice, for good measure.

When one of my hands goes under his head and the other tilts the vial to his lips, I bite on the inside of my cheek, speaking to him softly.

"Here. This will help," I instruct, and guide the liquid into his mouth with careful precision.

He doesn't respond, only making a twisted face when the taste reaches his tongue.

"I know it's not good. Just a bit more." I eye the glass carefully and pull it away when I'm sure he's taken enough. Spinning, I return it to the table to sift through for an appropriate medicine for pain.

Jade holds up two options. Worldlessly, I dip my chin at the one on the right and grab it.

I face Killian again, examining his screwed up face.

"This one won't taste well either, I'm afraid," I warn him, screwing off the lid.

The dropper I pull out is empty, so I fill it, then place my fingers on his jaw to open it, viewing his mouth.

I count the drops as they hit his tongue. When I finish, I release my grip on his face. A calm finally washes over me the moment the bottle leaves my hand, taken by Jade.

"Clean cloths, soap, and water bowls, please," I say cooly to Declan, who waits at the ready a few paces away.

I nod to Bash near the foot of the bed, and he follows the younger man to help.

That's when I inspect the marks up and down his chest. Then his abs. Then the few stretching over his biceps.

My insides roll at the amount of slices carved into him. A fit of nausea starts to rise. He must not have given up whatever it was Luca wanted. The slashes are everywhere, at odd angles. Some short and shallow. Most long and deep.

He resisted for so long. Between his broken arm and these, I can't imagine the pain he's in.

A nudge from Jade interrupts my thoughts.

I hadn't noticed the feeling of pinpricks behind my eyes but I blink rapidly to clear the feeling.

"They're back with supplies," she says, already reaching for a cloth from the stacks Declan and Bash place on the bed on each side of Killian.

I take in a deep breath as I reach for one too, reigning in my focus.

One at a time, I gently wipe down his wounds, holding back winces at the atrocious cuts.

He's going to have scars, lots of them.

Jade and I clean the wounds so thoroughly my wrists and fingers ache when I finally place my last cloth down a few hours later. I look over his face and hair, ensuring I got the last of the crimson off of him there too.

Bash and Asher, who haven't left the room since we started, help us roll him to the side as we wrap a large, clean, cloth bandage around the entirety of his middle.

They had done the same earlier, moving his body gently, when I decided the blood soaked into his pants was too gruesome to leave on him.

We all worked in silence; Killian passed out shortly after I started dabbing at the wounds on his torso, and the rest of us didn't speak until I asked the guys for their assistance.

"Thank you. For everything," I say, exhaustion pulling me down. I view the three of them with all the sincerity I can summon.

"Of course," Jade responds, reaching over to place a palm on top of mine. "Let us know if you need anything else, at all."

I dip my chin as way of acknowledgement, then give her a half hearted smile. She leads Asher and Bash out, but before she can close the door, a pale hand gently interjects.

Princess Callista enters, striding over to my place in one of the dining room chairs Declan brought for Jade and I to sit in while we worked on Killian.

"I am so sorry to leave you at such a time but I must return to the palace. I have been gone for a long while, and I must be seen by my father before word spreads to him of Luca's death. I don't want suspicion to arise," Callista says, a hand against her heart as she spies Killian's resting form on the bed.

"I understand completely. I appreciate all of your help and insight."

She eyes me carefully, considering her next words.

"I hope this is the beginning of a long-lasting allyship, if not friendship, if I am to be so bold," she begins. "I do not know what my father will do next, when he inevitably discovers my half brother's fate. However, I will stay in touch and send word of anything I can. Anything that may help."

The lilting of her voice is as regal as ever.

Possibilities float through my head but I put them to rest to find the right words to say.

"I believe an allyship *and* a friendship are well in order," I say on a barely-there chuckle.

She steps closer, crouching down, and taking my hands in hers. Another contemplative look crosses her face.

"I know I did not see it with my own eyes…" she trails off, moving her eyes away for only a second before returning them to me. "I overheard your friends discussing what happened. To discover a new ability well past puberty… I have seen great things in your future."

If I had the energy, I would have fallen out of my chair.

"Y-you have the power to… see forward? But it-it's so rare," I stutter.

Her lips tilt up at the edges.

"I, like Luca, am able to wield the mind. A part of that just so happens to detect a semblance of a person's future. It's not particularly strong, nor does it allow me to see much detail," she says grimly, but goes on. "I learned he wasn't as lucky as I to inherit such a gift."

"I never thought I would ever meet a seer-" I start, but catch myself when I think back, remembering I have, technically.

He stood beside King Kairos. The elderly man in the long, white robe.

The first day I ever laid eyes on Killian.

I shake my head, forcing myself to focus on Callista. "I appreciate your candor. Safe travels. I hope to hear from you soon."

The Princess grins demurely, releases my hands, and stands.

"I look forward to our growing relationship. Farewell," she says, then leaves the room with a walk much more elegant than the one I had seen from her on our way to the hidden outpost.

My gaze lands on Killian after the door clicks shut behind her. I watch as his bandaged chest raises and falls in perfect time.

Time crawls by, slow and agonizing while I wait for him to wake.

I wait for the medicine to wear off, for him to be in pain again. I know in my gut he will need another dose.

So, I wait. And wait. And wait even more.

Sleep must have taken me at some point because I fling my head up off the bed at a dizzying speed. The darkening room spins while I grapple with my mind. I stare at the spot on the edge of the bed where my arms had been, under the weight of my head.

I peer up, out the small window above Killian's bed, and see the navy, lavender, and soft pinks that come after a freshly set sun.

I hadn't meant to sleep so long. Or at all.

"I knew you had a crush on me."

My head whips down when I hear Killian's sleepy voice.

"You're awake!"

He chuckles, then winces when I state the obvious.

"I am. And I see you had the time to undress me," he starts, raising his eyebrows at me while gesturing to his body with his uninjured hand. "At least you didn't completely frisk me, I suppose." He brushes his fingers against the waistband of his undershorts.

The urge to roll my eyes into the back of my head is *extremely* tempting, but I resist.

"I had help, of course. From Asher and Sebastian." I smirk, lifting my own brows at him.

He releases another chuckle, followed by a groan.

It's my turn to wince when the sound of pain comes from him. I reach for the same vials as before, using my other hand to feel his head.

"Your fever doesn't feel as bad, but some of those wounds I cleaned were most definitely infected. Likely the cause of it," I tell him, opening the medicine.

This time he releases a groan of annoyance, not agony.

My heart feels a hair lighter seeing his stubbornness back, even if only a little bit.

"Bottoms up," I say, tipping in the liquid when he reluctantly opens his mouth. The stare he gives me as I do sends shivers down my spine and flittering soaring through my stomach.

"For pain." I hold up the second bottle, and drop medicine on his tongue like before.

His gaze holds on me the entire time.

"It'll make you sleep for a while again. I'll leave, and let you get some more rest." I don't add that I have no desire to leave his side, but I feed him the lie anyways.

I move to leave my chair but his uninjured right arm flies out, his hand grabbing mine.

Twisting to him, I wait. Wait to see what he will say to convince me to stay. Even though he doesn't need to say a word. I would stay with him forever, no questions asked.

I... want to stay with him forever.

The admission fills every part of me, making my heart beat in record time as I stare at him.

I gaze into his crystalline eyes, ones that lighten and darken depending on the brightness, or his mood, then his chocolate curls which rest against the tops of his strong shoulders. I peer at his soft lips, ones I hadn't truly expected to collide with mine, but welcomed with so much joy.

"Don't."

The single word leaves his lips and he tugs my arm closer to him. The rest of me follows, the front of my thighs hitting the bed. Then, his hand lets go of mine.

His fingers move to my hip, then slide around to the edge of my lower back. He gently pulls me, and I hesitantly sit down beside him.

His bright eyes plead with me, bouncing between myself and the suddenly narrowing space beside him. He slips his arm further around my waist.

Honesty spills from my lips. "I don't want to hurt you."

"You won't. I promise. Besides, you *just* gave me more pain medicine," he smiles smugly.

I let out a disgruntled huff, and with extreme caution, I lay down next to him.

I try to make myself as tiny as possible, although the curves of my body make me feel like my efforts fail.

I suck in a breath when my stomach and breasts brush against the side of his torso. The fear of pressing against his injuries eats away at me.

Lifting my chin up, a gulp passes down my throat, and I look into his eyes. He dips his face close to my own, his sapphire eyes gleaming at me.

"Relax, beautiful," he whispers, his warm breath hitting my flushed cheeks.

I do my best to listen to him.

My concentration eventually shifts from the awareness of my body taking up space beside him to the calming sounds of his even breathing.

The cadence soothes me, allowing me to remember he's alive, here next to me. And the thought replays over and over in my head until sleep conquers me once again.

Chapter 46

"Please don't hurt yourself," I tell Killian as he begins rising from the bed. I rush over to him, leaving the door open behind me.

Bare feet on the wooden floor, about to push up to stand, he pauses. The incredulous look covering his face tells me all I need to know.

But that doesn't mean I'll listen to it.

"I was going to bring you breakfast in here. You don't need to get up so soon if you're not ready." I know my words are meeting his ears, but he's too headstrong for his own good.

I sigh. "At least let me help you up," I say, giving in.

The hand of his uninjured arm grabs onto my hip when I shift to stand directly in front of him. I use my own hands to hold his elbows as he stands. When he comes to his full height, I stare up into the shining, blue seaside of his eyes, reading them.

I have to admit, I love being a taller woman, but there's something about a tall, powerful man that makes a chill run down my spine and the beat of my heart pick up in the best way possible.

And the way he grabbed my hip, a curve of mine other men have given me such crap for, like it was the most natural thing in the world. It made my insides melt.

"I'm not that fragile, you know," he starts, pushing a strand of hair behind my ear, pausing there.

I feel redness crawling to my cheeks at the motion.

"A little beating won't take me down so easily," he continues, a grin popping onto his face.

This man never makes me stop rolling my eyes.

"You had a fever from an infection in your wounds. Your arm is broken. I don't think that's a 'little beating' Killian," I say, gesturing to his left arm, the one I moved into a proper sling not long before I went to check on breakfast.

His fingers from his other hand slip down past my ear, onto my neck, and he pulls me closer.

My front flush now with his makes the heat in my face worse.

"I don't want to hurt you." The same words I spoke last night repeat when I feel the thickness of the bandage around his middle rub against my thin top.

"Stop saying that. You aren't. And you never could," he says, a serious look filling his eyes.

He guides me closer, tilting my head back slowly. His neck cranes down to meet me. When his lips meet mine it's as if the whole kingdom, the whole world, everything around us, disappears.

This kiss is gentle, lighter than the previous one. His lips are just as soft as I remember. It only lasts for a moment before he pulls back. And I long to return to it the second he moves away.

"Breakfast?" he asks, righting my focus.

"Mhm. Oatmeal alright? There's not a ton of food up here for all of us."

"Sounds perfect. I'm starved."

I step back, going to the dining chair I moved against the wall this morning.

"Here, you want this?" I ask him, holding up a clean, black shirt.

"What the hell do I need that for?"

"I didn't know if you wanted to hang out with your trainees half naked but if you do, I surely have no problem with it." I smirk when the words leave my mouth.

I gesture to the pair of sweatpants covering his bottom half that I helped him into in the middle of the night when his fever finally broke. "As long as you've got those on, it's fine."

A matching smirk climbs onto his lips at my remark.

"Do I detect a bit of jealousy?"

I consider his question for only a moment before I chuckle.

"Absolutely." I wink at him, tossing the shirt down and grabbing his hand when we leave the bedroom.

Upon our arrival in the dining hall, conversations come to a screeching halt, all eyes pointed towards us.

I stop in the doorway when I notice. Killian continues onward, and his hand connected with mine forces me forward. I follow behind him until we reach the far end of the table where all five of my friends eat breakfast. Jade is the first to wave at us to sit down.

"Sit, sit. Let me get you both some oatmeal," she says, collecting her empty bowl and standing.

"You don-," I begin but am swiftly cut off by a stern look from her. I sigh, sitting in an empty chair beside Bash.

Piper's green gaze meets mine when Killian takes the seat on my other side, her eyebrows dancing up and down at me.

"Good morning sunshines. Sleep well?" She winks.

My face feels warm again. Killian laughs lightly next to me, squeezing my hand still gripped by his.

"Well enough," he says cheerfully.

His tone grows dark when he looks over the table to her left, to Rowan. "How are you?"

A loaded question, but Rowan's lips tilt up.

"Been better, but I'll be fine. Glad to be back with my people," she says, eyeing those of us around her before they stop on Piper. She brings their clasped hands up from under the table, kissing the back of Piper's lightly freckled one.

Jade pops back in the room at the same time, two bowls in hand. She slides them across the table to us, then takes the seat she left next to Rowan.

"Thank you," Killian and I say at the same time. Chuckles fill the space at our twinned response.

The warmth of his hand leaves when he reaches for his food, and I miss it more than I thought I would.

I try to distract myself by shoveling the warm oatmeal in my mouth. It doesn't completely work, but it does make me realize how hungry I am now that the nerves in my stomach have settled after an extremely long couple of days.

"So, are we going to talk about you suddenly being able to wield shadows now?"

The question nearly makes me spit the food out of my mouth.

My eyes square on Asher, sitting at the head of the table, tan arms crossed over his chest as he gives me a speculatory look.

Quiet fills the space while I search for an answer.

But I don't have one.

I have no idea how it happened. Or why now.

I shrug my shoulders and finish the last few bites of my meal. All six of their gazes remain on me the entire time.

Thanks guys.

I eventually push my bowl away, sighing.

"I don't know. I was... mad. Upset. I didn't even know they were coming from me until I looked down," I explain, inspecting my palms on the wooden surface.

"It just came over me. All the emotions flooded in at once."

"It was pretty badass. If I do say so myself," Piper says, a grin shining across the lower half of her face.

"I wonder why now though. Our abilities come forward throughout our childhood, through puberty. I've never heard of anyone discovering a new ability after seventeen," Jade thinks aloud, her mouth twisting up.

"Me neither," Bash says.

I meet his dark, narrowed eyes at my right. Scanning the table, thoughtful, confused looks peer back at me when a chorus of similar responses follow Bash's.

My scan lands on Killian. His eyes ripple. A mixture of deep, jewel-toned blues swirl with lighter, brighter, sky blues.

"Doesn't matter. We'll just have to teach you how to control them," he states proudly.

He places his hand atop mine, and a calm washes over me now that the warmth has returned.

I stare at his fingers as they push through mine, lacing them together, and a thought comes to mind. Uncertainty rises in me. Is it too soon to bring up? Will I trudge up more pain for Rowan and Killian by asking them?

My face must distort due to my racing mind because I hear Killian ask me what's wrong.

I view Rowan, who stares back with gentle eyes.

Then, I look to Killian.

His eyes bore into me. So far into me I'm positive they are searching my soul.

I lick my lips, and ask.

"What did Luca want from you? What did he question you about?"

He turns away, brow furrowing, and I immediately regret my line of questioning. An apology almost escapes me. However, his answer rings aloud first.

"He wanted to know about the King's seer, my father's right hand man. It is well known that he sees, but Luca was searching for a specific answer. A specific thing the old man saw." Killian's face reads of confusion. He stares off in thought, then wets his lips with his tongue.

"Luca was positive I knew something. The truth is, the old man only speaks to the King. To my father, and to his father before him. He has never spoken a word to me in my entire life," he explains, facing me again.

My mind races. The only image I have in my mind of the seer pops into my head. That first day, when he silently stood beside the King wearing white, nondescript robes.

Killian's voice drags me from the memory before I can begin to theorize what it was Luca wanted to know.

"Speaking of, any word from the castle, or the King, on anything that's transpired these past few days?"

Silence falls. When his gaze roams the table and no one answers, those blue eyes land on me.

I shake my head, squeezing his hand at the same time.

"I wish I could say I'm entirely surprised, but I'm not. I know I'm just a pawn in his game and while the other side made a big move, he just sat back and watched it play out. I can't wait to get back and hear what his excuse was."

A sarcastic, haughty laugh escapes him, his head shaking side to side.

Out of the corner of my eye, I see the faces of my friends distort. They must have realized the same as me in this moment.

We learned several weeks ago, when we discovered the child army, that there's some sort of rift growing between Killian and his father. How long it's been in place is unknown, but he has never admitted his true feelings aloud before.

Killian's shoulders shrinking inward towards his ribs catches my attention and I watch as he winces from the burst of laughter.

"You need to take it easy." I look pointedly at his torso.

A disgruntled sigh and a very discrete nod later, he agrees.

"Yeah, no having fun. No laughing. You are only allowed to once she gives you the go ahead. *She's* in charge now," Piper chuckles, giving me a wink.

"She's right, you know," I say, eyeing Killian. I giggle when he rolls his eyes, even though a grin spreads over his mouth. His bright blue stare then turns to me, his eyes burying themselves into me, into my heart and soul.

"Whatever you say."

That evening, I lay in bed beside Killian once again. After a day filled to the brim with talks of Norfell, Luca, King Kairos, training, and everything in between, I'm thankful for the reprieve.

Even if my mind has yet to slow.

"I can practically hear the gears in your mind cranking," Killian says. "What are you thinking about?"

He brushes a strand of hair behind my ear. The action makes my face warm and the blood pumping through me speed up. I bite my lip in consideration, taking a beat before answering him.

"You really meant what you said about your father earlier, didn't you? If you despise him even a fraction as much as the rest of us, why do you do his bidding?"

His breathing stops. It only lasts a moment.

He inhales deeply when it starts again.

I look up at him but can't see the full reaction on his face from where I lay in the crook of his arm.

He begins to push himself up to sit and I back away, allowing him access to his one movable arm. When his back is flush with the wall, he studies the fingers of his broken left arm.

I wait patiently. I cross my legs, raising up at his side.

I don't believe I've ever seen him hold back.

"I do it for my family..." He still doesn't move his eyes up.

"For your piece of crap father?" The words flow from my mouth before I can stop them.

"No. *Never* for him."

The stern look that follows is one I've seen before in practice. But only when he's some combination of impatient, annoyed, and upset.

"I didn't mean t-"

"He holds the fate of those I care for the most over my head," he interrupts my apology.

I sit up straighter. Woah.

"I do it for my sisters, and my mother. He threatens to force my sisters into servitude or an arranged marriage. They're none the wiser to his threats. Still, I want them to have the choice in what they do with their lives. Where they go. Who they marry," he explains, voice on the verge of cracking.

He moves his stare to his lap, inhaling. When his eyes return to me, the distraught filling them threatens to tear my chest in two.

"He hides my mother's whereabouts from me. Only bringing her to a dinner once every few months to prove to me she's alive, and to remind me his claws are dug so deep into her, there's no carving them out. The last *six* times I saw her, she was drugged so heavily she could barely finish her meal or complete a sentence."

A crack runs through my heart. My gust twists, then drops.

"He even holds my grandmother's fate over me. My mother's mother. He says 'no one would suspect a thing at her old age.'"

The crack deepens, splintering. My body feels heavy, the weight of this information pulling me down.

"Oh, Killian. I'm so sorry," I say, moving towards him.

I scoot closer, my knees touching the outside of his thigh. I place my hands over his, hauling his uninjured one into my lap.

He looks away, opening his mouth then closing it again. Chewing on the healing split in his lip, his eyes flash back.

"He also threatened to turn my sisters into soldiers for his army, seeing as they're multiwielders too," he pauses, briefly. "I'm sorry. I'm sorry about your conscription. Your capture and being forced into his army. Your friends too. I see the way you care for them."

A rush of air fills my lungs.

I never expected this, especially from the man who runs his father's army. My mind spins. Clockwise first. Then counter. Words bubble up, then fail me.

I truly don't know what to say.

As if he reads my mind, which I know he doesn't because I don't feel him trying to pry into my head, he speaks again.

"You don't have to say anything. Or accept my apology," he starts, shaking his head. "I have felt stuck for so long. I felt as if I had no other choice. No other choice but to protect my family."

Understanding settles over me.

I was there once. When a dagger was held to my aunt's throat. I gave up, bending to the will of the King's Guards. Because I had no other choice.

"I get it. I've done the same," I begin. I tell him of my capture, and the events leading up to it. I tell him everything, beginning with the death of my parents.

He listens intently. Brow furrowing and raising as I explain, his eyes never leaving my own. At some point his hand shifts over mine, and he slowly rubs his thumb over the back of my knuckles while I talk.

The gesture means more than I can express right now, maybe ever.

We sit in a beat of comfortable silence when I finish. Laying out our lives for one another, something more than just understanding or acknowledgment grows between us.

Here I thought I had already fallen.

Now, I have completely and utterly crashed. All of me into all of him. And without a doubt, I know it.

I know that I have more than just feelings for him.

Killian breaks the quiet. "I'm so sorry for my father's actions. How it resulted in your parent's death."

"Thank you, but don't need to apologize for him." My lips pull up into a reassuring smile.

And it's the truth, he doesn't. I mean it, with every bone in my body.

He then reaches his fingers up to touch the end of my caramel braid draped over my shoulder.

"You're beautiful."

The touch feels familiar. I think back, racing through memories. And I land on why it does. He did this before launching our rescue plan with Luca. Fluttering takes flight inside me.

"You're strong."

The butterflies increase, spinning and flipping all around in my stomach at his words.

His hand slides to my neck, then my cheek. I lean into his touch, a smile blooming so large it makes my face ache.

"You're incredible."

He tilts his head and presses his lips into mine. Gentle at first, then harsher. Desire seeps out of him as he moves his soft lips against my own.

Tingles flow over my arms and down my back.

Kissing him is like a dream. One I never want to wake up from.

He pulls me closer, his fingers reaching around the back of my neck.

I move in, lifting my hands to the top of his chest and slowly climb onto his lap, straddling him, ever careful of his injuries.

I stretch my fingers higher, tangling them into his loose waves.

I lightly bite his bottom lip, and he opens, colliding his tongue with mine. He explores my mouth and I, his. Tasting. Devouring. As if hunger has taken me over. As if I'll never be able to kiss him again.

He cups the back of my head, bringing me impossibly closer. He presses his lips into mine feverishly. Like he can't get enough of me either.

Gently, he bites and pulls my bottom lip between his, sucking it for only a moment before releasing it.

Sparks light up within me, running across my limbs, over every hair on my body, lighting me on fire.

His lips linger on mine for a second longer, then he pulls back. Resting his forehead against my own, our breaths tangle together. He tips his face closer, brushing his nose against mine.

Heat covers me. My face, my body. Unlike anything I've ever felt before.

And I can't get enough of it.

Killian's lips hover, closing in. But he speaks before they touch my surely swollen ones.

"I knew there was something special about you the moment I met you."

"You mean when I spit on you and cursed at you?" I question on a giggle.

His chuckle mixes in. "Yes. I knew you had some fight in you, that's for sure."

Our laughter draws to a close, and he continues.

"I've come to realize… I would take down *anyone* who dares to stand in my way of you. I would crawl through any obstacle, any fight, any thing, to meet you at the ends of the earth, if it meant I could see you one last time. Your stunning, forest green eyes. Your flawless, teasing smile. Your perfect, beautiful curves."

He slides his hand down to my neck, then my back, wrapping his forearm around my hips, tugging me a hair closer.

Warmth flares through me again at his touch.

"I don't know the exact moment it happened, but I do know I've felt it for some time…" he trails off, peering at my lips, then stares longingly into my eyes.

"I love you. And I would do *anything* for you to allow me to stand at your side."

All the breath in my lungs disappears. Words clog in my throat.

So instead, I kiss him.

I slam my lips into his, and he meets me with the same hunger. I slant my lips, deepening the kiss, teasing his mouth with my tongue.

He takes control, pushing his tongue over mine and into my mouth.

And I nearly fall into him as he does.

I wrap my arms around his neck. He brings me flush with his chest, his grip tightening around my waist.

I gasp and pull away, not wanting to press against the wounds under the bandage covering his torso. His eyes fill with immediate concern.

"I-," I start, carefully placing a hand against his bandaged abdomen. "You need to heal."

Bringing my face close to his again, I softly press another kiss over his perfectly soft, full lips.

When I back up, the sapphire in his eyes swirl, like a galaxy far off in the sky.

"And… I love you."

The grin that covers his face is instantaneous, and so incredibly stunning.

His hand lands on the side of my neck once more and the kiss he plants on me in the next moment is truly, utterly life changing.

Chapter 47

The hallway stretches on forever. It feels even longer than it did my first day in this place.

Although, I suppose being dragged along the shining, tile floor by King's Guards would make the time go by faster than simply walking the length of the space.

Killian's hand brushes mine and I scan his face, then the sling that holds his opposite arm.

His fever hasn't even been gone seventy-two hours but he insisted we get back to the castle. He was restless.

He hasn't said as much, but I can tell he's been itching to confront his father. The rage he feels for the man has come to the forefront of his mind.

I can only hope he reigns in his vexation when we finally enter the throne room.

I glance over to Rowan, using my right hand to reach out and grip her own.

What her and Killian endured eats away at me, the guilt lying heavily on my shoulders, even though they've reassured me a dozen times.

I'm unsure the feeling will ever fully leave.

Rowan squeezes my palm, dipping her chin to me as I silently check in. I bring my hand back to my side when we finally approach the massive double doors leading to the throne room.

Killian releases his hold on my hand and he shoves the doors inward, a single hand pressed against the seam where the two meet.

I inadvertently suck in a breath at the sight of King Kairos upon his throne.

His face doesn't show a sliver of surprise at our group. His glare spreads over each of us, not lingering more than a moment. I can feel when his eyes land upon me, then turn on Rowan and Piper at my side, before moving behind me to Asher, Bash, and Jade.

His pupils grow, shrinking the dark brown of his irises when they shift to Killian last. They retract a second later.

The King's brows raise, signaling his impatience, and the question of why we stand before him.

Killian tilts his head to the side, waiting his father out.

The silence is excruciatingly loud.

Several minutes later, the King sighs.

"What is it, Killian? Anything to report from your mission?" His voice is gravel, as if it's been used too harshly, too often.

"I don't know. Does it *look* like I have anything to report?" Killian's voice drips of sarcasm, and his blatant defiance sends a chill down my spine.

King Kairos shifts in his seat, sitting up straighter. His brows come together, forming lines across his aging forehead.

"I wouldn't be able to tell past your *attitude*. So, I ask again, how did the mission go?"

"Wouldn't you like to know. Since you clearly had no intention of assisting me when I was taken hostage by Norfell," Killian spits.

My eyes widen so large I swear they will burst out of my skull.

The King's eyes narrow further, inspecting his son, then lets out a haughty laugh.

"Oh my boy, you really thought I wouldn't do *anything*? I *was* devising a plan. However, it seems your trainees got to you first. How well you have trained them," he says, gaze sliding to me in suspicion.

His stare unsettles me.

And some part of it tells me he's lying.

Everything in me comes alive, and I can't let it go. He didn't know of Killian's capture.

I'm sure of it.

His eyes hone in on me further, and then I feel it.

King Kairos runs a finger down the shield I have firmly in place in my mind.

It creeps along the edge of my shield, and he scrapes a nail over it, solely to let me know he could try. He could try to pry open my mind, but he won't.

The warning is clear.

"I don't think I believe you, *father*."

The claw running along my mind's shield disappears the instant Killian's voice booms across the room.

Killian's boldness invigorates me.

But it's also setting me on edge.

The King hasn't been brash thus far, but I fear his son's brutal honesty may change that.

Silence falls once again. King Kairos faces his son, leaning forward in his throne, gripping the armrests with his hands full of gaudy, gold rings.

The tension strung between the King and the Prince is pulled so taut, it could snap at any moment.

The King tilts his head, like a serpent surveying its prey before a strike. The gleaming, golden crown upon his brow doesn't shift an inch with his movements.

"Believe what you wish, *son*," Kairos fumes, finally resting his back against his chair.

The King's hands release their grip on his throne and fold together in front of him.

A smirk forms on his lips before he continues. "I'm glad you're back. Safe and sound after all."

He looks away, disinterested, and waves a hand at us. "You may leave. Now."

Killian whips around, leading us out of the throne room. He pauses for the briefest of moments in front of the gigantic, open doors, peering at his father over his shoulder.

When he faces forward again, I hear him under his breath whisper, "Disgusting tyrant."

But if the King heard him, he made no show of it, ordering the doors closed after our exit.

"It was freeing to finally say something to him. It had been building for quite some time," Killian admits. "I didn't mean for you all to be there when I couldn't hold my tongue. Thank you."

He dips his chin to Asher, Jade, and Bash across the table from us. Then he does the same to Piper and Rowan on my right.

His uninjured hand comes to cover mine that rests atop his muscled thigh under the table.

My heart flutters. The simple touches I'm not yet used to send my insides swirling.

"I knew your dad was a dick but his intimidation is no joke," Asher laughs, digging his fork into the pile of roasted meat on his plate.

A moment of quiet passes, uncertainty building as the remainder of my friends eye each other with trepidation. Until Killian releases a belly laugh, nodding his head in agreement.

"He is quite the asshole. And he thrives off of sitting upon that big, scary throne of his."

Chuckles spread over the table, mine included.

I let my palm on his leg be swept up into his hand. A squeeze of it from him sets my insides flickering, like a blaze being ignited.

I spear the vegetables on my plate, humming when the roasted herbs on them hit my tongue.

"My father is a problem. There isn't a doubt in my mind about it. But now we also have a new problem. Norfell," Killian thinks aloud. He bites into his own dinner, releasing my palm to use his fork.

"I suppose we will have to wait and see which of the two we'll be facing first," he says with a shake of his head.

I raise my hand, sliding it up his forearm and grip his bicep, then use my other to rest it on Rowan's shoulder.

My eyes roam over the table.

Asher's golden hair sits perfectly in place after being constantly disheveled on our mission.

Jade's blush returns to her cheeks, as opposed to the joyless lines drawn there only days ago.

Bash's face is warm and whole again since freezing out in the snow while finding Norfell's hideout.

Piper's eyes are finally clear, free of the irritated redness from the amount of tears shed.

Rowan's here, alive, and by my side once more, just as we started this journey.

And Killian, the most unexpected thing to come of any of this, may be physically broken and bruised, but he seems more ready for a fight than ever before.

"We will figure it out together."

I say the words without a second thought. And I mean them.

I don't have to worry about what's to come, although my stomach may beg to differ, because I know with each and every one of these people at my side, we can survive anything.

The nods and grunts of agreement over mouths full of food from them all warm me, filling me with undeniable hope.

Killian's eyes find mine. Those surreal, sapphire irises look at me, a confession swarming beyond them. They turn to the rest of the table, the others pausing when they sense the seriousness building in him.

"My father. I'm finished being a pawn in the chaos he calls Orellia. I can no longer stand by and watch him destroy the lives of the people he is meant to care for. I have done it for too long. For the sake of my family, for protecting them," he starts, bleeding into the confession of heeding his father's wishes for the sake of his sisters, mother, and grandmother.

Asher and Piper's faces distort with disgust. Jade balks at his words. Rowan sighs, shaking her head. Bash looks away, hiding whatever emotions cross his features.

While I may have heard his confession before, it doesn't make the words any easier to hear.

And as much as I'd like to say I would have done different, I know in my heart, in my soul, that I too would have done anything to protect those I love most.

"I'm finished with him. And," Killian pauses, lowering his voice and leaning forward into the table. "It's time to take him down."

A smile cracks on Piper's face as she raises her glass, water nearly swashing over the edge of it. "Count me in."

A giggle bubbles up my throat and I lift my own cup in the air, nodding to her.

"Count *us* in," Rowan corrects, smirking at the strawberry blonde.

"Me too," Jade chimes in.

"And me," Asher follows.

"Same here," Bash agrees, facing the rest of the table.

I spy Killian's throat bob as he takes in the raised glasses before him. A grin fights for purchase on his face, and he lets it win. Raising his own cup, he takes in each and every one of us.

When his gaze makes its way to me, I can't hold back the beam as my lips pull upward.

We clink our cups together, the clanging a sound I know I will never forget.

"Cheers!"

Thank you for reading *By the Order of the King!*

Follow the author online and stick around to find out what happens next
in the second book of The Orders trilogy: *By the Order of the Throne*

Find Shelby Ann Harms on Instagram at @readsbyshelby and on TikTok
at @readsbyshelbyy

Acknowledgments

I honestly don't know where to begin because this has been such a long time coming. From working sporadically on this story throughout the last year and a half of my college career to finally finishing it during the summer after graduation, this story has come so far from where it first started.

I am so grateful for my friends and family that have helped and encouraged me along the way. To my best friend Amanda, thank you for putting up with my random texts at all hours of the night when I was overthinking the wording of certain sentences. To my beta readers Sedona, Jasi, Nikki, Margarita, Sarah, Gaby, Tina, and Yari, thank you for all of your feedback and advice, it helped more than you'll ever know.

Thank you to my two book clubs, Bound to Books and Mytherra, for all of your constant support. Thank you to my street team, Shelby's Faeries, for helping spread the word of By the Order of the King.

I couldn't have done this without all of you. I can't wait to see where this journey takes me. Onto more fantastical stories!

About the Author

Shelby Ann Harms is a born and raised Californian with a degree in Communication Studies and a passion for storytelling that manifested as a child. She loves all things fantasy and romance, and considers herself a fangirl at heart. When she's not writing, she is most often found reading, crafting, binge watching one of her comfort shows, or spending time with loved ones, including her two cats, Teddy Bear and Jasper Binx.

www.ingramcontent.com/pod-product-compliance
Lightning Source LLC
Chambersburg PA
CBHW031110160726
47991CB00004B/1322